The Darkness Within

ETHERYA'S EARTH, BOOK 3
By
REBECCA HEFNER

Copyright © 2019

RebeccaHefner.com

This book is a work of fiction. Names, characters, places and incidents are the product of the author's imagination and are used fictitiously. Any resemblance to actual events, locales or persons, living or dead, is coincidental.

Copyright © 2019 by Rebecca Hefner. All rights reserved, including the right to reproduce, distribute or transmit in any form or by any means.

Cover Design: Susan Olinsky Design
Editor: Megan McKeever, NY Book Editors
Proofreader: Bryony Leah, www.bryonyleah.com

For everyone who loves a tortured soul...because perhaps we all possess one...

Table of Contents
Title Page and Copyright
Dedication
Map of Etherya's Earth
Prologue
Chapter 1
Chapter 2
Chapter 3
Chapter 4
Chapter 5
Chapter 6
Chapter 7
Chapter 8
Chapter 9
Chapter 10
Chapter 11
Chapter 12
Chapter 13
Chapter 14
Chapter 15
Chapter 16
Chapter 17
Chapter 18
Chapter 19
Chapter 20
Chapter 21
Chapter 22
Chapter 23
Chapter 24
Chapter 25
Chapter 26
Chapter 27
Chapter 28
Chapter 29
Chapter 30
Chapter 31
Chapter 32
Chapter 33
Chapter 34
Chapter 35
Epilogue
Acknowledgments
About the Author

ETHERYA'S EARTH

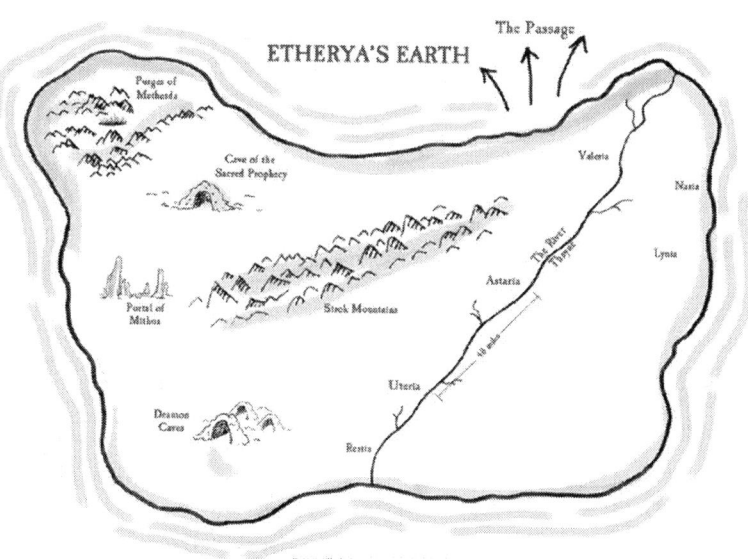

The Passage

- Purges of Methenda
- Cave of the Sacred Prophecy
- Portal of Mithos
- Stock Mountains
- Deamon Caves
- Valeria
- Nasta
- Astaria
- The River Thayat
- Lynia
- Utaria
- Restia

HUMAN WORLD

Prologue

Two centuries after the Awakening

Darkrip sat in the murky cave, the sole light emanating from the torch on the nearby dirt wall. His father, the Dark Lord Crimeous, was several miles away, conducting his nightly torture session.

His father wasn't aware of this particular cave and that made it a welcome hiding spot for Darkrip. He'd started coming here when he needed to breathe, feeling that his lungs were going to collapse from the evil that coursed inside him. Existence so far had been filled with death and destruction. When his beautiful mother had perished, he clung to them, thriving on the wicked thrill that he felt every time he crushed another's soul.

But one death bled into another, one harem woman violated turned into so many faceless others, and he felt himself drowning from the ever-present stench of death. His father's blood was so malevolent, comprising half of his nature, making him wonder if he should just jump in the Purges of Methesda and end it all. Wouldn't that be better than living in this wretch of a world?

He'd thought he could kill his sister. After all, she shared half his father's blood too. It was imperative that every trace of the Evil Lord be removed from the world if it had any chance of thriving. When he'd tried to kill her in her sleep, his mother's blood had coursed through his body, rendering him unable to complete the deed.

Determined to prevail, he hired their old caretaker, Yara, to complete the grisly task. She was one of the few people Evie trusted, and Darkrip gave Yara specific instructions on how to murder her before she could call upon her evil powers. Sadly, Yara had failed.

Now, Evie was gone, lost to the world of humans. Inside, he felt what he could only identify as regret. He questioned whether he would ever see her again. Cursing himself, he sat on the dirt floor of the cave, brainstorming ways to kill his powerful father. Since the bastard could dematerialize at will, manipulate things with his thoughts and read others' images in their minds, the task was extremely difficult.

Darkrip shared all of those powers, but with his mother's Slayer blood, he would never be as mighty as his father. Frustrated, he rubbed his forehead with his fingers. Snapping his head around, he narrowed his eyes at the faint noise behind him.

Suddenly, a bright light pierced the darkness. Darkrip's heart began to pound as he stood, facing the unknown with strength and curiosity. Out of the brilliance, his mother appeared. Unable to believe the image, he blinked quickly several times and shook his head furiously.

"My sweet boy," she said, walking up to him and cupping his face. "It's so wonderful to see you."

Wetness clouded his eyes as he gazed down at her. "Mother?"

Rina's pink lips turned up into a dazzling smile and her olive-green irises glowed with love. "I've missed you so."

Unable to stop himself, he pulled her into a firm embrace. "How are you here?"

Pulling back, he ran a hand over her silky, raven-black hair.

"I made a deal with Etherya. It was imperative that I see you."

"What kind of deal?" he asked, filled with dread. He knew the goddess to be spiteful, evidenced by the awful curse she'd placed on him when he was only a teenager.

His beautiful mother sighed, her expression sad. "I promised her I would spend eternity in the Land of Lost Souls, instead of the Passage, if she let me appear to you."

"No," he said, palming her cheek. "You won't find any peace there. You need to be in the Passage. After all he put you through, you deserve that."

"My dear son, you always were so protective of me. For better or worse, the decision has been made. Let me tell you what I've come to say, as I don't have much time."

Darkrip nodded, hating that his mother would have to suffer for eternity. She had been tortured so thoroughly by his father, and he wished for nothing more than serenity for her.

Releasing him, she straightened her spine. "You tried to kill Evie. It's unacceptable. She is your sister, and I need you to protect her."

"I know," he said, rubbing the back of his neck, filled with shame at his mother's scolding. "I thought I was doing the right thing by ridding the world of father's blood."

"No," she said, glossy hair flying as she shook her head. "You must protect her. She has a tough road ahead, but she is very important. I need you to promise me, son."

"I promise. I'm sorry. I regret it immensely."

Rina nodded. "I need you to be patient. You're going to have to wait several centuries. Let Evie stew in the human world during that time. Leave her alone while she comes to terms with what she is. In the meantime, earn your father's trust. It's imperative he trust you if we are to defeat him."

"Have you seen the future?" Darkrip felt his eyes grow wide.

She nodded. "Bits and pieces. Eventually, you will learn of the prophecy. Miranda will become the savior we need. She will reunite the species again and help forge a path toward your father's death." Lifting her chin, Rina's eyes filled with warning. "But it will not be easy. You must bide your time. If, after several centuries, you don't see her act, then do what you must to spur her along."

"Okay," he said, swallowing thickly.

"You cannot torture and kill anymore, Darkrip. I know that your father encourages you to do these things, but they are heinous and beneath you. I refuse to have a son who chooses hate over love." Lifting her hands, she caressed his cheeks. "You have so much of my father in you. Please, let that half win. You have to let it guide you. I need you to give me your word. No more death from your hands."

Darkrip inhaled deeply. "He urges me on. It's so difficult—"

"I know," she said, her eyes filled with understanding, "but you have to be strong. It will be hard for you to hide your lack of evil from him but it can be done. I want your word."

"You can never understand how hard it is for me to control that part of myself."

Anger flashed in her irises. "Don't tell me I can't understand your father's malevolence. He used it to torture me for decades. I only regained my sanity, and all of my severed appendages, when I entered the Passage. I understand your struggle, but I need your word. I sacrificed an eternity of peace for an infinity of suffering so that I could come here and get it from you. If you ever cared for me at all, you'll give it to me."

"I loved you, Mother," he said, his heart filled with sadness. "I don't know how to live in this world without you. When you died, I lost the ability to care about anything else."

"That's not true, son. You'll see. One day, many centuries from now, you will have the life that you deserve. The road there will be filled with pain and suffering, but you will have it." Lifting her face to his, she gave him a sweet kiss on his full lips. "Now, promise your mother."

"I promise," he said, vowing to do right by her. "I won't torture, although I can't promise not to kill. If I have to, I will. But you have my word that I will do my best to live by my Slayer half. I hope that your visions are true. If not, we are all doomed."

Her magnificent face glowed as she smiled up at him. "Good boy. I love you so, Darkrip. When the time comes, help both of your sisters. They will need it. Follow your intuition."

Wrapping her thin arms around his neck, she gave him a hug. As he closed his eyes and tried to hold her, she disappeared. The agony of her departure burned in his chest, and he rubbed his hand over his heart.

Determined to listen to his beloved mother, he dematerialized out of the cave and back to the room he kept near his father's main lair.

Chapter 1

The Vampyre compound of Astaria, 1000 years after the Awakening…

Arderin stood on top of the concrete platform, the gray slab feeling cold at her feet although she wore pretty black two-inch ankle boots along with her thin-legged jeans. Heden, her younger brother, stood next to her, chatting with Lila and Miranda.

The two women couldn't look more different, but both were stunningly gorgeous. Lila was tall—three inches taller than Arderin's own six-foot frame—and she had a voluptuous body that screamed "sex appeal." White teeth flashed in the sunlight as her blond head tilted back, laughing with Heden. They had a close bond and Arderin sometimes wondered if they even saw her when they were laughing and joking with each other.

Lila's lavender irises twinkled with mischief as she and her brother discussed the "bangin' chick" he'd hooked up with last night. Arderin hoped he'd caught seventeen STDs from the mindless, brainless woman. Heden's self-healing body would cure them instantly but the thought made her feel better somehow. He was an incredible flirt and got laid constantly. It annoyed the hell out of her, since eligible men barely ever looked her way. She might as well be a damn nun.

Miranda was watching the platform, absently chewing on her bottom lip. Missing Sathan, she was excited for him to come home. The silky, straight strands of her raven, shoulder-length bob blew in the breeze, and her olive-green eyes were filled with anticipation. A curve extended from her stomach on her five-foot-six frame, as she was ten and a half months pregnant with their first child. It was the first-ever Vampyre-Slayer hybrid. Being that Slayer fetuses gestated for nine months, and Vampyres for fifteen months, they didn't know exactly when the baby would come. Arderin hoped it would be soon if only so Miranda could have some peace. She was freaking huge.

"What time is their train coming in?" Miranda asked. "I told Darkrip I'd have dinner with him tonight, but I still have a ton of licenses to process for the new Slayer settlements at Naria and Lynia. I'm probably going to be late."

"Supposedly three minutes ago," Heden said, looking at his watch with his ice-blue irises. The color mimicked hers as well as their brother Latimus'. Sathan, the oldest brother, had pitch-black irises, but all four of the Vampyre royal siblings favored each other with their black hair and angular features.

A commotion sounded from the underground station, and Arderin knew the train had arrived. Sure enough, several people charged up the stairs. Finally, she saw her two oldest brothers. Both so tall and massive, they were a formidable pair as they climbed the stairs.

Once the last stair had been surmounted, Miranda launched herself at Sathan, wrapping her legs around his waist as she placed tiny pecks on his full lips. Her oldest brother chuckled, pleased to see his bonded mate. Murmuring for her not to jump since she was pregnant, she scolded him back and stuck her tongue in his mouth for a blazing kiss.

Lila, raised as an aristocrat and always so proper, didn't fling herself at Latimus but instead seemed to float into him as they melded into a warm embrace. Aligning their bodies, she gave her bonded mate a heated kiss under the mid-afternoon sun.

"It's not like they went to Centurion," Arderin said, rolling her eyes and referencing the next closest planet in the solar system where Etherya's Earth resided. "They were only at Valeria for two days."

"Hey," Heden said, pulling her to his side with his beefy arm. "Don't get all sad, little toad. It's nice to see our idiot brothers happy."

Arderin scrunched her face at the stupid nickname. He and Sathan had called her that for centuries, and she'd given up trying to get them to stop. "They're so in love. All of them. I wish I was. They all get to have amazing sex and be so happy. Meanwhile, I'm wasting away on this stupid compound destined to die a virgin. Someone kill me."

Heden chuckled. "Is it that bad?"

"Yes," she said, leaning into him and letting him squeeze her. Although she thought all three of her brothers to be massive morons half the time, she loved them immensely. The four of them shared a tight bond and had since their parents were murdered at the Awakening, over a thousand years ago.

"Hey, little one," Latimus said, releasing Lila and approaching her. "Give me a hug."

"Hey," she said, walking into his embrace, loving how he stroked her hair in his brotherly way.

"Why are you sad?" he whispered in her ear.

"Because everyone's in love and I'm a loser," she whispered back.

Laughing softly, he squeezed her with his beefy arms. "You're *my* loser. So, at least that's something."

Pulling away from him, she swatted his chest. "You suck."

Kissing her forehead, he smiled down at her. "It will happen, little one. Don't be sad."

"Arderin, do you want to have dinner with me, Sathan and Darkrip?" Miranda asked.

Great. Another in a long line of pity dinner invites from her sister-in-law. But she guessed it beat eating alone like a shriveled-up old grandma.

"Sure," Arderin said with a shrug. "Thanks."

Releasing her, Latimus shook hands with Heden, patting him on his broad shoulder with his free hand.

"Did we miss anything important?"

"Nah," Heden said, casting a sly glance at Arderin. "Except our sister's ever-present dramatics."

"Shut up," she said, punching him in his hulking upper arm. "I'm not dramatic." It was a lie, of course, as she knew herself to be one of the most melodramatic people on the planet. But wasn't that better than being a total bore? Sure that it was, she scowled at her brother.

"I missed you, Arderin," Sathan said, approaching to hug her with his colossal arms. "Stop giving her shit, Heden," he muffled into her hair as he squeezed her. "She's finally being nice to me."

Stepping back, she regarded her three enormous brothers.

Latimus, with his straight black hair and widow's peak, pulled into a tiny tail with a leather strap, tallest at six-foot-nine. The warrior.

Sathan, with his thick hair and dark irises, his hulking frame only slightly shorter than Latimus'. The king.

Heden, with his ice-blue eyes and goatee under his mop of wavy black hair, a few inches shorter than his older brothers. The jokester.

By the goddess, she loved them all terribly.

Deciding that it aggravated the living hell out of her, she raised her chin and huffed at them.

"I'm going inside. Screw all of you. Miranda, I'll see you at dinner."

Flagrantly pivoting, she sauntered back to the house, the heels of her boots sticking in the crunchy grass. Snickers sounded behind her, and she turned to give them all a look of death. They stood firm with laughter in their eyes, faces filled with mock innocence. Bastards.

Throwing her waist-length, curly black hair over her shoulder, Arderin resumed walking back to the main castle, determined to clutch what was left of her dignity.

* * * *

Lila held her bonded's hand as they rode the train from Astaria to Lynia, where they now resided. It was the Vampyre kingdom's smallest compound and most charming in her opinion. She'd fallen in love with it, as she'd fallen in love with her strong warrior over the past year.

Technically, she'd been in love with Latimus her entire life. A thousand years of hidden feelings and painful regrets. Etherya had declared her the king's betrothed when she was only a baby, but she had never loved Sathan romantically. When he had fallen for Miranda, she had moved to Lynia, away from Latimus, whom she believed would never love her back. So thankful that they had let go of their fears, she squeezed his hand and gazed into his sky-blue eyes.

"I missed you so much. Jack is excited to see you."

"I missed you too, honey," he said, kissing the top of her head. "Thanks for coming to meet me at Astaria."

"Sure. I had to bring some paintings for Miranda to drop off to Aron this weekend anyway." Shyly, she looked up at him and bit her lip. "I went shopping in town yesterday before heading to the shelter. I bought some special...things for us to use in the whirlpool bathtub."

"You little cock tease," he whispered in her ear, his deep baritone making her shiver. "Do you ever think about anything but fucking me?"

"Be quiet," she said, swatting his chest. Her face felt enflamed with ten shades of red. "There are other people in this car."

"I don't give a shit. I'll flip you over right here—"

Covering his mouth with her pale hand, she tried to give him her best look of mortification. "Stop it," she scolded.

Staring down at her with laughter in his eyes, he nipped at her hand. Removing it, she sank into his large body, loving how he held her.

After a few moments, she said, "I'm worried about Arderin."

"I know," he said, pulling her into him. "We were her two closest confidants, and now, we're together all the time. It must be hard for her. We have to make sure we check in on her."

Lila nodded. "I invited her to come and stay with us next week, but she said she's working on some skin regeneration thing with Nolan."

"That's good. I'm glad she has something that makes her happy. Her intellect is remarkable. Have you seen how fast she reads the medical books that Sadie and Nolan give her?"

"Yes. She's unbelievable. I love that she wants to be a doctor. Sathan struggles with it though, since she wants to train in the human world, and he's forbidden her to go there."

"He and Heden don't understand her. They focus on her dramatics and tantrums, which are really fucking annoying." He arched a raven-black eyebrow. "But under all that, she's an extremely intelligent, remarkable person who can do anything she sets her mind to."

Lila squeezed his hand. "You've always loved her so."

"I have," he said, full red lips forming a smile. "She was the only one for so long."

"You love your brothers. And, maybe, you always loved me just a little bit."

"I loved you the most," he said, rubbing the tip of his nose against hers. "But I thought you were in love with my brother, you little temptress. It was awful."

Sighing, she placed a peck on his lips. "Well, now we're bonded. Almost a month already. You can't get rid of me now."

"Never," he said. "You're stuck with my surly ass forever. I hope you realize what you've signed up for. I'm a huge asshole."

Laughing, she shook her head. "You're my asshole."

"You cursed," he said, his mouth dropping open. "I think I'm going to start a swear jar. What would your etiquette school teachers say?"

"I'm pretty sure they would've told me not to bond with you in the first place, but that stone's already been thrown, so..."

"Damn straight. You're mine. Besides, how would you survive without me fucking you five times a day? You're insatiable."

"Enough," she said, scowling up at him. "You don't get to seduce me and then make fun of me because I like it."

"Are we having our first fight after being bonded?" he asked, mischief twinkling in his gorgeous eyes. "I hope so. We can have fantastic make-up sex."

"You suck," she said, resting her head on his shoulder.

"You know I do," he whispered in her ear.

Once at Lynia, they hopped into a four-wheeler with one of his soldiers, who drove them to their pretty five-bedroom house by the creek. They shared a glass of wine on the porch, surrounded by the beautiful purple flowers that she loved, until their adopted son came barreling through the yard.

"Hi, guys," Jack said, running up to give Lila a hug as she stood up from the rocking chair. "I'm so glad it's Friday. I hate school."

Releasing Lila, Jack turned to Latimus and squealed with laughter as he playfully picked him up and threw him over his shoulder.

"No hating school around here, kid. You've gotta get good grades if you're going to be in my army."

Squirming, Jack laughed as her gorgeous man tickled him. "You don't need to be smart to be a soldier."

"Hey," Latimus said, increasing the tickling. "You'll pay for that." Running into the yard, he gently threw him on the ground and started wrestling with him. Lila watched the boy's red hair flop around, joy etched into every inch of his freckled face. Loving them both, she sipped her wine and watched them play.

Thinking of Arderin again, she absently fingered the rim of her wine glass. There was such sadness in her lately, which wasn't typical of her usually vivacious friend. The thought that finally loving Latimus would cause her best friend any pain spurred an anxious burn in Lila's belly. Knowing how left-out she felt made her heart hurt. Arderin had been there for Lila almost her whole life, supporting her when her parents died and when Latimus hurt her terribly. Wishing she could do something to help her, Lila wracked her brain.

Latimus called her name from the yard, pulling her from her thoughts.

"What?"

"Jack says you have to wrestle us to see who's stronger."

"Oh, no," she said, shaking her head. "I'm wearing a white sweater." Tugging at the V-neck, she smiled. "No wrestling for me today."

Latimus lowered his head and whispered to Jack. Trepidation filled her when the boy nodded, excitement pulsing from his small body. Her warrior lifted to his feet and began slowly approaching her.

"No," she said, standing and placing the wine glass on the wooden banister. "I don't want to get dirty—"

Black army boots made ominous sounds as he plodded up the porch stairs toward her. Backing toward the front door, she held up her hand.

"No, Latimus, I don't want to ruin this sweater—"

"I'll buy you a new sweater, honey," he interrupted, mischief in his ice-blue irises.

Lila's soft-spoken pleas were no match for her man. Grabbing her waist, she shrieked as he threw her over his shoulder. Pounding his lower back with her fists, she threatened him with murder. Walking back to Jack, he gently threw her to the ground, and her son pounced.

Unable to stop it, laughter swelled as she wrestled with her sweet boy. He was so precious, and her heart pounded with love for him. Latimus grabbed them both and embraced them, rolling them on the soft green grass. Eventually, they tired and lay panting, looking up at the late afternoon sun.

Lila turned her head on the ground to look at her bonded. *I'm going to kill you*, she mouthed to him.

Can't wait, he mouthed back, chucking his eyebrows.

Once the sun set, she made spaghetti for Jack, and they drank Slayer blood before he went to his room to do homework. Although Vampyres only needed Slayer blood for sustenance, Jack loved the taste of food, pasta being his favorite. Later, once he was fast asleep, Lila walked into their room, looking at her naked bonded mate lying on the bed.

"No way," she said, shaking her head. "You are *not* getting laid tonight. I'm still pissed that you ruined my sweater."

"Yeah," Latimus said, throwing his arm behind his head as it rested on the pillow. With his other large hand, he grabbed his thick shaft. "Too bad. I need to put this somewhere."

Saliva gathered at the back of her throat and moisture rushed between her legs. He knew that she loved it when he played with himself in front of her.

"Nope," she said, walking into the bathroom and closing the door.

It took about three seconds for him to slam it open and grab her. Carrying her to the bed, he gently threw her on top.

"You're going to pay for that, honey. Now, be a good girl and open your mouth."

Pursing her lips, trying to contain her smile, she shook her head on the soft comforter.

"Yes, you little temptress," he said, leaning over her. Desire swam in his eyes as he placed the head of his shaft on her sealed lips.

The scent of him, musky and spicy, filled her nostrils, and she almost came in her tight jeans. He was magnificent as he loomed over her.

Closing his eyes, he inhaled deeply. Lifting his lids, he gazed into her. "Your arousal smells so good. Open your mouth, you little tease."

Loosening her lips a bit, she shyly stuck out her tongue, bathing the tiny hole in the center of the sensitive head with her saliva.

"Goddamnit, woman," he said, clutching her wrists and pinning her arms above her head as he leaned into her. "I'm sorry about your sweater. I swear, I'll buy you a hundred more. Please, stop teasing me."

Unable to control her laugh, her mouth opened, and he took advantage. Groaning, she sucked him into her as deep as she could. There, as he held her hands above her head, Lila forgot all about her ruined sweater.

Chapter 2

Darkrip sipped his red wine as he sat at the long mahogany dinner table. Miranda sat to his left, Sathan at the head and Arderin across from him. Every so often, Arderin would lift her glass, placing her pink lips on the rim to take a sip, causing his shaft to twitch in his black pants.

His obsession with her was becoming dangerous. As the son of the Dark Lord Crimeous, he knew that he was playing with fire. And yet, he couldn't seem to avoid the spitfire little princess.

Somehow, she was always there. In the places he found solace, or the spots he'd come to think of as his own. It was as if the universe had given her a GPS, he her sole destination.

He knew her wish to avoid him was as strong as his. Feeling his lips twitch, he thought of all the times she'd looked upon him with disgust and threatened murder at the hands of her brothers if he even spoke to her. But they also had an undeniable energy that passed between them. Sometimes, he felt it pound so ardently through his veins that he had to clench his fists as he verbally sparred with her.

But, oh, how fun it was. Dramatic and impetuous, arguing with the Vampyre princess had become one of his favorite pastimes. Her gorgeously defined cheekbones would redden, and her ice-blue eyes would flash with rage. Every so often, as she defiantly scolded him, tiny flecks of her spittle would escape from her plushy lips. His skin would sizzle as they landed on his face, and he would restrain himself from pulling her in to taste her fully.

The little brat should've been terrified. After all, he was the son of the Dark Lord and capable of killing her with one flick of his hand. If he wanted to, he could hold her slender body hostage and ravage her as she struggled. God, he'd had the fantasy so many times. It might have made another man feel shame but he, with his evil blood, could never feel such emotion. Instead, he reveled in the fantasies, usually imagining raping her as he jerked his never-softening shaft.

It seemed safe somehow, allowing his mind to wander there, as he knew he would never actually perform the malevolent deed. His mother's blood was too pure. Stealing a glance at Miranda, he let himself feel emotion for her as it pulsed through his body. It was so strange, as he hadn't felt any emotion toward any living soul on the planet since his beautiful mother died, all those centuries ago.

Miranda was a mirror image of her. Sometimes, it fucked with his head. Usually, until his half-sister's ire started to inflame, in her always stubborn and passionate way. That's where they differed. He remembered his mother, Rina, to be sweet and pliant. His father had successfully tortured any remnants of her fighting spirit out of her. When she'd finally died, she had been so broken. Meanwhile, his sister had probably never even heard the word pliant. Feeling his lips curve into a smile, he sipped his wine as he watched her chat with Sathan and Arderin, her hands waving in their always animate way.

"And what are you laughing at?" Miranda asked, turning her green-eyed gaze to him.

"Nothing," Darkrip said. "You just always use your hands when you talk. I'm trying not to lose an eye."

"Ha ha," she said, playfully scowling at him.

They finished dinner, and Miranda asked if she could walk him through the castle before he turned in for the night at his cabin, which sat on the outskirts of Astaria. Not needing to walk, as he could dematerialize anywhere, he acquiesced since he wanted to speak to her privately.

Strolling down the dimly lit hall of the castle, she looked up at him.

"We'll have the combined council meeting on Monday. Sathan said they didn't find much in the archives at Valeria, but there were a few things that we can look into."

Darkrip nodded. "I'm interested to hear what they found. It's going to be very difficult to locate her."

They were referring to their sister, Evie. Rina had also borne her in the caves, when Darkrip was eight-years old, and she was now the key to killing Crimeous. The ancient soothsayer prophecy stated that a descendant of Valktor, their grandfather, would kill the Dark Lord with the Blade of Pestilence. Both Miranda and Darkrip had attempted and failed. Reaching out to Evie was the next logical step.

Unfortunately, their evil sister wanted nothing to do with the world of immortals. She had been living in the land of humans for almost eight centuries. Whereas Darkrip had found the strength to suppress his father's wicked blood, Evie thrived on it. Worry ran through him as he thought of finding her.

"I know you're concerned about tracking her down," Miranda said, taking his hand as they entered the barracks warehouse. "But we don't have a choice. We have to find her and convince her to help us."

"I know," he said, sighing. "She will be extremely resistant. She detests all of us and everything to do with our world. But she also hates my father, so, hopefully, we can find an angle there."

"We'll find one. I'm excited to meet her. I know you think she'll hate me, but I don't care. As you always like to point out, I'm really fucking stubborn. I'll win her over if it kills me."

Coming to a stop at the garage doors that led from the barracks to the green meadow where the troops trained, he turned to face her. "I have no doubt that if you set your mind to it, you'll accomplish it, Miranda."

As she smiled up at him, he felt a jolt in his solar plexus. It was as if his mother was looking into him with her olive-green eyes.

"And how are you otherwise?" she asked. "Are you okay in the cabin? Do you need anything?"

He shook his head. "Your husband has been very kind, although I know he doesn't like my presence here."

The flawless features of her face scrunched together. "Well, he's not the boss. I am."

Chuckling, Darkrip nodded. "Oh, I know it. You wear the pants in that relationship. Latimus and Heden chide him for it all the time."

"What can I say?" she asked, flinging her dark, bobbed hair. "He knows what he has to do to keep his woman happy."

"Well, as I told you when we first met, it's a good pairing. His calm and thoughtful nature is good for your impulsiveness, and your fearlessness gives him strength."

Inhaling a deep breath, she closed her eyes. "And I just fucking love him. With my whole heart." Lifting her lids, she grabbed his hands. "I want you to find that with someone too."

Squeezing her hands, he let them go, not wanting to touch her for too long. Touching created an intimacy between people, and he was already too close with her; felt too much for her. It made her a target for his evil father, and he didn't want to expose her to any danger if at all possible.

"Love would be a wasted emotion for someone like me. I'm not capable of feeling that deeply."

"I think you love me," she said softly.

"I care for you, Miranda. More than I should. It makes you vulnerable, and I hate that."

"You're a good man," she said, slipping her arms around his waist. He didn't hug her back but let her sink into him. The comfort that he took from her felt good and he reveled in it. He had rarely felt any comfort in his long, lonely life.

"You lie to yourself too easily," he said. "I think that's advice your father gave you as well. Don't lie to yourself about me. Use me to find Evie and kill my father. After that, who knows what will happen?"

"I know. You're going to fall in love with a wonderful woman and build a life that our mother would've wanted you to have."

Smiling in spite of himself, he pulled her away from him by her upper arms. "That's enough for tonight. I can't have you filling my head with silly fantasies that will never happen. Go upstairs to your Vampyre. I'll see you tomorrow."

Closing his eyes, he transported to his cabin. Once there, he threw off his clothes, brushed his teeth and lay down upon the bed, naked. Grasping his always-hardened cock with his hand, he gently moved it back and forth, thinking of Arderin as he usually did now when he performed this deed.

For a moment, just one sweet moment, he lowered his lids. In the darkness, he imagined coming home to her, the sunset at her back as she ran to him and gave him a passionate kiss. He would carry her inside and fuck her, begging her to thrust her fangs into his neck. She'd wrap that slender body around him as she pierced him, pulling blood from his quivering body. Moaning, he let himself revel in the fantasy until his seed spurted upon his stomach.

Then, he returned to reality. The thick stalk of his cock rested on his abdomen, still turgid and angry even after he'd achieved release. The goddess Etherya had cursed him when he was only a teenager to go through life with a never-softening shaft so that he would always be reminded that he was a child of evil and rape. It disgusted him, causing him to drown in self-loathing whenever he took any time to dwell on it.

A harsh laugh escaped his lips as he remembered he could never have any of the things he rarely let himself fantasize about. A wife to go home to, a happy life, children to care for. As if he would ever procreate. It would be immensely irresponsible, not to mention extremely evil, to bring any children into the world with even one drop of his father's blood. Evie had shown them that. Children were something he could never have, and he took that vow very seriously.

Sighing, he got up to wash his release off his stomach. Afterward, he crawled under the covers and turned off the bedside light. Most nights were filled with nightmares of his father raping and torturing his sweet mother. The images were burned into his brain, the pain so thick and severe that he usually awoke sweaty and gasping. Praying that tonight would hold no dreams, he fell into a restless slumber.

* * * *

On Sunday, it rained—a rarity for the immortal world on Etherya's Earth. They lived in a mostly temperate climate, filled with warm, sunny days and soft breezes. Darkrip liked to jog around the Vampyre compound of Astaria, usually charting a path through the open meadows that separated the cabins by the walls. Today's weather wouldn't afford him that, so he decided to convey to the gym inside the barracks at the main castle.

Immediately, he gritted his teeth when he materialized. The scent of innocence and purity threatened to choke him. Goddamnit, he was extremely annoyed with this almost daily occurrence of being forced to be in her presence.

Arderin was off to the side, her bare feet on a purple yoga mat that sat atop a larger blue gymnastics mat. The wall mirror beside her showed her reflection, and he clenched his jaw. Just what he needed. The ability to see her gorgeous body from multiple angles. Mentally cursing, he stalked toward the treadmill.

Eyes closed, her legs were stretched wide and straight as she bent at the waist, showing him a front-and-center view of her vagina, had her black yoga pants not been covering it. Earbuds hung from her ears, and he assumed she was listening to some human garbage. She must have sensed him because her body tensed, and she opened her eyes. They locked onto him through the V of her outstretched legs, her head hanging upside down, her black curls held into a messy bun that almost touched the floor. Ice-blue eyes pulsed with anger.

Straightening, she turned and pulled the buds out of her ears. "What in the hell are you doing here? Are you watching me?"

"I came to use the treadmill," he said, gesturing to it with his head. "It's pouring outside."

"Well, it looks to me like you came to gawk at me while I do yoga. You scared the crap out of me."

Slowly, he approached her, closing the ten-foot distance between them. "Good. You should be scared of me. It worries me that you're not more so. I'm extremely dangerous."

She rolled those dazzling eyes. "Oh, please. My brothers would gut you if you touched one hair on my head."

He smiled, loving how she always threatened his slaughter at the hands of her hulking brothers. Although they were fierce, his powers were far superior. "Would they? I imagine I'd snap their necks before they even had time to try."

Fury crossed her features, and her nostrils flared. "Don't threaten me or my brothers. I'll tell Miranda, and you'll be gone so fast you won't even remember you were here."

Breathing a laugh, he crossed his arms over his chest. "Is that so?"

"Yes."

"I don't think so, princess. You all need me a lot more than I need you. Let's get that straight."

"I don't need you for anything, you son of a bitch."

Lifting an eyebrow, he contemplated. "Hmmm. I actually think you do. I need to find my sister and convince her to kill my father. Without that, none of you will ever have peace. So, yeah, I think you need me, you ungrateful brat."

"Don't call me names," she said through clenched teeth. "I'm so tired of you treating me like shit."

Inhaling a deep breath, he studied her. Little splotches of red darted the smooth skin of her cheeks. She had a few tiny freckles across her nose, and he wondered why he'd never noticed them. "I don't mean to," he said after a pause, "but you drive me insane. You're always so combative with me."

Her mouth opened in shock. "*I'm* combative with *you*? You've threatened to rape me and shove your...*thing*...in my mouth. That's extremely fucking rude. Are you serious right now?"

Feeling the corner of his mouth turn up in a mischievous smile, he chuckled. "I guess you're right. That is pretty rude. You're just so infuriating." His eyes darted over her face. "I also told you that you were one of the most intelligent people I've ever met, and I think you could rule the planet. Or do you only remember the bad things?"

"I remember," she said, her tone sullen. "But I didn't believe you when you said them. I thought you were trying to trick me into leaving you the hell alone."

"I was," he shrugged, "but that still doesn't make what I said less true."

They stared at each other, two wary opponents deciding whether or not to let down their guard.

"I have ten minutes of yoga left. Do you want to come back when I'm done?"

The thought of someone as powerful as he changing course for someone like her equated to capitulation in his mind. He would never let her win like that.

"No, I'll just jog now if you don't mind sharing the gym with me. I'll leave you alone."

"Fine," Arderin said, replacing one of her ear buds. "But don't watch me. It makes me uncomfortable."

"I won't," he lied, knowing he'd never be able to keep his eyes from darting to her perfect, yoga pant-clad body. "What are you listening to?"

"Hailee Steinfeld. She's awesome. Her songs are so empowering."

"Never heard of her."

"Well, you probably didn't get much exposure to human pop music in the Deamon caves."

Laughter bubbled up and he shook his head. "No. My father was too busy torturing and raping to get his jam on."

She gave a sad smile, a subtle compassion shining in her sky-blue eyes. Not wanting her to feel any sort of emotion for him, he harshened his tone. "Go on. I'll leave you alone."

Giving him a proper scowl, she replaced her other earbud and resumed the yoga. Hopping on the treadmill, he set the pace on the electronic screen. Beginning to jog, he noticed that he could see her out of the corner of his eye. She was now balancing on one leg, her opposite foot placed on her inner thigh, her hands together in prayer in front of her chest.

Good. She'd better pray he never acted on his ridiculous attraction to her. If he ever did, he was afraid for her life. Touching one cell of her body would render him unable to let go, and the consequences would be disastrous. Of that, he was sure. Picking up the pace, her scent surrounded him as he ran, wishing he could so easily run from her.

Chapter 3

Monday morning, Arderin rose, thankful for the gorgeous sun after yesterday's downpour. Wanting to stretch in the sunlight, she threw on her yoga clothes and headed to the barracks. After grabbing her mat from the gym, she headed outside to the hill that sat under the elm tree. She knew it to be Sathan's favorite place, beautiful and serene, and offering a nice view of the main castle.

Opening her mat, she sat cross-legged and closed her eyes, straightening her spine. She'd started doing yoga a few years ago, spurred on by the energetic and inspiring human yoga instructors she followed on Instagram. It filled her with a sense of calm—a good thing for someone as dramatic and passionate as she. Inhaling deeply, she reveled in the warmth of the shining orb above. The glowing sun shone on her skin and Arderin basked in the simmer. After living in the darkness for so long, it felt magnificent.

Vampyres had only regained the ability to walk in the sun recently. Etherya had cursed them to live in the darkness for a thousand years due to the War of the Species and their raids on the Slayers for their blood. Now that Sathan and Miranda had united the tribes once more, Slayers freely banked their blood, and huge barrels showed up daily. Smiling, she thanked Etherya, showing her gratefulness.

Vampyres needed to drink what equated to ten pulls from a vein every two to three days or they would perish. Since drinking directly from a Slayer's vein would afford the Vampyre the ability to read that person's thoughts and feelings, as long as the Slayer's blood coursed through them, Arderin's father had outlawed direct drinking before the Awakening. Sathan had continued the ban, now that the species were reunited, although she knew he drank from Miranda's vein when they mated. Her fiery sister-in-law was possessive of her brother, and Arderin was pretty sure she wouldn't let any blood inside him but her own.

Arderin was so proud of Sathan, although she was slightly annoyed with him at the moment. It was the usual pattern they'd fallen into since Arderin longed to be a doctor. She'd always been fascinated with healing, feeling it a noble profession. When Nolan, Astaria's physician, had come to live on their compound over three centuries ago, she had become his student, her curious and eager mind soaking up everything he could teach her.

It was hard for Sathan to understand her desire to heal since Vampyres possessed self-healing abilities. She understood that. But now that Slayers lived at Astaria and more would be moving to their satellite compounds in the future, there was a need to have more than two physicians in the land of immortals. She'd been begging Sathan to let her train in the human world for centuries. They were extremely proficient at medicine, and the Slayer doctor, Sadie, had trained there throughout the past few centuries, off and on.

Arderin smiled as she thought of Sadie. She'd become one of her best friends. She was extremely kind and always up for learning about all of the human pastimes Arderin loved. Although humans were pretty much useless, and unaware of the immortals' existence on Etherya's Earth, they produced some amazing music and technology. She always enjoyed helping Sadie use Instagram or find an awesome filter on Snapchat. Since her friend was badly burned on half her body, she was self-conscious about her appearance. Wanting to cheer her up, they always snickered when they found the filters that made them look so cute in their selfies.

Standing, Arderin reached to the sky, beginning her half-moon poses. Her brothers, Lila and Miranda would all be on the train to Uteria by now. They had called a meeting of the combined Slayer-Vampyre council to discuss what Sathan and Latimus had discovered in the archives at Valeria. The Vampyres kept separate records there lest Astaria be raided by the Deamons, although the chance was small. Etherya had erected a protective wall around Astaria, wanting to safeguard Sathan after their parents had been killed. Also, Latimus was a kick-ass warrior who would never let those bastards in.

Shifting into a dancer's pose, she stretched toward the sky, looking toward the hills in the distance. Darkrip's cabin sat out there, and her face scrunched into a scowl. Bastard. He'd scared the crap out of her when she'd found him watching her in the gym yesterday. As was always the case when he was near, her heart had slammed in her chest and proceeded to pound as she verbally sparred with him.

She didn't know why she was so affected by him. He was evil, the child of the Dark Lord, and she tried her best to hate him. But he was also Miranda's half-brother, Slayer blood coursing through his muscular body along with the vile Deamon blood. Although she felt his darkness, he also possessed a pulsing energy that sizzled. Drawn to it, she was always enraged by their vocal scuffling and, if she was honest with herself, a bit aroused.

Lowering to her knees to begin camel pose, she cursed herself, hating that she was attracted to someone so contemptible. But he was exceedingly handsome and always so well-dressed. How someone raised in the Deamon caves could develop a love for Italian loafers and expensive, tailored clothing was a mystery to her. Yet, his firm body was always draped in attire that accentuated his toned frame.

Deep green eyes, the color of olives, always seemed to melt as he chided her. His lips were thick and full, and she'd be lying if she said she hadn't imagined them nibbling on her own. Or maybe somewhere else. Hmmm. Dark, buzzed-cut hair sat atop his pointed ears, inherited from his father. They should've disgusted her, reminding her of what he was, but she always had the urge to lightly clamp on them with her teeth for some insane reason.

She'd never told anyone of her attraction to him. It was pointless, as she'd never act on it. He was a monster, regardless that Miranda believed his good side overrode his malevolent one. Arderin would never believe that, considering the way he treated her.

Knowing that she wanted to train in the land of humans, he'd offered to transfer her off the compound many times...for a price. He had the ability to transport her to the ether, and once through, he could convey her anywhere in the human world. Until now, she'd rejected his offers. She was pretty sure what his price would be and vowed that he would never touch her.

Sitting, she stretched her legs in front of her, grabbing her big toes with her two longest fingers and pulling. Finishing her set, she leaned back on her arms, breathing in the blue sky. It glowed with stripes of ocean blue, ice blue and every shade in-between. The streaks formed a gorgeous tapestry that she hadn't seen since she was so very young. Only three years old during the Awakening, Arderin had grown accustomed to only seeing the daylight sky in her dreams. The splendor above her was remarkable.

Sighing, she watched the clouds. Loneliness threatened to choke her, and her eyes welled with tears. Everyone seemed to have a purpose but her. They were all so happy while she struggled with her inability to get Sathan's blessing or assistance to travel to the human world.

He wanted her to focus her efforts in the Vampyre kingdom, since she was royalty and had a responsibility. Sathan felt that her duties should entail helping him and the governors of the other compounds mobilize their people. Being quite social media-savvy, he wanted Arderin to organize the younger subjects of the kingdom and enroll them in projects that would better their world. But she truly felt in her heart that the path to helping her subjects would be through medicine. What if Heden wanted to go to the land of humans? Would Sathan forbid him? Anger simmered as she stewed, contemplating the answer.

A red bird landed on the grass beside her mat, and she called to it. "Hey, little bird. Are you enjoying the sun?"

It studied her, shifting its tiny head back and forth several times.

"Me too. Although I wish I had someone to enjoy it with. Maybe we can enjoy it together." The bird flew away, symbolizing her inability to be anything but alone.

Arderin wanted to be in love so badly. Seeing her brothers in love was amazing and she longed to feel the same. Sadly, very few men of the kingdom had ever expressed interest in courting her. Narrowing her eyes, she contemplated why. She was attractive—this, she knew to be true. The belief didn't stem from arrogance, just a knowledge of the basics of bone structure and general appearance. Her features were perfectly placed, her nose angular and pert, her cheekbones pronounced. Ice-blue eyes formed a pretty contrast with her raven-black, waist-length curls. Looking down her body, she admitted she was lucky in that she was lithe and slender. So, why in the hell was no one interested?

She'd had a handful of suitors in the past. All aristocratic men, none of whom she'd even come close to falling in love with. Being a passionate person, she'd had some epic make-out sessions, but had never let anyone get past second base. Eventually, each man had tried to push her toward bonding and having children, neither of which she'd been ready for. Perhaps that was why she had so few prospects. The men of the kingdom who wanted to start a family had figured out that she was a waste of their time.

Or maybe they were scared of her brothers. After all, Sathan was king, and Latimus was the most powerful soldier who had ever walked the planet. Pretty intimidating for a would-be suitor. Seeing her brothers so happy had her reconsidering her desire to settle down and she hoped some of the handsome men of the realm would grow a pair and court her. The prospect of finding someone to love and start a family with didn't seem as daunting as it once had.

Her friend Naran, whom she'd known forever, had been trying to court her lately, although his attempts were so lame. He always asked her to dance at their royal parties, so formal and meek. Feeling the corners of her lips turn up, she found herself wishing he would spar with her like Darkrip did. Now, that would be interesting. Instead, the man just bored her to tears. Too bad. She was so tired of being a virgin, and thought she might do the deed with him, if she wasn't so afraid of falling asleep right in the middle.

Snickering to herself at the thought of drooling in slumber while her dull friend attempted to bone her, she rolled up her mat. Strolling back to the main house, she deposited it in the gym and showered in her chambers. Once dressed, she plodded down the grand spiral staircase from her second-floor bedroom and through the now-unused dungeon. Once past the cells, she found Nolan, looking through a microscope, clad in his always-present white lab coat.

"Hi," Arderin said, approaching him. "Whatcha got today? Are we close?"

Turning, he smiled at her, the ever-present twinkle in his kind brown eyes. "We are. The skin seems to be regenerating to about eighty percent with our current formulation of Vampyre self-healing blood, saliva, Slayer blood, CBD and essential oils. It's a huge advancement but the last twenty percent is elusive."

"Hmmm," she said, bringing her fingers to tap on her chin. "What else could we possibly need?"

Nolan leaned back on the counter, crossing his arms. "As we've discussed, I think the only way we can get to one hundred percent is by getting the cell regeneration formula from the genetics lab that we identified in Houston. Unfortunately, I can't go to the human world to get it, and if we send Sadie, we'll blow the surprise."

Arderin nodded, the wheels in her mind turning. Nolan was an anomaly. A human that lived in the immortal world, he'd tried to save Sathan from an injury over three centuries ago and accidentally discovered their hidden part of Etherya's Earth. The goddess had given him a choice: immortality in the land of Vampyres and Slayers, unable to ever rejoin the land of humans, or death. He'd chosen immortality, something that Arderin was grateful for. Although she suspected he was lonely in their world, she cared for him immensely and ingested the medical knowledge he gave her like a parched traveler in a dry desert.

"I really don't want to ruin the surprise," she said, feeling her eyebrows draw together. "Sadie is such an amazing person who does so much for everyone else and never thinks of herself. I want us to be able to give this gift to her so badly. But the formulation has to be perfect."

"I agree," he said with a nod. "I'm excited to do something nice for her too. It's been wonderful to work with another physician, and she's phenomenal."

Arderin studied his thick brown hair and prominent chin. He was quite handsome, for a human. She wondered if his motivations toward Sadie were purely platonic. Could he be interested in her romantically as well?

Filing that away in her curious brain, she stepped to look at the sample under the microscope. Tiny cells, burnt only minutes ago, had regenerated to be quite smooth again. "I have to find a way to convince Sathan to let me travel to the human world."

Nolan sighed beside her. "I'd hate to see you guys get into an argument. You've been getting along so well."

Arderin rolled her eyes, training them on his. "Because he's in love and stuck in la-la land all the time. He doesn't have time to drive me nuts now that Miranda's pregnant. He's more protective of her than he is of me at the moment. I'll feel her out. Maybe she can be swayed to let me travel there. He'd do anything she asked him."

Nolan lifted a tawny eyebrow. "He's pretty set on keeping you safe, here in the kingdom."

"Well, it's not his life. I told him recently that I've grown tired of letting him have a say. If he's not careful, I'll just go. It will be much more difficult to travel there without his help and support, but I'm getting tired of his crap."

Nolan smiled. "Well, I wish you the best in your efforts to sway him. If anyone can, it's my curious and stubborn little student."

Arderin felt her lips curve. "I'm so happy you're here, Nolan. I know you must feel lonely. Believe it or not, I feel lonely too. More often than not lately. You can always come to me if you want to hang."

"Thanks, sweetie," he said, running a hand down her hair. "I don't want you to feel lonely. I'm always here for you too." His six-foot height was the same as hers, and she smiled into his eyes and gave him a firm hug.

"Okay, I'm off to find some Slayer blood. I'm starving. Let me brainstorm. I'll figure it out."

With a nod, he turned back to the microscope, and she departed the infirmary, determined to get to the human world or bust.

Chapter 4

Darkrip materialized into Miranda's royal office chamber at Uteria. The room held a long mahogany conference table and the other members of the council milled around. He noticed Kenden, Miranda's chestnut-haired cousin, chatting with Aron and Larkin as he drank coffee from a white paper cup. Aron was a Slayer aristocrat. Larkin was the resilient soldier who commanded the combat troops at Uteria.

Lila was smiling at Miranda as she rubbed her rounded abdomen. Miranda threw her head back and laughed at something the woman said, and Darkrip's heart squeezed. No one laughed quite as heartily or fully as his beautiful sister.

Latimus and Sathan stood chatting, arms crossed against their beefy chests. They made a formidable pair indeed. Although Arderin's threats to have them murder him were pithy, they still could likely beat the shit out of him before he gained his wits and ability to use his power to destroy them. Deciding that would expend too much energy, he reminded himself that was one more reason why he'd never touch the obstinate little princess.

Miranda gave Lila a friendly hug and walked toward the head of the table. "Okay, guys, let's get started."

Sathan sat to her right, his usual seat when they met at Uteria. In return, he always sat at the head when they held their combined council meetings at Astaria. Latimus sat to her left, Lila sitting next to him. Although Darkrip didn't like many people as a general rule, the blond-haired diplomat had always been so kind to him. A recent battle with his father had led to him almost striking her and he still felt quite guilty about it. Strange, since a creature like him rarely felt any emotion, especially one as ridiculous as guilt.

"Hi, Darkrip," Lila said, cordiality swimming in her stunning lavender irises as he sat beside her. "How are you?"

"Fine," he said, forcing himself to smile at her, uncomfortable with her graciousness toward him. Especially after he'd almost killed her. Swallowing thickly, he waited for Miranda to speak.

She was still standing, making eye contact with each of them as she spoke. "Thanks to everyone for coming together this morning. One of the security systems for the train from Naria to Lynia went offline this morning, so Heden is at Astaria repairing it. He sends his regards. Today, I want to discuss what we've found and chart next steps. Sathan and Latimus spent two days going over the archives at

Valeria, and Aron and Kenden searched the manuals here. Sathan, why don't you go first?"

"There wasn't much," he said, as Miranda sat. "The archives at Valeria aren't as extensive as the ones at Astaria, but we did find a few things." Opening the notebook that sat before him, he touched the white page with his thick index finger.

"There's a mention from the fourth century of a woman with flame-red hair who came to meditate for several consecutive decades at the statue of the Great Buddha in Kamakura, Japan. The archivist noted that her hair never turned gray. It's quite possible that it was Evie."

Latimus nodded across from him. "There's also another entry from the seventh century that details a pale woman turning into a dragon. It's a fairy tale that circulated around the villages of Japan for centuries. The dragon was said to breathe fire the color of the woman's hair and originated in the modern-day town of Zushi. It's a coastal town that's also located close to the Great Buddha statue. The dragon was described as quite evil, to scare children into behaving. We were thinking that perhaps Evie murdered some of the locals and this was the resulting fairy tale, passed down through the ages. If so, Japan could be a place she frequents quite often."

Sathan looked around, connecting with everyone as he continued. "There were no more mentions of her in Japan, although we did find some mentions of a red-haired woman in France and Italy. Since that's where Kenden found her, that makes sense."

Kenden tilted his head in acknowledgement. "Yes, I knew to look for her there from the mentions in our soothsayer manuscripts. After looking over them again with Aron, we did find a fable that the soothsayers wrote, warning children to obey their parents lest a woman come to abduct them. The story warned that she would snatch them under the light of the red sun if they misbehaved. Knowing that Japan uses that symbol on their flag, it could be a confirmation that she favors that location."

"Okay," Miranda said with a nod. "Anything else?"

"Unfortunately, that was it on our side," Kenden said. "Most of the mentions of her in our manuscripts reference France and Italy."

"Same here," Sathan chimed in. "That was all we could find as well."

Miranda stood, and Darkrip sensed her restlessness. "So, the next logical step would be to look for her in Japan. Darkrip, we need to get you there. I'm wondering if I should come with you."

"No," Sathan said, his dark eyebrows drawing together. "You can't travel while you're pregnant, Miranda. We've discussed this."

Her nostrils flared with frustration. "I know. But she hates Darkrip since he tried to kill her. I feel like having me there would soften the blow or something."

"I appreciate your faith in me," Darkrip said, his tone sardonic. "But I assure you, she'll talk to me if I find her. If for no other reason, then to try and murder me back. She's nothing if not vengeful."

"And if she won't listen to you, how will that help our cause?"

"Let me try first," Darkrip said, moving his gaze to make eye contact with everyone in the room. "She hates our father, and we are united in that. Let me at least try to see if her hate is strong enough to sway her to our cause. We share an understanding of our father's evil that Kenden didn't have when he found her. It could be enough to pull her to our side. It's worth a shot before I drag you to the human world, Miranda."

"Okay," his sister said, inhaling a deep breath. "Do you all agree that this should be our next step?"

Everyone gave an, "Aye," heads nodding.

"Then that's what we'll do. Let's all wish Darkrip well and hope that he's successful. Given that our grandfather's blood courses through him, I expect he will be. Thank you all for coming. I value your council and know that we're on the right path to killing that bastard. For now, let's adjourn. I'm going to head to the main square to peruse today's street fair, if anyone wants to join me."

Latimus stood and addressed Kenden. "You still want me to help Larkin with the orientation for the new Uterian soldiers today, right?"

Kenden nodded, standing. "If you don't mind. I need to do the final walk-through on the house today." He was building a house close to his shed, on the outskirts of Uteria, so that he no longer needed to live in the main castle.

"Sure," Latimus said. Leaning down to kiss Lila, he asked, "Are you going to go to the street fair with Miranda?"

His bonded nodded and gave him a peck back. "See you at the train platform at three."

"Okay, honey. I'll miss you." Darkrip had to restrain himself from rolling his eyes. Those two were so in love it made him want to throw up in his mouth.

Lila seemed to float out of the room behind Miranda, with Sathan and Aron accompanying them. Larkin and Kenden followed behind, chatting about the new long-range walkie talkies they had purchased for the soldiers to communicate more effectively.

Not bothering to stand, Darkrip decided he'd sit and stew a bit longer.

"Do you want to help me orient the troops?" Latimus asked him.

Darkrip contemplated. It would give him something to do besides wallow in his always constant rage and self-hate.

"You're adept at using the TEC. I wouldn't mind having your help to show the twenty new soldiers we have."

"What the hell," Darkrip said, standing. He had an eternity to concentrate on what an abomination he was. Why not help out the Vampyre commander? They'd grown quite cordial to each other lately, and Darkrip was impressed at the mighty army the man had built.

"Great. C'mon."

Striding together, the warrior dwarfed his six-foot-two frame. But that was okay. Darkrip could still kill him with a thought. Smiling at the nasty image, he let him lead the way to the sparring field.

* * * *

Two hours later, Darkrip was actually enjoying helping the troops learn how to deploy the TEC. It was a powerful weapon against the Deamons, its ability to latch onto their foreheads and plunge a blade into the vestigial third eye between their functional eyes deadly. It killed every Deamon with one discharge—except his powerful father, who was unfazed by the weapon.

As he trained three Slayer soldiers on the device, he saw the man to his left struggling. "You need to hold it like this," he said, addressing the soldier. "Otherwise, it might detonate in your hand."

The soldier fiddled with the weapon, accidentally dropping it to the ground. As he bent and picked it up, it seemed to shoot out of his hand, right into the side of Darkrip's abdomen.

Sucking in a huge breath, he waited for the pain. And then he felt it. Pleasure on the highest level coursed through his body, causing his heartbeat to accelerate. It was another trait inherited from his wretched father. While others felt agony at the infliction of pain, Darkrip felt an immense joy. It was extremely evil and disgusted him thoroughly.

Latimus ran over, placing his hand on Darkrip's shoulder. "Are you okay?" he asked, worry lacing his ice-blue eyes.

"Yeah," Darkrip said, pulling the contraption from his side. Blood gushed behind, swamping him with a wave of bliss. Looking up at the Vampyre, he saw the realization resonate in his eyes.

"We're okay here, troops," he said to the three soldiers Darkrip had been training. "Take ten."

"Sorry, man," the offending soldier said, his eyes filled with guilt. They stalked off toward the nearby barracks for their break.

"I have a first-aid kit—"

"It's fine," Darkrip interrupted the commander, holding his hand over the gaping wound. "That's what I get for trying to be nice and help people. The universe just isn't ready for that."

Latimus' irises darted over him. "I understand that you're not feeling pain. But the wound needs to be treated."

"I'll be fine. It's time I get back to the cabin anyway. This Mr. Nice Guy shit just isn't me." Closing his eyes, he transported to his cottage. Pulling off his bloody shirt along with the rest of his clothes, Darkrip assessed the wound in the bathroom mirror. It was bad. A long, deep laceration ran down his entire left side. Cursing Vampyres for being the only immortals with self-healing abilities, he washed out the wound with a soapy cloth and applied the long bandage that he'd pulled from his bathroom cabinet.

Lying on his bed, Darkrip threw his arm over his eyes. The cut at his side throbbed, his dick throbbed—hell, his whole body throbbed. Wishing for nothing more than to never feel anything again, he drowned in self-loathing. Eventually, he fell into sleep.

Chapter 5

Darkrip angrily rubbed his eyes as he awoke. Feeling gritty, he lifted the bandage and looked at his laceration. It stared back at him, red and angry. Cursing himself for even agreeing to help Latimus in the first place, he rose from the bed and clenched his teeth at the sight of his near-to-bursting cock. The twisted pleasure-pain from his wound combined with his sick need to masturbate was driving him insane, reminding him of what a vile, nasty creature he was.

Looking out the curtains, he saw the moon. Good god, he'd slept for hours. His injury pulsed, and he realized he didn't have the proper tools to treat it in the cabin. Checking the clock on his bed stand, he noted that it was almost midnight. Throwing on some sweat pants, he conveyed to Nolan's infirmary, mindless of his bare chest. Since it was so late, no one else would be there.

When he reached the infirmary, he found a counter with cabinets above and all the appropriate medical supplies. Pulling out a needle and thread, he sat on the infirmary bed to start stitching. God, the wound was ugly. He inspected it, sewing the enflamed tissue together, hating the pleasure that shot through his body with each needle prick into his skin. And then, he stilled...right in mid-prick...

She was *here*. Her scent invaded his nostrils like an unwelcome army attacking the thick layer of protection he had built around himself. With a growl, he lifted his head.

Arderin stood inside the entrance to the infirmary, her eyes rounded as her pink lips formed a silent 'O.'

"Get out," he gritted through his teeth. He hated that his tone was so harsh, especially after their recent cordial conversation in the gym, but he detested showing vulnerability to anyone. That he would show it to her, the woman who seemed to pervade his every thought, was humiliating. Vowing to scare her away, he bristled, hoping she'd scamper off and leave him to drown in his self-loathing.

Her ice-blue irises lowered to the gash, where his hands were still frozen in mid-sew, and then lifted back up to his. "You're hurt." Her voice lacked the harshness he'd come to expect from her.

"Very observant, princess."

She took two tentative but long strides toward him, her chin held high. "Who hurt you?"

"Arderin," he said, squeezing his eyes shut as her smell overwhelmed him. "I would leave now, if you know what's good for you."

Opening his eyes, he observed that she swallowed visibly as she closed the remaining distance between them. "I think that's the first time."

"What?" he asked, his tone somewhere between exasperated and furious.

"That you called me by my name and not 'princess' or 'brat.' Now, I'm really worried." Her lips curved into a half-smile as she looked down at him, her expression filled with concern. He felt scrutinized, as if he was a bug under a microscope.

"I'm not your latest science experiment. Get out."

Arderin grabbed the needle and thread, grazing his hands as she took them. Fire sparked through his entire body from her brief touch. "You can't sew yourself if you don't clean the wound first," she instructed as if he were a child, not the son of the Dark Lord who could pulverize her into a million bits with one thought.

"I cleaned it earlier. I've been injured thousands of times in the Deamon caves and sewn myself up just fine. Not all of us have the luxury of playing doctor for a day."

Her eyes narrowed. "Since you're in pain, I'll let that one go. Give me a sec."

Pivoting, she opened the windowed cabinets above the counter, pulling out a bottle of alcohol, some gauze and some bandages. Dragging over a tray that sat atop thin legs with wheels, she sat everything on top. Coming to stand in front of him, she gave him an irritated look.

"Move your hands."

Realizing that he was still holding his hands in front of his wound, he moved them, sitting the palms flat on the bed. Opening the bottle of alcohol, she poured a generous amount on the white gauze. Lifting those gorgeous eyes to his, she said, "This might hurt." Her perfect features were laced with extreme focus as she touched the gauze to his wound.

It did indeed hurt, but that pain sent an agonizing burst of pleasure through his veins, compounded by her scent. Hating himself, he closed his eyes in shame.

Her short gasp indicated that she'd realized what he had so desperately wanted to hide from her. He wasn't sure why, but he'd wanted his sick pleasure kept from her.

"I am the son of the Dark Lord," he muttered to her, his eyes opening to form angry slits. "You should expect that I would feel pleasure from pain."

She shrugged her slender shoulders and continued cleaning him. "Guess you're lucky."

Darkrip scoffed. "Yes, none are as lucky as I," he mocked.

Arderin lifted her icy irises to him, filled with the quick flare of anger that he'd come to expect from her. "Most people would give anything to feel pleasure where there should be pain. Perhaps *you* need to change your perspective."

"Perhaps *you* need to close that bratty mouth before I do it for you."

Her nostrils flared as she stared back at him. Inhaling a large breath, she just shook her head in disapproval and lowered her focus to his wound again.

As she cleaned him, Darkrip felt something in his chest that he refused to acknowledge. His nostrils clung to the smell of her fruity shampoo and he had visions of pushing her head into his lap. Fuck.

Her thin fingers were steady as she began to stitch his wound. "How did this happen?" she asked, her ministrations never ceasing.

"I was helping your brother orient some of the new Slayer troops to the TEC. One of them misfired into my side."

"Yikes," she said. He could tell she was holding in a laugh. "No good deed goes unpunished, huh?"

Breathing out a laugh, he shrugged. "Guess not."

"Okay, you're all done. Let me just bandage you up."

As she opened the dressing on the table, he inspected her work. It was flawless. Impressed with her medical skills, he allowed her to place the long white gauze strip over his stitches. With the thin pads of her fingers, she rubbed over the bandage, making sure it bonded with his skin. Unable to take it, he grabbed her wrist, stilling it.

"That's enough," he said, pulling her wrist from his burning body. Her touch consumed him. "You'd be wise not to voluntarily touch me. I think you know that."

Her perfect features formed a scowl, and she pulled her wrist from his grasp. "Well, you're fucking welcome, asshole. That's the last time I try to help you." Turning, she began cleaning up the table, muttering to herself.

Knowing that he was playing with fire, he stood to his full height. Aligning his front with her back, he brushed against her. She stilled instantly, snapping her head so that she watched him from the corner of her eye.

"I appreciate you helping me. I'm not trying to be a jerk. But you know of my curse. It drives me to want things I can't have." Unable to stop himself, he pushed his erection into her lower back. "I'll never be able to erase the image of you clutching my cock in your hand after the battle with my father. It felt amazing." Closing his eyes, he nuzzled her soft curls with his nose. "God, I want to fuck you so badly. Remember that next time you come near me. I've exhibited extreme control around you and enjoy our little spats more than you realize, but I'm every bit the monster you think I am."

Breathy pants exited her frozen body. "If you're such a monster, why are you warning me?"

Lowering his lips to her ear, he whispered, "Because you matter. Don't take that for more than what it is. I don't want to hurt you. Be cautious." Chill bumps dotted the pale skin of her slender neck as she shivered. Knowing he was so close to crossing a line from which he could never return, he closed his eyes and dematerialized back to his cabin.

* * * *

Arderin clutched her hand over her beating heart once Darkrip disappeared. Inhaling several deep breaths, she told herself to calm down. Lifting her hand, she traced her ear where his lips had touched her so softly. By the goddess, she wanted him to lick her there.

Feeling a rush of wetness between her thighs, she clenched them together. Telling herself that she was insane, she cleaned up the bedside table and counter and headed to her room. Prepping for bed, she brushed her teeth, washed her face and donned her silky nightshirt. Crawling underneath the covers, she let her mind drift to Darkrip.

Finding him injured had sent a shock through her body. For one moment, before he'd become aware of her presence, she'd seen him hurt and vulnerable, struggling with self-hate as he sat on the infirmary bed. What must it feel like to loathe yourself every minute of every day? And how difficult must the war within him be? His father's evil battling his mother's good. That, along with the curse that the goddess placed on him, must be extremely torturous for him. Being a clinician, she understood that always being in a constant state of arousal was maddening. While arousal was enjoyable in short bursts, being constantly hard and straining to mate would be awful. Feeling sorry for him, she sighed.

He had a nice body, that was for damn sure. Broad shoulders ran into a solid six-pack. What would it feel like to run her fingers over the ridges of his abdomen?

Remembering the heat that emanated from his body as he brushed against her back, she lowered her hand to her core. Running two fingers through the wetness, she pulled the moisture up to her little nub and began rubbing. As she pleasured herself, she imagined him nibbling on her ear, the image strong under her closed eyelids.

"Oh, god," she moaned, increasing the pressure and pace of her hand. What would he be like in bed? Allowing herself to imagine, she could almost feel his hard body over hers. His never-softening shaft would pound the hell out of her. "Yes," she whispered, her taut body so close.

Throwing her head back, she gave in to the climax. Shuddering on the bed, she let herself enjoy it. Although Vampyre women were taught to save their virginity for bonding, Arderin saw no harm in giving herself pleasure. Why the heck not? Men jerked off all the time. She was enthralled by sex and couldn't wait to enjoy it with someone she cared for and trusted, hopefully sooner rather than later. She was so damn tired of being a virgin.

Sighing, she pulled the covers close, relaxed and sated. Cuddling into the pillow, she fell to sleep.

Chapter 6

The next morning, Arderin found Miranda on the treadmill in the gym. Heavy metal blasted out of her earbuds, and she approached slowly, not wanting to startle her.

"Hey," Miranda said, pulling the white knob out of one ear. "What's up?"

Arderin glanced at the treadmill screen, which indicated forty minutes had passed. "Wow, forty minutes. That's awesome. How much longer do you have? I can come back."

"Since I can only walk on an incline, now that your brother implanted a Vampyre inside me, I usually do a full hour. I miss running so much. But I can hop off if you need me."

"No, I'll come back when you're done."

Twenty-five minutes later, Arderin returned to see her sister-in-law toweling off the bronzed skin of her flawless face. Lifting her water bottle, she chugged the entire contents, gesturing to the open spot beside her on the workout bench.

"Oh, boy. This must be bad," Miranda said, noticing Arderin's hesitation. "What do you need?"

Straightening her spine, Arderin said, "As you know, Nolan and I have been working on the skin regeneration formula. It's going really well, and we want to surprise Sadie with it once it's ready."

Miranda smiled. "So awesome. What do you need from me?"

Arderin bit her bottom lip. "The formula is only about eighty percent effective. It won't help someone as badly burned as Sadie unless it's at one hundred percent. There's a human genetics lab in Houston that has a formula we need. It's the only place on Etherya's Earth that has developed something this advanced. I need to travel there to get it."

Miranda's eyes searched hers. "Arderin—"

"Before you say no, let me remind you that Sathan has no problem letting anyone go to the human world but me. As a fellow feminist, I would hope you'd support me."

Inhaling a deep breath, Miranda stood and ran her hand over her silky hair, pulled into a tiny ponytail at the nape of her neck. "You know I struggle with Sathan's protectiveness too. He's a barbarian half the time, especially now that I'm pregnant. But he's had to protect everyone his whole life and is still haunted by your mother's murder. His wariness to let you travel there stems from something so good. He would die if something happened to you."

"I know," Arderin said with a nod. "But he's got to relax. I'm my own woman and I've let him make this choice for me for centuries. I understand that we are a traditional society, but I'm done having him or anyone dictate my life. If he won't help me, I'll go on my own."

Miranda stayed silent, the wheels of her mind churning. "I want to support you, Arderin. You know that I think both of our kingdoms are stuck in the damn fourth century. But these things take time. I love you as if you were my own sister, but he's my husband. I have to honor his wishes."

Rage flew through Arderin and she stood. "Even though you know it to be wrong?"

"I know it to be dangerous," she replied, her eyes narrowing. "I have no desire to go to the human world and never have. I don't understand your obsession with traveling there. How would you protect yourself? How would you travel to the ether? You've never learned to drive. If you rode a horse, he would perish before you returned. What if something happened while you were there, and we were unaware? You know that the ether prevents us from communicating with anyone over there. Have you thought about any of this?"

Arderin flared her nostrils, hating how wise her sister-in-law was. Of course, she'd thought of those things. Well, sort of. Okay, not really, but she would figure it out. She was nothing if not resilient and her mind was sharp.

"I'm not an idiot, Miranda. I'm pretty sure I can learn how to drive a four-wheeler on YouTube."

Miranda breathed a laugh. "I'm not sure it's that simple, but you're right. You're extremely intelligent. I just worry for you." She clutched Arderin's hand. "I understand your desire to do this. I think it has more to do with struggling to find your independence than securing the formula for Sadie."

A warning flashed across Miranda's features and she squeezed Arderin's fingers. "Don't snap at me, Arderin. I see the words forming and I'm telling you not to go there. I'm your ally here, although you don't believe it."

"Not if you won't help me convince Sathan to let me go!" she said, yanking her hand from her grasp. "Otherwise, you're just keeping me prisoner like he is!"

"Good grief." Rolling her grass-green eyes, she placed her hand on her hip. "When you're in the human world, maybe try out for Broadway or something. I think we need to channel that dramatic energy into something useful."

Unable to control herself, Arderin breathed a laugh. "Stop joking. I'm serious."

"I know," Miranda said, gesturing for Arderin to sit beside her on the bench again. "Sit down and let me think." Staring absently at the ceiling as Arderin complied, she rubbed her extended abdomen over her workout gear. "I want so badly to help you. I'm just struggling with the fact that I don't want you to go there either. If something happened to you, I would never recover. You're my sister, and I love you."

Damnit. Her heart clenched at the Slayer's reverent words.

"Our little man is coming soon. He needs his aunt. Please, don't leave us."

Her eyes welled with tears as Miranda's thin hand moved over her belly. She was so happy for them and beyond excited to meet her nephew. "I already love him. I promise I'll be safe and won't get hurt. Please, Miranda."

Chewing on her plushy lip, she said, "What if I could offer you a compromise?"

"And that being?"

"Darkrip is heading into the land of humans at the end of the week to try and find Evie. I could ask him to go to Houston and retrieve the formula for you while he's there."

"It's an extensive formula that only a physician would recognize. I don't think he has the medical knowledge to ensure he'd retrieve the right one."

"Could you show him the image in your mind? Surely then he could find it."

Arderin grimaced, hating to allow the man into any part of her mind, although she knew he could read the images there without her permission. "I could, but I still wouldn't have confidence that he would locate the correct one. If he fails, then they would relocate the formula to somewhere else with tighter security, and Nolan and I would have to start from scratch."

Looking at the floor, Miranda's lids blinked several times as she considered other options. "Okay," she said, lifting her gaze. "I think I'd be okay with you going if Darkrip accompanies you. At least he could protect you, and his ability to dematerialize would ensure you extra protection."

Standing, Miranda said, "I'll try to convince Sathan. It won't be easy, and I'm pretty sure it's never going to happen. If he won't agree, I have to support his decision. We're a team and we love you."

"Okay," Arderin said, jumping from the bench as excitement coursed through her. Although she was loath to travel with Darkrip, she would acquiesce if it helped her get to her destination. "Thank you, Miranda. I know he'll agree if you ask him. Let me know how it goes." She threw her arms around the Slayer, giving her a tight hug.

"Geez, you're strong. Don't choke me before I can sway him."

Chuckling, she pulled back and smiled. "I love you."

Miranda arched a black eyebrow. "Let's see if that sentiment is still the same when he says no."

Arderin felt the corners of her lips curve. "You can do it."

Laughing, she nodded. "I'll try my best."

Hoping that she would be successful, Arderin bounded from the gym, an extra bounce in her step.

* * * *

That evening, Sathan watched his wife prep for bed. Although she was performing the same mundane routine she did every night, he sensed something was off. Finished with brushing her teeth, she padded over to their walk-in closet and removed her clothes, throwing them in the hamper. Naked, she walked toward the dresser and pulled out one of his large black t-shirts. He knew she liked sleeping in them because they held his scent.

"Hey," he said, approaching her and pulling the shirt from her hand. Stuffing it back in the drawer, he closed it and looked at her in the reflection of their dresser mirror. Sliding his hands up the sides of her stomach, he rubbed her silky skin as his palms came to rest on her extended abdomen.

"Hey, yourself," she said, desire swimming in her gorgeous eyes as she stared back at him in the mirror. "There's nothing like being fondled by a naked Vampyre before bed. Are you gonna do something with those hands, or do I have to make you?"

Smiling, he lowered his chin on the top of her silky head. The pads of his fingers traced over her smooth skin. "You look so beautiful like this."

"Like a fat cow? Good grief. I need to get you to an eye doctor."

He chuckled and slid his hands up to her bare breasts, swollen and large with her pregnancy. Feeling himself start to pant, he latched onto her nipples with the thumb and forefinger of each hand. Tugging slightly, his shaft pulsed on her upper back as he smelled the responding wetness that rushed between her thighs.

"Like my gorgeous bonded. I'm so lucky to have you, Miranda."

"Who says you have me, blood-sucker?" she said, her grin wide. "I'm my own woman."

"You are. I love that about you. You don't let me get away with anything, you stubborn little minx."

Closing her eyes, his wife enjoyed his ministrations on her breasts. He hadn't drunk from her in three nights and was ravenous for her. He'd decreased his drinking of her since she was pregnant, not wanting to tax her body any further. She still offered every night, telling him he was an overprotective caveman. Lowering his mouth to her neck, he began to lick the skin over her vein, preparing it for his invasion.

Her eyes snapped open. "My blood's probably out of you since you haven't had me in a few days, so be prepared for what you're about to see. Arderin and I had a talk this morning, and I need to discuss it with you."

Narrowing his eyes, he stared into hers. What was his sister discussing with her? Deciding to find out, he plunged his fangs into her neck. Pleasure swamped him as her blood, so pure and vibrant, coated his tongue. Closing his eyes, he lost himself in the sensation. She moaned beneath him, and he gently pushed her to rest on her elbows over the dresser. Latched onto her, he shoved his cock into her wetness.

"Sathan," she cried brokenly.

He growled against her, unable to break his connection with her succulent neck. By the goddess, she tasted so good. Sliding his hands from her breasts to her collarbone, he cupped her shoulders, needing to pull her into him as he loved her. The wet tissues of her channel clutched his shaft, the choking pressure sending jolts of pleasure up his spine. Lowering one of his hands, he began rubbing the tiny nub below the juncture of her thighs.

"Harder," she commanded. Unsure whether she was referencing his shaft or the pressure of his fingers, he increased both. His little Slayer loved it when he didn't hold back, although he was always mindful to be careful with her now that she was pregnant. He'd never let anything happen to her or his child.

She tensed below him, and he knew she was close. Pulling his fangs from her, he whispered in her ear. "Come for me, sweetheart."

Throwing her head back, she began to climax, the muscles of her core flexing around his engorged cock. He watched her reflection: eyes closed, lips full, mouth open, blood trailing down the tan skin of her neck. God, he loved her.

Letting himself go, he spurted his release into her, giving a loud wail. Laughing, she reached up and fisted his hair. "Everyone in the house will hear you."

"I don't give a shit," he moaned, burrowing his face into her shoulder. His hulking body convulsed above her as they trembled. Upon regaining his sanity, he licked the wound at her neck, closing it with his self-healing saliva.

"You've got a lot of nerve fucking an old pregnant lady that way," she teased, her forehead on her crossed arms on top of the dresser, her body replete and sated.

Unable to control his laugh, he nuzzled her nape with his nose. "You're the hottest pregnant lady I've ever seen. Except for your swollen ankles. Those are pretty rough."

"Screw you," she said, snuggling her rear into his front.

Smiling, he lifted and pulled out of her. Grabbing some of the tissues on the dresser, he wiped his seed from her. Content, he lifted her and carried her to the bed, laying her on their soft sheets.

As he stared down at the glossy strands of her hair splayed on the pillow, the images from her conversation with Arderin began to form in his mind, now that her blood coursed through him again.

Scowling, he gazed down at her, lying on her side since her belly was so curved. "No, Miranda."

She rolled her eyes and gave him an exasperated glare. "Can you at least cuddle with me before we start arguing? Or am I only good for baby-making and blood-sucking?"

His lips turned up slightly, but his tone was serious. "Don't turn this into a joke. I'm not letting her go to the human world. It's not happening."

"Get in the damn bed," she said, extending her arms to him. "I'm not arguing with you while you brood down at me. It's annoying."

Scrunching his features at her, he lowered beside her and turned off their bedside lamp. In the darkness, he pulled her to him, spooning her since she could only lie on her side. Nuzzling his nose into her silky hair, he gently rubbed his palm in lazy circles over her distended abdomen.

"If Heden wanted to go to the human world, what would you say?"

"He has no desire to go there, so it's a moot point."

He could almost feel the heat of her anger as it rushed through her warm skin. "Don't play word games with me. You know what I'm asking."

Sighing, he contemplated. "It's not because she's a woman—"

"I think it might be."

"Don't interrupt me, Miranda. I'm not discussing this with you if you won't let me speak."

"Fine. Go ahead." Her thin arms squeezed him as she wiggled her butt into his warmth.

Inhaling a breath, he chose his words wisely. "It's not that she's a woman. Sadie goes to the human world, and I'm fine with that."

"She did that before she met you."

"Yes, but I don't have a problem with it. Arderin is more complicated. I know you all think I doubt her, but I assure you, I don't. Hell, she's probably smarter than the three of us put together," he said, referencing his brothers. "But she's easily angered and overdramatic and that can lead to danger. I only want her to be safe. She can go anywhere she wants in the immortal world, but the land of humans is too dangerous."

Miranda stroked his thick forearm. "I'm worried for her to go there too. I agree with you that it won't be as safe for her there. That's why I have a solution."

"I can't wait to hear this," he muttered.

"Hey," she said, pinching his skin through the prickly black hairs on his arm. "Shut up and listen to your brilliant wife."

Chuckling, he placed a kiss on her head. "Go ahead."

"I think Darkrip should take her when he goes to find Evie. He can transport her there safely and protect her while they travel."

Thick muscles tensed as he listened. "No."

"You're pissing me off by saying 'no' to everything right away. Careful, Sathan. I'm not asking your permission. I'm discussing this with you as your partner. It's only going to work if you're reasonable."

"Sorry," he murmured, trying to tamp down his anger. "I just don't like the idea of him accompanying her. I've already told you that I've caught him watching her several times. He's attracted to her."

"She's a gorgeous woman. I know it's hard for you to see her that way because she's your little sister. He'd have to be dead not to notice her."

Sathan clenched his teeth, wanting to kill anyone who dared look at his sister in any way but platonic. His bonded chuckled below him, further inflaming his ire.

"She's going to marry one day and have amazing sex, darling. I know it's hard for you to accept, but it will happen."

"No one is good enough to touch her."

"Good grief. What will you do when we have a daughter? Will I have to fight you to let her leave the house?"

"Yes," he said, feeling his lips form a pout. "I'll banish anyone who touches her."

The waves of her laughter surrounded him, and he pulled her close, loving how ardently she challenged him.

"She's determined on this. We need to find a way to let her go."

After several moments, he said, "What if something happens to her? By the goddess, Miranda, I would die. I'm not sure I can take the chance."

"You have to trust her. She's her own woman. I know it's hard for you, but your mother raised you this way. What would she want?"

Calla's magnificent face blazed into his mind, so much like Arderin's. "She'd tell me I was being an overbearing misogynist."

Laughing, Miranda nodded against his chest. "Then I think you have your answer."

His heart pounded with fear as he thought of Arderin in the human world.

"Oh, sweetheart," Miranda said, looking up at him as she smoothed her hand over his cheek, noticing the hammering organ in his chest. "I know you're afraid. But Darkrip will protect her. I told her that was the only way I'd feel comfortable with her going."

Filled with terror, he rubbed his chin against his wife's hair. "Okay. Let me talk to both of them. I want to get their commitment on several things before I even consider this."

"You're doing the right thing." Snuggling into him, she gazed into his eyes. Now that he'd adjusted to the darkness, he could see the love swimming in hers. "I'm proud of you. We'll get you out of the fourth century if it kills us."

"Goddamnit, woman," he said, stroking her distended belly. "You're infuriating."

"Don't I know it." Raven-black eyebrows waggled as she gave him a breathtaking smile.

"I love you so much," he whispered.

"I love you too," she said, placing a sweet kiss on his lips. Sliding back to cuddle into him, she drifted off as he stared at the wall, too worried for his sister to sleep.

Chapter 7

After finishing her morning yoga routine, Arderin checked her phone. There was a text from Heden with a funny SNL clip that he thought she'd love. One from Lila asking her if she wanted to come over for dinner one night next week. Contemplating, she realized she would. Their home was beautiful, and she loved Jack to pieces. Deciding she'd text her back later, she read the text from Sathan.

Sathan: Miranda and I talked last night. Meet me in my office at noon to discuss.

Her heart burst in anticipation, praying that her sister-in-law had been successful in her efforts to sway him.

Arderin: Okay, see you then. Love, Your Favorite Sister ☺

Hoping that would butter him up a bit, as well as make him smile since she was his only sister, she headed inside to shower. Donning some cute sandals, tight black jeans and a thin-strapped, silky tank top, she headed downstairs.

"Hi," she said, knocking on the open door of his office.

"Hey," Sathan said, looking up from the paperwork he was furiously scribbling on. "Come on in."

As he motioned to the chairs in front of his mahogany desk, she sat in one of them.

"Just give me a second to finish this," he said, signing his name on a few of the pieces of paper. Stacking them on the desk, he sat back in his leather reclining chair.

"You have a lot of nerve going behind my back to Miranda, sis. Pretty smart, but it pissed me off."

Always quick to anger, Arderin felt her nostrils flare and told herself to stay calm. "I would say it was brilliant. The fact that we're here would indicate so."

His expression was impassive. "Well, I've decided not to let you go."

Furious, she stood and leaned over his desk. "Are you fucking serious right now?"

He studied her, and as his gaze roved over her face, she realized her mistake.

"Crap," she said, rubbing her fingers over her forehead. "You were testing me. Asshole."

Lifting a black brow, he said, "Yes. Your laser-quick tantrums are one of the reasons that I'm hesitant to let you go to the human world. If you lose your temper there, you might get killed."

Sighing, she sat down, feeling defeated. "I know. I'm a passionate person, Sathan. What do you want me to do? Be a boring old hag? So, sue me. It doesn't mean I'm not smart or capable enough to go to the human world."

The wheels of his mind seemed to be spinning, long and contemplative. "Tell me about the formula and why this is so important to you."

She told him about Sadie, how caring and kind she was, and did her best to make a compelling case. When she was finished, she stared at him, fidgeting her fingers in her lap as she waited.

"You're such a good person," he said, smiling. "Mother and Father would be proud."

"Thank you," she said, pride swelling in her chest. She had always longed for all of her brothers' approval, but none more than Sathan's.

"Giving the dog to the two little Slayer boys was also pretty awesome. Those kids were so happy when they left the barbeque."

Arderin grinned. Several months ago, she'd adopted an adorable black and white shaggy puppy named Mongrel. He'd proceeded to grow into a rather large beast that seemed to have a proclivity for breaking expensive antique heirlooms around the castle. It had almost driven their sweet housekeeper, Glarys, quite insane. The little terror also had a hilarious pastime of peeing on Latimus' leg every time he was nearby. Well, she thought it hysterical. Her serious brother, maybe not so much.

During one of the barbeques that Sathan held to encourage interspecies mingling, two young Slayer boys had begun to play with Mongrel. Taken with their laughter and sincere joy, she'd offered their mother the opportunity to adopt him. The woman informed her that their father was a soldier who had perished in one of Crimeous' recent attacks on Uteria, her brown eyes welling with gratitude at Arderin's proposal. She'd felt it was the right thing. The boys seemed thrilled with the dog, and Mongrel would be able to thrive in the open field behind their house, rather than being cooped up in the castle.

Smiling, she said, "I miss the little terror, but I think Latimus might have killed me if I kept him any longer."

Sathan chuckled. "I've never seen him as mad as when the bugger pissed on his leg. And I've seen him fight Crimeous." Studying her for a moment, he pondered, "Your cause is noble, and I want to support you. However, I have conditions."

"Okay." Scooting to the edge of her seat, she nodded furiously. "I'm listening."

"First," he said, straightening in his chair and holding up his index finger, "Darkrip has to accompany you the entire time."

Realizing she had no control over taking the trip with the man who vexed the hell out of her, she nodded. "Okay. What else?"

"You can go for no more than three days. That should give you more than enough time to have Darkrip transport you inside the lab to retrieve the formula."

"I agree. I'm fine with that timeframe."

"Third," he said, holding up three fingers. "I want everything left as it was. Humans have no idea we exist, and I don't want them anywhere close to figuring it out. We've got enough problems with Crimeous and the Deamons. When you take the formula and whatever else you need, make it look like a break-in and have Darkrip disable any cameras from the security systems with his mind. Got it?"

"Got it," she said with a nod.

Leaning back, he inhaled deeply. "Okay. If you can do that, then we're good. I'm going to ask Darkrip to escort you back to the ether and make sure you get home safely. Once he does, then he can go find Evie."

"Thank you, Sathan. I promise I'll do everything you ask. I'm so grateful you're supporting me in this."

"You're welcome. I know you don't believe this, but I'm not an ogre. I just love you very much and want you to be safe."

Tears welled in her eyes and she stood, walking over to him. "I love you too. I'm sorry I've been so awful to you."

"Shh..." he said, standing and hugging her.

Snuggling into him, she reveled in his warm embrace.

"You're my little sister. It's hard for me to see you as a grown woman, but I know I have to. Bear with me, sis. I promise I'm trying."

"I know," she said, nodding against his chest. "You've had to protect everyone in the kingdom for so long. I'm so happy you have Miranda. She's able to help you with that burden. I know you want me to help you here more, and I promise I will."

"Wow, I should say 'yes' to you more often."

"Shut up," she said, swatting his chest. Lifting her chin to gaze at him, she said, "Thank you."

"You're welcome, little toad," he said, kissing her forehead.

"I hate that nickname," she said, scowling.

"I know. But I'm pretty sure you'll acquiesce to anything right now."

Smiling, she nodded. "Yep. Call me whatever you want. Did you talk to Darkrip? When can we leave?"

"I'm speaking to him later this afternoon. I'll let you know. Now, I need you do something for me." When she arched an eyebrow, he continued. "The Slayers that live at the wall are getting acclimated, but they don't visit Astaria's main square as much as I would like. I want us to be one kingdom. Can you send out an Insta-story thing and get them all to come to the main pub tomorrow night? Tell them that it's open bar all night. I'll be covering the tab. I want Slayers and Vampyres to mingle."

"Got it. I'll blast social media. You'll have more people there than you know what to do with."

"And I expect you, as the kingdom's princess, to be there and to help me."

"Absolutely."

"Damn. This is amazing. Keep this up, and I'll send you to the human world once a week."

Laughing, she pulled away from him and lifted her phone from her back pocket. Shaking it, she said, "Challenge accepted. Let me get to work on this social blast."

Pulling up Instagram, she bounced from the office.

* * * *

As the sun was setting over the mountains that lined the horizon behind his cabin, Darkrip materialized to the main castle. Intrigued as to why Miranda had summoned him, he plodded down the hallway outside Sathan's office. After knocking, he heard her call to enter.

"Hi," she said, giving him one of her brilliant smiles. "Thanks for coming."

"Hey," he said, sitting in the chair beside her. Sathan sat behind his mahogany desk in a high, leather-backed chair.

"Thanks for coming, Darkrip," the king said in his deep baritone. "We have something of great importance to discuss with you."

"Okay," he said, alarmed but interested.

Miranda informed him of Arderin's wish to travel to the human world and the formula she needed to recover for the Slayer physician.

"Good for her," he said, not understanding what this had to do with him. "I hope she has a pleasant and safe journey."

"That's why we wanted to talk to you," his sister said.

"Okay," Darkrip said, becoming annoyed at the drawn-out antics. "Just tell me what the hell you need, Miranda. You know I can't stand dramatics."

She lifted her chin. "We want you to accompany her on the journey. We only feel comfortable if she has you with her at all times to protect her."

His eyebrows drew together. "Seriously? She's more than capable of going by herself."

"I worry for her safety," Sathan said, leaning his elbows on his desk and resting his chin on his fists, fingers laced together. "I won't let her go unless you go with her. I'm immovable on this."

"I understand your need to protect her, but you underestimate her ability to travel on her own. She's a capable and intelligent person. Look at how she escaped from the Slayer soldiers when Miranda held her captive."

"I agree," Miranda said, "but my Neanderthal husband is firm." Sathan glowered but remained silent. "I'm united with him on this and want her safe. Please, do this for us." Reaching out, she placed her hand over Darkrip's forearm.

Rolling his eyes, he sighed. "I don't really have time for this right now. I need to find Evie."

"I know," Miranda said. "But we've told her that she can only go for three days. Once you return her through the ether, you can go find Evie."

"This is ridiculous," he said, unable to contain his frustration. "Just let her go on her own."

"No. It's with you, or not at all," Sathan said.

Darkrip scowled. "What makes you think I'll keep her safe?" Training his gaze on Sathan, he felt his eyebrows draw together. "You don't strike me as the type who wants an evil Deamon protecting your sister."

Sathan stared back at him, unfazed. "I trust the Slayer part of you. We are allies, and you are my wife's brother. I have done my best to accept you."

"I was under the impression that you're not exactly thrilled with my presence here."

Sathan shrugged. "I don't have the luxury of choosing my allies. You are a powerful one and you are family. I trust you to take care of Arderin."

Darkrip contemplated, realizing he was quite ingratiated at the Vampyre's words. Interesting. He'd been telling himself he didn't give a crap that Miranda's husband hated his guts. Guess that wasn't entirely the case.

"Did she agree to my protection? I can't see her being on board with that."

"She did," Miranda said with a nod. "Do you two not get along?" Worry laced her tone.

"We get along just fine when she's not driving me insane. She's as stubborn and hardheaded as you are."

Breaking into a huge smile, she said, "Thank you. I consider that a compliment."

Darkrip's eyes darted back and forth between them. "I'll agree, but on my terms. I only want to travel to the human world once. I can't dematerialize through the ether, so I have to walk through like everyone else. I'll help her get the formula and then I'll secure her a hotel to stay in while I go look for Evie in Japan."

"No," Sathan said, shaking his head. "I only want her there for a few days."

"Take it or leave it, man. I'm happy to help because Miranda's asking but I'm not letting you dictate my actions once I'm in the human world. We have a huge battle before us, getting Evie on our side, and I want to approach her as we discussed. I'm not altering my plans for a spoiled Vampyre princess. It's just not happening."

"Fine," Miranda said, looking at her husband with a pleading expression. "We can agree to that—right, Sathan?"

The Vampyre gritted his teeth, the corded muscles of his neck threatening to pop out. "Yes. That's fine. I need your word that the hotel in Houston will be secure and you'll be thorough in erasing your tracks when retrieving the formula."

"You have it."

"Okay. You're planning to leave on Thursday, right?"

"Yes. Early morning."

"Arderin will be ready. I'll ask you to drive to the ether in one of our four-wheelers if you don't mind. I want her to take some pictures of the open land along the way, as we've been discussing possibly building another compound between Astaria and Uteria."

Nodding, Darkrip stood. "I'd like to speak to you privately for a moment," he said to his sister.

"I'll walk you to the kitchen. I'm starving." Rounding the desk, she gave Sathan a blazing kiss.

As they headed to the kitchen, Darkrip gazed down at her.

"I'm attracted to her, Miranda. I'm not sure this is a good idea."

"I know. I've watched you around her for some time now. She's gorgeous, so I can't say I blame you for being attracted to her," she said, her grass-green eyes so genuine. "But I know you won't hurt her. I believe in your Slayer half. I trust you."

Shaking his head, he couldn't help but smile. "One day, I'm going to blow your faith in me to bits. You give me too much credit."

"Never," she said, leading him into the kitchen.

"How can you be sure I won't touch her?"

Her lips formed a sad smile. "Because you've convinced yourself you don't deserve her. It makes me sad but you're as stubborn as I am, even if you won't admit it. She'll be safe with you. Thank you for doing this for us." She squeezed his hand.

"You know I'd do anything you ask, Miranda."

"I know," she said, her teeth glowing as she beamed. "I think there's some pasta and egg salad in the fridge. Want to have a picnic on the counter?"

Unable to tell her no, they sat and ate, enjoying each other's company.

Chapter 8

When Thursday rolled around, Arderin told herself not to be a scared-ass pansy. Yes, she was traveling to the land of humans for the first time. Yes, she was traveling with the son of the Dark Lord, who drove her insane ninety-five percent of the time. But she was going, and that was something. Excited, she dressed in black ankle boots, dark blue jeans, a black tank and red cardigan.

Since one could only carry a small bag through the ether, she packed her toiletries, nightshirt and a change of clothes and headed to the kitchen. Once there, Glarys handed her a large metal thermos filled with Slayer blood. Hugging the woman, whom Arderin loved dearly, she kissed her on her ruddy cheek and headed to the barracks.

Latimus was there, chatting with Darkrip. Knowing her brother, he was probably threatening the Slayer-Deamon's life if he let anything happen to her. Approaching them, she said, "You didn't have to come."

The corner of Latimus' full lips curved. "Sathan is finally letting you go to the human world. I had to see it. I never thought it would happen."

"Don't doubt your sister," she said, smiling at him.

"Come here," Latimus said, dragging her through the open garage doorway to the meadow, leaving Darkrip to stand by the vehicle.

"I need you to promise me you'll be safe."

"I promise," she said with a nod.

Ice-blue irises darted between hers. "I can't lose you, little one."

"You won't," she said, throwing her arms around his thick neck. "I'll be smart."

Hugging her, he said, "If anything happens, I want you to know that I'll come for you."

"Nothing's going to happen." Pulling back, she stared at him. "I'm sure it will be the most boring and uneventful trip to the human world ever. I mean, I'm going to grab a few medical vials, not save the world," she said, beaming up at him.

"Maybe," he said, his tone cautious, "but I need to say this. If you get in a jam and think there's no way out, don't give up. I'll always save you. It's important that you hear me say that."

"Okay. I won't give up. But Darkrip will be with me. I don't want you to worry."

"Have you met me? Get over yourself. I love you, Arderin." He placed a small envelope in her hand. "Lila wanted to wish you off, but she had to be at the shelter today. She wrote you a note."

"Thank you," she said, her eyes welling at how many people cared about her. "I love you too. Tell her I'll come to dinner when I get back. I miss Jack. My little buddy's so cute and I need some new Snapchat pictures with him."

"Snapchat. Twitting. I don't know how you put up with that human rubbish," he muttered, and she grinned.

"It's called *'tweeting'* but thanks for showing your age, old man." Giving him a peck on the cheek, she embraced him in one last hug.

Arderin's phone emitted a *ding*, and she smiled when she read Sadie's text.

Sadie: I'm so happy you're going to the human world! Still not sure how you convinced Sathan to let you accompany Darkrip but great job! Can't wait to hear all about it.

Arderin gnawed her lip as she typed her reply. She'd told Sadie that Sathan had allowed her to accompany Darkrip so that Arderin could help him use social media to search for Evie in the human world. Being that Darkrip wasn't nearly as tech savvy as she, Sadie had believed the flimsy excuse. Arderin was so excited to procure the formula for her always-thoughtful friend. Thanking her for the well wishes, Arderin shot a text back.

Sathan and Heden appeared by the four-wheeler, and she rushed back to embrace them. They both looked at her with apprehension and concern, causing her heart to melt. After one last hug with Miranda, who had just come from the gym, Arderin climbed into the passenger seat. Buckling the seatbelt, she clutched her bag in her lap.

Dark curls flew in the wind as she turned to wave goodbye to them. When they approached the compound wall, a small section opened. Latimus must've been watching them on the security cameras. Waving to the sky, hoping he'd catch her on screen, they drove through the opening in the stones.

Arderin glanced at Darkrip's muscled arm as he maneuvered the long stick shift that rose from the floor. Bare below the sleeve of his t-shirt, his skin was quite tan. Imagining running her tongue over it, she began to feel hot and looked away. By the goddess, she really needed to get some action.

They drove in silence down the River Thayne, past the Slayer compounds of Uteria and Restia and then another thirty miles southeast to the wall of ether. Along the way, they stopped so she could snap pictures for Sathan with her phone. Finally arriving at the thick wall of ether, Darkrip placed the car in park and shut off the engine.

"Well, princess, we made it." Opening his door, he jumped from the vehicle and grabbed his pack from the small truck bed in back.

Exiting, she walked around the front of the four-wheeler, clutching her bag to her chest. He placed the keys in his bag, slung it over his shoulder and began walking to the ether.

"Wait," she said, grabbing his arm.

Darkrip stilled and then slowly turned to face her. "I thought we had a discussion about you touching me."

"Oh, please," she said, rolling her eyes. Dropping her hand, she said, "I want to thank you. Don't make it difficult."

He arched an eyebrow, making him look incredibly handsome. "Are you under the impression that I'm the one in this twosome who makes things difficult?"

She couldn't stop her snicker. "I'm not going to let you bait me, but good try." Inching closer to him, she tilted her head slightly since he was a few inches taller. "Thank you for agreeing to my brother's ridiculous terms. I'm sure you were less than thrilled to be tasked with accompanying me. I know you think I'm annoying and selfish and all the other words you've used to describe me since I met you. What you're doing for me is amazing, and I really appreciate it."

"Wow," he said, his deep voice acerbic. "Did you give that same speech to your brother? No wonder he acquiesced. You're a great little actress, princess."

Anger rushed through her. "Can't you just let me thank you?"

"What's the point? We're stuck together anyway. Let's get this show on the road. I'm ready to find my sister and don't want to waste any more time talking."

"Asshole," she muttered. What a bastard. Huffing, she walked toward the ether.

"You need to clutch your bag tightly," he said behind her, giving her body a rush as she felt the heat from his. "If you don't, it won't come through with you."

She nodded, unwilling to look at him since he hadn't accepted her attempt to thank him.

"The ether is extremely challenging to navigate. You're going to want to stop. Don't do it. Once you stop moving, it's incredibly difficult to get going again. I'll be behind you and will push you if needed."

"I'd rather you not touch me," she said, still angry at him.

"Then don't stop walking." He muttered something about her being a spoiled princess.

"Fine." Finished with talking, especially to his rude ass, she clutched her bag to her chest and entered the waxy ether.

Man, he wasn't kidding. The stuff was thick, and she found herself struggling to breathe. A dense coat of what felt like plushy plastic surrounded her, and she silently screamed at her muscles to keep moving forward. Concentrating on placing one foot in front of the other, she closed her eyes.

Feeling nauseous, Arderin pushed her shoulder forward, then took another step. Opposite shoulder, step with opposite foot. When she attempted to take her next step, her damn foot wouldn't budge. Cursing, she mentally gathered all her energy, shooting it to her leg.

Frustrated, she felt tears well in her eyes and self-doubt coursed through her. Had she come this far and expended all this energy convincing Sathan to let her travel just to die in the ether? Choking in air, she willed her limbs to move.

Suddenly, Darkrip was behind her. His firm hands pushed her, and she rejoiced that he was helping her. Wide palms covered her back as he slowly forced her through. And then, as if it was all a dream, she was under the blazing sun of the Texas sky.

Inhaling a deep breath, she turned to observe him walk through. Panting, she threw her bag on the grass and doubled over, resting her hands on her knees.

"Thought you were gonna go down," Darkrip said.

"Me too," she said, unable to spar with him since he'd helped her. "Damn, that was rough."

"It gets easier after the first time. Are you okay?" Placing his hand on her back, he rubbed her in concentric circles with his steady hand.

"Yeah," she said, cursing her beating heart. Although, she wondered if it was pounding from the ether or from his touch. Turning her head, she locked onto his emerald eyes. "Are you comforting me?"

Darkrip retracted his hand as if she were a hot stove. Feeling the corner of her lip turn up, she chalked one up for the win. He must've not realized he was performing the kind gesture. She wondered how many other caring impulses he tamped down to keep people at a distance. Deciding she'd explore that as they traveled, she straightened and threw her hair over her shoulders. Something flashed in his eyes, and she hoped it was desire. After all, he'd told her he wanted to sleep with her. He probably wasn't immune to the image of her flicking her long hair.

"Ready?" Arderin asked, lifting an eyebrow and trying to look sexy.

He scoffed and shook his head. "Let's get one thing straight, little girl. I told you I wanted to fuck you to shock you into being afraid of me. You're an attractive woman, and I'd have to be blind not to notice that. But you have another thing coming if you think you could ever entice me or satisfy me in bed. I have no interest in bedding an innocent virgin who doesn't know the first thing about pleasing a man. I have proclivities that you could never even dream of and I'll never touch you that way. Doing so would be a waste of time, and I have other priorities in my life. So, thanks for the come-hither expression, but I'm all set. Got it?"

His words hurt her so deeply that Arderin felt like he'd slapped her. It was as if he was confirming all her fears as to why no one would court her. Hating him more than she ever had, she cursed the tears that welled in her eyes. Unable to control them, she pivoted, afraid he would see one of them fall.

"Got it," she said, taking in the beautiful park before them. Darkrip had scouted the place before they arrived, and it was a perfect launching point.

"Good," he said behind her, although his voice was gravelly. For a second, she hoped he felt guilt and then squashed that thought. A monster like him would never feel that emotion.

"The hotel I want to reserve for us is across the street. Let's go, princess. I don't have all day."

Picking up her bag, she straightened her shoulders and began walking across the grass, not giving a damn if he was following her.

* * * *

Darkrip watched the little princess's curls sway in the warm Southern breeze as she stalked in front of him. Something burned in his gut, and he wondered if it was the beginning stages of remorse. Not really ever experiencing that emotion, he had no idea what it felt like. But probably something like the piece of shit he felt like right now. Yeah, that sounded right.

Arderin stopped at the intersection, the red hand telling her not to walk. Cars whizzed by as the sounds of the Houston summer surrounded them. Music blaring from nearby apartments, birds chirping in the trees above, a revved motorcycle engine in the distance. The human world was incredibly busy compared to the more sedentary, country living of the immortal world.

"You should be taking this all in," he said to her, admiring her stubbornness as she refused to turn around and acknowledge him. "It's your first time in the human world. I thought that curious brain of yours would be more excited."

"I am," she said with a shrug. "I just want to get to the hotel and drop this bag off. After that, I'll explore."

Fuck. He'd ruined her first taste of the one place she'd been dying to get to her whole life. Feeling like an ass, he decided he'd make it up to her once they checked in. "Okay, let's go."

The hand on the directional turned green, and they crossed the street and entered the lobby of the hotel. Pulling out the fake IDs and fully functional credit card that Heden had created for them, he showed them to the man at the front desk.

"Well, hello, Mr. Osmond. May I call you Donald?" the concierge asked, reading the ID. Darkrip nodded.

"Have you stayed with us before?"

"No," Darkrip said. "I need a room for myself and one for my sister for five nights."

The man picked up Arderin's ID and glanced over it. "Okay...*Marie*. Wow, your parents must have had some sense of humor. Let me get this reservation started."

As the man typed, Darkrip couldn't help but notice Arderin's snickering. "What the hell is so funny?" he asked softly, through clenched teeth.

"Heden," she said, shaking her head and wiping the corner of her eye. "He's freaking hilarious."

"I don't think I get the joke," he muttered.

The clerk finished their reservation and gave them two plastic keys. "You're in adjoining rooms on the fourth floor. The elevator's through there." He pointed down the hallway. "Do you have any questions?"

They shook their heads and wended toward the elevators. Once inside, Darkrip pushed the button for the fourth floor and proceeded to watch her double over with laughter when the doors closed.

"I fail to see what is so hilarious."

"They're a brother-sister singing duo from the twentieth century. It's so funny."

Shaking his head, he took her in. Body quaking with laughter, reddened cheeks, white teeth with glowing fangs. He couldn't help but grin.

"I guess I'll take your word for it."

They exited the elevator, and he handed her a key. "You're here. Let me set my bag down and get settled and then I'll come over. We need to form a plan."

Nodding, she took the key from him, his fingers on fire where her soft skin brushed his.

Once inside, Darkrip set up the human cell phone Heden had given him, making sure he could access the internet. When he was set, he headed to her room.

Arderin let him in, not making eye contact. Stalking to the center of the room, he turned off the TV, which she had blaring for some insane reason.

"Hey!" Coming to stand in front of him, she placed her fists on her hips. "I was watching the Kardashians! I never get to see new episodes unless Heden does a favor for me on my birthday and beams them to the tech room. Turn it back on!" She grabbed at the remote in his hands.

"This isn't a vacation, princess," he said, tossing the remote on one of the double beds. "We have shit to do. I want to talk about our itinerary."

She gave him a look of death, spurring the crooks of his lips to curve against their will. Her impertinent expressions were vexingly adorable. "Fine." She collapsed into a sitting position on the bed. "Let's plan."

Sitting on the bed across from her, they decided he would transport her to the genetics lab tonight. The darkness would ensure few people would see them. They went over the map of the lab that she and Nolan had downloaded from the internet so he could visualize exactly where he needed to materialize with her. Once they had the formula, she would stay in Houston while he traveled to Japan to find Evie.

Firm in their plans, he asked her what she wanted to do for the day. After all, they had many hours until nightfall, and he was starting to get hungry. As she bit her lip, contemplating, he imagined her performing the act on his nipple. Or his ear. Or, hell, anywhere on his pulsing body if he was honest.

"I'd really like to go to a honky-tonk bar and do some line dancing. Isn't that what they do here in this part of the human world?"

"I don't know. I don't ever really come here for fun. I've only been to gather intel on weapons and to help my father kill more effectively."

He thought she might've shivered at his answer. Standing, she extended her hand to him. "Well, today's a new day. C'mon."

Filled with dread at having to function in the human world, he took her hand and let her drag him out of the room.

* * * *

Several hours later, Darkrip was convinced that humans were the most stupid beings that ever lived. The men all wore large metal belt buckles with images of bulls on them. The women all had fake tits and painted faces. Although everyone they'd come into contact with had been cordial, he couldn't quite squelch his distaste for the inferior species.

They'd had lunch at a barbeque place with picnic tables covered in red and white checkered tablecloths. The food hadn't been half-bad. Not needing food, Arderin had still stolen his fork and tried a large bite. Once he resumed eating, he couldn't help but enjoy the taste of her on the utensil way more than the meat.

Then, they'd walked around the city, joy evident in her ice-blue irises. She possessed a sense of wonder at everything from the tall buildings to the various cars that sputtered in the street to the people who tipped their hat and said hello. He wondered if he'd ever known someone with such a genuine sense of innocent curiosity. In spite of himself, he was charmed by her.

Now, they were sitting in a darkened bar with a mechanical bull off to one corner. A song came on the juke box, and a man approached them.

"Excuse me, sir, but we have a request of the little lady." The human tipped his head toward a table of friends behind him. "The record on that bull there is sixty-three seconds, and we think this pretty little thing might just beat it. What do you say, darlin'? You up for a challenge?"

Darkrip observed the man smile at Arderin beneath his wide-brimmed hat.

"This little lady never shirks a challenge," she said, her smile full of mischief. "I accept."

"Come on, darlin'," he said, extending his hand to her. Pulling her toward the bull, the cowboy navigated her over the plushy mats and onto the pommel. Darkrip had never seen her beam so wide, her white teeth threatening to blind everyone in the dim bar. She wore tiny white concealers to cover the tips of her fangs, ensuring she wouldn't stand out in the human world.

The man tugged some sort of lever, and Arderin grabbed onto the ball of the saddle with one hand, the other held high in the air. Thick muscles hardened as Darkrip observed her lithe body move. She undulated atop the fake animal, slender hips grinding into the leather. Back arched, husky laughs escaped her throat as the motions below her grew fiercer. It was impossible not to imagine her atop him, gyrating over his straining body. God, what he would do her. His fist would latch on to those thick curls, bowing her further so he could reach a place so deep inside her virgin body. The image was so vivid he almost came in his pants. Christ.

As he watched her struggle to stay buoyant, his heart seemed to yearn for her. Impossible, since it had been blackened and hardened long ago. Wrestling with why the damn thing was trying to resuscitate itself, Darkrip admitted that what he felt for her was more than simple attraction. He'd convinced himself that he just wanted to fuck her because she was gorgeous. But somewhere along the way, he'd become attracted to her spirit and spunk as well. Yes, she was a spoiled brat half the time, but she was also so loving and innocent and sincere. All the things his mother had been. Feeling the sadness wash over him, he allowed himself to think of Rina.

How awful it must be for her to suffer in the Land of Lost Souls. Wishing he could save her, Darkrip sipped his drink, chewing on the small cubes of ice. How different would his life be now if she had lived? If he hadn't been spawned by his wretch of a father but a different man?

Sighing at his ridiculous musings, he chugged the drink and set the empty glass on the counter. Throwing some bills on the bar, he went to retrieve Arderin.

The cowboy was helping her up from her position on the cushy pad.

"Fifty-four seconds, darlin'," he said, clutching her hand as he led her back onto the solid ground outside the circle. "You're a natural. One day soon, you'll break that record." He winked at her, causing Darkrip to want to rip the man's throat out with his bare hands.

"Come on," Darkrip said, grabbing her forearm. "It's almost ten p.m."

She gave him an insolent scowl and then smiled up at the cowboy. After giving him a hug goodbye, they headed outside.

"That was so fun!" Lifting her arms, she twirled around under the full moon. "I wish you would've danced. Or ridden the bull. You would've been great!"

Darkrip rolled his eyes. "I'm not really into having fun."

"Oh, everyone's into having fun, grumpy."

He shook his head. "Not me. Ready to get the formula?"

"Yep," she said with a nod.

"Okay, I'm going to transport us to your room so you can grab your bag. Then, I'll take us to the lab." Approaching her, he stopped only a hairsbreadth away. "I need to hold you in order to transport you."

"Okay," she whispered. The pale skin of her throat bobbed as she swallowed.

"Put your arms around my neck."

Complying, she slid them over him, clenching her hands behind his nape. Arousal snaked through him, and he reminded himself of their purpose. Placing his arms around her waist, he pulled her close, aligning their bodies. He almost groaned at her throaty gasp. Closing his eyes, he conveyed them to her hotel room.

Arderin grabbed her bag and came back to embrace him. Lifting those innocent eyes to his, she stared into him. His shaft pounded against her stomach, urging him to grab her silky hair and stuff his tongue in her wet mouth. Controlling himself, he grabbed her bag and sandwiched it between them. With a thought, he whisked them to the darkened room of the lab.

Once there, Darkrip disabled the facility's security cameras with his mind. Nodding to her, she illuminated her flashlight and began looking through the hundreds of vials that sat on the counter. Minutes later, she seemed to find what she was looking for and stuffed a few of the minute tubes into her bag. Leafing through the pages on the counter, she also absconded a few of those. Darkrip figured they had the written formulations for the solution that she and Nolan were after.

"Okay," she said, coming to stand before him. "I have what I need."

Suddenly, the door swung open behind them. "Freeze!" the uniformed security guard yelled, holding up what looked to be a taser. "Don't move, or I'll shoot!"

Darkrip's irises darted around the room. Sure the security guard had alerted others of their intrusion, it was imperative that they escaped on foot. Disappearing into thin air was *not* on the agenda. Freezing the guard with his mind, Darkrip grabbed Arderin's hand and dragged her through the door.

Together, they ran, her thin hand clutching his, navigating through the twists and turns of the dim, fluorescent-lit hallways.

"This way," she said, pulling him in the opposite direction from where he was headed. "I remember it from the map."

"You're sure?" he asked, contemplating the hallway as they panted.

"Yes," she said with a confident nod.

Trusting her, they fled down the squeaky floors toward the main lobby. Alarms rang overhead as they burst through the glass entrance doors. Charging toward the side of the building, Darkrip drew her to him and closed his eyes, searching for outside cameras with his mind. Certain they were out of range, he shut his lids and shuttled them to the hotel.

"That was awesome!" Throwing the bag on her bed, Arderin followed suit, flinging herself to lie on her back. "We did it."

"We did. Holy shit. I was sure we were screwed."

"I feel like we're in a TV show," she said, sitting up to perch on the side of the bed. Red splotches darted her cheeks, making her look so young and achingly beautiful. Sliding her fingers around his wrist, she drew him toward her.

"Hang out for a while. It's still early. I'm sure we can find some human smut to watch on Bravo."

His tense body ached as he looked down at her, wanting so badly to unzip his pants and thrust himself into that angelic mouth. Resisting every impulse to touch her, he gently disengaged from her grasp. "I'm glad you have what you need. I'll come to say goodbye before I leave for Japan in the morning."

"Wait," she said, following him as he bolted toward the door. After exiting, he turned to face her.

"I know you hate accepting my thanks, but I'm so grateful to you." Guileless eyes swam with sincerity, her body enveloped by the door frame.

Each cell in his ice-covered heart shifted. If he wasn't careful, she'd tear down every wall that he'd erected. It would be a disservice to both of them, since they had no future. She, an innocent virgin, and he, the malevolent son of the Dark Lord. Never had there been such an improbable pair.

Wanting to push her away, his tone was harsh. "Lock the door behind me."

Stalking to his room, he dematerialized his clothes to sit in a pile on the floor. Collapsing on the bed, he threw his arm over his eyes as he grabbed his turgid cock. It was the closest he'd ever come to being with her, having her situated in the room next door, only feet away. Taking solace in the small comfort of her proximity, he let the fantasy take over as he relieved himself.

Chapter 9

The next morning, Darkrip knocked on Arderin's door promptly at eight a.m. Eyes puffy with sleep, she opened it and stared up at him. He'd never seen anything more striking than her slumber-swollen face in the pale morning light of the hotel room.

"I'm leaving," he said, his voice curt, hating that he wanted her so badly.

"Okay. I'll stay near the hotel while you're gone. I hope you find her."

"Me too." Something akin to worry for her filled him. "I know you like to challenge me, but please, honor your word to stay close. Humans are wily bastards. I don't want you hurt."

Pink lips formed a smile. "Would you miss me if something happened to me?"

"No. But Miranda would kill me."

She scrunched the features of her face at him. "Oh, fine. I promise. You be safe too. I actually *would* miss you if something happened to you."

His heart slammed at her words, and he cursed himself a fool. Closing his eyes, he barreled himself across the world.

* * * *

Two days later, Darkrip exited the train at the seaside town of Zushi. Not wanting to call attention to himself, he'd chosen traditional forms of transportation since his first materialization in Japan. Hailing a taxi outside the train station, he informed the driver of his destination. Thankfully, the Japanese man knew English, as that was the human language with which Darkrip was most familiar.

Arriving at the edge of the cliffside park, Darkrip gave the man four thousand yen, telling him to keep the change. When the taxi drove away, he observed the park. It seemed quite deserted, as the sun was about to set. Most locals were likely sitting down to dinner, their children done with the outdoors for now.

Walking through the line of trees, he came to a clearing. Off in the distance, the waves of the ocean could be heard, singing their song of approach and retreat against the stony shore. Coming to the top of a hill, he gazed before him, seeing the horizon as it sat above the sea.

Darkrip saw her, sitting atop the rocky cliff, as if an artist had placed her there to be the subject of one of his masterpieces. Thin arms stretched behind her, palms flat on the rock, supporting her willowy body. The fire of her hair threatened to burn the sky around her as it fell below her shoulder blades, since her head was tilted slightly back.

Although he couldn't see her face, he imagined her eyes were closed as she breathed in the beauty. Tiny dotted clouds soaked up the golden and ruby rays from the sun as if they were sponges. The orb sat low on the horizon, enflamed and angry as it fought to stay afloat. He understood now why this country used the red sun as the symbol on its flag. The sphere was magnificent as it splattered colors across every inch of the sky, showing its strength.

Slowly, he walked toward her, stilling a few feet behind her.

"Hello, Darkrip."

Her posture remained the same, face tilted to the sky, eyes closed. Her slender, jean-clad legs hung off the side of the cliff.

Carefully, he sat beside her. Not too close, lest she push him off.

"Hello, Evie."

The corners of her lips turned up slightly as she sat, lids still shut. Inhaling a deep breath, he mirrored her, resting his hands on the stone and lifting his face to the sky. They sat like that for minutes, the only sound coming from the nearby birds.

"It's one of my favorite places in the human world," she said, only her lips moving. "I've seen the sunset in Positano, Maui, Kenya and so many other beautiful places. But nothing beats the sunsets of Japan. They're always filled with rage but also possess such beauty. If we understand nothing else, we understand that dichotomy, don't we, brother dearest?" Lowering her head, she pierced him with her olive-green gaze.

"That we do," he said with a nod.

Sighing, she ran a hand through her thick scarlet hair. "I should've known not to come here. I've been here so often that surely one of the soothsayers saw me and wrote it down in one of the stupid archives the immortals insist on keeping. I've never understood their desire to document their tragic history. What a waste of time."

"Then, why did you come?"

Her lips pursed and her eyebrows drew together. "Maybe I wanted to be found. I don't think I realized that until right now."

Darkrip swallowed. "You look well."

Facing him fully, Evie arched a scarlet brow. "Do I? You look like shit. Still walking around with that horrid curse?"

Unable to stop himself, he breathed a laugh. "Yeah. The goddess fucked me over pretty hard."

Grass-green irises darted over his face. "Your obsession with the Vampyre princess is dangerous."

He nodded, understanding that she had the power to see many things, as he did. "Yes."

"Why don't you just rape her and get her out of your head?"

Inhaling deeply, he shook his head. "I can't. The part of her that's in me is too good," he said, referring to their mother. "I made a promise to her over eight centuries ago, right after you left. She took a hold of me, and that part of her is my voice now. The evil tries but it hasn't won in a very long time."

"Good for you," she muttered, turning to look back over the ocean. "It controls the hell out of me."

"You haven't killed in a while. Except for the old Italian man. You couldn't just let him die in peace?"

Her eyes narrowed. "He pissed me off. There are consequences for that."

"You cared for him."

"I was fond of him, for a brief moment. There might have been a flash of regret when I snapped his neck. But he was old and had lived a rich and full life."

Darkrip stared at the sun, half-sunk below the horizon. "I regret hiring Yara to kill you. It was stupid and rash. Mother appeared to me afterward and made me promise to find you and make it right."

"How did she appear to you?"

"She agreed to live in the Land of Lost Souls if Etherya would let her speak to me. It was a huge sacrifice."

Evie pulled her legs to her chest, crossing her arms around them. "She always loved you. It was plain to see."

"She loved you too."

Scoffing, Evie shook her head. "No, she loved you. And Miranda. She always called me by her name. It was devastating until the evil took over. Then, it was just infuriating."

"When you were a baby, she used to call me over when she was feeding you. I would watch you drink from her, and there was such love in her eyes. She would touch my face,"—he lifted his hand, gently touching Evie's cheek—"and say, 'Take care of my Evie, son. She's so small and I love her so.'"

His sister grabbed his wrist, pulling it away from her face. "Your lies won't help your cause."

"You know I tell the truth," he said, resting his palm flat on the rock again. "You were always the best at discerning lies."

She shrugged. "So what? You come here, tell me mommy loves me, and I go kill our father for you? Is that how this works?"

"You must want to kill him as badly as I do."

White teeth chewed on her lower lip. "I definitely hate the bastard. That's for damn sure."

"Then, help us," he said, hearing the plea in his voice. "I know you hate me. I can accept that. But there are so many that need our help. We can rid the world of his evil."

Releasing her legs, she crossed them and tilted her head. "Why in the hell do you care? What's in it for you?"

Darkrip struggled to find the answer. "I don't know. A lot of things, I think. I want so badly to honor the promises I made Mother. I'm so tired of living in a world filled with death and war. And I've grown quite fond of Miranda. I want to help her bring peace to her people."

"And maybe marry a pretty little princess and have lots of blue-eyed brats?"

He exhaled a soft chuckle. "You know I'll never procreate. That would make me as evil as Father. I'll never bring another soul into this world with his blood."

"So, what's so great about Miranda? Tell me about our sister."

Darkrip smiled. "She's a little firecracker. Smart and strong. Stubborn as hell. She alone is responsible for uniting the species again. I've never met anyone as fearless."

"She's a dead ringer for Mother," Evie said, her expression contemplative. "I saw it when I captured the videos of you all."

"Yeah, you really fucked everything up with that. Nice job. Miranda almost died fighting Father."

"Her cousin pissed the hell out of me. What an arrogant ass to think that he could ask me to help with their pitiful wars. He's lucky I didn't murder him."

Darkrip's eyebrows contracted. "You're attracted to him. Shit. I didn't see that coming."

Evie rolled her eyes. "He's easy on the eyes, okay? I'm attracted to most men under the age of fifty who are passably handsome."

He studied her. "There's a different energy around your images of him, though."

"Well, I haven't fucked him yet. Maybe one day. Until then, I'm interested. Leave it at that."

Darkrip filed away her attraction to Kenden, knowing that he could possibly use it in the future.

Throwing her head back, she laughed. "I see your mind working, brother. It's not going to happen. I want no part of saving the immortals or helping our sister."

"She's amazing, Evie, and determined to meet you and make you care for her. I've tried my best not to, but she wins me over every damn time. I doubt you'll be able to resist her, especially with her likeness to Mother."

"Screw Mother. She was weak and broken."

"Yes. At the end, she was. You really only got to see that part of her. I knew her when she still had a bit of spirit left. I see where Miranda gets it." Grabbing her hand, he squeezed. "Where *you* get it. You have so much of her in you. You just won't let yourself accept it."

Throwing his hand away, she stood. "Like you? Mister '*reformed Deamon?*'" Lifting her hands, she made quotation marks with her fingers. "You're an abomination. Don't tell yourself otherwise."

He rose, facing her above the waves that crashed on the rocks below. "I know I am. But I'm also strong enough to make a choice. And I choose to be like her. I won't let myself be like him. You have the power to make the same choice, if you're willing to take that path. I know you can do it. I have faith in you, Evie."

He swore he saw wetness glistening in her green eyes, if only for a moment, and then it was gone.

"Others have told me I have goodness too. They were all wrong. I'm a monster. So are you. The only difference is that you delude yourself, and I never will."

Shaking his head in frustration, he grabbed her upper arms. "You're capable of so much more. Come back with me. Let me help you. Regardless of what you believe, I care for you, in the meager way that I even understand how to. Be strong enough to make a different choice."

"Don't fucking touch me," she said through clenched teeth, flinging his arms away. "I'll never go back there. You wasted your time trying to find me."

Quick as lightning, she grabbed the collar of his shirt. "Don't bother me again. And this is for trying to kill me." Giving a loud grunt, she gave him a heaving push, plunging him off the side of the cliff. Cursing, he let himself fall for a second and then dematerialized back to the top. As he reappeared, he watched her storm away. She could've transported herself from the cliff, but sometimes, one just needed a good, angry stomp-off.

In spite of himself, he laughed at her retreating form. She was more like Miranda than she knew. Both of them were little hellions who made life disastrous for anyone who crossed them. Determined that they would meet one day, he evaporated to find Arderin and head home.

Chapter 10

It took about five minutes for Arderin to become bored. She showered, styled her hair and played around with her makeup, mimicking the style of a human influencer's tutorial she'd watched last week on Instagram. Even the Kardashians couldn't keep her attention, and after an hour, she grabbed her bag and headed to the hotel lobby.

Heden hadn't given her a phone that could access data in the human world like he'd given Darkrip. She'd give her brother hell about that when they returned. Heading to the hotel business center, she sat at one of the desktop PCs and got down to business.

Sadie had informed Arderin that she should look up Dr. Sarah Lowenstein when in Houston. She was a Board-Certified Internal Medicine physician that Sadie met on her last journey to the human world. Although they'd trained together at Yale, Dr. Lowenstein was now an attending physician at Houston Methodist Hospital.

Clicking through the screens, Arderin pulled up the doctor's profile, memorizing her features and getting a lay of the land for the massive hospital's layout. Heading back to her room, she called the cell number that Sadie had given her.

"Hello?" a warm female voice answered.

"Hi, Dr. Lowenstein? This is Arderin. I'm a friend of Sadie Duran's." Arderin smiled at the surname, which Sadie had designated her own when she traveled to the human world. Last names weren't employed in the immortal world. Instead, one was known as the son or daughter of their father. Sathan, Son of Markdor. Miranda, Daughter of Marsias, and so on.

"Aw, how wonderful," the woman said. "I haven't seen Sadie in ages. How's she doing?"

"She's doing great. I told her I was coming to Houston, and she suggested we meet. I'm hoping to become a doctor, and she said I should pick your brain."

"Fantastic. Today's a bit busy but I could spare half an hour for lunch. Can you meet me in the lobby at Methodist Hospital at noon?"

"Absolutely," Arderin said, heart swelling in anticipation. After they exchanged details, Arderin counted the US currency Darkrip had left for her. Five hundred dollars altogether. Enough for her to get into a bit of trouble, she thought with a smile.

She met Dr. Lowenstein in the bustling lobby promptly at noon, as passersby hurried around them.

"Arderin?" the doctor called, thrusting her hand out. "Your hair is absolutely gorgeous. When you said long, curly black hair, you weren't kidding."

"Thank you," Arderin said shyly, shaking her hand. "It's so nice to meet you, Dr. Lowenstein." She was pretty, with shoulder-length brown hair and light-green eyes, set behind black, wide-rimmed glasses.

"Sarah, please. Dr. Lowenstein is my dad. A fact he never lets me forget when he chides me for becoming an Internist rather than a Surgeon."

"Parents can be infuriating that way," Arderin said. "My oldest brother is an overprotective Neanderthal. It would be maddening if I didn't love him so much."

"Ain't that the truth," she said, showcasing a slightly Southern accent. "Follow me and don't mind my drawl," Sarah said, leading her toward an elevator. "I'm originally from New Jersey but when you live in Texas long enough, everyone picks up a bit of the twang."

They chatted companionably as the elevator whisked them to the fourth floor. Sarah led them to a lounge that had a buffet lunch spread on a large white table.

"Medical reps," Sarah said, her smile wide. "Gotta love them. They bring us lunch every day and keep me fat. C'mon, let's grab some food, and we'll sit and talk."

They filled their plates with salad, sandwiches and soups, and sat at one of the round pop-up tables that filled the lounge.

"So, where is Sadie practicing now? She never wanted to be tied down to one place and always seemed to be traveling to help underprivileged patients around the world. Last I heard, she was in a remote area of Nigeria setting up a clinic."

"She's opening clinics in various rural areas of Africa," Arderin said, confirming the story that Sadie had told the human physicians she trained with so they didn't question her absence. "The areas have no cell service, so she's quite cut off from the world."

"Good for her. She's such a caring person, with a deep well of compassion. I hope she's happy."

Arderin thought of Nolan and his possible attraction to her dear friend. "I think she's on the right path, for sure." Smiling, she chewed a bite of her salad.

After getting to know each other for a bit, Arderin began asking about Sarah's journey toward becoming a physician.

"It's not easy," she said, swallowing a spoonful of soup. "Especially for women who want to '*have it all*' and all that jazz. I'm married with two kids and find it hard to balance everything. But my husband is an author, and he works from home, so that makes it easier on us than most."

"And what did you think about Yale?" Arderin asked. "It's supposedly one of the best human—I mean, best schools for medicine in the world." Biting her lip, she waited, hoping the woman hadn't caught her slip-up.

"Yale was wonderful. Sadie and I sure got into some trouble there. Although, she never seemed phased. It's like that woman's seen a thousand lifetimes of drama and just smiled through it all. Anyway," she shrugged her shoulders, "it's really phenomenal but I hated the winters."

"Were they that bad?"

"Yeah, they were pretty rough. Being from the Northeast, I could handle it, but Sadie didn't seem thrilled. There are also great residency programs in California, Florida and Texas. It just depends on what you're looking for."

Arderin contemplated. She'd never seen snow and was used to temperate climates. Plus, she loved wearing her cute little ankle boots and would never be able to wear those on an icy day. Could she survive in a cold winter climate?

"Have you decided on a specialty?" Sarah asked, yanking her from her thoughts.

"Not yet. I know a fantastic surgeon who's pushing me toward general surgery, but Sadie is so great with her clinic. I think I might be leaning toward office-based medicine rather than surgery."

"Good," Sarah said, nodding as she wiped her hands with her napkin. "We need more primary care physicians. They're a dying breed."

"So, you're happy with the specialty you chose? And your practice here?"

"As a pig in shit," Sarah said, grinning. "I've never wanted to be anything but a doctor and get so much joy from helping people. If you have that same calling, I'd urge you to pursue it. It fills a hole inside that nothing else ever could."

"Thank you, Sarah," Arderin said, noticing the other woman stand. Following suit, they trotted over to dispose of their paper plates in the large gray trash can. "I really appreciate all your help."

"Sorry, I have to run," she said, placing a stethoscope over her neck. "It's the life of a physician. But, please, contact me anytime you have questions. I'm always happy to help another burgeoning doctor." She held out her hand.

Brimming with gratitude, Arderin threw her arms around her, hugging her tight.

"You and Sadie, both huggers," Sarah muttered companionably. "Gotta love it. Be well, Arderin. Grab more food if you want and then just take the elevator back to the first floor. See ya soon." With that, she was gone, flitting through the door with a flash of her white lab coat.

Arderin grabbed a cookie from the buffet table and munched on it as she rode the elevator back to the lobby. Once outside, she lifted her face to the warm sun, inhaling a deep breath.

Loving the sounds that surrounded her, she felt a sense of peace in front of the busy medical center. She could make a life here, in the human world, at least as she trained. One that was happy and fulfilling, preparing her to answer her calling to help others heal. Just imagining it made her heart threaten to burst. Determined to figure out a way to convince Sathan to let her study in the human world, she set about finding a taxi to take her back to the hotel.

* * * *

Once back at the hotel, Arderin searched the desktop computer in the business center for information on the best medical schools in the human world.

There were some in London, Australia and Sweden, but most were in the US. Scrunching her nose, she decided that although Yale and Johns Hopkins both seemed great, their East Coast winters probably wouldn't be to her liking. If she was going to leave her family for years to train, she wanted to be somewhere that allowed her to do yoga under the sun. After regaining the ability to walk under the shiny orb, she didn't want to spend several months of the year sequestered indoors.

Clicking the mouse, she grinned. California. Now, that's where it was at. Maneuvering the arrow around the screen, she took detailed notes on various residency programs. Locating the medical school applications for the programs at UCLA and Stanford, she printed them. Folding the papers, she stuffed them in her bag.

Back in her room, she attempted to watch TV again but found herself restless. Needing to explore, she headed out into the bright afternoon sun. A few blocks from her hotel was the bustling downtown of Houston. She spent hours walking from store to store, loving the pretty clothes and jewelry. Although she'd never developed a burning desire for food, she nevertheless ordered a hamburger at one of the self-proclaimed "local joints" downtown. Sitting alone, she savored the taste of the juicy meat slathered with toppings.

Later that evening, she visited a few bars, excited to see the nightlife in the human world. Some had line dancing, some had karaoke. All were extremely entertaining. As she danced with one of the many gentlemen who asked her, she became lost in the simplicity of a warm night in the land of humans. Anticipating her future, she danced deep into the morning.

Chapter 11

After three days, Darkrip returned. When Arderin pulled open the hotel room door, his face was impassive.

"Did you find her?"

"Yes," he said.

"Okay," she said, rolling her eyes. "And?"

He sighed. "She wasn't cooperative. Come on. I want to get you back to Astaria and update Miranda."

Muttering at his unwillingness to tell her anything, Arderin grabbed her bag. Sadness coursed through her as she contemplated returning to the immortal world. Although she loved her family desperately, she felt she'd barely gotten to see anything of the land she'd dreamed of visiting for so long. What if Sathan didn't want her to return? It had been difficult to get him to agree to this trip. Mustering her determination to sway him, she followed Darkrip to the park.

Once there, his low-toned voice washed over her. "Close your eyes and concentrate on visualizing the last spot we were before we came through the ether. See the four-wheeler and the surrounding foliage in your mind." He aligned his front with her back, and the heat from his body made her shiver. "Ready?"

Arderin nodded and lowered her lids. Forming the image, she stretched out her hand, surprised to feel the thickness of the ether.

"Go," he said, nudging her with his body.

Anger flashed through her and she wanted to tell him to fuck off, but she stayed silent and began wading through the viscosity. It was stifling, but now that she knew what to expect, she didn't feel like she was going to suffocate. Thank the goddess.

A few moments later, she was through. Needing air in her lungs, she dropped her bag on the green grass and rested her hands on her knees, inhaling large gulps.

"Something's wrong," Darkrip said above her. "The four-wheeler's gone."

Standing to her full height, she looked around the open field. The vehicle had indeed vanished. Feeling her brow furrow, her heart began to pound.

"Maybe someone came upon it and stole it?"

"Not likely," he muttered. "Text Latimus that we're through the ether and the four-wheeler is gone. After that, I'll transport us back to Astaria."

"Okay." Pulling out her phone, she did as he requested.

"Come on," he said, pulling her close by her wrist. Threading her arms around his neck, he closed his eyes, and she felt herself being *whooshed* through the air. Seconds later, her body slammed to a stop.

Pain coursed through Arderin, and she grunted. Falling onto what felt like dirt-covered ground, Darkrip's muscular body crashed on top of hers.

"Shit," he muttered, pushing himself off. Green eyes alert, his head rotated to take in their surroundings.

Sitting up, she allowed herself to adjust to the dimness. Snapping her head in all directions, she was able to see that they were in a cave of some sort.

They sat in the middle of a natural lair, the dirty ground stretching about thirty feet in each direction. Rocky walls formed a dome that held them in, and several torches were lit along them. A pond sat on one side, the blue water seeming to glow in the light of the torches. The pond was about ten feet long and twenty feet wide, stretching to one of the stony walls.

"What the hell happened?" she asked.

"I don't know," Darkrip said, shaking his head. "We should've ended up at Astaria. I used to come to this cave to escape my father."

Fear coiled around Arderin's heart, thick as a snake, as an evil laugh came from the shadows. Gasping, she turned her body, still sitting on the cold ground, toward the sound.

"Hello, son," the Dark Lord Crimeous said, his voice gruff and wicked. Appearing from thin air, he slowly sauntered toward them. Tall and thin, his gray skin was pasty. Reedy eyebrows sat atop beady eyes and a long nose. Lifting his lips in a sneer, Arderin noticed that his yellow teeth had been filed into sharp points. He wore a flowing gray cape, the collar surrounding his pointed ears.

Terror, blazing and encompassing, enveloped Arderin. Never had her body been wracked with such violent tremors. Evil washed off the creature in waves, causing bile to burn in her throat. Unable to control her need to scream, she inhaled a breath.

Darkrip covered her mouth with his firm hand, cutting off her shriek. Shoving her behind him, he stood, facing his father.

"You son of a bitch. How did you interfere in my materialization?"

Crimeous chuckled. "I've grown so powerful, son. Don't you understand? It's only a matter of time before I torture you all to death."

"Why did you bring us here?" he asked. Arderin rose, lurking behind Darkrip but allowing her curious brain to absorb what was happening while her heart pounded inside her chest.

"You used to come here to hide from me. Smart, as I didn't know of this cave for centuries. But when you almost died after the battle with Miranda, the shield you erected in your mind was down for several minutes. I learned of this place and that your mother came to see you here. How sweet. I miss Rina sometimes. She was always so tight as I fucked her."

Arderin could feel the rage vibrating off of Darkrip's powerful body. "Don't you *ever* speak of my mother again. I'll kill you for what you did to her."

Throwing back his head, the Deamon gave an awful laugh. "Of course, you won't. You've already tried and failed. And who is left? Evie? I'm more scared of a rag doll."

"So, are we to fight?" Darkrip said, lifting his hands. "Is that why you brought me here? Let's get on with it then. I don't have all fucking day."

"Oh, no, son. I have much bigger plans for you. A brilliant idea has recently formed in my mind. So magnificent that I'm disappointed I didn't think of it before. A child with the combined blood of Valktor, Markdor and myself would be invincible. A warrior I could train to exterminate every last Vampyre and Slayer upon the Earth."

Lips curved, the Dark Lord continued. "You have been sequestered here to impregnate this Vampyre. Her father's blood and self-healing abilities combined with my powers will make the progeny exceptionally powerful. When the child is ready, I will take it, as I took Rina, and train it to kill every wretched immortal that Etherya has spawned." Lifting his palms toward the sky, he closed his eyes. "It will be splendid. I can already *feel* the glory."

"You're delusional, but I've come to expect that. I'll never procreate. You know that as well as I do."

Crimeous cackled. "I don't believe you'll be able to squelch your attraction to her, but we'll see. I've erected a barrier around the cave that won't allow you to dematerialize. Eventually, I think you'll fuck her, or rape her, and she'll bear the spawn that I need. Careful that I don't just do the deed myself. Your grandfather's blood is needed for the child. Consider it a gift that I'm letting you have her."

Arderin wanted to retch at his words, sickened by the thought of the wicked creature ever touching her. Darkrip's arms extended behind him, pulling her into his back. Tears welled in her eyes at his protection of her.

"I'm stronger than you will ever be. Fuck you, old man. You'll never get a child out of me."

Arching an eyebrow, his penetrating irises raked over them. "We'll see. Have fun, Darkrip. If you don't do as I ask, you'll die here. There's no way out unless I am wounded, which is highly improbable given Latimus and Kenden's inability to create a weapon that can maim me. They could still blow open the cave, but I find that doubtful since it's so secluded. You'll be long dead before they locate you. Give me a spawn. It's your only option if you want to live." Closing his eyes, the Deamon disappeared.

"Fuck!" Darkrip yelled, releasing her and walking forward. Pacing, he palmed his forehead.

"Hey," Arderin said, lifting her hand to his shoulder. "We have to stay calm." Difficult, since her blood was racing through her body.

"Why don't you at least try to dematerialize? Let's not take his word for it."

Olive-green eyes latched onto hers, filled with fury and frustration. Inhaling a deep breath, Darkrip nodded. Closing his lids, she saw his pupils darting underneath. After a few moments, she realized it was futile.

"Crap," she whispered, looking around the cave. "We're trapped here."

A muscle corded in his firm jaw as he clenched his teeth. "Let me look around. I'll try to find an exit of some sort. Stay here and catalog our rations. I think I have three granola bars in my bag, and I need to know how much Slayer blood you have."

"It will only stay drinkable without refrigeration for twenty-four hours."

"I know," he said, his expression wary. "Catalog everything and let me look around. I'll be back in a bit."

When he started to walk away, she grabbed his forearm, calling his name.

"Yeah?"

"Thank you for shielding me from him. That was very brave."

"Don't thank me yet. We very well could die in here, princess. I'm determined to not let that happen. See you in a bit." Wrenching his arm from her grip, he walked through the dimness and into what looked to be an entrance to a cavernous hallway.

Straightening her spine, Arderin gazed at their two bags on the ground. Inside were all the rations they had to survive. Steeling herself, she began logging the contents.

* * * *

Darkrip cursed his father, Etherya and every other god he knew as he walked through the small tunnel. It was the second one he'd found, leading from the lair, and it was also a dead end. Closing his eyes, he tried to dematerialize again, but it was no use. His bastard father had erected a powerful barrier indeed.

Hating the creature more than he ever had, he went back to find Arderin. She sat on the ground, her tight jeans and thin green sweater somehow still pristine in the dirt. For a moment, he took her in and worry coursed through him. It would be extremely difficult not to touch her the longer they were sequestered together. Clenching his jaw, he affirmed his resolve.

Coming to sit beside her, he asked, "What have we got?"

Ice-blue eyes latched onto his. Although they were slightly tinged with fear, there was a resolute strength there that he admired. "Three granola bars, some Skittles that I bought at the hotel lobby and my bottle of Slayer blood. Although, as we discussed, it will only be good through tomorrow."

Darkrip nodded. "I'll see if there are any fish in the pond. If so, I can eat those. Perhaps there are some rodents in the cave that I can eat as well."

Her perfect features scrunched together. "Gross."

"Well," he said, shrugging, "you do what you have to when you're stranded in a cave with no food."

"I guess so," she said, biting her juicy bottom lip. His always-erect shaft pulsed at the action. Wetness seemed to shine on the pink flesh, illuminated by the torches along the wall. White fangs taunted him as he imagined her scraping them over the sensitive skin of his neck.

"We need to set some rules for our captivity."

"Okay," she said, blinking as she cautiously observed him.

"You know of my curse. I need to relieve myself every few hours. I know this might be embarrassing to discuss but, believe me, it's better if we get it out in the open. If I don't attain proper release, it makes it harder for me to control the evil half of myself."

Her flawless face filled with compassion, and he wanted to tell her he didn't deserve it. Instead, he let her speak.

"I'm a clinician. I understand how frustrating it must be to be in a constant state of arousal. I'm not embarrassed. I'll give you privacy."

"Thank you," he said with a nod. "There's a tunnel over there that extends about fifty feet. I'll go there every few hours when needed."

"Okay," she said. Those probing irises studied him, and he felt himself drowning in them.

"I also need to make sure you don't touch me. It's imperative that we keep physical distance. I haven't given into the evil in many centuries, but I don't want to hurt you."

She nodded, ever so slowly, and he couldn't take the sentiment in her eyes.

"I don't deserve your sympathy, Arderin. I'm a monster. You need to remember that. You have an inquisitive mind and good heart, but I'll never be someone like you. Please, be wary of me."

When she opened her mouth to argue, he placed two fingers on her soft lips.

"No, princess. Don't fight me on this. I'm not worthy of it." Standing, he wiped off his pants. "I'm heading into the tunnel. See you in a bit."

Those curious eyes watched him as he exited, her gaze so strong that it burned his back. Hating himself, he found a spot to sit so that he could relieve his turgid phallus.

Chapter 12

Latimus' troops were on their lunch break when he received the text from Arderin that the four-wheeler was gone. Worried for her, he strode to the main castle to find Sathan. Locating his brother behind the mahogany desk in his royal office chamber, he showed him the text.

"Are they back to Astaria yet?" Sathan asked.

"No," Latimus said, shaking his head.

His brother cursed, standing to run a hand through his thick, wavy hair. "Okay, if they're not back within the hour, let's assume something happened to them. Crimeous hasn't attacked any of our compounds in a while. It's possible he's been plotting to kidnap them upon their return."

"Agreed," Latimus said, dread filling his soul. If anything happened to his sister, he'd be devastated. She'd been the sole light of his world for so long, and he would fight until his dying breath to save her.

An hour later, Latimus dismissed the troops early from training. Calling Kenden, he informed him of Darkrip and Arderin's disappearance and asked for his help. The calm Slayer commander was ready and willing.

Loading into a Hummer with Sathan, they stopped at Uteria to pick up Kenden. Miranda was spending a few days there and came to meet them outside the large wooden doors to the compound.

"Where do you think they are?" she asked, rubbing her arms as she crossed them over her large abdomen.

"I don't know," Latimus said, hugging her. "But we'll find them."

Nodding, she looked at Sathan. They embraced, but Latimus observed Sathan's tense shoulders. Miranda had talked him into letting Arderin travel to the human world, and he could see his brother struggling not to blame his wife.

As the three of them drove to the ether, Latimus regarded Sathan.

"We'll find her," he said, his tone firm. "You can't blame Miranda. She loves her too."

"I know," his brother said, a muscle ticking in his jaw. "But I never should've listened to her."

Kenden cleared his throat from the backseat. "I'm not trying to butt in, but when my cousin sets her mind on something, it's happening. I think we all know that. Her motivations were pure. She loves Arderin so much."

Sathan sighed, gripping the handle above the passenger-side door as they traversed the open meadow. "I'm just disappointed in myself that I didn't better ensure her safety."

"I know," Latimus said, patting his shoulder as the other hand steered. "We'll find her. I promise. Don't take it out on your pregnant wife, man. You've got enough to deal with."

Sathan ran his hand over his face and nodded. Arriving at the ether, they jumped out to inspect the tracks that Darkrip's four-wheeler had left in the grass. Latimus noticed a fresher set of tracks that stretched in the direction of the Deamon caves. Under the light of the afternoon sun, the men set about following them.

* * * *

Arderin was determined to escape the musty cavern. Holding up her cell, she tried to text Latimus but there was no service. Realizing only half the battery life was left, she turned it off and put it back in her bag. Roaming around the cave, she felt along the ridges of the rock wall with her fingers. Surely, there was some kind of exit, if only they could find it. She explored for what seemed like hours and then came to sit on the ground by their bags.

Darkrip returned from the tunnel, and she figured he'd been gone so long because he'd been searching for an escape as well. Hope began to die in her heart as he sat beside her, his expression resigned.

"We can't give up," she said, reaching to grab his hand.

He pulled away from her, causing her to scowl. "I know. I'm trying to think if I ever told Miranda about the location of this cave. I told her that our mother appeared here to me centuries ago, but I can't remember if I told her where it was."

Arderin pulled her legs into her chest, hugging them as she rested her chin on her knees.

"What did she say when she appeared to you?"

Darkrip studied her, the green of his eyes seeming to melt in the dimness. They were absolutely mesmerizing, and Arderin found herself wondering how it would feel for him to stare into hers as they made love. Mentally shaking the thought away, she waited for him to speak.

He seemed hesitant to tell her, and she realized he'd probably never had a confidant. Someone whom he could tell his stories to. She'd always had her brothers and Lila, and his reluctance caused empathy to swell within.

"I'm not trying to pry," she said, her tone gentle. "I just know that she was very important to you. I'd be honored if you would tell me, but I won't force you."

Sighing, he sat back, resting his weight on his palms. "She told me to stop torturing and killing. She didn't want to be the mother of someone so terrible."

Arderin did her best to retain an impassive yet understanding demeanor. "Judging by comments you've made to me, it seems you listened to her."

"I've tried," he said, looking down at his crossed legs. "It's been extremely difficult. The part of him that flows through me is awful. It urges me to do things that are unspeakable."

Rubbing her cheek on the denim of her jeans, she felt her heart squeeze. Although he swore he was evil, he'd chosen to live by the lightness of his better half for centuries. She wished he would give himself credit. It was quite amazing.

"Well, I've only seen the good part of you. Even when you're driving me crazy and telling me I'm a brat. Which I am, about seventy percent of the time."

"Only seventy percent?" He lifted a raven eyebrow and the corner of his full lips turned up. It made him look unbearably attractive.

"Okay, maybe seventy-five," she said, smiling broadly.

"You're infuriating, princess, and I think you know it. But you're incredibly fun to spar with. I like that you don't take my shit. Most people are fucking terrified of me."

"Oh, please," she said, waving her hand. "You're harmless. Look at you with Miranda. You're a puppy dog."

Chuckling, Darkrip shook his head. "She does something to me, that's for sure. She's a dead ringer for Mother. I rarely feel emotion, but I feel it for her. It's so strange."

"I'm glad you found each other. You deserve to have someone who cares for you."

His features hardened, and he sat up. "Listen, we have to be honest about what's going on here. I can't dematerialize and I can't break through whatever shield my father has erected. I tried to reach Miranda's mind to tell her where we are, but all of my powers are useless."

Wetness filled her eyes, and she blinked to hold back the tears. "We have to keep trying to find an escape. Latimus promised me that if something happened, he'd save us. We can't give up."

"We won't. That bastard won't get the best of me."

Arderin toyed with her bottom lip, struggling with a mixture of embarrassment and the need to speak frankly. "Should we discuss why Crimeous trapped us here? His ridiculous ultimatum?"

Darkrip exhaled, his gaze probing and firm. "It's my fault. I've tried to shield my thoughts about you. When I saw Evie, she could read them, clear as day. I should've anticipated that my father could read them as well."

Her ears rang as blood coursed through her body at his words. "What thoughts?" she asked, the words almost whispered.

Lids blinked in succession over those olive-green irises. "You're too smart to ask questions that you already know the answer to, princess."

Arderin swallowed, feeling her throat bob. "You always seem so determined to stay away from me. I thought it was because you hated me."

"Hate certainly isn't a word I'd associate with you, Arderin. You're...*important*," he said, seeming to grapple with the word. "I'm harsh to you for your own good. You don't want someone like me in your life. And you certainly don't want someone thinking even half of the thoughts I do about you."

Her tongue darted over her parched lips. Tingles rushed to her core as his eyes filled with desire at the gesture. "I'm not the innocent angel you think I am. I have thoughts too."

"Enough," he said, shaking his head and holding a palm up. "This discussion is futile. We obviously won't ever give my father what he wants. Knowing that, we need to work together to find a way out of this cave. We only have a few days of rations. Once your blood is gone and my food is gone, we're screwed. I think we can drink the water from the pond. It looks safe enough. But we need sustenance."

Giving in to the tense moment, she accepted his change of subject, knowing they would have to discuss their mutual attraction. The longer they were sequestered, the more it would consume them. Just sitting next to him caused little pangs of desire to throb in her belly.

"I'll alert you if I see any small animals," she said. "We can keep you alive, and if I have to drink your Slayer blood, I can."

"No," he said, warning flashing in his eyes. "Drinking from me would be worse than death. You'll be exposed to all of my thoughts and memories. Torture and violence like you've never imagined. I won't do that to you. It would be better if you went to the Passage."

"Wait," she said, feeling anger bubble in her chest. "You'd rather let me die than drink from you? Are you serious right now?"

"You don't understand what you're asking. Someone as innocent as you never could. I won't let one drop of my Deamon blood inside you, Arderin. Not one fucking drop. It's vile and malevolent."

She stood, her temper enflaming. "Then, you're a murderer, no better than your father!" Pointing her finger in his face, she began yelling. "How dare you? My brother trusted you to protect me! As long as you have food, I need to drink from you. It's the only way I'll survive."

Standing, he grabbed her finger. "Don't shout at me," he sneered, throwing her arm back at her. "My father's blood ruined my mother, and I'll be damned if it ruins you too. And if you don't like it, then too fucking bad."

"Asshole!" she screamed. "You're despicable!"

Rolling his eyes, he shook his head. "I don't want to waste what time I have left arguing with a spoiled Vampyre. I need to get some sleep if I'm going to resume searching for an escape tomorrow. Leave me the fuck alone. Got it?"

Gritting her teeth, she watched him walk to the mouth of the tunnel he'd gone to earlier, twenty feet away. Lying down, he rested his head on his bag and closed his eyes. Giving a *harrumph*, she crossed her arms and sat on the ground, fuming.

After a while, her anger turned to exhaustion and she lay down. Pulling her nightgown from her bag, she turned it into a makeshift pillow and allowed herself to sleep.

Chapter 13

Miranda sat with Sathan, Latimus and Kenden in the conference room at Uteria. A dark cloud of despair seemed to permeate the chamber.

"If you think Crimeous has sequestered them in one of the Deamon caves, then we have to search there," Miranda said. "Ken, can you make a list of the all the lairs you think he would hold them prisoner?"

"Yes," her cousin said, nodding. "I have about twenty in mind."

"Okay," she said, struggling to hold back tears. "And maybe we can add Darkrip's secret spot to the list. He told me that Mother visited him there. Perhaps, if they escaped, he would go there to regroup. I think he felt a sense of peace and calm there. If I remember what he told me, it lies several miles from where Crimeous used to torture our mother."

"I know which lair he used for that," Kenden said. "We found it in one of our attacks when we were attempting to recover the Blade. Latimus and I will form several groups of soldiers and have them search within a twenty-mile radius of that lair."

"Thank you," Miranda whispered, unable to control her voice. "I think our path is clear. Let's get on this right away."

They stood, Latimus and Kenden exiting the room with urgency. Sathan walked to the window and looked out over the meadow that ran behind the castle. His broad shoulders were stiff with worry and frustration, and Miranda wanted to crumble into a ball on the floor and melt away.

"Sathan," she called, her voice hoarse. "Are you ever going to look at me again?"

His massive chest expanded as he inhaled, refusing to turn around.

"What do you want me to say, Miranda? I was terrified something would happen to her."

Wanting to comfort him, she tentatively approached and slid her arms around him. Clutching his back to her distended front, she rested her forehead between his shoulder blades. "I'm so sorry. I don't know what to say. This is so fucking terrible. I only wanted her to be happy. Please, don't hate me."

Exhaling, he slowly turned, pulling her close. Resting his forehead on hers, his black irises seemed to pierce her. "I love you, Miranda. You know that. But right now, I'm extremely pissed that I listened to you. What if she dies?"

"Don't think that way," she said, stroking his cheek with her palm. "You can't think that way."

With glassy eyes, he regarded her. "I just can't do this right now. I need to be alone. I'm going back to Astaria. I'll see you when you arrive in a few days."

Miranda felt her heart shatter into a thousand pieces as he disentangled himself from her and began walking toward the door. "So, that's it, then? You're going to blame your pregnant wife for your sister's disappearance. That's really freaking fair."

"Don't," he said, turning and motioning with his hand. "I don't want to argue with you. I don't blame you, but I'm afraid I'm going to say something that I'll regret. Leave it at that. I'll see you in a few days."

As his large frame exited, she fell into a chair and lowered her head onto her crossed arms, resting on the table. Hating herself for ever agreeing to let Arderin travel to the human world, she let herself cry.

* * * *

Arderin awoke to unfamiliar circumstances, her teeth chattering. Man, she was *freezing*. Wrapping her arms around herself, she pulled her legs into her chest and willed herself to stop shaking. As her eyes darted around, she remembered the circumstances that had led her to the cave. Feeling hopeless, she draped her long hair around her compacted body, hoping it would give her extra heat.

No such luck. Forget dying from lack of Slayer blood. She'd most likely freeze to death at this rate.

"Come on," a deep voice said behind her. "For god's sake, your teeth are going to fall out if you don't stop chattering." Darkrip pulled her into his warm body, spooning her as he held her tight. "Good girl. Calm down. The faster your heart beats, the more you shiver. Relax. I won't let you freeze to death before we can have at least one last epic argument."

Thankful for his warmth, she tried to breathe a weak laugh, but it froze in her windpipe.

"It must be nighttime outside. It would make sense why the cave has gotten so cold. The sun won't be warming the ground above for a few hours. Let's track it so that we can differentiate when it's day from night. It would be best for us to search for an escape during the warmest times, so we don't have to divide our energy trying to stay warm."

Nodding, she reached up and pulled her phone from her bag. Turning it on, she started the timer. As the light from the phone faded, she soaked up his body heat. Eventually, she stopped trembling, and he began to pull away from her.

"No," she pleaded, turning her head to look up at him. "You're so warm."

His expression was derisive. "No touching, remember? I only wanted to stop your shivering." Rolling away from her, he stood and brushed off his black pants and button-up, collared dress shirt. "I'm heading to the tunnel. I'll keep searching for an escape in a few hours."

Turning over so that she could watch him retreat, she imagined him jerking off. She'd already seen his six-pack when she'd stitched him up. Boy, was it yummy. Would the skin of his hand brush it as he tugged on his shaft with his fist? When he spurted his release, would it land there, needing to be licked away by her tongue?

Feeling a rush of wetness between her thighs, Arderin acknowledged her yearning for him. It had always been unwelcome, especially because he didn't seem to want her back. After their recent conversation, she understood how badly he desired her. It was enough for his evil father to force them into shared captivity and demand they spawn a child.

For one moment, Arderin imagined them in different circumstances. Darkrip, a willing suitor, who'd been born of an aristocratic family. Lacking Crimeous' malevolent blood, he would be able to court her and shower her with playful affection. After a passionate engagement, they would bond. The night of their ceremony, he would spread kisses over her body, readying her for his invasion. Those striking eyes would stare into her, filled with love and reverence as he took her virginity.

By the goddess, she could envision it so clearly...

Scoffing, she sat up and rubbed her palms over her jeans. Living in fantasyland wasn't going to do her any favors. As reality set in, Arderin admitted that Darkrip would never let himself fathom that type of existence.

Anger swelled as she remembered their argument. How could he not let her drink from him? No, she wasn't as experienced as he, but she wasn't an idiot. She possessed a voracious intellect and had seen much in her life. She wasn't afraid to see Darkrip's innermost thoughts and memories. Although they must be terrible, they were worth seeing if they saved her life. She was smart enough to comprehend that the actions of his youth had been a result of his father's influence. How could he deny her the opportunity to survive?

Wracking her brain, she understood that she needed to study him. There must be more behind his reluctance to let her drink from him. Determined to figure it out, she also needed to begin the day's search for an escape. Confident in her ability to use her fastidious mind to figure something out, she got to work.

* * * *

Evie sat atop the withered mountain, the fresh autumn air filling her nostrils. This place, nestled in the Appalachian Mountains of Western North Carolina, was almost as calming to her as the cliffsides of Japan. Almost. Narrowing her eyes, she wondered if she'd ever truly feel peace again.

First, the arrogant, handsome Slayer had come looking for her. That had angered her terribly, and she'd tried to show him not to fucking mess with her. She'd plotted her revenge, hoping to scare the immortals into leaving her the hell alone. Sadly, Miranda had lost her unborn child in the skirmish with Crimeous. Remorse and a heavy dose of shame washed through Evie at the thought. Although she was a despicable creature, she drew a line at harming children. Unfamiliar with the reticent emotions, she glowered before her, jaw clenched.

Next, her asshole brother had shown up, shattering the tranquility of the Japanese sunset. Bastard. Couldn't he find someone else to harass? He'd tried to kill her once, for the goddess's sake. Of course, he'd failed, but it still rankled her anyway. Staring at the multicolored, dying leaves, Evie imagined strangling him.

And yet, there was something inside her that was clawing to get out. Restless, it kneaded and clanked at every wall she'd thrown up inside her blackened heart. As the blood coursed through her body, she let herself feel it.

There, so deep inside, in a place she'd long forgotten, was a kernel. Of hope and curiosity and wonder. Were there people in the immortal world who really needed her? Could her poor excuse for a life actually have some sort of miniscule purpose?

She'd always just assumed she was destined to float. Alone, in a sea of strangers, no one ever wanting anything to do with her. But what if she was wrong? What if she was the one to fulfill the prophecy?

Killing her father would be epic, for sure. He'd raped her repeatedly in front of Rina, hoping to torture her further by hurting her child. But her mother had been too far gone for any of that to register. It was a waste, really. She'd long ago released any sort of emotion from the battering her body received from her father or any of the other men who had succeeded in her youth. Once the evil had taken over, she'd made men pay a hundred-fold. Growing into her body, and her malevolence, she'd realized that *she* had the power; *she* controlled any sort of sexual encounter. Thankfully, that had somehow liberated her from the atrocities of her past.

Straightening her spine, she observed the cotton ball clouds in the sky. They seemed to form rabbits and hearts, crosses and frogs. A soft breeze blew by, caressing her face and whipping her red hair. Her father had once told her it was the same color as Etherya's. Surely, another lie spawned from his hateful lips.

Internally clutching her revulsion of the despicable creature, she contemplated whether she could align with her brother and the stupid immortals to defeat him. Still unsure, she dissolved back to her condo in France to pack up her belongings. Just in case.

Chapter 14

A few days later, Darkrip ejaculated on his abdomen with a groan. Panting, he wiped the wetness away with an extra t-shirt he'd stowed in his bag. Crumpling it, he pulled up his pants, tucked in his shirt and began the short trek back to the lair. He'd ditched the belt when they'd realized they were trapped, but he'd always enjoyed being well-dressed, and the habit of tucking in one's shirt didn't just vanish after several centuries.

Living in the Deamon caves for all those years, the one thing he could control were his clothes. The first time he'd visited the human world, he'd gotten a taste for tailored shirts, expensive loafers and fitted pants. The desire to wear them had never ceased.

Stopping in front of the pond, he washed the shirt. Wringing it out, he went to sit beside Arderin's sleeping form. Irritated, he rubbed his fingers over his forehead. She'd had the last of the Slayer blood two days ago. One more day, and she'd perish. Although he'd acknowledged their imminent death, he hadn't really believed it. Someone as powerful as he could always find a solution. And yet, as the hours ticked by, his despair had grown.

There were no fish in the pond, but he'd found a rat. Arderin had refused to watch him eat the damn thing, and he'd almost laughed at her prissiness. Even when possible death was looming, the spoiled Vampyre princess retained her haughtiness and self-righteousness.

During their time together, he'd also realized her strength. She was tireless in her search for an escape. Every morning, when the cave started to warm, she would rise and tinker to hatch a new escape plan.

First, she'd whittled down the tip of her plastic hairbrush with a nail file to form a sharp point. For hours, she had chipped away at the rock wall, hoping to break through. Although the action had been futile, Darkrip admired her gumption as she gritted her teeth and pounded with her slim arm.

Next, she'd taken her phone into the narrowest points of one of the tunnels that branched from the main lair. Maximizing the volume, she'd blared the speaker so that one of Miranda's heavy metal songs vibrated against the low-hanging rocks. Hoping to cause a collapse and create an opening, frustration appeared in her expression and reddened cheeks when the stones remained firm.

Every time she lay down to rest, her slight shoulders hunched in dejection. Fear and resignation seemed to constantly war in her magnificent ice-blue eyes, causing Darkrip to feel disparaged that he hadn't saved her yet.

Although he chided her for being spoiled and annoying, he actually liked her immensely. Her feisty spirit was consuming, and he hated the possibility that the Earth would no longer experience her smile or quick temper. A soul as pure as Arderin's deserved better than dying in this squalid cave.

Thinking of Sathan and Miranda, he knew they must be distraught. Hating that he'd let his sister down, he tried to send her messages with his mind, frustrated when they didn't reach her.

Arderin's pale cheek rested on her hands as she slept on her side. Allowing himself to touch her while she slept, he ran a feather-light finger over the curve of her chin. Smacking her pink lips together, she sighed and smiled, her eyes never opening. God, she was the most stunning creature he'd ever beheld. What he wouldn't give to fuck her, just once.

Gently clasping her shoulder, he shook her awake. Swollen sky-blue eyes gazed up at him, causing his heart to pound.

"I thought you might want to write a note to your brothers, so that it's found if we don't escape and they locate our bodies."

Her features drew together, and tears welled in her baby-blues. Sitting up, she regarded him. "We can't give up."

"I know, princess," he said, his tone morose. "But let's be prepared just in case."

With a huff, she crossed her arms over her perfect breasts, hidden by the V-neck of her sweater. "I'm not wasting time doing something so dreadful when we're going to be found. I told you, Latimus will come for us. We have to forge ahead."

She looked so impertinent, like a spoiled queen whose jester hadn't pleased her. It should've turned him off. Instead, he felt his lips curve.

"Man, you are some kind of brat."

Those eyes locked onto his. "Sathan used to call me that when we were young."

And then it happened. The gravity of their situation washed over her stunning face. As her chin quivered, her eyes brimmed with tears. Letting them fall, she cradled her face in her hands.

"We're going to die," she wailed, shaking with her cries. "All because I couldn't listen to him and just stay in the kingdom. I'm so fucking stubborn. He always told me that one day I'd get myself into a situation he couldn't save me from. Goddamnit!"

Looking to the roof of the cave, she groaned in frustration. "Fuck you, asshole!" Darkrip assumed she was yelling at his father. "Come back here and let me fight you. I'll kill you for what you've done to me and to Lila and everyone I love. Aargh!"

"Okay, okay," Darkrip said softly. He awkwardly rubbed her upper arm. "You have every right to be upset, but let's channel our anger constructively and use it to find an escape."

"Stop being so flippant," she said. He felt himself drowning in her damp irises. "We could die in this fucking cave. Don't you even care?"

"Of course, I care. I just don't know how dramatics will help. Now, here," he said, thrusting a pen at her that he'd pulled from his bag. "Write them a note. I think it will make you feel better."

She pulled some folded white papers from her bag, straightening them out on her thigh and flattening them with the palm of her hand.

"What are those?"

Her broken smile almost shattered his deadened heart. "Applications to medical schools in California. I printed them out at the hotel in Houston. I was going to try to convince Sathan to let me attend one. Guess that bird's flown the coop."

Darkrip swallowed, sadness swamping him that she would most likely never see her brothers again.

"I'm sorry," he whispered.

"For what?" she asked, innocent sincerity swimming in her gorgeous irises.

"For not saving you. One as powerful as I should have. I promised Sathan I'd protect you. I let everyone down."

"No," she said, scooting closer and cupping his cheek. "You've been amazing. We'll keep trying. I know we'll find an escape. Two people as stubborn as us won't accept defeat."

Her tongue darted out to bathe slightly curved, pink lips with moisture. Slowly, she lifted her face toward his.

"No," he said, pulling her hand from his face. "It's not happening, Arderin."

The lightning-fast anger that he loved so much contorted her face. "Why the hell not? We're obviously attracted to each other, and I'm curious. Don't you want to kiss me?"

Fuck yes. More than anything he'd ever wanted in his godforsaken life. And yet, Darkrip was determined not to touch her. One kiss, one taste, would never be enough. She'd wrap that slender body around him and drown him in lust. His desire for her was too great, and consummation would give Crimeous exactly what he wanted. No way in hell.

Touching one inch of her perfect body would ensure her downfall. Whether she realized it or not, he was saving her. Although he cared about little in the world, he cared enough about her to deny her.

"Wanting has nothing to do with it."

"God, you're annoying!" she snapped, snatching her arm away. "So, I can't kiss you and I can't drink from you. I deserve to know why you won't save my life."

Fear coursed through him as he thought of everything she'd see if she imbibed his blood. Although it was temporary, lasting days until the liquid exited her body, she would be privy to all of his past atrocities. Every shameful act of his youth, before he'd given his pledge to his mother. There was a malevolence in those actions, completed so long ago, that he didn't want her to see. Someone as guileless as she never should.

But the decision also stemmed from his desire not to show her any weakness or vulnerability. Their relationship was a dance of wills and constantly reclaiming the upper hand. It went against Darkrip's every fiber to allow her to see him exposed. Never had someone seen into the dark depths of his soul. Allowing one such as she, who would surely hate him, was impossible.

He couldn't live with her revulsion. He'd lived with vitriol from so many others in his destitute life. Self-loathing had always consumed him, forcing him to contemplate ending his existence more times than he cared to admit. Only his promise to his mother, to help Miranda, had given him something to aspire to. Something to hope for.

And now, Darkrip reluctantly admitted, he craved something else. For the gorgeous princess who sat in front of him, with her innocent, wide eyes, to think him capable of having some good inside. Somewhere along the way, that had become extremely important. Knowing that she would never see him as anything other than an abomination if he let her see his most sinister moments, he solidified his vow to never let her drink from his vein.

"Stop asking questions that you know I won't answer," he said gruffly, wanting to anger her so that she left him the hell alone. "I told you, I'm not touching a virgin who hasn't the first clue about pleasing me. And I'll never let you drink from me. It's a gift, whether you want to admit it or not. Now, go on," he said, jerking his head at the papers. "Write to your brothers."

Scowling, she clutched the pen and began to compose.

* * * *

Furious that she was letting Darkrip direct her to do anything, Arderin swiveled cursive letters across the white paper.

To Heden, closest to her in age. Only two years younger, he was her contemporary. Always the comedian, he could make her laugh even when she was consumed by her dramatic temperament.

To Sathan, her protector. Arderin's resemblance to their mother cemented his obsession with making sure she didn't share Calla's fate. He'd watched over her for all these centuries, frustrating her but also filling her with such love.

To Latimus, her favorite. Although she loved all three of her brothers immeasurably, he just seemed to get her. Whereas Sathan scolded her or Heden teased her, Latimus always found a way to burrow into her heart and connect with her. Confident that he would save her, she wrote as sentiment overwhelmed her.

Tears blurred her vision as they drenched the papers she scribbled upon. Family was so important to her and she missed them terribly.

Once finished, Darkrip took the sheets and placed them in his bag. "It's waterproof. On the off chance that the cave floods, they'll be protected better in my bag."

"Fine," she said, annoyed that she couldn't stop crying.

"We'll keep trying," he said. "I just want you to be prepared."

Rolling her eyes, she gave an irritated growl. "Prepared to die a virgin in a gross, smelly cave. Awesome. What an end to a wasted life."

Darkrip's lips twitched, exasperating her even more.

Lifting a small rock, she threw it across the cave. "Whatever. You don't know anything. You've had an exciting life full of adventure and great sex. I'm going to die a shriveled-up, untouched spinster. It's pathetic."

Her head snapped as she regarded him though a cloud of red. "Are you *laughing* at me?"

"I'm sorry," he said, tears of mirth clouding his eyes. "I've seen so many people perish, and never has one been concerned about dying a virgin. You've got some interesting priorities."

"Oh, shut up. Why would you understand anyway? You're freaking hot. I'm sure you've had so many women you can't even remember. I'm completely unfuckable. It's awful."

That statement only exacerbated his laughing. Arderin set about imagining every which way she could strangle him. After several moments, he regained his composure. Grabbing her chin, he turned her face toward his.

"You're right. I've fucked more faceless, nameless women than you could fathom. Not one of those times did it involve any sort of care or concern. I've never once finished inside a woman because I'm so terrified of spawning a child with my father's wretched blood. Fucking isn't all it's cracked up to be, princess."

Curious eyes darted between his. "Then, be with me and let it be different. Why not comfort each other before we die?"

"I can't," he said, his voice scratchy. "You don't want someone like me. Regardless of what you tell yourself. I'm an abomination. You used to think so."

"I never thought so," she said, her tone sincere. "You just made me so mad. But I began to realize that you also challenged me more than anyone I've ever met. It was awesome. I think I've been attracted to you for some time."

He grinned, making him look so appealing in the dim light of the torch-lit cave. "Well, I'm flattered, but we can't act on our attraction. I would be the embodiment of every part of my father's evil if I touched you. I'm sorry."

"Oh, fine. Screw you then. I'm taking a swim if you won't kiss me. At least I can die a clean, withered old virgin." Standing, she pulled off her sweater and threw it in his face. Then, she slid off her tight jeans. Turning to face him, she stood before him in her lacy yellow bra and tiny thong.

Arderin knew she should be embarrassed. But she was nothing if not confident and felt that he should have to suffer from their forced separation, if only a little. Or, judging by the way his pupils darted over her breasts and the juncture of her thighs, maybe a lot.

Lifting her chin, she pivoted and entered the pond. Satisfied that he was now as miserable as she, Arderin allowed herself to enjoy the swim, knowing there might be very few pleasures left in her life.

* * * *

Miranda returned to Astaria, Kenden driving her in one of their Hummers. She hadn't seen Sathan in several days and missed him terribly. Since Arderin and Darkrip were still missing, he'd spent quite a bit of time helping Latimus and Kenden search.

Their phone conversations had been quick; their texts short. Feeling tears well in her eyes, she gazed out the window of the vehicle, seeing nothing.

"You need to make him talk to you, Randi," Kenden said, squeezing her hand as it rested on the seat between them. "You're over eleven months pregnant and due to give birth any day. You two need to be united as we search for them."

"I know," she said, swiping a droplet from her cheek. "But he hates me."

"Stop it," he said, clutching her harder. "I've never seen anyone who loves a person more than Sathan loves you. He's just hurting right now. You need to be strong for him and make him see reason. If anyone can do it, you can. You're the strongest of all of us."

Turning her head, she smiled at him. He'd always been so sure of her strength and valor.

"Why have you always had so much faith in me?"

"Because you're the most incredible person I've ever known." He gave her a brilliant smile, flashing his perfect white teeth. "I mean, you're a pain in the ass most of the time, but I love you more than myself."

Laughing, she pulled his hand up to give it a sweet kiss. "I love you too. You were the only one I had for so long. Now, I have you and Sathan and Darkrip. It's so amazing. Maybe the universe is just punishing me for finally being happy."

"Never," he said, always so confident. "Sathan will come around. Especially if you make him. You can do it, Randi."

Pulling into the barracks warehouse at Astaria, he came around and helped her from the car. She felt like a freaking blue whale and struggled to shuffle into the house. Knowing she would find her husband in his royal office chamber, she traversed the hallways of the large castle until she came upon him.

Sathan was furiously writing on one of the several papers that lined his desk. Head hung low, she marveled at his thick hair and wide shoulders. God, he was magnificent. Wanting so badly to hug him, she entered the room.

"Hey," she said, coming to sit in one of the chairs in front of his desk.

"Hey," he said, setting down his pen. "How are you feeling?"

"Fine," she said, rubbing her abdomen. "Except my husband is being a huge asshole to me. Otherwise, I'm good."

The corner of his broad lips turned up. "Is that so?"

She nodded, hating that tears were welling again. Goddamnit, pregnancy hormones really were the worst.

"Do you need me to kill him?"

Swallowing thickly, she shook her head. "No. I love him too much. And I'm about to have his baby, so I guess he'll have to keep me until then. Afterward...well, I'm not sure."

His handsome face was overcome with an expression of such love that Miranda slowly felt her shattered heart beat again. Standing, he walked over to her. Turning the chair with her in it, he knelt before her. Lowering his head to her lap, he wrapped his massive arms around her waist.

She couldn't see his face, since it was buried in her pregnant mom-jean-clad thighs, so she ran her fingers through his dense hair. Stroking him, she reveled in holding her mate, whom she'd missed so much for what felt like forever.

"I think his youngest brother's still single," she said, carrying on their teasing, "so, if he leaves me, I guess I can pass off the baby as his."

Laughter reverberated off her legs. Lifting his head, he beamed up at her, his fangs making her quiver. "If he touches one hair on your head, I'll kill him."

Chuckling, she caressed his hair. "Well, I might not have a choice. My husband is pretty upset with me right now."

Placing his arm under her knees, and one behind her back, he lifted her. Sitting in the chair, he placed her on his lap. Resting his forehead against hers, he softly kissed her lips.

"I'm not upset with you, sweetheart," he said, rubbing the skin between his eyebrows against hers. "I'm just fucking distraught. I'm so worried she's dead. But I had no right to take it out on you. I'm so sorry."

"Shh..." she said, placing her arms around his beefy neck. "I know this is your worst nightmare. I'm terrified too. But I want to be here for you. Please, let me."

"Okay," he said, nodding against her. Leaning in, Sathan pressed his lips to hers, groaning when he slipped his tongue inside her mouth. Desperately wanting to taste him, she thrust her tongue against his, needing to connect with him in any way possible.

"Miranda," he whispered, licking her mouth everywhere. "Please, forgive me. Every time I think I have this bonded thing down, I fuck up again. I swear, I'll get it right one day."

"Where's the fun in that?" she quipped, nibbling his lower lip. "Make-up sex is my favorite."

Chuckling, he nodded. "Mine too." Kissing a path down her neck, he began to lick her skin. "I haven't had you in days. I need you." Placing his fangs over the vein, he pierced her.

"Oh, god," she purred, feeling wetness surge to her core. "Yes, Sathan. It feels so good. I need you inside me."

He pulled on her vein, sucking her life-force from her body. Finally, when he was sated, he licked her neck to close the wounds.

"You're so wet. I can feel it through my pants," he growled.

Suddenly, she tensed. "Oh, shit," she said, feeling her eyes grow wide.

"What?" he asked, fear entering his dark irises.

"Darling, I need you to call Sadie and Nolan."

"Are you okay? Are you hurt?"

Placing her hand on his cheek, she struggled to remain calm. "I'm pretty damn sure my water just broke. Now, be a good husband and call the fucking doctors."

His quick gasp and wide eyes would've caused her to tease him mercilessly on any other day, but this was no laughing matter. Biting her lip, she watched her beloved husband grab his phone from the desk and frantically call the physicians.

Chapter 15

Darkrip woke with a start. Never had he felt the sense of foreboding that he felt at this moment. For the son of the Dark Lord, the importance of that sensation couldn't be overstated.

Looking to his left, he saw her curly dark hair first, spread around her like a halo to an angel. Sharp, breathy pants exited from her lips as she lay still. So very still.

"Arderin?" Rolling over toward her, he placed his fingers at her neck, feeling her pulse, which was extremely faint.

Gentle, ice-blue eyes lifted to his, and she spoke so softly, "I'm dying."

Emotions that he'd convinced himself he was incapable of feeling battled inside him. After all the days of telling himself he wouldn't let her drink from him, the urge to save her was overwhelming. Wracking his brain, he tried to remember all the reasons he couldn't save her. There were so many. He just had to think.

Coming up with absolute shit, he resigned himself to his fate. It had been the same when he'd tried to kill Evie all those centuries ago. His mother's blood was just too good. It overrode all of the excuses and justifications for his death-filled decisions.

Resting on his left elbow at her side, he lifted his right hand to cup her cheek. "I won't let that happen."

She coughed and sputtered, causing his heart to tighten. He thought the damn thing had disintegrated in his chest long ago, but apparently not. She was so pallid. Although that was normal for a Vampyre, in the waning light of the cave, she appeared as pale as death.

"I need Slayer blood," she said, a humorless smile forming on her lips. "I can't go on without it, and you've already sworn you won't give me yours."

Darkrip stared at her, letting the feelings swirl inside. Fury at his father for forcing them both into this impossible situation. Self-loathing that one as powerful as he hadn't been able to save them yet. Fear for her and her imminent death. And, if he was honest, fear for himself. Throwing away a thousand years of acquired wisdom, he was going to let the little imp drink from him.

Inhaling a deep breath, he spoke, his voice firm with resolve. "You're going to take my vein, Arderin." He shook her face with his hand, forcing her to open her fluttering eyelids. "It's going to be tough to swallow, so I need you to concentrate on forcing it down."

Turning her head slightly, she pushed her cheek further into his hand, forcing a tender caress that he had not the time nor the inclination for. "Do you hear me?" he asked, his tone almost angry. "I'm going to puncture the vein at my wrist and then I want you to drink. The Deamon part of my blood will be rejected by your body. You're going to have to make sure you swallow it even though it's against your will."

Her expression was filled with such openness, such peace, that he wondered if he should just let her pass. After all, he had killed so many in his time. Why should she matter? What was one more?

But he knew he was kidding himself. She was nothing like the nameless others he'd known before her. If he was honest, he'd begun to think of his life in two parts: before her, and after her. Before her, he had been lost on a journey to nowhere, drowning in endless death and destruction. After her...well, after her, he had begun to notice things again. The smell of the grass by the riverbank at Astaria. The sounds of laughter at the nightly dinners shared by his sister, her husband and their family. The feeling that enveloped him every time he caught a singular pair of ice-blue eyes studying him, then quickly looking away when she was discovered. He had noticed it all. And for one such as him, whose every day had been filled with ruin and pain, wasn't that just a small bit of amazing?

In reality, she'd brought him back to life. Given him something to experience besides pestilence and hate. Couldn't he at least extend her life? Even if it meant damning himself in the process?

After she drank from him, there would be no more curious sideways glances, that was for sure. No more attempts to kiss him with her perfect lips. After seeing his worst atrocities, she would most likely never want to be in his presence again.

Knowing all of this, he still lifted his wrist to his teeth. Biting sharply, he tore the flesh, reveling in the pleasure-pain that the action caused. Placing his left hand underneath her slim neck, he placed his right wrist at her mouth.

"Drink," he said.

She hesitated and studied him, still the curious scientist even in her almost comatose state. "Why are you saving me?" she whispered.

Choosing not to answer, he touched his bleeding wrist to her lips and commanded, "Drink".

Watching her pink lips close over his pulsing wound was almost his undoing. After all, he was still a man, and she was the epitome of everything feminine and beautiful in this sometimes-horrid world. Latching on, she began to suck him, causing his ever-hard cock to pulse and strain toward her. A normal person might feel shame at the throbbing arousal. Instead, he just watched her, hoping that she would be able to bear the half of him that was pure evil.

Lifting her head, she began to cough violently and then rolled away from him and began dry heaving. "No!" he shouted, turning her face back to his. "You will take this blood, Arderin! Concentrate. I know it it's vile, but it will save your life, and I need you to take it. Do you understand me?"

Nodding, she latched back onto his wrist. Her eyes locked onto his, and he found it impossible to look away. It was as if she was pleading with him, asking him to help her will the blood into her body. "You're doing great," he said encouragingly as he stroked her hair. "Keep going. I know it's awful, but it's going to make you feel better."

Soft lips sucked his tan skin, and he couldn't help but imagine them sucking another place on his always-straining body. After a few moments, she released his wrist, laying her head back on the ground. "No more," she pleaded, and he nodded.

"Okay, let's see how you do, digesting that amount. How do you feel?"

"Queasy," she said, looking up at him with those eyes that were his undoing. "But better. I think I just need to lie here for a minute."

"Okay," he said, and began to untangle himself from her.

"No. Stay," she said, pulling him toward her with weak arms. "Please."

She had no idea what she was asking of him. Now that her lips had touched his skin, the desire to plunge inside her was coursing through him. "Arderin, I can't—"

"Please," she pleaded again softly, still dragging him toward her. "I know you won't rape me. You always vow you'll never touch me that way. I'm freezing. Please."

Lowering himself, he pulled her back into his front and let her fall to sleep. Listening to her breath for what seemed like hours, he finally felt himself grow tired. Yawning, the mighty and malicious son of the Dark Lord allowed himself to descend into slumber while holding another for the first time in his long, desolate life.

Chapter 16

Sathan observed his bonded mate as she lay on the bed, the hospital gown glowing white against her bronzed skin. In anticipation of the birth, they had converted one of the upstairs rooms into an OR so that all precautions could be met. Nolan and Sadie had helped with the preparations and were furiously buzzing around the chamber.

Vampyres were larger than Slayers, so Miranda's pregnancy had been difficult. Carrying the first ever Slayer-Vampyre child had caused her severe morning sickness for the first several months. More recently, she'd been extremely tired, and her abdomen was so distended that Sathan sometimes wondered how she balanced to walk. Although, his snarky little wife could do anything she put her mind to, so he shouldn't have been surprised that she'd kicked the ass out of her pregnancy.

Sadie had slapped a pair of scrubs to his chest when he'd carried Miranda in. Informing him that the birth would most likely be bloody, he'd changed into them and was now sitting by his wife's side. Her olive-green eyes were fraught with pain, and her teeth were clenched as she grunted. Throwing her head back on the pillow, she wailed as another contraction hit.

"You're doing great," he said, bringing her hand to his face and squeezing. Feeling helpless, he tried his best to soothe and encourage her. "You've got this, Miranda. You're so amazing."

Lifting her head, those green irises latched onto him. "I swear to god, I'm debating ever fucking you again. What the hell? I feel like my insides are being ripped out. Ahhh..." Hips arching in pain, she bowed off the bed with another contraction.

Sathan felt like an absolute piece of shit. He wished so badly he could experience the pain for her. "You're doing great, sweetheart. I'm here."

"Fuck. You," she gritted through her teeth. "Go away. Get mad at me again or something. I swear, I hate you right now." Panting, she slapped her free hand to her forehead.

Chuckling, he maneuvered her palm to his cheek. "I love you, Miranda. By the goddess, you're unbelievable. You can do this."

"Okay, let's keep up the pep talks," Sadie said, coming to the other side of the bed. "I'm going to push the epidural now, Miranda. You ready?"

Miranda nodded, her silky black hair sliding over the pillow. With her unburned hand, Sadie injected a vial of liquid into Miranda's IV.

"Okay, let's hope that works. It might not, due to the extreme circumstances of the birth, but we'll keep our fingers crossed. Let me know if you start to feel numb in your legs."

Miranda nodded, rubbing her forehead with her fingertips. "Not yet. If it doesn't work, just kill me. I'm fucking over this. Who needs an heir anyway? Give my kingdom to the Vampyres. I'm done."

"Stop it," Sathan said, shaking her hand. "I don't want to hear you talk like that, Miranda. You know I'd die if I lost you. Soon, we'll have our son. I'm so proud of you. You've given me everything I've ever wanted. I can't believe how lucky I am to have you." His eyes welled with moisture, but he didn't care. His wife was so damn precious.

"Goddamnit. Stop saying nice shit. It makes it really hard to hate you. Oh, god—here's another one—ahhh!" Her hips arched off the bed again, and Sathan clenched her hand for dear life.

The contractions continued for what seemed like a small eternity. Frustrated that the epidural wasn't working, Sathan asked Nolan to inject her with more.

"We can't," the kind, chestnut-haired doctor said, clutching Sathan's shoulder. "She's strong as an ox. She can take it. Keep encouraging her."

Filled with worry, Sathan sat back on the bed at Miranda's side.

"Well, so much for the epidural," she said, her voice calm since she was in between contractions. Exhaustion lined her face. "You owe me for this, big fella."

"I'll give you anything. Everything. By the goddess, sweetheart, you amaze me." With his broad hand, he stroked her cheek.

Suddenly, one of the monitors began to beep. Sadie rushed to Miranda's side, her face lined with worry.

"Nolan, I need you. Sathan, please move away from the bed."

Following her orders, he stepped back, and Nolan swooshed in to take his place. Miranda's body jerked and then she collapsed on the bed, her eyes rolling back in her head.

"No!" Sathan screamed, rushing to her.

"Let us work!" Nolan said. Lifting his lab coat-clad arm, he pushed Sathan back. "Heden is outside. Bring him in if you need to. I need you to let us treat her."

Scowling, Sathan stomped to the door and pulled it open, finding his brother sitting outside.

"How's she doing, man?"

"I need you to come in and make sure I don't rush the bed."

"Okay." He came to stand behind Sathan as they watched the doctors work on a now unconscious Miranda.

"Why is there so much blood?" Sathan asked, his eight-chambered heart splintering in his chest as he saw the rivulets of blood coming from between Miranda's legs. "Answer me!" he screamed at Nolan.

"Whoa, dude," Heden said, latching onto Sathan's massive upper arm. "Calm down. Let them focus. I'm here. She's going to be fine."

"We're going to have to do a C-section," Sadie said.

"Agreed," Nolan said. Latching onto Sathan's gaze, his tone was firm. "You and Miranda have both stated that if we must choose between the baby and saving her, we should choose the child. I'm going to do my best here, Sathan. It's possible we'll have to perform a hysterectomy if there's too much damage."

"Whatever you have to do," Sathan said, willing to sacrifice future children as long as his wife and son survived. A heart-wrenching decision, but there was no other choice in his mind.

"Okay," Nolan said with a nod. Turning, he picked up some alcohol-laced white pads from the sterile tray behind him. After rubbing them over Miranda's distended abdomen, he used a sponge to spread orange liquid over her belly. Grabbing the scalpel that sat on the tray, he placed it on Miranda's stomach and looked at Sadie. "Time of insertion for C-section twenty-two forty-seven."

Sadie nodded. "Confirmed."

Placing his hand over his mouth, Sathan watched them cut into his beloved wife. Unable to control himself, he sank into his brother, feeling his solid arm surround his shoulders. "I can't lose her too," he said, thinking of Arderin.

"She's going to be fine, bro. I know it."

Taking comfort from his brother, he prayed to Etherya.

* * * *

Arderin awoke to unfamiliar circumstances yet again. As the surroundings came into focus, she realized she was in a different cave. Eyebrows drawing together in confusion, she tried to get her bearings.

She remembered swimming in the pond. Then, she'd thrown her clothes back on and fallen asleep. She'd woken with a gasp of air and realized she was dying. As if in a dream, Darkrip had let her drink from his wrist. Hadn't he? Or had she dreamed that and died anyway, stuck in some kind of purgatory before heading to the Passage?

Pushing herself up on her arm, she lifted her head toward the sounds coming from above. The rock sat about twelve feet high, not allowing her to see what was making the noise from atop. Standing, she slowly approached.

A naked creature with gray, pasty skin was jutting his hips between the legs of a woman. Bile filled her throat as she realized what she was witnessing. As if in slow motion, she tilted her head, the woman's face coming into view.

Gasping, she brought her fingers to her lips. It was Miranda. No! Shaking her head, she looked around the lair of the cave. Where were Sathan and Latimus? Why weren't they here saving her?

Miranda's grass-green eyes locked onto hers, filled with crazed pain and madness.

"It's okay, sweet boy," she said.

Confused, Arderin shook her head.

"Shut up!" the pasty man screamed, backhanding Miranda so hard a tooth flew out of her mouth.

Arderin tried to yell, 'Stop!' but was frozen, unable to move or speak.

Miranda gave a weak attempt to fight back, trying to jab her fingers in the man's eyes. Cackling with sin, the creature grabbed her hand and bit off her index finger, spitting so that it landed on the floor in front of Arderin.

Looking down, she picked up the finger. Rotating it in her hand, she felt herself place it in her pocket.

"Keep that to remember what a weak waste of a Slayer your mother is," the beady-eyed man said, his hips gyrating at the same unending pace. Glancing over, she saw that Miranda was unconscious. Thank the goddess. At least she could black out from the abhorrent torture for a few minutes.

The creature looked at her again, his expression curious. Pulling out of Miranda, he floated down, lifting Arderin's chin with his reedy fingers.

"So, he let you drink from him," he said, his black irises roving over her face. "Interesting. He cares for you more than I thought."

Now fully aware, Arderin realized she was stuck in some sort of vision. Rina was on the slab above, not Miranda. Expecting to feel fear in the face of the Dark Lord, Arderin instead felt a violent rage. "Fuck you, asshole!" she said, trying to shove his chest, unable to move her arms. "I'll fucking kill you."

"So passionate," he said, placing his hands on top of her head. He tried to push her down to her knees, and she struggled with every ounce of strength she had.

"No!" she screamed when she felt her knees hit the ground.

His wicked laughter surrounded her as she tried to flail her arms to strike him.

"No! No! No!"

Jerking, she felt someone clench her shoulder. And then, her body was rolling back and forth on the ground. Flinging her arms anywhere they would go, she fought off her unseen assailant.

"Arderin!" Darkrip's voice seemed so far away, as if spoken through the ether.

"Wake up, Arderin! You're having a nightmare."

Inhaling a huge breath, she opened her eyes. Panting, she saw Darkrip's handsome face above hers, filled with concern.

"You're having a nightmare," he repeated, stroking her hair. The action was so soothing coming from the terrible scene she'd just witnessed.

"What the fuck?" she asked, unable to comprehend how it had been so real.

His striking green eyes darted over her face, lips drawn thin. Finally, he said, "You were stuck in one of my memories. Now that you've had my vein, they'll course through you along with my blood. I'm sorry. It's one of the reasons I didn't want to save you. They're awful."

Lifting her hand, she caressed his cheek. "How old were you in the memory I just saw?"

Closing his lids, she saw his pupils dart back and forth as he searched the images in her mind. "Ten or eleven, I think. We didn't really celebrate birthdays in the Deamon caves."

"Oh, Darkrip," she said, compassion for him threatening to choke her. "How terrible. To see her violated like that?"

"It's all I saw for the first thirty years of my life. Thank god she finally perished. If she hadn't, I think I would've gone mad."

Unable to control her tears, she felt one slide down her cheek. "It was obvious she loved you. She looked so much like Miranda."

"Yes," he said, nodding. "It's uncanny."

Lifting her arms, she tried to wrap them around his neck.

"No," he said, dragging them away and sitting up. "I don't deserve your sympathy. I've done things just as terrible as he has. They'll come to you, and I don't blame you if you hate me once you see them. I'm a monster."

Closing her eyes, she allowed his memories, thoughts and feelings to assuage her.

There were the ones from centuries ago where Darkrip used his muscular body to violate and mutilate bound Deamon women. She assumed they were from the harem that Crimeous kept. Latimus had told her of it ages ago, confiding his hatred and distaste. As Darkrip tortured the women, his father stood behind him, spurring him on. She could feel his revulsion as the Dark Lord urged him to do the terrible deeds.

There were images of all that he had killed over the centuries. So many snapped necks, knives that gutted abdomens of Slayer soldiers, eight-shooters that decimated Vampyres. Each time a man would perish, a thrill unlike anything Arderin had ever experienced would rush through Darkrip's body. She felt the sensation now, true as if she had committed the acts herself. Feeling vomit burn her throat, she continued to search the memories and images.

Long ago, Rina had come to him, asking him to live by his Slayer side. Although the evil clawed at him, he'd remained true to her. Love, pure and absolute, filled her gut as she experienced what he felt for his mother.

And then there were the centuries of deceiving his father. Still killing alongside him, convincing him that he was wicked. Biding his time until Miranda was ready to claim her throne and reunite the species.

There were so many memories of fucking faceless women, each of them bound, as he tried to relieve his turgid shaft. After each coupling, he would send them back to the harem, place his arms over his eyes and drown in despair. How had he lived like this for so many centuries?

It was all too overwhelming for Arderin. Although she considered herself a worldly person, she'd never seen anything as squalid and desolate as his memories. Never felt anything as deplorable as the demons that lived inside him, urging him to harm others, even if he didn't listen.

Unable to control herself, she rolled over and proceeded to retch on the dirty ground.

"That's an appropriate response," he muttered behind her. "Get it all out, and I'll give you some more blood. For now, I need to relieve myself. I'm going to try and find another rodent to eat as well. Sorry, princess, for shattering your innocence."

As she vomited, she heard him shuffling behind her, and then, he was gone. Unable to control her raging emotions, she buried her head in her arms, drew her knees to her face and began to cry.

Chapter 17

Kenden detonated the explosives on the soft ground. As the grass and foliage blew to bits, he assessed the makeshift entrance.

"It's wide enough for you too," he said to Latimus. "Come on."

They both attached their harness to the nearby tree and lowered themselves in. Once inside, Latimus illuminated the flashlight from his belt. Through the narrow walkway, they navigated, until they came upon a lair.

Kenden noticed the wooden desk, a chair and a bookshelf filled with jars that looked to contain body parts in formaldehyde instead of any reading material. A rock slab sat off the side, about twelve feet high. Four posts sat at the corners of a long stone, atop the rock slab.

Approaching the bookshelf, Kenden observed a tuft of red hair encased in a locket that sat beside the jars. Could it be Evie's? It looked to be the same stunning red that sat atop her flawless face. Deciding he'd like to give it to her if he ever saw her again, he grabbed the trinket and gently placed it in the pack on his belt. Sentimentality surrounded him as he thought of Rina cutting the lock from her little girl to save it for her future.

"This is where he tortured my aunt," Kenden said, emotion almost choking him.

"I can't imagine what she must've endured," Latimus said, patting him on the shoulder. "Darkrip said she survived for decades. She had a strength that was indomitable."

He nodded. "Miranda has so much of her inside. I was twenty when she was taken, so I remember her. She was remarkable. God, we've all endured so much death and torture. I'm so tired of it all."

"I know," Latimus said, absently staring at the slab. "All I can think is that he's torturing Arderin the same way."

"No," Kenden said, straightening his spine. "We can't think like that. Darkrip is powerful and will do his best to protect her."

Latimus rubbed his forehead with his fingers. "I hope so. We have to find them. Let's get back to the top so we can check in."

Padding from the lair, they reattached their harnesses, and the automatic retractors pulled them up. Kenden dropped enough TNT into the opening to blow up a small island. Packing up their gear, they retreated several yards away. From atop a nearby hill, Kenden detonated the explosives, destroying the lair and all that surrounded it for thirty feet.

"Good riddance," he muttered.

Larkin crested the hill, walkie talkie in hand. "I just heard from Alpha and Beta team. Both found caves but they were deserted. They destroyed them."

"Good," Latimus said. "Let's keep moving. Team Charlie and Delta are further off, so we should hear from them soon. We'll find them."

"Ten-four," Larkin said. Heading down the hill, he lifted his walkie to check in on the teams.

"I promised her I'd save her if anything happened," Latimus said, swallowing thickly. "I have to keep my word."

"You will," Kenden said, inhaling a deep breath. "Let's go."

Lost in thought, they trudged down the hill.

* * * *

Arderin lifted her lids, puffy after her pre-slumber crying jag. Raising her fingers, she rubbed her eyes. Sitting up, she searched for Darkrip. The cave was empty, so he must be relieving himself. Sighing, she ran her hands over her jean-clad thighs. His memories and feelings assaulted her as his blood coursed through her body, and she did her best not to let them overwhelm her.

Inhaling a deep breath, she straightened her spine. Calling upon her yoga training, she placed her hands together in prayer in front of her breasts. Chest rising and falling, she attempted to form some sense of peace.

Behind the darkness of her closed lids, she concentrated. Although his blood was evil, there was also such a latent goodness in it. Allowing herself to focus on that, she felt every cell in her body strain toward the part of him that was Rina and Valktor. It was so pure, so true, and it gave her such a sense of calm that she felt her lips curve into a smile.

"Didn't think I'd come back here to find you smiling now that my evil courses through you."

Slowly, she lifted her lids. Darkrip sat across from her, his olive irises filled with slight hesitation and a hefty dose of worry.

"That part of you is awful. I won't sugarcoat it. But I was meditating to find the part of you that is your mother and grandfather. It's so much stronger than the wicked part. It's not as pulsing or angry, but it's resilient and consistent. Latimus always tells me that strength doesn't come from force but from peace. There's a beautiful peace in your mother's side."

His eyes tapered. "Wow. You've got quite an imagination. Tell yourself what you want, but it's disgusting. We both know it."

She shrugged, lowering her hands to sit on her thighs. "It's done now. And although part of it is awful, I truly appreciate you giving me your blood. I was pretty close to biting the bullet there."

His pupils darted back and forth between hers. "I shouldn't have done it."

"So, why did you?" she snapped.

"I'm trying not to contemplate why. I wasn't ready to see you go. Let's leave it at that."

"Fine," she said, standing and brushing off her legs. "Well, we have to find you some more food if we're going to survive. I'm going to head off to the other tunnel and see if there are any dead rodents."

He nodded. "I also need you to think about how long you want to go on like this. I saved you, but it's most likely temporary if I can't find food. Eventually, I'll die, and you along with me."

"Latimus will save us. Now, I'm going to find you something to eat."

Pivoting, she grabbed one of the torches that seemed to endlessly burn somehow and headed down the tunnel.

Two hours later, she returned triumphant, having found a dead rat in the tunnel. Although picking up the damn thing had almost made her lose the meager contents of her stomach, she took it back to their spot by the pond.

As she exited her tunnel, he was exiting his. He must've been searching for an animal there as well.

Coming to stand before him, she offered him the rat. "Bon appétit."

The derisive look he gave her made her chuckle.

"You can do it."

"I've ingested much worse in my father's caves. You don't want to know."

"Well, enjoy. I'm washing that thing off my hands."

While he cooked the rat with the fire from one of the torches, she used the shampoo from her toiletries bag to wash the dead rodent from her hands. When he was finished eating, he disposed of the bones behind one of the rocks against the wall and approached her as she sat by the pond.

"Can I use your soap?"

"Sure," she said, thrusting the tiny shampoo bottle up at him.

Grabbing it, he cleaned himself and brushed his teeth with the little tube and brush he'd carried over.

Once finished, he sat back on his hands, his legs outstretched, as they both gazed at the azure water.

"How is it so blue since we're so far underground?"

"I don't know," he said. "It's one of the things that always drew me here. There's a serenity about it."

Nodding, she pulled her knees into her chest, resting her chin on top. It was a nice moment, spent in silence.

"I understand now why you didn't want me to drink from you," Arderin said softly.

"Is that so?"

Resting her cheek on the denim at her knees, she stared into him. "You thought I'd hate you."

He shrugged, showcasing an indifference that Arderin was sure he didn't feel. "Don't you? What I've done in my past is wretched. I'm surprised you're still speaking to me."

Compassion coursed through her. Had anyone ever shown him any deference? Ever understood that a person is the product of their environment? His memories showed that he never left the Deamon caves until two centuries of his life had passed. Arderin refused to believe he would have committed the atrocities of his youth if he'd known better. Tentatively, she slid her hand around his wrist, squeezing.

"I'm smart enough to understand who you are and that your actions are a result of your circumstances. Once you made the choice to live in your goodness, you became your true self. It's insulting that you didn't give me enough credit to draw that conclusion."

His gaze dropped to her fingers grasping his wrist and then lifted to drill into her. "I don't let anyone see what's inside me. Vulnerability and openness are everything I detest. I knew you'd come to despise me once I showed you the true darkness within."

Smiling, she gnawed her lip. "Well, you were wrong yet again. Let's remember that, next time we argue. It seems I'm always right."

Darkrip rolled his eyes. "Right," he scoffed.

"I am," she said, squeezing his wrist again. "And you misjudged me. I'm honored to see inside you. It's made me admire you even more."

Gently surrounding her wrist, he disengaged her hand. "You have so much empathy," he said, seeming perplexed. "It's...difficult for me to accept." His Adam's apple bobbed as he swallowed, appearing to struggle to find the right words.

"Well, have some faith in this spoiled, aggravating princess," she teased. "You saved my life, and I'm grateful. If you weren't so terrible at accepting my gratitude, I'd thank you."

"Don't waste your breath," he muttered, but his lips quirked into a half-grin. A spark of affection swam in his grass-green eyes, giving her hope that they were on the path to becoming friends. How much he needed one and, now that he'd saved her, how desperately she wanted to be one to him.

They sat in companionable stillness until her stomach growled.

"I think I need to drink from you again."

"Okay," he said, rotating toward her and lifting his wrist.

Contemplative, she turned to face him. "I want to drink from your neck."

His eyes narrowed. "No."

"And why not? It's what our fangs were designed for. Drinking from the wrist is boring. I want to experience *some* new things before I die a tragic death."

"Because it creates a connection that I'm not interested in sharing with you," he said, his tone firm. "I told you, I don't want to touch you unless absolutely necessary."

"What connection could it possibly create? After all, I'm just a stupid virgin with no chance of enticing you or pleasing you in bed. Isn't that what you said? So, what's the big deal?"

Feminine mischief coursed through her body as he studied her. He could lie all he wanted but he desired her. His muscles seemed to be straining toward her through his clothes.

"Take off your shirt. I don't want to ruin it."

"It's not happening—"

"Oh, for god's sake," she said, reaching for his top button and opening it. She continued down his shirt, unbuttoning several, until his hands grabbed hers. "You'd think you were the innocent wallflower here. Are you afraid to let me have your vein?"

"You don't know what you're messing with, princess. I won't let you provoke me."

"I'm not provoking you," she said, pushing his half-buttoned shirt off his shoulders. "I'm just going to drink from you. Now, be a good Slayer and expose your neck."

His hand lodged in her hair, fisting it so hard that tears prickled her eyes. Gasping, she lifted her chin, her face inches from his.

"Stop being a fucking coward," she whispered.

"Fuck you," he said, his nostrils flaring.

Baring her fangs, she grabbed the back of his head, pulling it toward her. Before he could stop her, she plunged into his neck. Pulling the life-force from his pulsing vein, she felt him shudder.

Relaxing his hold on her hair, he pushed her into him, moaning as her lips moved against his skin.

"Goddamnit," he groaned, pulling her body toward him. Stretching out her legs, she straddled him, his thick shaft resting in the juncture of her thighs. Wishing they could lose the barriers of their clothes, she moved her hands between them, struggling to unbutton his pants.

His hands seized her wrists, stilling her. Moving them behind her back, he held them prisoner with his strong grip. Bringing his free hand back around, he unbuttoned her jeans, the move skilled and practiced. Dragging the zipper down, he slipped his hand inside.

Arderin purred against his neck, pushing her core into his fingers. Navigating around her thong, he slipped his middle finger inside her wetness.

"Yes," she murmured against his skin, placing tiny kisses along his vein.

"I'm going to make you come," he said, moving his finger in and out of her tight channel. "Don't stop drinking from me. It feels so good."

Latching back on, she felt him insert another finger. Squirming, she arched to feel the friction she needed. The heel of his hand began a maddening circle on her clit as his fingers invaded her. By the goddess, it felt amazing.

"Good girl," he said, the deep timbre of his voice forcing a rush of wetness onto his fingers. "You're so slick. Would you be like this if I fucked you?" She moaned at his dirty words. "Would you coat my cock with all that silky wetness?"

"Yes," she said, placing tiny kisses along his strong jaw until she came to his lips. "I'd squeeze you so hard if you were inside me."

Growling, he nipped at her bottom lip. "How in the hell are you still a virgin?"

"Maybe I was waiting for you." Opening her mouth, she pressed against his lips, her tongue charging inside. His came to meet it, battling as they stroked each other. Licking and panting, he increased the pace of his hand.

"I'm so close," she breathed into his mouth, lapping at his wet tongue. "Let go of my hands so I can climb onto you."

"No," he said, clutching her wrists tighter. "Now, come for me, princess. Rub your sweet little pussy on my fingers and come all over my hand. Damn, you're drenching me."

Throwing back her head, she let the pleasure overwhelm her. Daggers of desire coursed through her as she trembled. Growing closer, she pushed herself onto his fingers. The nerve endings around her tiny nub were on fire, and she closed her lids, imagining him pounding her with his shaft.

"I'm coming," she cried, gyrating on his fingers. "Oh, god. Yessss..."

Her body bowed and then began convulsing, tiny mewls escaping her lips. Unable to control them, she gave in to the sensation, joy sweeping through her thin frame. Thrusting into him, she let the wave take her. Slowly, the stars that were bursting behind her eyelids began to dim.

Panting, she lifted her head to look into his stunning eyes. They were filled with desire and passion. "You're so fucking gorgeous," he said softly.

"Let go of my wrists."

He complied, and she reached for his hand, still at her core. Pulling him from her, she lifted his hand to his thick lips. Pushing his fingers inside his mouth, she forced him to taste her.

Eyes never leaving hers, his tongue lapped up every drop of her from his own skin.

They sat like that for a while, gazing into each other, regaining their ability to breathe normally. Blood trickled from the punctures on his neck.

"Let me close your wound," she said, leaning in to lick him, her self-healing saliva closing the bite marks in seconds. She reveled in his shiver as her wet tongue coursed over his skin.

Lifting her head, she regarded him. "Well, what the hell are we going to do now?"

Darkrip breathed a laugh, genuine emotion swimming in his irises. "I have no fucking idea, princess. You're something else."

Feeling the corner of her lip turn up, she lifted her palm to run it over his head. "Your hair's growing in. I like the buzz cut, but the black color's nice." Gently, she caressed his short, soft hair.

"You like the tips of my ears."

She nibbled her bottom lip. "How do you know?"

"I've seen images in your mind. You imagine biting them. You've got some pretty interesting fantasies for a virgin."

"I think we've just proven I'm a virgin in name only," she said, grinning at him. "I'm enthralled by sex and think it's something that should be enjoyed with someone you care about."

Sighing, he pulled her hand from his head. "I don't want you to care about me. It's a waste of your time, and I don't deserve it."

"You saved my life. I can't think of anyone who deserves it more."

He shook his head at her. "What is it with all you immortals trying to convince me I'm a good person? Between you and Miranda, I'm a fucking saint. Believe me, one day, you'll realize how awful I am. Don't set yourself up for that. It will make it that much harder when you grasp the truth."

"Don't tell me what to think or feel." Cupping his cheeks, she placed a soft kiss on his lips. "I like kissing you."

"I like it too," he said, pulling her hands away. "Too much. It's going to get cold soon. Let's bundle up."

Standing, he offered her his hand. After he pulled her up, she buttoned her jeans and returned to the spot where she usually slept.

"Will you at least hold me, so I don't freeze to death?" she asked, lying down.

"No. I don't cuddle, princess. You should've figured that out by now."

"Whatever," she said, rolling her eyes and lying on her side. "You'll hold me when I start shivering. You always do."

He muttered something about her being a bossy spoiled brat and then lay down at his spot, several feet from her.

Hours later, he pulled her shuddering body to his chest. The brightness of her resulting smile could only be seen by the rock wall of the cave.

Chapter 18

Lila sat beside Miranda as she fed baby Tordor, his red lips pulling from her swollen breast. His name paid homage to the last half of his great grandfather's and grandfather's names: Valktor and Markdor. Sathan and Miranda had chosen the name together, and Lila thought it so fitting for the strong little prince.

"He's so beautiful," Lila said, unable to stop the tears from welling in her eyes.

"I know," Miranda said, kissing the top of his head, swathed with black hair.

"I've imagined feeding my own children so many times."

Miranda squeezed her hand. "I'm so sorry, Lila. I know how this must hurt. I wish I could give you back the ability to have children. It's so fucking awful."

"Shh..." Lila said, clenching her hand. "I'm very lucky and have so much. Latimus loves me more than I ever thought possible, and Jack is such a precious little boy. I don't have anything to complain about."

"You're awesome," Miranda said, her white teeth radiant as she smiled. "I'll never understand how you took the man I met when we went to get the Blade and turned him into a domesticated sap. It's freaking amazing. You're Wonder Woman."

Lila gnawed her lip, trying to contain her grin. "He was always so sweet. I knew that from when we were kids. He just needed me to remind him."

Miranda chuckled. "Well, great freaking job. I'm so happy for you guys." Her eyebrows drew together. "Hey, little buddy, this isn't a buffet. Stop biting my nipple. Ouch."

Tordor gnawed for a bit and then his tiny features squished together as he yawned.

"Okay, I think that's my sign to leave. Our little man needs a nap. Do you want me to put him in the bassinet?"

"That would rock," Miranda said. "Thanks."

Nodding, Lila lifted the baby from her arms and grabbed the burping towel from the bassinet. After patting his back and hearing him exhale the wispy burps, she gently placed him in the bassinet. Swaddling him, she stroked his cheek until he fell into slumber.

"God, you're a natural at this crap. Please, help me. I put off having kids as long as I could. Now, I'm screwed."

Lila laughed. "You'll get it. I've never seen you unable to accomplish anything you put your mind to."

"Hope so. I'm sure my caveman husband will knock me up several more times before I beg Nolan to tie my tubes."

Lila smiled at her always funny friend. "Thank the goddess that Nolan was able to save your ability to have more children."

"Yeah," Miranda said, relief crossing her face. "Sathan said it was touch and go there for a minute. I'm so thankful. Although, we're not having another kid for a while. Mom over here needs a break."

Grinning, Lila pulled her phone from her pocket and read the text from her bonded mate. "Latimus, Kenden and Sathan are back. I'm going to go greet them. I need to head home for tonight's literacy meeting anyway."

"Thanks for coming. I hope they found something today. They've been missing for almost three weeks. I'm trying not to lose hope."

"Me too," Lila said, coming around to give Miranda a hug. "Now, get some rest, and I'll come to visit you again soon."

With one last squeeze, Lila headed down the spiral staircase and through the door that led to the barracks. Latimus was rinsing off a four-wheeler with the hose attached to a nearby spout.

"How'd it go today?" she asked, approaching him.

"Hey, honey," he said, leaning down to kiss her. "Let me just finish this. We trekked through a lot of mud today." He rinsed off the back of the vehicle, turned the spout and laid the limp hose by the wall. Stalking toward her, he pulled her into his thick chest.

"Hey," she said, squeezing him as tight as she could. "It's all right, sweetheart."

Lowering his forehead to hers, he looked into her eyes. "We still haven't found anything. It's fucking awful."

"You promised you'd find her, and you always keep your word. You'll do it, Lattie. I know you will."

The corner of his lips lifted. "Your faith in me is what's keeping me strong. I'm so honored to have you by my side."

"You'll always have me," she said, placing a soft peck on his lips. "And I love her too. I know you'll prevail. There's no other option."

Hand-in-hand, they strolled to the train platform. Lifting to her toes, she kissed him. "You'll be home late?"

He nodded. "We're conducting another night search with the copter. I won't get home until after midnight."

"Be safe. I love you so much. Please, wake me when you get home. I want to comfort you."

He smiled down at her. "I couldn't do this without you. Thank you, Lila."

"One day, this will all be a bad memory. You'll see." Giving him one more soft peck, she descended the stairs and boarded the train home.

* * * *

Arderin regarded the note Lila had written her, admiring her pretty handwriting.

Arderin,

I'm so thrilled for you to enter the human world. I know it's been your wish for so long. Please, don't forget about those of us who love you here in the immortal world. I've sensed your sadness lately and need you to remember that Latimus and I love you with all our hearts. You are the most important person to us, along with Jack, and you will always hold a special place in our lives. Please, come home to us safely.

Love, Your Best Friend Lila

Letting her tears fall, she swept one away with her fingers. Lila always had a way with words, and she missed her terribly. Pulling out her pen, she wrote on the back of the card:

Lila,

If I don't make it, please know that your words gave me solace during my last days. I've always felt extremely lucky to have you in my life. I love you like my own sister. Please, take care of Latimus. He'll be devastated that I'm gone, and I need you to promise to get him through. You've always been so strong.

Love, Arderin

P.S.—Darkrip is hot. I want to bone him so bad. I had to tell someone. Sadly, I'll still probably die a virgin. If so, wish me lots of sexy times in the Passage.

Knowing her proper friend would smile at that, even through her sadness, she placed the note back in the envelope. Restless, she rubbed her upper arms. Where the hell was Darkrip? He'd disappeared down the tunnel a lifetime ago. At least, it felt that way to her.

Curious, she slowly trudged through the cavern that he always retreated into. In the distance, she saw the light of his torch. As he came into focus, her breath became more labored.

His shirt sat on the dirt floor, the hardened abs of his stomach glistening in the torchlight. Although he'd lost weight, he still was extremely cut. Black pants were open, pushed to his thighs, and his thick cock rose out of the hole in his boxer briefs. Eyes closed, he jerked his shaft tirelessly. The image was so sexy that Arderin felt herself gush inside her jeans.

Quiet as a mouse, she came to stand before him. Lowering, she placed her hands on his knees, spreading them as his feet sat flat on the ground. His eyes shot open, and he gritted his teeth. Stilling his hand, he panted as he regarded her.

"You're supposed to leave me the fuck alone when I'm doing this."

Compassion swamped her. She could feel the shame pulsing off his body. How did one live with such self-revulsion?

"I'm so sorry she cursed you like this," she said, shaking her head. "It's awful. You never did anything to deserve it."

"The first two centuries of my life were an abomination. Don't feel sorry for me."

"But you've turned so good, for so long. There has to be some redemption in that." Gently grasping his wrists, she pulled them away from his straining phallus. "Let me help you."

He studied her through narrowed lids. "Well, go ahead. I'm not a fucking saint. If the most beautiful woman I've ever seen wants to jerk me off, I don't have enough willpower in my body to say no to that."

Hesitating, she regarded the pulsing veins and thick head of the throbbing stalk. His was the only cock she'd ever seen. Were they all that large when erect?

"Get on with it, or go back to the lair. I don't do foreplay, princess."

Scrunching her features, she scowled at him. Closing her hands around his shaft, she began to move them up and down.

"Fuck," he rasped, leaning his head back to rest on the rock wall.

Never having jerked a man off before, she had no idea what to do, but it seemed pretty straightforward. Squeeze, move, repeat. Concentrating as if her life depended on it, she increased the pace.

A chortle burst from his throat, and she locked onto his eyes. "Are you laughing at me?"

"You're just so fucking curious about everything. You're doing it right, believe me. Just relax. It feels good."

Inhaling through her nostrils, she fixated on her ministrations, determined to make it good for him. After several moments, his body tensed, and a muscle in his neck corded. "I'm coming," he said through gritted teeth. "Point it toward my stomach so I don't blow it everywhere."

Following his command, she jutted her hands all around his hardened, silky skin. Reveling in his deep-throated groan, her eyes grew wide as his white seed began to spurt all over his stomach. The purple head coughed it everywhere, all over his toned abs and lower chest, and then came to rest below his navel.

Always the inquisitive scientist, she traced the pad of her finger through the wetness.

"Careful, princess," he warned, watching her through slitted eyes.

Collecting the moisture on her finger, she lifted it to her mouth. Latched onto his gaze, she inserted her finger onto her tongue and tasted it. Swishing it around her mouth, it tasted quite salty.

"Good fucking grief," he said, shaking his head. "You're too much. I think you were made to fulfill men's fantasies. Holy shit."

Smiling, she licked her lips. "You taste good."

He just stayed silent, green irises studying her. After several moments, he pushed her away, bringing his shirt to his abdomen to wipe off his release. Standing, he buttoned his pants.

"Come on," he said, extending his hand to her. Pulling her up, he ran a hand down her soft tresses. "You're making me want things I can't have. It's not fair."

"I want you too," she admitted softly

Resignation crossed his features. "The second we consummate, you'll be a target. You know that as much as I do. My father could materialize and snatch you anytime. Do you want that to happen? Trust me, he won't be as restrained as I am."

Remembering her nightmare, where Crimeous was torturing Rina, she shivered. "Of course, I don't want that."

"Then, let's stop wasting time wanting things that are futile."

Understanding that he wanted to protect her, she nodded. "Okay. I guess I'll have to accept that I'm never going to have awesome sex. No matter how badly I want to."

Surprising her, he placed his arm across her shoulder and began walking her slowly back toward the pond. "Believe me, I want it too. But I can't put you in danger like that."

"I know," she said, leaning her head on his shoulder. "Thank you. I wish my brothers could see how much you've done for me."

"Uh, yeah, let's not let your brothers know that I finger-fucked you and let you jerk me off. I'm all set, thanks. Don't need that drama in my life."

Snorting, she imagined her brothers' reactions if they found out those little tidbits. Man, they'd murder him. "Good call. They'd cut off your balls."

Chuckling, he squeezed her. "Yeah, I need those. Let's keep this between us."

Once they had prepped for sleep, she rolled on her side, prepared to freeze until the last possible moment when he would pull her close. Instead, he lay down and pressed his back to hers.

"This is about as close as I get to cuddling. Take it or leave it."

Snuggling her butt against his, she said, "I'll take it."

Sliding her hand behind her, she curved it over his hip. After a while, he fitted his hand in hers, threading their fingers together. As the cave grew colder, they fell asleep, clutching each other's hands.

Chapter 19

Sathan sat in the tech room, watching the video of Arderin passing through the wall for the thousandth time. Her smile had been so bright as she waved, Darkrip beside her in the four-wheeler. Clutching his chin, he tried to control its trembling.

"Enough, Sathan," Heden said, pounding through the door. "You've got to stop watching this shit. Latimus and Kenden said they've already accessed seventy-five percent of the terrain they scouted. They're going to find her."

Sighing, he ran a hand through his thick hair. "It's been over four weeks. At this rate, how can they even be alive?"

"Darkrip will most likely let her drink from him. As long as he can find food, they can survive for quite some time."

The thought of the Dark Lord's blood coursing anywhere through his sister's body made him want to vomit. "Eventually, they'll give up hope. How could they not? What if Crimeous is raping her right now?"

"Dude, stop it. I mean it." Grabbing his shoulder, Heden shook him. "I won't let you do this. You have a new baby and a wife who almost died giving birth. Go, be with them. Let them remind you of all you have. I know they're going to find her."

"Okay," Sathan said. "I just don't want to burden Miranda. She went through so much with the birth."

"Um, yeah, she's about a million times stronger than anyone I've ever met, including any of us. Let her comfort you. That's what being married is about."

Sathan contemplated his youngest brother. "You're right. She always reminds me that she's stronger than I'll ever be. I can't wait until you bond one day. It will be amazing to see your mate put you in your place."

"Whatever, man, I'm awesome. She'll be so in love with me she won't be able to see straight. And I'll make sure she can't walk straight, if you catch my drift." He waggled his eyebrows.

Chuckling, Sathan shook his head. "Latimus would kill you for joking at a time like this."

"Eh, he's much more chill now that Lila's turned him into a pansy. I'm not scared of him."

"I'll remember that next time he has you in a headlock. Thanks for pulling me away from this. I'll see you later."

Stalking to his bedchamber, Sathan found Miranda sitting on the bed in one of his large black t-shirts. Naked underneath, she was applying some sort of salve to her C-section scar.

"Hey, sweetheart," he said, lowering to sit beside her on the bed. "Want me to rub that on for you?"

"No," she said, scowling up at him. "You stuffed a Vampyre in me, and now, I'm all flabby and gross and scarred. I don't want you to see me like this. It's awful."

Smiling, he stilled her hands. Pulling them to her sides, she relaxed onto her palms. Lifting the shirt, he lowered his face and placed several soft kisses over the folds around her scar.

"You're so gorgeous" he murmured, loving that her body had held their son. "I wish you could understand how I see you."

"You can fuck me," she said, arching a raven-colored brow.

"Sadie said we have to wait six weeks, Miranda. I don't want to hurt you."

"Six weeks is torture. What's the point of being married if you can't bone? Go away then, and let me try and resuscitate my disgusting belly."

Tordor chose that moment to start wailing from the bassinet.

"See? Even he thinks I'm gross, and I give him all his food. Jerk."

Placing one more kiss on her stomach, Sathan approached the bassinet and lifted their son. Cooing to him, he brought him over to Miranda. Sitting back on the pillows, arms outstretched, she said, "Give him to me."

She pulled off the shirt as he sat on the bed. Handing over the baby, she latched him to her breast. Sathan watched his beautiful bonded mate feed their son, so similar to how she fed him through her vein. By the goddess, she was unbelievable, giving them both the life-force they needed.

"I don't deserve you," he said, running his fingers through her hair.

Lifting those magnificent irises to his, she smiled. "Stop it. You know I was only teasing you. I love you, Sathan." Her eyes welled with tears. "We have a son. After what we went through with the first baby, I feel so lucky."

"Me too," he said, caressing her cheek. "We should take him to the riverbank soon, to visit the baby and Rina."

Centuries ago, Miranda had buried pieces of her mother at the riverbank on the outskirts of Uteria. When she'd fought Crimeous recently, she'd been unaware that she was pregnant with their first child and had sadly lost it. Needing to mourn the baby properly, they had erected a small headstone at Rina's spot so they could remember them both.

"I'd like that," she said, a tear sliding down her cheek.

"Don't cry, sweetheart." Kicking off his shoes, he cuddled beside her. Placing his brawny arm around her shoulders, he pulled her into his chest. Watching his son's tiny lips move over his wife's breast shifted parts inside of him that he didn't even know existed.

"We made a baby," he said, nuzzling her silky hair with his nose.

Tilting her head back, she locked onto him. "We made a baby." They were the same words they had said upon learning of their first child.

"He looks just like you," she said, biting her lip.

"Except for the eyes. Thank the goddess he has yours." Caressing his son's soft hair, he asked, "Did Sadie say whether he'll need blood or not?"

"She said that we just need to monitor him. For now, he's doing fine with my milk. Sadie said it might be because it contains proteins that my blood has. As long as he continues to grow, she wants me to just keep breast feeding him. We're winging it here, huh?"

Chuckling, he nodded. "Yep. Hopefully, we'll get it right. With you as his mother, how can we not?"

Sliding his hand from his son's head, he caressed a path to her free breast. Gently, he squeezed the tip, causing some milk to drip. Wetting his finger with it, he drew it to his mouth.

"Mmmm..." he said, ingesting it.

"Okay, blood-sucker," she said, shaking her head at him. "Leave some for your son."

"But it tastes so good," he whispered, resting his forehead on hers. "Another place for me to suck you. It's so hot."

"Um, yeah, super-hot. My vagina's about to hit the floor, and I look like a butchered cow. Man, you've got some serious fetishes."

"Shut up, woman," he said, lowering to give her a blazing kiss.

They smiled into each other until the worry entered her eyes.

"How much have they traversed so far?"

"Seventy-five percent," he said, rubbing his forehead against the soft skin of hers. "I'm praying they find them over the next few days."

"They will," she said, her belief evident in her tone. "I know it, sweetheart."

"If my strong wife believes it, then I know it will happen."

"I believe it. And if you can't, then I'll believe it for both of us."

Drawing on her strength, he held her and his son close, hoping she was right.

* * * *

Despair set in as each hour ticked by in the cave. Although they were determined to escape, Darkrip didn't know how much longer they could survive like this. The small rats he was eating barely gave him enough sustenance. Every time Arderin drank from him, he felt his strength drain dangerously low. That, compounded by his all-consuming desire for her, threatened his sanity. Although they searched tirelessly, an escape seemed elusive. A dream they both shared but silently knew might never happen.

At times, he would hold Arderin as they sat on the cold ground and rub his hand over her hair as she cried onto his chest. Soothing her, he urged her to grasp onto hope. Once her tears dried, his strong princess would stand, slim body filled with resolve, and resume chipping at the rocks with whatever makeshift tool she'd fashioned from her meager supplies. Darkrip would help her, understanding that she needed the encouragement. Hell, he needed it just as desperately.

Some moments, she turned on her phone, the screen shining upon her magnificent features as she scrolled. She showed him pictures of her brothers, of Miranda and Lila, and of Jack. It was a nice way to cherish memories as they clung to the anticipation of rescue.

Weeks into their captivity, he could sense death looming for them both. Arderin's skin had become frighteningly pale. It should've made her less attractive, but instead, she possessed an almost ethereal glow. Unable to lie to himself, he inwardly acknowledged his feelings for her.

He'd come to care for her. Something he'd thought irrevocably impossible. But these weeks in the cave with her had been some of the happiest of his life. Strange, since they should've been so dreary. Darkrip had become enamored with her gorgeous eyes, lightning-quick temper, throaty laugh and haughty pout. Every time they slept, the need to hold her hand as his back pressed against hers consumed him. Never thinking he would need companionship, it was quite the miracle. She'd tunneled her way into his deadened heart and made it beat again.

As he watched her brush her teeth in the pond, he reminded himself of his restraint so far. The Universe was cruel, not letting him have her just once. Cursing all the gods, he let himself drink in her image, gorgeous in the light glimmering from the cobalt water.

Standing, she seemed to float over and place the brush and paste back in her bag. Stuffing all the contents inside, she pulled the string closed and tied it.

"If they ever find us, at least they can say I was tidy." With a weak smile, she lay on the ground.

Watching her from his sitting position, he lifted his hand to caress her cheek.

"Don't tell me you're ready to have sex with me now," she said, a teasing light in her baby-blues. "I'm not sure I have the energy."

Inhaling a deep breath, he studied her. "We can't. But I want you so badly."

"Even though I'm overdramatic and drive you completely insane?"

The corner of his lip turned up. "You're the most exasperating person I've ever known, princess. It's been amazing sparring with you. I think I'll treasure our arguments the most if I'm lucky enough to make it to the Passage."

"That's so fucked-up. I love it." She was absolutely adorable as she smiled. How was he supposed to think clearly when those pink lips curved up at him?

"Let's get some sleep," he said, lying down. "I'm exhausted."

"Me too," she said, snuggling her back into his.

Allowing himself one small pleasure, he reached behind and laced their fingers, resting them on her upper thigh. "We'll resume hacking at the rocks in a few hours," he mumbled. It was a lie. He knew they might not awaken. They were both so thin; so cold.

"Sweet dreams," she whispered. The words were filled with sadness, as if she understood the gravity of their situation.

Only of you. The words echoed in his mind. He'd only ever had sweet dreams of her.

Latching onto them, he fell into unconsciousness.

Chapter 20

Arderin awoke, her mind hazy and clouded. Basic instincts pulsed inside her starving body. Breath. Hunger. Sex. Survival.

Claws of death scratched at her, urging her to drown in the murky depths. Hot. She was so fucking *hot*. She'd had enough medical training that her muddled brain understood she had a fever. Most likely from her starving body's efforts to survive. Fire scorched her, and she dragged off her jeans and shoes, needing to expose her burning skin to cool air. Rolling onto her back, her arm flailed, searching for something. *Someone.* Wasn't there someone trapped in this hellhole with her?

Finding a warm body, she snuggled into it, feeling a thick thigh cover hers. Wrapped in the strength of the male frame, her head tilted back. Eyes closed, unable to open due to the sticky sleep that pervaded them, her lips searched for their mate.

A warm, wet mouth covered hers, shooting thrills of joy through her dying body. It caught her tiny mewls, drinking them as if they were the sustenance it needed. By the goddess, she'd never tasted anything as savory as her phantom lover's kiss.

Still in a dream, his hand slid down her side and latched onto the button of his pants. Releasing it and lowering the zipper, her lover set himself free. Slithering his palm over her naked thigh, he dragged it over his leg, opening her. Gasping, Arderin lifted her lids.

Darkrip's olive-green irises stared back at her, *into her*, filled with lust and desire. The bottomless orbs swirled with limitless emotion. Anger, frustration, affection, arousal—they all warred in the eyes of the man she'd come to care so deeply for.

Not knowing where the energy came from, she pushed him onto his back. Sliding over him, she spread apart, straddling his hips, aligning her wetness with his straining shaft.

Nostrils flared as he secured her hips with his broad hands. There, they stayed, eyes locked together, for eternity. Or maybe only a moment. Inhaling a deep breath, Darkrip clenched his teeth and thrust into her.

Her spine bowed, head thrown back as her lids closed from the pain of his invasion. Feeling him throb inside her, she stayed still, frozen, unsure what to do.

Ever so slowly, he pulled himself from her tight channel. As he pushed back in, she felt tiny pangs of pleasure. Testing, she began to move with him, slightly, tentatively.

His breathing was labored below her as she moved atop his body. Blood pounded in her veins as she caught onto the rhythm. Her untried body understood; the undulation of her hips swaying to the intrinsic knowledge of the dance older than time.

Darkrip snaked a hand under her sweater. Fingers delved beneath the cup of her bra, pinching her straining nipple. Releasing a moan, Arderin's pace increased, needing more. Sitting up, he yanked the sweater over her shoulders and devoured her mouth. Tongues mated as their joined bodies strained toward ultimate pleasure. Where she'd originally felt pain, now, she felt such joy as his smooth skin traveled up and down her innermost place.

Breaking their kiss, he trailed a path down her cheek with his lips, landing on the tender skin of her upper shoulder. Biting her, he mimicked the action that brought him so much pleasure when she drank from him. Burying her face in his neck, instinct took over as she plunged her fangs into him.

Blood flooded her mouth as his thick cock stretched her. They were one; bound together by death and captivity and an unfaltering attraction that could no longer be denied. Embedded into him, she rode the wave of her desire.

The head of his shaft began hammering a spot inside that seemed to house every nerve-ending in her straining body. Moaning against him, she grasped his short hair, fear moving through her as she came so close to losing control.

"Let it happen," Darkrip whispered in her ear, causing her to shiver. "Let go, princess. I've got you."

"It's too much," she cried, unable to stop her hips from gyrating. God, she needed him *there*...and *there*...but it was so consuming; trepidation welled inside that she might shatter in his arms.

"Never too much," he gritted, sliding his hand down her abdomen. Resting the pad of his thumb on the little nub below her strip of dark hair, he began rubbing in concentric circles. That, combined with the ceaseless pounding of his shaft, broke her.

Tossing her head back, she flew apart in his arms. Unable to control her body, she rode him like the bull in the Texas bar. Raw and open, she succumbed to the orgasm. Fire burst behind her eyelids as she gulped breath into her heaving lungs. His deep baritone whispered indiscernible words as she lost all hold on reality. Feeling him shift below her, she embraced him in an unbreakable hold.

Face submerged in his neck while her arms clutched him, he struggled beneath her.

"I have to pull out," he groaned. "Goddamnit, Arderin. Let go."

"No," she cried, not understanding where the word came from. How could one still speak when their body was falling apart? "I need you inside me."

His fist clenched her thick curls as his other hand grasped the globe of her ass. She could feel the war of his straining muscles as the battle raged within. He attempted to pull away again, and she wrapped her legs tighter around his waist, locking at the ankles. Squeezing, she vowed to never let go.

Cursing, he began to come, groaning her name as he shot himself inside her. Her still-trembling body took it all, loving how his torso ground into hers with each pulsing jet. Submerged so deep within her, she squeezed him with the walls of her core as he growled. Never had she seen him so vulnerable. It shifted something in her gut as she held him. Feelings, overwhelming and profound, washed over her. They were frightening and new. Too consuming to analyze.

They shuddered together, faces hidden in each other's necks, as they fell back to Earth. Back to the cave, and to the reality that they'd just given Crimeous exactly what he wanted.

"Fuck!" Darkrip said, the word vibrating against the top of her shoulder.

"Hey," she said, caressing his back with her palm. "It's okay."

Inhaling a large breath, he lifted his head to stare down at her. "We just cemented our death, Arderin. What the hell were you thinking?"

Anger coursed through her as she still sat atop his hardened shaft. "You're blaming *me*?" she asked. "Are you fucking serious?"

Frustration lined his features as he lifted her away from him. The cold, dirty ground felt hard beneath her as she struggled to contain her fury. Concern flooded his gaze as it swept over her inner thighs.

"You're bleeding," he said, lightly touching her there. "Did I hurt you?"

"Yes," she said, too raw to lie. "At first. But then, it was...*incredible*," she almost whispered. "I'm sorry you're pissed."

Sighing, he shook his head. "I'm pissed at myself. I can't believe I finished inside of you. My father's likely seconds away from appearing and kidnapping you. Do you understand the gravity of this, Arderin? We have to kill ourselves. I won't let him take you."

Fear choked her as the magnitude of what they'd done registered. "Shit," she whispered.

"Put on your clothes," he said, standing and closing his pants. "Use this to wipe off the blood." Reaching into his bag, he thrust a t-shirt at her.

Arderin followed his directive, mostly because her mind was muddled with terror at the thought of Crimeous abducting her to his lair. After glimpsing his torture of Rina, she had no doubt he'd revel in doing the same to her.

"I'm sorry I can't give you flowery words and love letters, but this is serious. I need to drown you in the pond. My mother's blood won't let me kill you, so we need to tie our bags to your feet so you can't resurface."

Hopelessness consumed her. "I'm not ready to die." Tears welled in her eyes.

"Well, you shouldn't have fucked me then. I don't know what else to say. We're screwed."

Fury at his callousness swelled within. "Don't you care that you took my virginity? Don't you care about me at all?"

Sentiments warred across his handsome face, slightly softening it. For a moment, she thought he might embrace her; comfort her. Then, his features hardened into the mask she'd become accustomed to before they were trapped.

"I don't have the luxury of feelings right now. I'm sorry, Arderin. I wish things were different. I wish I could be the man you pretend I am in your fucked-up head. But I'm not. I won't let him torture you like he did my mother. Discussing this any further is futile. Put everything you have in your bag, and I'll load it up as well. I'll tie it to your ankles, so you won't be able to kick your way free."

Desperation closed her throat as she shook her head. There had to be another way. Surely, if she just thought for a moment—

Suddenly, a malevolent cackle echoed in the dimness.

The Dark Lord appeared feet away, the bottom of his purple cape flowing above the squalid ground. Pointed teeth looked like nasty fangs as he smiled at them, evil straining from his beady eyes. Slowly, he sauntered toward them.

Arderin had never been so scared. Securing the button on her jeans, frightened tears welled in her eyes. Darkrip pushed her behind him, dragging her front to his back. After the intimacy they'd just shared, the protective action threatened to shatter her pounding heart.

* * * *

"No!" Darkrip screamed. "I won't let you hurt her."

"I can't believe it," Crimeous said, his voice so low and contemplative. Piercing irises studied Darkrip. "I never thought you would actually consummate with her. It's magnificent."

"I'll kill her. If I have to, I'll murder her before you can touch her. I won't let you take her," Darkrip said, wishing to all the gods it was true. His mother's blood would never let him perform the heinous act. Bile rose in his throat as he surreptitiously scanned the cave, thinking of ways he could kill his father before he dematerialized with Arderin.

"It won't happen, son." Approaching him, Crimeous placed his thin, gray hand on his shoulder. "Your Slayer half is too pure. You couldn't kill this Vampyre now if you tried. I think you have feelings of love for her. They course through you so strongly. I don't understand them, as I've never felt any emotion like that."

Darkrip flung his hand from his shoulder. "Don't fucking touch me," he said through gritted teeth.

"Come back to the caves with me, son. Let me teach you all the dark magic I've learned. It's so powerful. The thrill is like nothing I've ever imagined."

Lowering his lids, Darkrip let the Dark Lord's feelings of viciousness and supremacy course through him. They were consuming and so very evil. The magnificence of the power he would gain from aligning and learning from his father tempted him more than he'd allowed in centuries. Until Rina's beloved face appeared in his mind, reminding him of the promise he gave her.

Training his gaze on Crimeous, he said, "Fuck you, asshole." Darkrip's eyes wandered around the lair, trying to see if there was a rock or sharp stone he could use as a weapon.

"I'm so omnipotent. Don't you see? It's futile for you to attempt to fight me."

"How did you interfere with my powers?"

"I've been studying the dark magic of humans for some time. I created a poppet of you, placed it in a hexagram and cast a curse on your ability to dematerialize. For the cave, I drew on some of the black magic and voodoo spells of the Creoles in New Orleans. It allowed me to create a shield that your powers couldn't break through. The humans are quite insignificant, but they have a great malice that runs through their black magic."

Darkrip filed that knowledge away in the dim hopes that he survived.

"So, what are you going to do now? You won't know if she's pregnant for several weeks. Even you aren't potent enough to see her future like that."

Arderin tensed behind him, and he squeezed her forearm, urging her to stay quiet.

Crimeous shrugged. "There are many ways to torture a pregnant woman and not harm the fetus. Your child will have so much power. It will give me limitless dominion over this world and possibly even others. You have done me a great service."

"You'll never lay one hand on her. Now, give me back my powers and let me fight you, hand-to-hand."

"I told you, your abilities will only return if I'm wounded, causing the spells to be broken. You've lost, Darkrip. It's time to admit defeat." Crimeous' expression was impassive. "There were occasions when you pleased me, son. I hope Etherya finds it in her rotten heart to let you into the Passage." Out of thin air, an eight-shooter appeared in his hands. Training his gaze upon Darkrip, he aimed.

Bracing for impact, Darkrip clutched Arderin, hoping to shield her from the bullets. From above, an explosion detonated. Rocks and dirt seemed to fly into every crevice of the cave. Rotating, he pushed Arderin to the ground and covered her with his body.

Above him, metal clashed and discharges burst. Lifting his head, he saw Latimus approaching his father. The massive soldier held up a long sword, the blade emitting a bright light.

The Dark Lord wailed as Latimus thrust the weapon into his chest several times.

"The blade is a solar simulator, you son of a bitch!" Latimus yelled. "I'll fucking kill you with the light of the sun." Mercilessly, he pounded Crimeous until the Deamon threw his head back and vanished.

"Fucking asshole!" Latimus screamed, flinging the weapon to the ground. Running over, he crouched beside them.

"It's okay, man, we've got you." Clenching his shoulder, Latimus gently pulled him off Arderin. "Is she dead?"

Darkrip shook his head. "I think she fainted, but she desperately needs Slayer blood."

"Can you dematerialize?"

Closing his eyes, Darkrip transported outside the cave. Appearing back inside, he nodded. "Let me take her to Nolan's infirmary." Placing his arms under her limp body, he held her to him.

"Thank you, man," Latimus said, his eyes glassy. "Thank you for keeping her alive."

"Don't thank me yet," Darkrip said, swallowing thickly. "There's a lot of shit that you don't know. I'll see you at Astaria."

Holding his princess to his chest, he transported her home.

Chapter 21

Arderin gasped a large breath into her straining lungs and sat up to assess her surroundings. After a moment, she realized that she was in the infirmary at Astaria. IVs attached to her arms streamed Slayer blood into her starving body.

"Hey there, little student," Nolan said, coming to stand beside her. His kind brown eyes were brimming with tears as he ran his hand down her curls. "We almost lost you. I'm so happy you're home."

"Nolan!" Grabbing onto his white lab coat for dear life, she pulled him to her and squeezed him until he started to cough.

"Wow, you're really strong. Remind me never to get on your bad side."

Laughing, she placed her hands on his cheeks. "I'm alive. I can't believe it. We were so close to dying."

"I know," he said, nodding. "Darkrip told us everything. You were so strong and brave. I'm so proud of you."

"Oh, Nolan, I love you." Embracing him again, she spoke into his broad chest, "I'm so happy to be home."

"I love you too. Thank goodness you're back safely."

They hugged for another minute, and then, he released her. Walking to the counter that sat behind the bed, he pointed to a stack of papers.

"The vials you retrieved from the lab couldn't be salvaged due to lack of refrigeration, but you were so smart to grab the written equations. We got it, Arderin. I was able to create the composition we needed. The skin regeneration formula is one-hundred percent effective."

"Holy crap, how long was I out?"

"Almost two days. I was worried sick, and working on the formula gave me something to do while I waited for you to recover, so,"—he grinned sheepishly—"I finished the serum."

"Awesome," she said, throwing off the sheet and standing to walk toward the microscope that sat on the counter. The tubes in her arms held her prisoner to the IV pole a few feet away. Feeling woozy, she grabbed onto the head of the bed.

"Whoa there," he said, supporting her around her waist. "Lean on me. I'll walk you over. Grab the IV pole and drag it along."

Allowing him to support her, she slowly traversed to the microscope that sat atop the counter and lowered her head to look inside. "It's so smooth, and the veins are circulating blood through the specimen." Lifting to look at him, she said, "By the goddess, Nolan, we did it!"

Nodding, he smiled, his white teeth so bright. "We did it. I can't wait to show Sadie."

"Oh, my god. She's going to die. I'm so excited."

Ushering her back to the bed, he urged her to lie down. "Let's get you healthy before we tell her. I want you to take a few days to rest."

"Okay," she said, nodding against the pillow. Gazing up at him, she couldn't read his expression. "What's wrong?"

Sitting on the bed, he held her hand. "I did a full exam to make sure you were okay. There were traces of blood on your thighs. Did he rape you?" Concern drenched his chestnut irises.

"No," she said, squeezing his wrist. Biting her lip, she tried to contain her smile. "It was mutual, believe me. We've been attracted to each other for some time. Darkrip was so protective of me, Nolan. Even though he didn't want to, he let me drink from him. It was a huge sacrifice, allowing me to see his terrible past. He saved my life."

Inhaling a breath, Nolan studied her. "Is it possible you're pregnant?"

Arderin felt wetness in her eyes as emotion swamped her. "Yes," she whispered.

"Okay," he said, his tone filled with understanding. "I'll monitor it in your chart. You consummated only recently, right?"

She nodded.

"Let's do a pregnancy test in four weeks. If you miss your next period, let me know."

"Damn it," she whispered, chewing her lip. "It was so careless. We were so close to dying, and I woke up in a daze...It just happened..." She struggled to find the right words to describe the circumstances that led to the all-consuming experience.

"Sex is a normal affirmation of life when one is facing imminent death. I don't blame you for wanting to be with him. It's only natural."

"Thank you, Nolan. Please, don't tell anyone."

"You know that anything we discuss is covered by doctor-patient confidentiality. And if you don't want to tell anyone, then I hope you'll come to me whenever you need to talk. This is a huge secret, and I'm here for you."

Love for him swept through her. In the three centuries she'd known Nolan, he'd become like one of her brothers. He'd spent so much time teaching her medicine, always patient and thorough. Realizing how lucky she was to have him, she felt a tear slide down her cheek.

"Don't cry, sweetie," he said, wiping it away.

"They're happy tears. I'm just so thankful that you're here. I want you to have a full life. I hate that you're stuck here in a world that isn't yours. What can I do to help you?"

"Keep smiling at me like that. And help me give the serum to Sadie. That's what will make me happy."

"You care for her."

"Yes," he said with a nod.

"As more than a friend?" she asked.

He looked toward the ceiling, features drawn together. "I don't know. As a very intelligent colleague and one of the nicest people I've ever met, for sure."

"Okay. We'll leave it at that for now. But I'm a pretty good matchmaker. Ask Latimus. I single-handedly helped him bag Lila. If you want my help, you just have to ask." She wiggled her eyebrows.

Chuckling, he said, "Well, let's focus on getting her the serum first. I'm excited to see her reaction."

"Me too."

Their conversation was interrupted by the sounds of her three massive brothers pounding into the infirmary. They all rushed her, pulling her into their beefy chests and clutching her close. Tears streamed down her cheeks as she held them, soothing them and assuring them she was okay.

Thankful to have such an amazing family, she finally let herself accept that she was going to live.

* * * *

Darkrip sat on the stool at the high island counter in the kitchen at Astaria. The room was large, fit for the castle in which it resided, and he reveled in the food that Glarys had prepared. The housekeeper, a lovely woman with kind, light-blue eyes and white hair, had informed him that he must eat everything she prepared to regain his strength.

Looking at the feast before him, he took a moment to revel in how lucky he was to still be alive. As he munched on the succulent chicken, he closed his lids as the flavor drenched his tongue.

"Good boy," Glarys said, patting him on the cheek as she breezed by. "We'll get you strong again. We're so thankful that you saved our beautiful Arderin. If you need anything at all, you just tell me."

Darkrip narrowed his eyes, watching the woman hum as she rubbed a wet cloth over the counter by the sink. Would she be so benevolent toward him if she knew he'd boned the little princess's brains out? Hmmm. He didn't think so.

Swallowing the chicken, he reached for the pasta salad, spooning a heaving portion on his plate. Stuffing a bite in his mouth, he deliberated as he chewed. It was quite possible that Arderin was pregnant. They wouldn't know for several weeks, so he'd have to keep an eye on her. That would be tough, since he was determined to never touch her again.

Their sexual encounter in the cave was the most disastrous mistake of Darkrip's life. Now that they had survived, it took all his strength not to strangle himself. What a fucking idiot he was. He'd made a rash decision, swept up in the emotion of the moment. All these centuries, he'd been so careful to never impregnate a female. Now, he'd gone and thrown away all of his self-restraint.

It would be impossible to let her have his child. If she was pregnant, he would have to convince her to have an abortion. Spawning another creature with his father's blood would create an imbalance leading to more death and destruction. He would never allow it to happen.

Sighing, an image of Arderin's flawless face entered his mind. His stubborn little Vampyre would most likely fight him on aborting the child. He would just have to do his best to explain to her the abomination it would become. Vowing to sway her, he took a swig of the smooth scotch Latimus had given him. Damn, he should save Vampyre princesses more often. People did really nice shit for you when you did stuff like that. Huh.

Deciding he was near food-coma status and ready to sleep, he thanked Glarys and disappeared to his cabin. After preparing for bed, he rummaged around awhile, feeling restless and perhaps a bit...lonely? Did he miss Arderin, after being near her for all that time in the cave? He certainly hadn't forgotten the feel of her slender body wrapped around him, giving him what was surely the most pleasurable moment of his life.

Resolved that the resulting pangs of longing in his gut were bullshit, he decided that his delusional mind just needed rest. Pushing away the memory of the scent of her hair and the smoothness of her skin, he lay down on his soft sheets, thankful that he was no longer sleeping on the dirty ground.

Chapter 22

Arderin set about resuming her life, grateful to be alive. And yet, her survival had created a dangerous situation that she felt ill-prepared for. After consummating with Darkrip, she was now Crimeous' number one target.

The blood of their child would be irrepressible, creating a spawn the likes of which the Earth had never seen. Combining Crimeous' powers, Markdor's self-healing pure blood and Valktor's pedigree, it would be undefeatable. The prospect was daunting.

Not because of the child. No, Arderin thought, absently staring out the window of the sitting room as her palm rested on her abdomen. The baby would be beautiful. An amalgamation of Arderin's beauty, inherited from her mother, and Darkrip's handsome features. If they focused, they could teach the child kindness, humility and restraint.

But the threat would always loom. Even now, Arderin felt it close around her throat. An invisible hand, choking her with fear. At least Astaria had an impenetrable wall. One built by Etherya after her parents' murder to protect the Vampyre royal offspring. So far, Crimeous hadn't been able to break through.

Shivering, Arderin thought of the ugly creature. If she was pregnant, he would stop at nothing to abduct her and raise the child to be a mighty soldier in his battle to destroy the immortals of Etherya's Earth. Straightening her spine, she vowed that would never happen. Balancing her fear with her joy at retuning home, she pivoted to see her family enter the sitting room.

Taking Tordor from Miranda's arms, Arderin cooed to him, resting him atop her thighs as she sat on the couch. Speaking unintelligible words, she smiled, enthralled by the infant who looked so much like Sathan.

Miranda sat beside her on the couch, conversing with Sathan, their voices filled with slight resignation. They were discussing the security on the trains, confirming Heden had elevated it even more now that Arderin and Darkrip had escaped.

"We need you to sit and debrief with the council, Arderin," Miranda said. "We've called a meeting for Wednesday morning at ten a.m."

"Okay," she said, not lifting her gaze from Tordor. "I know we're on high-alert now, especially after we escaped. But can we just have one night where I don't have to think about that bastard? I missed you guys so much and just want to chill."

"Sure," Miranda said, compassion in her voice. "We all need a night to relax. I told Glarys to pop open the fancy red wine."

Arderin's lips curved, mouth watering in anticipation of tasting wine again. "You're just so freaking cute, aren't you?" she asked, rubbing her nose against Tordor's as he lay atop her legs. "I can't wait to show you to the world. You're the sweetest baby that ever existed."

"No Insta-whatevering of our child, Arderin," Sathan said, a tender warning in his dark eyes. "I don't want him plastered all over the social media of the immortal world."

After scowling at him, she looked back down at Tordor. "Your daddy's a big grouch, isn't he? We'll show him. I'm going to make you the biggest influencer in the Vampyre kingdom. He won't know what hit him."

"I mean it, Arderin," Sathan murmured.

"Stop torturing my husband," Miranda said, her expression filled with mischief. "That's my job."

Laughing, Arderin nodded. "Don't I know it."

Jack surged into the room, toy sword in hand. "Uncle Sathan!" he yelled, climbing up on his lap. "Did Lila tell you about my race at school? I won first place!"

"No way," Sathan said, hugging the boy.

"Yup," he nodded, red hair swishing about his head. "I beat all the boys and broke the record for the fastest time. They don't let the girls race with us because they're so slow. They have their own race." He rolled his eyes dramatically.

"Hey," Lila said, entering the room and smoothing out Jack's mane with her fingers before sitting in the chair to Sathan's left. "Girls are really strong too. Don't count us out. Look at your Aunt Arderin. She survived in a secluded cave for weeks."

Squirming on Sathan's lap, Jack's eyes grew wide. "Were you scared?"

"Yeah," Arderin said, nodding as she reveled in his cuteness. "I was really scared. But I knew I couldn't give up. I needed to come home to you guys. I thought about you all the time, Jack. Wanting to see you helped me survive."

Sliding off Sathan's lap, he ran toward her. "I'm so glad you're okay," he said, throwing his arms around her and Tordor.

"Oh, be careful around the baby, sweetie," she said, pulling him to her side and hugging him with her free arm. "I'm so happy too. Thank you." Heart bursting with love, she kissed the soft tresses atop his head.

"The training's done for today," Latimus said, strolling into the room. "I'm starving. Are we having dinner?"

"Yep," Miranda said, standing. "Glarys prepared some Slayer blood and food for us. It should be ready in the dining room."

"Did I hear something about food?" Heden said, popping his head around the entryway to the sitting room.

"Of course, he only shows up when there's something to eat," Arderin muttered, standing and handing Tordor to Miranda.

"Hey, little toad," Heden said. "Leave me alone. I didn't do anything to you."

She stuck her tongue out at him, causing him to playfully scrunch his face at her.

"Okay, kids, enough," Miranda said. "Let's go. This baby is heavy."

"Do you want me to take him?"

They regarded the nanny, Belinda, who strolled into the room. Miranda and Sathan had hired her a few weeks before the birth of their son. She came with impeccable references from Restia, where a family had used her services for forty years until all their children had married. Arderin regarded her slight frame, her height similar to Miranda's five-foot-six stature. She had dirty blond, shoulder-length hair and pretty brown eyes.

"That would be great," Miranda said, handing Tordor to her. Holding the child, Belinda followed them to the dining room and tended to him, sitting with the family while they ate their dinner.

"Where's Darkrip?" Arderin asked. She longed to see him and make sure he was okay. It had been days since their return, and she had the distinct impression he was avoiding her.

"I asked him to come, but he said he already ate," Miranda said. "I wish he'd join us. He should be part of these family dinners."

Deciding that she would track him down tomorrow, Arderin nodded. "I'll ask him to join us next time I see him. We became close in the cave, obviously. He never let me give up. I wish you guys could've seen how supportive he was."

Her brothers all gave each other a look, driving her positively mad.

"What?" she asked.

"Nothing," they all muttered.

Rolling her eyes, she informed them they were all morons and poured herself a hefty dose of Slayer blood. Sitting back, she contemplated her family. So thankful to be home, she reveled in Miranda's melodic laugh when she threw back her head. Lila's soft smile and beautiful lavender irises. Sathan's scowl as Miranda teased him. Latimus glaring at Heden when he threatened to cut off his man bun while he was sleeping. Jack smacking his lips together as he ate the penne vodka Glarys had prepared. They were all so precious to her.

Rubbing the pad of her finger over the rim of her goblet, Arderin realized that something was missing. *He* was missing. She ached to see him, to hold him, being that she'd had the luxury for so many weeks. She didn't appreciate it then, but she was determined to grab onto it now, for dear life if she had to. She wanted to lay with him again. To have him look into her with those melting green eyes as he thrust inside her. By the goddess, she burned for it. Resolved to make it happen, sooner rather than later, she sipped the blood and smiled.

* * * *

Darkrip ran under the light of the blazing sun, determined to regain the strength he'd lost in the cave. The open meadow gave him a sense of peace, and he wiped his brow as he panted. His heart pounded under his bare chest and sweat dripped down his legs under his jogging shorts. The plushy sneakers crunched the green grass as he strived to keep up the blistering pace.

Approaching the forest that surrounded the River Thayne, he decided he'd jog there for a while before returning to his cabin. The broken tree stubs on the ground and raised roots gave him some extra obstacles to overcome as he ran. Appreciating the cross-country terrain, he darted under the thick overhang of trees.

Her scent swamped him immediately, causing his heart to slam in his chest. Clenching his teeth, he searched for her. Arderin was leaning against one of the tall redwood trees, one ankle-booted foot resting on the bark while she supported her weight on the other.

Telling himself not to be a coward, he jogged over to her, stopping only a foot in front of her.

"Those don't look to be appropriate footwear for jaunting about in the forest."

She shrugged. "I think they're cute. And it's not like I'm running a marathon. You, on the other hand," she said, extending her arm, index finger outstretched, "you're sweaty and hot." She ran her finger over his pecs, slightly scratching him with her nail. It drove him wild, his cock twitching in his shorts.

"What do you want?" he asked, snatching her finger and holding it in a death grip.

Her eyes narrowed. "Why are you avoiding me?"

"I'm not," he said, releasing her hand.

"Don't play games with me," she said, straightening to her full height. "I haven't seen you since we returned. I wanted to thank you. You saved my life."

"You're welcome. Now, leave me the fuck alone."

"God, you're infuriating. You're avoiding Miranda too. If you're not careful, everyone will start to suspect what happened in the cave."

"Believe me, they have bigger fish to fry. My father will be furious that we escaped, make no mistake about that. I anticipate he'll attack one of the compounds soon."

Worry entered her ice-blue eyes. "Well, at least we're safe here at Astaria. He'll never be able to break through Etherya's wall."

Darkrip nodded. "It's imperative that you stay on the compound. You're in imminent danger, now that we consummated. Until we know if you're pregnant, you have to stay safe."

Her pale cheeks dotted with red splotches, and he found the corner of his lips turning up. "Are you embarrassed? I never thought I'd see the day."

Rolling her eyes, she gave him a caustic glare. "It's just all so surreal. We were so stupid. I can't believe I wasn't more careful."

Sighing, he rubbed his fingers on his forehead. "We were steps away from death. It's pointless to waste time regretting something we can't change."

"Well, I grabbed some condoms from Nolan's infirmary. For next time."

Anger welled in his chest. "There's not going to be a next time, princess."

Her raven-colored eyebrow arched. "Is that so? I thought you might say that. Coward."

"Call me whatever names you want, I don't give a shit. I'm not fucking you again. It was extremely careless of me, and I won't put you in danger like that."

Her plushy lips curved into a smile. "So, you want to protect me?"

Frustration consumed him as he ran a hand over his face. "Sure. Whatever you need to tell yourself. Just know that it won't ever happen again."

The little imp stepped into him, brushing her body against his. It took all of his willpower not to groan as she lifted her chin, her mouth a hairsbreadth from his. "Maybe you should kiss me to remind yourself how good we were together."

Every muscle of his taut body screamed to pull away from her. Mortified that he would even consider shrinking away from her, he pushed further into her body. "Don't provoke me, little girl. You have no idea what you're messing with."

She brushed her open lips against his, causing him to shudder. "I know you want me," she breathed into his mouth. "Take me here, against the tree. You can have me."

Snaking his hand behind her waist, he fisted her hair with his other hand, causing her to gasp. "It's not happening. Stop approaching me. I won't tell you again."

"You're such a pussy—"

His thick lips closed over hers, inhaling the words as she clutched him to her with her slender arms. The strength of her embrace rocked him to his core as he plundered her mouth. Lifting on her toes, she extended her wet tongue to mate with his, giving a sexy mewl when he sucked it. Groaning, he let himself battle with her, sliding over every part of her sensual mouth, until he knew he had to let her go.

"Enough," he breathed, pushing her away by her upper arms. "I'm not the man you want to do this with, Arderin. We have our attraction and our captivity between us. That's all. It doesn't equate to love or caring or whatever you've made up in your busy brain. I don't want you to search me out again. I have an important task ahead of me, swaying Evie to our cause. Now that my father has learned to manipulate my powers, we need her more than ever. I can't have you distracting me."

Innocent eyes stared into his. "We could be so good together if you let yourself try. I know it seems impossible, but I've never felt this way—"

"No," he interrupted, shaking her. "Stop this. You have a second chance at life. At having everything you've ever dreamed of. Don't waste it on me. You'll build something much better, I know it. Now, I need you to promise me you'll leave me alone."

Her irises darted back and forth between his, filled with emotion and a twinge of hurt. It sliced a crack through his deadened heart.

"Please, Arderin," he said, softening his tone. "I need to focus, and you need to move on."

"And what if I'm pregnant? Miranda's called a council meeting later this week. I wanted to discuss with you whether I should tell them I might be pregnant. You and I need to be unified in our decision on that."

Licking his lips, he studied her. "I'll leave the decision up to you. You'll have more shit to deal with than me if your brothers find out we slept together."

Her eyebrows lifted. "I'd say you might have more repercussions. They're most likely going to want to slaughter you if they know you laid a finger on me."

Darkrip nodded, the action resigned. "No less than I deserve. I should've never touched you. You deserved so much better for your first time."

"Well, if that's the best you can do for an apology, I'll take it," she said. "But I don't regret being with you. And if I'm pregnant, I won't regret that either. I'd like to withhold the information from the council, for a few more weeks at least. Although, we now know that the purer the blood, the more likely a couple is to conceive a hybrid. And you and I have royal blood in spades."

"Then, we'll keep an eye on everything and deal with that when the time comes. I'll need you to be honest with me. It's imperative that we don't bring another child into the world with his lineage."

Confusion filled her expression. "You wouldn't ask me to abort it."

"I would," he said, nodding. "It's the only option."

Shaking her head, she stepped away, creating distance that he desperately needed. "I'm not going to discuss this with you now. It's a moot point until we know for sure anyway. But I'll tell you right now, I don't believe in abortion."

"Well, that's too bad. Do you really want a child with my father's blood? One who's conditioned to rape and murder?"

"With your blood!" she yelled, stomping her foot. "And Miranda's and your mother's. I don't think that would be terrible at all."

"Delude yourself all you want. If it happens, that baby is perishing. One way or another."

Lifting her chin, in her always-haughty manner, she said, "This discussion is over. Remember what I said about the condoms. I have plenty, whenever you're ready to stop fighting your obvious desire to fuck me again."

Exhaling a large breath, he placed his hands on his hips. "You're exasperating. I don't have the energy for you, princess."

"Oh, I think you will, when the time comes." Patting his cheek, she placed a soft kiss on his lips. "Can't wait. See ya soon." Flipping her gorgeous hair over her shoulder, she pivoted and sauntered toward the edge of the forest and onto the open field.

Lowering his head, he couldn't help but chuckle. She was something else. Deciding that he needed to run an extra mile to release the sexual energy she'd stirred up inside his throbbing body, he resumed jogging.

Chapter 23

The next day, Darkrip sat with Miranda, Sathan, Kenden and Latimus in the large conference room at Astaria. After recounting his meeting with Evie, he ran his hand over his short hair. He'd continued to let it grow out after returning home, denying that it was because Arderin had complimented it. No, it just saved him from having to buzz it as often. Of course, that was why.

"Now that your father has learned to manipulate your abilities, we need Evie more than ever," Miranda said, sitting to Sathan's right as he sat at the head of the long table. "Not only can she possibly fulfill the prophecy but Crimeous most likely won't be able to manipulate her powers yet."

"No," Darkrip said, shaking his head. "He all but admitted to me that he doesn't see her as a threat. It's a huge miscalculation on his part. She's extremely formidable. When she was young, she had powers that I never possessed. I once saw her cut off her own hand and regenerate it. I think she did it just to feel the thrill. My father never knew. Who knows what other skills she's developed over the last eight hundred years?"

"Okay," Miranda said, nodding. "It's time I put my foot down. Now that I'm not pregnant, I want to go with you to the human world to try and convince her." She held up a hand when Sathan tried to speak. "I know your first reaction is to say no, darling. So, let's get this out of the way. I'm the queen of our kingdom and have an obligation to help our people. It's high time I got on with it."

Sathan's black irises darted over her face. "I understand your desire to sway her in person. I'm just terrified for you to travel into the human world."

When Miranda opened her mouth to respond, Sathan grabbed her hand. "It's not because I'm afraid you can't handle it, Miranda. The goddess knows you're the most fearless of us all. I just worry that when you're over there, I won't be able to communicate with you. Now that we have Tordor, I want to make sure we explore every possibility. Can we at least discuss other options?"

Miranda gave him a soft smile and squeezed his hand. "Fine. Let's brainstorm."

"Honestly," Latimus chimed in with his baritone, "I hate to do this to you, Sathan, but I think getting Miranda in front of her would help. She's the most stubborn person I've ever met, and if she's determined to get Evie on our side, it will happen."

Sighing, Sathan sat back and ran his hand through his thick hair. "Kenden?" he asked, eyeing the Slayer commander.

"I agree with Latimus. Miranda has a way with people, and Evie's her sister. We need to let her do this."

"Well, dear, I hate to say it, but I think you've been outvoted." She shot him a sympathetic look. "I'll be safe. I promise."

"Okay," Sathan said, sitting up and lifting her hand to kiss it. "Let's make a plan. We need to make sure your travel is as short as possible, especially since you're breast feeding."

Nodding, she detailed how she could pump and bank milk that could be frozen and stored for their son. "But I only want to go for a short stint as well. Unlike Arderin, I've never had any desire to travel to the human world. I want to get in, convince our sister and get out."

"Then, let me go there first and locate her," Darkrip said. "It might take some time, but I'll track her down. Once I do, I'll come back through the ether, notify you and get you safely to her. You should go ahead and begin to store milk in preparation."

"Will do. In the meantime, we need to discuss Crimeous. He's gotten so strong. Where are we at on the production of the SSWs?"

It was the name they'd come up with for the Solar Simulator Weapons. Armaments, similar to traditional swords, whose blades consisted of solar lighting. Heden, a huge Star Wars fan, always referred to them as 'Deamon lightsabers.' He wasn't far off. Learning that Crimeous burned in the sunlight had been a huge advancement for them. The weapons maimed him more than any they'd ever invented.

"We've got two hundred in the barracks at both Astaria and Uteria. The welders and laborers at Restia, Lynia and Naria did a great job with the production, and we have five hundred more on order," Kenden said.

"Good," Miranda said. "Let's keep it that way. We're going to need them if—"

The walkie at Kenden's side buzzed before she could finish. Lifting it, he spoke into the receiver, "Repeat."

"Crimeous is attacking Uteria," Larkin's voice said, scratchy over the device. "It's drizzling here, so he must not be afraid of direct sunlight. The troops are responding, but you might want to send backup."

Latimus' phone buzzed, and he picked it up, reading a text. Standing, he gave a loud curse.

"What is it?"

"The Deamons are attacking Lynia. Mother-fucker! Lila and Jack will be home since it's almost dusk. Damn it!"

"Stay calm," Sathan said, standing. "Darkrip, can you transport Latimus to Lynia and then return here and get Kenden to Uteria?"

Nodding, Darkrip strode to Latimus. "Don't worry. We'll get there. Let's go." Placing his arms around the massive Vampyre, he transported him to defend his wife and child.

* * * *

Latimus emerged with Darkrip in front of the porch stairs of their pretty house. Giving him a nod, the Slayer-Deamon disappeared. Lila stood on the porch, staring off in the distance at the Deamons that fought in the open field. They were still over two-hundred yards away, but the screams of battle could be heard as metal clashed with metal.

"Hey, honey," he said, rushing up the stairs and embracing her. "Is Jack inside?"

"Yes," she said, her gorgeous violet irises laced with fear. Pride coursed through him as he noticed that they were also filled with strength and resolve. By the goddess, she was amazing.

"Okay, let's get you guys in the bunker."

When he'd built the house, Latimus had designed a shelter where she and Jack could hide in case of attack. The walls were built of osmium, an extremely dense platinum metal that Darkrip had assured him Crimeous couldn't materialize through. He'd also stationed ten soldiers to guard the house at all times, albeit from afar, so that Lila didn't feel stifled.

Walking in the house with her, they called to Jack. He barreled down the stairs from his bedroom, where Latimus assumed he was doing his homework. "We need to get you to the bunker, buddy."

His deep brown eyes grew wide, but he puffed his chest proudly, showing such courage. Latimus felt his heart melt. Their boy would make such a strong soldier one day. Leading them down the wooden stairs of the basement, he made sure they were safe and placed a kiss on Lila's lips.

"I'll see you when I'm finished. Keep your phone on. I love you guys."

"We love you," Jack said, causing Latimus' chest to constrict. Closing the thick door, he headed back outside.

Grabbing the AR-15 that one of his soldiers thrust at him, he charged across the open field. He had two hundred soldiers stationed at Lynia, and they were all earning their due at the moment. There were at least three hundred Deamon soldiers, although they would never be as strong or well-trained as the Vampyres. Crimeous had recently employed a cloning tactic from the human world, increasing his number of warriors, but they would never be able to defeat Latimus' soldiers. Of that, he was certain. He had the most well-trained troops on Etherya's Earth.

Running into battle, he unleashed the magazine of his gun on the Deamons, ready to decimate each and every last one of them.

* * * *

Meanwhile, Kenden was locked in a skirmish of his own with the Dark Lord. The surrounding battle was being handled mightily by the Uterian combined Slayer-Vampyre army, but he wanted to mutilate the bastard himself. Striking repeatedly with the SSW, he noted each time the weapon connected with Crimeous' skin. Always a thoughtful and curious student of war, he took mental note of how the weapon singed the tissue and where he could improve it to make it more effective.

Finally, Kenden began to tire and called to Larkin. "Break out your SSW and give me some help," he yelled. "We need to get him off the compound."

Larkin charged over, weapon pulled and illuminated, and began battering Crimeous. With one last wail, the Dark Lord vanished. Minutes later, the remaining Deamon troops were defeated. Giving orders to Larkin to start the clean-up, Kenden pulled his cell from his belt and called Latimus.

"Do you guys need me to come over?" Latimus asked.

"No," Kenden said. "We just finished. They're all dead. We need to increase the output of solar energy from the SSW. It's not searing his skin enough."

"Okay, we'll change the specs for the welders tomorrow." Silence stretched between them until Latimus spoke, his voice low and filled with resignation. "That's the first time he's attacked two compounds at once."

"I know," Kenden said, kicking the ground with the toe of his boot. "He's becoming arrogant and stronger than we ever imagined."

"We have to find Evie,"

"Yes. I'll speak to Darkrip. He needs to get to the human world ASAP."

"Let me talk to him," Latimus said. "I have other things I need to discuss with him anyway."

"Okay. Alert me know when it's done. I'm going to stay at Uteria tonight and help Larkin with the cleanup."

"Ten-four. Way to kick that bastard's ass, Ken."

"You too, man. You've still got it even though Lila's turned you into a lovesick sap."

Latimus chuckled. "Not you too. I already have enough chiding from my brothers. Why don't you go find a woman so you can all leave me alone?"

Laughing, Kenden said, "One day soon, man. One day soon. Talk to you later."

Disconnecting the call, he went to find Larkin and help with the aftermath of the battle.

Chapter 24

Miranda watched Belinda coo and coddle her son. The woman was an excellent and nurturing caretaker. Walking over to her, Miranda lightly touched her shoulder. She seemed to stiffen a bit and lifted her gaze. Her eyes were almond-shaped and quite pretty.

"Do you want to feed him?"

"Yes," Miranda said, stretching out her arms. Once he was in her embrace, she sat in the large wing-backed chair of the nursery they had built next door to their bedchamber. Unbuttoning her sweater, she latched him onto her breast. Love coursed through her as he drank, his green eyes shining.

"He's very cute," Belinda said.

"Have a seat," Miranda said, motioning toward the bed. "Tell me about yourself. How long have you lived at Restia?"

Belinda told her of her birth two centuries ago to a family of laborers. She had many siblings and had learned to take care of them while her parents worked. Eventually, she left in search of employment and ended up a nanny for the family who referred her at Restia.

"I don't mean to pry, but I hear you have a great journey ahead of you. I heard you telling Glarys that you need to store your milk to head to the human world."

"Yes," Miranda nodded. "My sister lives there, and she's important in our quest to kill Crimeous. I need to sway her to help us."

"Why does she need swaying?"

Miranda inhaled a deep breath, pursing her lips. "Because she's distrustful of everything and everyone. She's never had one person who cared for her or put her first. It must be awful. I hate that her life has been filled with so much pain. From the stories my brother told me, her early life was just terrible. I hope to change that."

"It's hard to change things that have happened in the past. Perhaps she won't be able to accept you."

"It will be hard for sure, but I have to try. I almost died in battle and went to the Passage. My grandfather was there. He asked me to find her and help her find her way."

"So, she must truly be lost."

"No one is ever lost if you love them enough. I'm determined to find her and love her, even if she doesn't want it. Although she instigated some pretty heavy shit recently, I find that I want to forgive her. I mean, if I can forgive the Vampyres for all their transgressions, I can certainly find compassion in my heart for my sister. It's the only way forward, and I'm so tired of all the bloodshed and hate. Also, I'm kind of insane, in case my husband hasn't already informed you." She gave her a huge smile.

"No," Belinda said, gently rubbing her hand over the comforter. "You're just...different. So few people in the world have your optimism and capacity to love. It's a great gift. Many people are only driven by the bad things."

"Well, I hope I can convince her to be driven by my mother's side. Darkrip has done a great job living by his Slayer blood for centuries. We'll see." Noticing that Tordor was done drinking, she placed him on her shoulder to burp him. Once done, she laid him in the bassinet and swaddled him to sleep.

"I think he'll be out for a few hours. Why don't you go take a long lunch? I'll watch him this afternoon."

"Thanks."

Miranda watched her leave the room, feeling a connection with her somehow. She'd always wanted to help her people and was happy that this nice young Slayer woman was in their employ. Knowing that Sathan was downstairs working on the budget for the updated SSWs, Miranda hopped into bed and allowed herself to read the juicy novel on her tablet for a few sweet, quiet moments.

* * * *

Latimus found Darkrip in the barracks gym. He knew he came there regularly when it rained, and it was pouring outside. He'd given the troops the day off from training after yesterday's battle, knowing it was vital that he speak to the Slayer-Deamon.

"Hey," Darkrip said, punching the button to slow the machine down. Eventually, he came to a slow walk. "Need me to jump off?"

"If you don't mind. I have a few things I want to discuss with you."

"Sure." Bringing the black belt of the treadmill to a stop, he grabbed the towel hanging from the rail and dried his face. Chugging the entire contents of his water bottle, he sat beside Latimus on the long work-out bench.

"What's up, man?"

"Your father has never attacked two compounds at once. He's becoming bolder. It's imperative that you find Evie and get her to help us."

"I know. I was going to leave at the end of this week."

"I think you should leave tomorrow. Unless you're waiting for something."

Darkrip shrugged. "Not really. I just figured it would be best to get my strength up, after losing so much weight in the cave."

A muscle ticked in Latimus' jaw. "Or maybe you want to sniff around my sister a bit longer?"

Darkrip arched a black eyebrow. "Do you really want to go there? I'm not sure you'll like what you find."

Clenching his teeth, Latimus regarded the man. "I'm not naive enough to think you didn't touch her. It makes me want to pound your face in, but my sister's no shrinking violet. If you did, she was most likely a willing participant."

Darkrip breathed a laugh. "Wow. You know her well. I'm convinced Sathan and Heden have no idea. They seem to want to believe she's an innocent spinster who knits all day and never even thinks of sex."

"They've never been able to see her like I do. I understand the direness you faced in the cave and the need to affirm your lives. I'm not happy about it, but I get it."

Darkrip rubbed the back of his neck. "This is so awkward, but if we're going to do it, then, yeah, she and I are extremely attracted to each other. I vowed not to touch her, but we were so close to death. I was dreaming, and then she was above me, and...she's the most gorgeous woman I've ever seen. I don't know what else to tell you. I understand if you want to kill me."

Latimus sighed, clenching his hands as his elbows rested on his knees. Staring at the floor, he shook his head. "I don't need to tell you that this has disaster written all over it. Sathan will banish you from the compound the moment he finds out you touched her. We need you as an ally. I can't have us divided."

"I know. I've already told her it's never happening again." Sitting up straighter, he patted his shoulder. "Look, man, I know you have no reason to trust me, but I'm intent on staying away from her. She deserves better than any life I could give her. I want her to move on and find someone that she can build a home and a family with. I obviously can never give her those things."

"I told Lila the same thing," Latimus said, cupping his chin. "In the end, it wasn't really true." Turning his head, he trained his gaze on Darkrip's vivid irises. "Do you love her?"

"Fuck, you guys and your avowals of love are so foreign to someone like me. I don't understand what that word means. It's not something that I can even begin to feel."

"Then, I need you to honor your word not to lay a hand on her."

"I told you, I'm trying. You need to tell her to leave me alone. I'm not the initiator, now that we're back at the compound. I know it's hard to see your little sister that way, but she's incredibly stubborn."

"I'll talk to her. In the meantime, I'd like to ask if you can leave tomorrow. Yesterday's attacks shook me. You need to locate Evie so we can get Miranda in front of her."

"Okay, I'll leave tomorrow morning. Let's not make a big deal out of it. I don't want any fanfare or goodbye hugs. That shit drives me nuts. I'll text you before I walk through the ether."

"Thanks. I won't say anything. I hope you're able to find her quickly. You know I'm here if you need help."

Nodding, Darkrip stood. "Thanks for being so understanding. I thought you were going to cut off my balls if you ever found out I laid a hand on her."

"Don't tell Sathan," Latimus said, standing to scowl down at him. "He'll most likely murder you." He crossed his arms over his chest. "If you cause her even one ounce of pain, I'll rip every tooth from your mouth and shove them from your ass to your brain. Got it?"

"Good to know the secrets of Vampyre soldier interrogation," Darkrip muttered.

Latimus shot him a glare. "Geez, man, I've got it. Look, I'm very fond of her. I don't want to hurt her. She's an amazing person."

Silence stretched as Latimus observed Darkrip's muscles tense and worry darken his expression.

"What is it?"

"You have to protect her," Darkrip said. "When I'm gone. She's a target now, until we know for certain whether she's pregnant. We decided not to tell the council, but now that you know, it's imperative you keep her on the compound. She's spirited and so damn hardheaded. I don't want my father to hurt her."

Latimus' eyebrows drew together. The man before him cared for Arderin, perhaps more than Darkrip wanted to admit. "I'll keep her safe. You have my word."

"Thank you," Darkrip said, running his hands over his face. "I need to shower and tell Miranda I'm leaving."

"Safe travels," Latimus said, extending his hand. "May the goddess be with you."

Darkrip shook it, appearing cautious and a bit surprised at the gesture of goodwill.

Resolute, Latimus stalked from the gym.

* * * *

Arderin chatted with Sadie as she lay on her bed, phone held to her ear as she absently threaded her fingers through her long hair.

"So, you're coming on Friday to check on Tordor?"

"Yup," Sadie said. "Nolan could do it, but I also want to check on Miranda's progress, and he thought she might be more comfortable having me do it. Plus, it gives me an opportunity to hang with you."

"Totally. I can't wait to show you the new Snapchat filters I downloaded. They're fantastic. Oh, and I have a Cosmo quiz for you to take with me. It's called,

Are You Good Girl Hot or Bad Girl Hot? I'm thinking I'm totally 'bad girl' but give off the 'good girl' vibe. You're 'good girl' all the way though."

Laughter swelled through the phone. "Well, I'm not really hot, so I don't even know if that one applies to me."

"Oh, whatever, Sadie, you're so hot. I don't know why you tell yourself you're not. Your eyes are the most remarkable I've ever seen. You have so many colors in your irises. They're absolutely stunning."

"You should've been a cheerleader in another life. You're great at it."

"Ha! Maybe I'll travel back to the human world and try out for one of their NFL cheerleading spots. I bet I could do it."

"You can do anything, Arderin. I'm so happy that you're okay. We were all so worried about you."

Sentiment for her kind friend welled in her chest. "Thank you, sweetie. I'm so glad I'm home too. I can't wait to see you on Friday."

They ended the call, Arderin's blood coursing with excitement about giving her the serum. Trotting down to the infirmary, she confirmed with Nolan what time Sadie would arrive on Friday. His resulting smile convinced her that he had romantic feelings for her.

Heading back upstairs, Arderin meandered into the kitchen to find some Slayer blood. After drinking, she wandered around the large castle, bored since it was raining. Walking past the sitting room, she heard Darkrip speaking with Miranda, his voice hushed.

"I'll leave in the morning. It might take several weeks to find her. Now that she knows I'm looking, she'll have covered all her tracks. I'll alert you as soon as I find her and help you through the ether."

"Okay," Miranda said. She heard shuffling and assumed they were embracing. "Please, be safe."

"I will." A *whoosh* of air sounded, and she realized he'd vanished.

Sinking back into the hallway wall, she watched Miranda stalk to the kitchen, unaware that she was listening.

Heartache, strong and true, coursed through her. He was going to leave without even telling her? After everything that happened in the cave? Yes, she was a big girl, but he'd taken her virginity, for the goddess's sake. Didn't he care for her at all?

Muttering that he was an ass, she clenched her teeth in fury. How dare he think he could have her and then just dismiss her like one of his harem whores? Fuck that. She was the daughter of Markdor and Calla and princess of the Vampyre kingdom. She deserved better than being pushed away by a callous man who wouldn't let himself care for her.

Wanting to confront him and make him admit that she was more than just some tramp, Arderin called upon the one thing that she knew he couldn't deny: his attraction to her. He'd admitted it to her multiple times. It was a weakness that she was damn well going to exploit.

Marching to her bedroom, she formed her plan. She would seduce him and maneuver him into a position of vulnerability. Once there, she would get him to admit that his attempts to push her away were futile and ridiculous. Whether he liked it or not, they were tied together. Especially if she ended up being pregnant.

Determined to get him to admit his feelings and to understand why he wouldn't tell her he was leaving, she donned her attire. Throwing some condoms in her pocket, she headed to the barracks, where Latimus kept the chest of tools he used to bind prisoners for torture. Straightening her shoulders, she padded through the back door of the barracks, out onto the expansive training field. Darkrip's cabin was far off, under the light of the just-risen moon, and she trudged toward it, never looking back.

Chapter 25

Darkrip gritted his teeth at the pounding on the door. Wanting badly to tell her to bugger off, he pulled it open, stopping her in mid-knock. Emotion-filled, ice-blue eyes pierced him as she held her fist high. The nostrils of her perfect nose flared under the moonlight.

"You fucking coward," Arderin said.

Rolling his eyes, annoyance at her always dramatic temperament shot through him. "I'm packing, princess."

"Oh, yes, I know," she said, arching her perfectly plucked brow. "For your trip that you were never going to tell me you were going on."

He sighed. "Can we save the tantrum for another time? I've got shit to do and don't have time for spoiled Vampyres right now."

Pain flashed across her face, making him feel like the biggest jerk who'd ever walked the Earth. He'd taken her virginity and dismissed her—not because he didn't care, but because his feelings for her were going to get her killed. His stubborn princess appeared to be balancing on a ledge between extreme hurt and intense anger.

Breezing past him, she made it to the center of the room, beside the king-sized four-poster bed, before pivoting.

"Why are you wearing a raincoat? It stopped raining an hour ago." He closed the door, warily eyeing her.

Untying the knot at her waist, she pulled open the flaps of the brown coat, wearing nothing underneath. Darkrip inhaled a huge breath, his cock straining toward her in his black slacks.

Throwing the coat to the floor, she said, "I've come here to say goodbye, you heartless bastard."

His eyes darted over her flawless body, unable to stop them. Her long, sensuous hair. That gorgeous face that haunted his dreams. Large areolas, darker than her pale skin, with rapidly firming, pebbled nipples. The small black strip of hair in between her barely-flared torso and thin thighs.

"I told you, I'm not fucking you again."

Breathing a laugh, she slowly lowered her upper body, reaching to pull something out of the pocket of the coat. The image she made, bent over and submissive, was so fucking sexy, and he was damn sure she knew it.

"Have you ever seen *Legally Blond*?" she asked, her sky-blue eyes twinkling with mischief as her hair almost touched the floor in her pretzeled state.

"What the hell is that?"

"It doesn't matter," she said, slowly lifting up, shiny objects dangling from her hand. Sauntering toward him, she patted his face. "You were just a victim of the *Bend and Snap*, my friend. Works every time."

Grabbing her wrist, he pushed her slightly away from him. "You have five seconds to exit my cabin—"

"Or what?" she asked, slowly backing toward the bed. "You'll lift me up and carry me? That's what I'm trying to get you to do, moron." Sitting on the bed, she held up two pairs of silver handcuffs. "Look what I found."

Darkrip clenched every muscle in his jaw, striving to remain calm. "I'm not here to fulfill some fantasy you read about in your silly human fluff magazines, Arderin."

"*My* fantasy," she said, shaking her head and giving him a *tsk, tsk, tsk*. "Oh, no, little boy, this is *your* fantasy. I saw it in your thoughts when your blood coursed through me. You like to bind your women and dominate them while you screw them."

Slipping over the gray comforter, she lifted an arm to the bedpost on the far-side and attached her wrist to it with the cuff. Turning her gorgeous face to him, she said, "I don't have the keys. You can unlock this one with your mind, or you can use this one on my other wrist." Lifting the cuffs, they balanced on her outstretched index finger. "So, what's it going to be? I don't have all night. Someone's got an impending trip to depart for."

In spite of himself, a husky laugh escaped his lips. How in the hell was he supposed to resist? He'd imagined her bound and submissive to him so many times.

"Goddamnit, Arderin."

Pink lips pursed, and then her tongue appeared, lathering them with wetness. "Don't you want to fuck me like this?" Jangling the cuffs, she beckoned to him. "I won't tell anyone. It will be our secret."

Unable to control the urge to touch her, he skulked toward her. Fisting her thick hair in his hand, he pulled her head back, reveling in her gasp. "You're playing with fire, little girl."

"So, burn the hell out of me," she dared.

"You fucking bitch." Although the words were harsh, he was sure she could see the admiration in his eyes. Damn straight. He admired the hell out of her for rendering him unable to push her away. It was astounding that one so innocent could manipulate one as evil and cunning as he. But she'd always been able to burrow inside him, the little imp. Hating how much he wanted her, he squeezed her hair harder. "I won't be gentle if you're shackled."

That raven eyebrow arched again. "I'd be disappointed if you were."

Growling, he pulled her face to his, giving her a hard kiss. Licking her tongue when she extended it, he grabbed the handcuffs. Clutching her wrist, he attached it to the other bedpost. With a thought, he dematerialized his shirt, dark pants and boxer briefs. Standing beside the bed, he ran his hand over her stomach, his dick twitching against his abdomen when her muscles quivered.

"Your body is so beautiful," he whispered, sliding his hand down to cup her, the small tuft of dark hair almost tickling his palm. "When did you go through your change?"

"When I was twenty-two," she said, her eyes glassy as her head rested on the pillow. No wonder she had the body of a goddess. He'd never seen a female figure more perfect. Slender and soft, she had ripe, perky breasts and slightly flared hips. She was a fucking wet dream come true.

Breathing hard, he extended his third finger into her tight, wet little channel, reveling in her moan. Her back shot off the bed to clench his finger, and he felt himself shudder.

"Do you want more?"

"Yes."

"How many?"

Her eyes grew wide and her mouth opened as she panted,

"As many as you can."

He nodded and placed his palms on her inner thighs, spreading her legs as wide as they would go. Sliding his hand back over her mound, he inserted two fingers, spearing them into her. After a moment, he inserted three.

She gave as good as she got, undulating against his hand with her lithe frame. With his thumb, he rubbed her nub as his fingers drowned in her warmth.

"God, you're voracious," he said, as her skin began to glisten with sweat. "Good girl. Fuck my fingers." With his free hand, he caressed her stomach and then higher, stopping at her hardened nipple to tweak it. Unable to take the madness, he removed his fingers, licking every drop of her from them.

Crawling on the bed, he straddled her hips. Sky-blue eyes watched him, and he reveled in the image before him. Thin arms were stretched out and restrained, as if she was an offering to him made by an ancient tribe wanting to appease their god.

"Pull at your binds," he growled.

The cuffs clanked against the wood of the bedpost. Seeing her struggle, although he knew it was just fantasy, was extremely hot to him. After all, he was the son of the Dark Lord, and although he'd made a promise to his mother, the urges and fantasies had never ceased.

"I've dreamed of raping you so many times."

"I know," she said, breathless. "I saw the images."

"And yet you still give yourself to me, even though you see how evil I am. Why?"

Compassion filled her eyes. "You're not as evil as you pretend to be. We both know that. Otherwise, you never would have saved my life."

He shrugged. "Maybe I just did it to keep your brother on my good side, since he's married to Miranda and lets me stay here."

Her lips turned up into a sexy smile. "Tell yourself whatever you want. You saved me because you care for me. And deep down, you're a good person. Otherwise, you would've raped me the night you sent me down the river to Miranda."

Darkrip thought of that night, the first he'd ever seen her. Even then, he'd been consumed by her beauty. "You were so gorgeous under the oak tree. I wanted you so badly."

"Well, now you have me." Lifting her hips under him, a bold look flashed through her eyes. "You can fuck me as hard as you want, as long as you want. I'm yours. There are condoms in the right-hand pocket of my coat."

"Fuck that. I don't do condoms. I'll pull out."

"As a future physician, I'm obligated to tell you that you have a much lower rate of pregnancy if you wear a condom rather than using the pull-out method."

"Stop talking."

"Make me." Darting her tongue over her pink lips, she gyrated her hips again.

"Goddamnit," he whispered, stroking his shaft as he sat atop her. As he panted, the paleness of her skin called to him. Keeping one hand on his cock, he traced the line of freckles between her apple-ripe breasts with the pad of the finger of his free hand. "These are pretty."

"My breasts, or my freckles?" she asked, her voice scratchy.

"Both." Leaning over her, he spat between her breasts, rubbing the saliva so that it coated the skin between. Lowering his cock between her tits, he pushed them together and began moving his shaft back and forth, the friction causing the nerve-endings there to sizzle with pleasure.

Her eyes shuttered as she watched him. Groaning, she said, "That's so hot."

"You like watching me fuck your pretty breasts?" he asked.

"Yes," she whispered.

Increasing the pace, he twirled her nipples between his fingers as he pushed the ripe mounds together over his straining cock. Needing more, he rose on his knees, placing the head of his dick against her sexy-as-sin lips. "Open your mouth, princess."

A surge of dominance ran through him when she complied. Needing to feel her, he pushed back to her throat. "Take it all," he commanded. "Open your throat and spread your tongue around my cock as I move."

Stunning eyes locked onto his as she obeyed his directive. "Relax. I won't hurt you. If you're going to play with someone like me, you need to know how to take it."

That enraged her, as he knew it would. His little Vampyre couldn't resist a challenge. Opening her wet mouth and throat to him fully, she proceeded to give him the best blow-job of his life. Saliva dripped from her lips as he moved back and forth, her tongue seeming to swipe over every cell of the straining organ. Her head maneuvered around the movement of his hips, causing friction to shoot pleasure to every nerve in his body.

"You're fucking great at this, princess. Damn."

Pleasure shot through her irises, and he chuckled.

"I'm going to come in your mouth. I want you to swallow every drop. Understand?"

Dark curls bobbed against the pillow as she nodded. Inhaling a huge breath, he increased the pace, feeling his balls tighten. Jutting his hips into her face in a frenzied rhythm, he felt his seed start to spurt. Those eyes never left his, and he refused to close his, needing to watch her consume his release. Shouting, he came all over her tongue, pushing himself down her throat. Purring, her throat bobbed up and down as she swallowed.

Regaining the ability to breathe, Darkrip popped himself from her mouth. Not needing time to recover, thanks to the goddess's curse, he inched down her slender body. Placing himself between her thighs, he slid his arms under the backs of her knees. Lifting her legs and spreading them wide, he impaled her with one hard thrust.

"Oh, god," she cried, throwing her head back on the pillow. He pounded her relentlessly, the tight walls of her pussy choking his flesh.

"Yes," he said, gritting his teeth with the pleasure. "Take it. Take my fucking cock. It feels like it was made for you."

The perfect globes of her breasts jiggled up and down as he hammered her. Unable to resist the turgid little nubs, he dropped down and took one in his mouth.

"Use your teeth," she commanded, lifting her head to gaze at him.

Wanting to piss her off, he extended his tongue and licked her nipple instead.

She groaned and begged him for more. Acquiescing, he bit the sweet, tight point. Lapping it, he sipped away the sting.

"I'm in charge here, princess. Don't forget that. I give the orders."

Increasing the pace, he hammered her as hard and fast as he could, wanting to make her come so that she couldn't boss him around. As she gave him a glare of death, he lowered his head and bit her again.

"Yessss..." she moaned, throwing her head back on the pillow.

Chuckling, he kissed his way to the other nipple and clamped it between his teeth, pulling it away from her body but careful not to hurt her. A ragged cry escaped her lips as he sucked on the tiny nubbin.

"Come," he said, his teeth still around her nipple. Pinching the little bud with them, his cock battered the spot deep inside where he knew she felt the most pleasure.

"I am," she wailed, a deep flush rushing over her soft skin. "Oh, god..."

The muscles of her tight inner walls strangled him, and he gave over to the orgasm. Pulling out, he jetted his seed all over her stomach. Heaving large breaths, he collapsed over her.

They lay like that for several minutes. With a limp arm, Darkrip reached over to pull some tissues from the box on the bedside table, wiping his release away from her stomach. Tossing them to the floor, he relaxed over her. Since her arms were still shackled, he found himself missing them around him. Wanting to compensate for that, he slipped his arms under her and held her to him, resting his head between her breasts.

"Aw, how sweet," she said, panting above him. "I knew I'd figure out how to get you to cuddle with me. I just had to bind myself up like a damn circus acrobat."

Unable to control his laughter, he shook his forehead against her collarbone. "Shut up, Arderin."

She wiggled underneath him, and he held her closer, unable not to. Although he was loath to admit it, he loved snuggling with her. Sighing, he let himself enjoy the moment. His beautiful Arderin lay bound, her body sated under him, her nose nuzzling his short hair. For one who'd felt such pain in his life, it was a welcome moment of contentment.

Lifting her long legs, she encircled him with them. He was wrapped in her like the sweetest present. Squeezing her, he placed a kiss between her breasts.

"I feel too much for you," he murmured against her soft skin. "It's dangerous."

"I can take care of myself, thank you very much," she said against his head, rubbing the smooth skin of her cheek over his hair. "And I feel so much for you. It hurt me that you would leave without telling me."

Inhaling a deep breath, he lifted his face to hers. Sliding over her, he realigned their bodies and touched his lips to hers. Their tongues mated as he told his pounding heart to calm down. "I was afraid this was going to happen if I told you I was leaving. I can't control myself around you. It's extremely careless of me. I'm terrified that I finished inside you when we were together in the cave. I can't have children or a life that is in any way normal. You have to understand that."

The emotion in her eyes was so pure. "Would it be so terrible to try? I feel like we could have so much together. I don't care that his blood runs through you. You're your own man, and I think I'm falling for you."

"No," he said, shaking his head. Dread filled him. "You can't let yourself care for me. I'm extremely evil and not worthy of any of that. I only fucked you in the cave because I was half-dreaming and convinced we were already dead."

"You just said you cared for me—"

"No, Arderin," he interrupted, placing his forehead on hers. "It's not in the cards for me. You're a brilliant, amazing woman and will find someone who can build a life with you and give you a home and children. Let yourself have that. I want that for you."

Those stunning eyes filled with tears. "Undo the binds."

Her anguish coursed through him, and he wanted to die at how pure and innocent it was.

"Arderin—"

"Now."

Closing his eyes, he unlocked the cuffs from around her wrists. They popped open, and she lowered her arms, bringing her hands to cup his face. "Why won't you even consider it?" she asked, the gravel in her voice breaking his unfeeling heart. "Don't you want to be happy?"

He shook his head. "I don't have that option. I never did. The moment I was born, I was destined to a life of pain and suffering."

A lone tear slid down the perfect skin of her cheek, and the organ in his chest constricted with agony. "Arderin," he whispered, wiping the wetness with the pad of his thumb. "I thought this might happen. I don't want you to waste your time caring for me. I don't deserve it."

Her nostrils flared. "I'll care for whomever I want to. And right now, I find myself caring for you. So, screw you."

His lips curved, and he placed a sweet kiss on her lips. "I wish I could care for you back. But I can't. I don't want to hurt you."

They lay like that for several minutes, gazing into each other's eyes, stroking each other.

"I'm leaving at dawn. I have to convince Evie to come here and help us. I'm determined not to come back until I have. It will take some time."

She nodded, black curls bobbing behind her. "I'll miss you."

"Don't miss me. Make a life for yourself. If you care for me as you say you do, then, please, let yourself be happy. I want that for you more than anything."

She swallowed deeply. "I'm staying here with you tonight."

"No. Go back to the castle—"

"Are you still under the impression that you can tell me what to do? I thought you were smart enough to have given up on that by now."

Sighing, he shook his head, unable to stop his grin. "I probably should have."

The brightness of her smile took his breath away. She was the most magnificent creature he'd ever beheld. Reaching over, she turned off the bedside lamp, plunging them into darkness.

"Stay right there," she said, placing her thin arms around his shoulders and squeezing him tight. "I finally got you to cuddle with me willingly, and I want to fall asleep in your arms."

Realizing that arguing with her was futile, he let himself relax, pulling her into him as he shifted on his side. She rotated and shimmied the round globes of her ass into his still-hard shaft. Sliding his hand up her stomach, he cupped her shoulder as his arm rested between her breasts. Spooning her, he reveled in the smell of her hair and the rhythm of her breathing. Nuzzling her soft curls with his nose, he sank into her.

It was one of the first nights in his dark, tortuous life that he didn't have nightmares of his father raping his mother. Instead, he dreamed of her. Sitting under the sunset, laughing as they played in the green grass with the children they would never have.

* * * *

As dawn flirted with the sky through the curtained window, Darkrip rose to dress. Finished packing his small bag, he looked to the bed to find Arderin watching him.

"You can stay here as long as you want," he said, sitting beside her on the bed. "I don't mind if you come here while I'm gone."

She nodded, and his heart constricted at the sentiment in her eyes.

"Let me up," she said, pulling off the covers. Stalking to the coat that lay on the floor, she pulled it on and tightened the sash. Reaching in the pocket, she pulled out a tiny box.

"Come here," she said.

Powerless not to, he walked over to stand in front of her. Opening the box, she pulled out a long chain that held a ring as its charm.

"My mother had four rings that we were supposed to inherit when we turned eighteen. When she was killed, we each got one. Latimus chose the amethyst because it reminded him of Lila's eyes. Sathan took the diamond, and Miranda had it resized and now wears it on her middle finger. Heden and I were very young, so our caretakers split the remaining two between us."

She lifted the chain, the ring slightly swinging back and forth as it dangled between them. "Heden got the opal, and I got the emerald. It seems fitting since it matches your eyes." Grasping his hand, she placed the ring and the chain in his palm. "I want you to have it."

"No," he said, shaking his head. "This will go to the man you bond with one day."

Anger flashed in her stunning eyes. "I'll give it to whomever I want, and I'm giving it to you."

"No, Arderin—"

"Take it," she said, closing his fingers around the ring. "You saved my life. I wouldn't be here if it wasn't for you. There's such honor in that, even if you won't let yourself accept it. I want you to have it."

Darkrip's irises darted back and forth between hers. "No one's ever given me a gift before."

Sadness swamped her expression. "Oh, Darkrip. You deserve gifts. And love. And everything you want. I hate that you don't believe that."

"Believing things like that will get me killed."

Pink lips turned up into a sexy smile. "I'll save you. I'm pretty tough."

Breathing a laugh, he nodded. "You are. But I can't take it." He tried to place it back in her hand.

"Goddamnit," she said, grabbing it from him. "Stop fighting me on this." Clutching the chain with both hands, she tried to slide it over his head.

"Arderin—"

"I'll fucking shove it down your throat, or you can wear it like I intended. Which one will it be?" Stubbornness emanated from her passionate eyes and lifted chin.

Chuckling, he sighed, loving how dramatic she was. "Fine. Put it over my damn head."

She did, smoothing the chain over his chest and touching the ring with her slim fingers. "It's yours now. Take good care of it. Don't let your bitch sister kill you. I'd like to see you again."

Lifting his hands, he cupped her cheeks. "I don't deserve this, but thank you." Placing a soft kiss on her lips, he stared into her. "I wish I could have a different life. Be a different man. You deserve that. Be happy, Arderin. Don't waste time thinking of me. I'll give this back to you when I return."

He kissed her again, allowing himself to taste her as their tongues slid over each other's. And then, he dematerialized to the ether, needing to let her go. Not only for now, but forever.

Chapter 26

Arderin felt the emptiness of his retreat as she stood in the middle of Darkrip's tiny cabin. Rubbing her upper arms, she absently observed the room. Slowly walking around, she languidly snooped through his meager possessions. Already missing him, she left the cottage and began walking back to the main house.

The grass was wet and squishy under her sandaled feet. Smiling, she remembered him walking in on her in the gym the last time it poured. Would he work out while trying to find Evie? She wasn't sure, as the task was extremely important and would be his main priority. She hoped he retained his muscled six-pack. Even though he'd lost weight in the cavern, his body was freaking *hot*.

Faint light stretched out over the sky, and she stopped to lift her face. Closing her eyes, she inhaled a deep breath. Remembering their loving, she placed her hand over her heart. He'd been so sweet to her, cuddling her to his firm body afterward. He could fight it, but she knew he cared for her. Rubbing her chest, unable to deny it any longer, Arderin acknowledged her love for him. Smiling, she reveled in it, determined to make him love her back. While he was away, she would thoughtfully build a case for their future, resolute to sway him when he returned.

Resuming her walk, she imagined their children. They would have dark hair and be absolutely gorgeous. Yes, they would have Crimeous' blood—but they would also have the blood of Rina and Valktor, Calla and Markdor. Surely, all that goodness would prevail over any darkness. Firm in her belief, she approached the barracks.

Upon entering, she opened the chest where Latimus kept his articles of captivity and placed the handcuffs back inside. Hearing a noise behind her, she pivoted.

"What are you doing, Arderin?" Latimus sat in the shadows, off to her side, cleaning a rifle. His expression was lined with fury as he regarded her.

"Nothing," she said, lifting her chin. "I just borrowed those for a new yoga pose I've been working on."

Ever so slowly, he lowered the weapon, sitting it on the floor. Approaching her, he stopped a few inches away, forcing her to tilt her head back to retain eye contact.

"A yoga pose," he said, his tone flat.

"Yeah. So?"

"He's Crimeous' son. You know the consequences of being with him. Is that what you really want for your future?"

Lowering her eyes, she stared at his broad chest under his black t-shirt.

"I can't help it," she said, hating that tears were welling in her eyes. "I think I'm in love with him."

Her brother cursed, his body tensing even further. "He doesn't have the ability to love you back."

"You believed that about yourself with Lila for centuries and look what happened. You guys are so happy now."

"Lila isn't the child of an evil Deamon. Your children would have his blood. What if they can't squelch their evil? Are you prepared to have a child who murders? How would you live with yourself?"

Anger flashed through her. "You murder! All the time, in your battles. You're not evil."

His eyes narrowed. "I have a darkness that drives me in battle, and I've struggled with that for ages. It's nothing compared to what Darkrip has. Half of him is extremely malicious."

"He saved my life, Latimus," she said, pleading for him to understand. "It was over for me, and he saved me. There's such goodness in him. You have to trust me. I know what I'm doing."

Exhaling a large breath, he pulled her to him. Clutching her to his chest, he stroked her hair. "He's going to hurt you, little one. I'm afraid, when that time comes, I'll kill him. I can't live in a world with someone who causes my sister pain."

"He would never hurt me," she said, so firm in her belief of her man. "I know it deep inside."

"I hope you're right," he said, pulling back to gaze down at her. "Otherwise, a lot of shit is going to hit the fan. I hope you understand that your actions affect many others. He's essential in our cause to defeat his father, and I need him focused on that."

"He's focused, believe me. He just left for the ether and won't return until he finds her."

Latimus nodded and let her go. "I just worry for you. I want you to be happy."

"I know," she said, smiling up at him. "That's why you've always been my favorite brother."

He chuckled, and her eyebrows drew together. "Why are you here so early? I thought you'd be home for breakfast with the fam since Lila's turned you into a domesticated pansy."

"Shut up," he said, scowling. "She took Jack to see his Uncle Sam at Valeria. They left early, so I headed here to organize some stuff before training starts."

"Got it," she said, so happy for him. "You really love them so much."

"I do," he said with a nod. "She's such a beautiful person. I want you to find a man who's good inside and out. You deserve that."

"He *is* good," she said. "You'll see. Now, I need to go shower. We put those handcuffs to good use last night."

Latimus rolled his eyes. "Don't want to hear it. In my mind, you're still seven years old with scraped knees. If you tell me any more, I'll have to break his neck."

Laughing, she shook her head. "I love you. Thank you for protecting me. You have for so long. One day, the three of you are going to have to accept that there will be a man who claims me, and I'll no longer be yours to defend."

"Never. You're our sister, and we'll always guard you to the death. Now, go, before I hear any more and cut off his hands so he can't ever touch you again."

She bit her lip. "Please don't tell Sathan. He'll never understand."

"I won't. But I need you to be smart, Arderin. Your emotion clouds your judgement. Please, be wary."

"I will." With a smile, she pivoted and sauntered away, through the barracks. But not before she got in her last jab. "And don't think for one minute I didn't get the handcuff idea from Lila. You're not innocent in this, bro. You guys are kinky. Like, for real." Snickering, she imagined him glaring behind her.

"That's none of your business. Freaking women. Can't keep their damn mouths shut."

Lifting her hand in a wave, she chuckled as she entered the main house.

* * * *

Sadie rode the train, excited to spend the weekend at Astaria. Tordor was the cutest little baby, and she always loved seeing Miranda. Arderin had become one of her best friends, and she'd promised to take her to the main square on Saturday night to make some 'bad decisions.' Chuckling, she smiled and stared out the window into the dark tunnel.

Furrowing her brow, Sadie thought of Nolan. If she was honest, she was looking forward to seeing him as well. He was such a nice man and a phenomenal surgeon. Gazing at her right hand, she looked at the stubs that used to be her pinkie and fourth fingers. They had been burned in the Purges of Methesda all those centuries ago.

Not having the digits precluded her from doing the meticulous surgeries that Nolan could perform. Always desiring to be a surgeon, she'd watched him operate on so many of the wounded Slayer and Vampyre soldiers since the kingdoms united. She'd trained with many exceptional surgeons in the human world and had never met anyone as skilled as Nolan.

Long ago, she'd accepted that she would never become a great surgeon and had chartered her path to becoming proficient at other specialties. She was now experienced in many areas, including general medicine, trauma, psychology, obstetrics and gynecology, to name a few. Allowing pride to course through her, she acknowledged her hard work and accomplishment.

Nolan was always the first to compliment her skills as a physician. Lately, he'd also been dropping compliments about her personally. That her eyes were pretty, that she had a nice tan, that he liked seeing her short brown hair without the ball cap on. Extremely uncomfortable with that, she always averted her eyes and changed the subject.

After all, her hair only covered half her head. The other half was so severely burnt that the hair follicles had died long ago. In fact, every nerve ending and skin cell on the right side of her body was dead. When she'd been burned, she might as well have died along with them.

Realizing ages ago that no one would ever possibly be attracted to her, she'd resigned herself to helping others. Understanding that she'd lost the ability to ever have a husband or family, she dedicated her life to healing people and ensuring their happiness.

Healing gave her a great peace. If she wasn't a physician, she didn't know how she would survive. It was her only purpose on Etherya's Earth. Happy she'd found the small piece that could sustain some sort of contentment for her, she grinned as the train pulled into the station at Astaria.

She was surprised to find Nolan waiting for her on the platform at the top of the stairs.

"Arderin told me you were arriving around noon. I thought you might want to grab some lunch with me."

She studied him, wondering why he was going out of his way to greet her. "I just assumed I'd settle in my room and then go examine Miranda."

"Well, I'm starving, and since Vampyres don't eat, I figured you might want to eat with me. Here," he said, extending his hand, "give me your suitcase."

Gingerly, she placed it in his hand. "It's not heavy. I can carry it."

"Although I haven't seen my mother in three centuries, I'm pretty sure she would kill me if I didn't offer to carry a lady's bag." White teeth seemed to glow as he beamed at her. "Now, come on. I set up a table for us behind the kitchen."

He led them through the barracks and into the foyer.

"Let me set this in your room. Hang out for a sec." Jogging up the stairs, he set the suitcase in the room that Miranda had prepared for her, located at the first door on the right. Trudging back down, he extended his hand to her. "Ready to eat?"

Lifting her stubbed hand, she brushed him off, confused by his behavior. "I can't really hold hands. But yeah, I could eat."

Nolan's brown eyes flitted over her face, half-hidden under her blue baseball cap. "Okay. Come on."

He steered them through the expansive kitchen and then through a door that led outside. A picnic table was set with a red and white checkered cloth. A nice spread of food sat on top, along with a bottle of white wine.

"I asked Glarys to prepare enough for us to have leftovers later, especially since Arderin's taking you drinking tomorrow night. You'll need some hangover food for sure."

Lowering, he gestured for her to sit across from him. Unable to do anything but comply, Sadie sat on the wooden seat. Lifting one of the pieces of sliced bread, he slathered mayonnaise over it with a knife and proceeded to stack it with bologna, salami, sliced cheese and a piece of lettuce. Lifting the yellow mustard bottle, he swirled some yellow lines on top. Stacking another piece of bread over the contents, he placed it on the plate that sat in front of him.

"Oh, sorry," he said, picking up one of the wine glasses that sat by the bottle. "Should've poured us some wine first. I'm just so hungry." He poured a generous amount into each glass, setting one in front of her. Lifting it, he smiled. "A toast?"

"Um, sure," she said, lifting her glass.

"To the two best physicians in the immortal world." Clinking his glass with hers, he smiled. "I won't mention that we're the only physicians. Let's just consider ourselves awesome." Taking a sip, he set the glass down and lifted the sandwich, taking a large bite.

Chewing, he regarded her thoughtfully. "Aren't you going to eat?" he asked after he'd swallowed.

Eyes darting around the table, Sadie acknowledged that she was indeed hungry. But she was also quite unsettled. Unable to account for his strange behavior, she tentatively reached for a piece of bread. Holding it with her left hand, she used the thumb and two working fingers of her right hand to hold the knife and lather it with mayo. After loading the contents and stacking the bread, she took a big bite.

"Good stuff," she said, swallowing it down. "Thanks. Didn't realize you'd planned to have a picnic today."

"I wanted to sit and hang with you," he said, shrugging as he took another bite. After swallowing, he said, "I rarely get to be in your presence unless we're operating or stitching someone up. It's nice to just chill."

"Yeah," she said, eating her sandwich. Not being that great at small talk, she listened to the birds chirp, hoping she wasn't boring him to death.

"So, tell me about your family. Do they live at Uteria?"

"My father was taken in a Vampyre raid about seven centuries ago. My mother never recovered from his abduction and died from pneumonia shortly thereafter. I was an only child, so that left me with no family."

"Wow," he said, setting his food down. "I'm really sorry. I had no idea."

"It's okay," she said, shrugging. No one ever really asked her about herself. It made her quite uncomfortable. "Miranda gave me a room at the castle, and I've stayed there ever since. It's a nice home, and she's been so wonderful to me."

"I'm sure you miss them," he said, lifting his sandwich to take another bite.

Sadie's teeth gnawed the unburnt side of her bottom lip. "They were ashamed of my burns. I don't blame them. They're so ugly. I always thought they wished I'd died in the Purges. So, yeah, I guess I miss them, but they weren't really nice people."

His brown irises swam with compassion. "Well, that sucks. What a bunch of assholes. Your burns aren't ugly. It's absurd that they let you believe that."

"It's true," she said, taking a sip of her wine.

"No, it isn't."

"Honestly, I don't really want to talk about this. Can we talk about something else? Why don't you tell me about your family? Sounds like your mom was a stickler for manners."

Nolan's eyes tapered, contemplating her, and then, he nodded. "Okay, I'll let you change the subject. For now. Yes, my dear mother was a stickler for manners and anything else proper. You have to remember that I followed Sathan through the ether back in the Georgian era of England. I grew up in the seaside town of Brighton. Everything back then was so proper. A lady wasn't permitted to show her ankles or go anywhere without a bonnet. It would've been scandalous."

She felt the features of her face scrunch. "That's so limiting. We were always lucky to have Miranda in our kingdom. She fought for women's rights for centuries, challenging her father when he was being a stick in the mud. I can't imagine that."

"Yup," he said, nodding. "It was all very rigid. But there was also a civility and chivalry that permeated every aspect of life. For example, if I was to court you, I'd have to ask your father for permission."

"But he's dead," she said, raising her unburnt eyebrow.

"So, I'd have to ask your next of kin. Or whomever you consider to be the closest. It would have to be a male though. Women had no power in that era. It was quite ludicrous."

"Hmmm," she said, looking to the blue sky. "Then, I guess you'd have to ask Kenden. He's about the closest thing I have to a brother."

"Then, I would ask him for permission to court you and take you all about town in my regal carriage. As a young, unmarried lady, I'd want everyone to see I was courting you so that all the men would know you were off-limits."

Enjoying their banter, she smiled. "Such a nice fantasy. Although, I'm sure the women you used to court were so beautiful. You'd want to make sure that no one saw me in your carriage."

His expression changed in an instant, his features falling into a mask of what appeared to be indignation.

"I'm sorry. Did I say something to offend you?" She didn't understand what she could've possibly said to affect him so.

"Why would you say that about yourself? If I was lucky enough to have you in my carriage, I would drive around the town ten times to make sure everyone saw that you were mine."

The words caused her heart to beat furiously in her chest and blood to pound through her scarred body. Why would he say something like that to her? Of course, it could never be true. She was so hideous that she'd given up on ever being attractive centuries ago. She hadn't worn makeup or nice clothes or grown her hair more than a few inches in ages.

Anger welled in her belly, and she wondered if he had an agenda. Was he upset that she saw his female patients at Astaria? Perhaps he preferred practicing alone. She'd always thought that he liked working with her, but she'd misread people before.

"I don't know why you're placating me, but I'm not going to sit here and let you say things to me that aren't true. If you'll excuse me, I'm going to go unpack."

Standing, she left the table, all but running to her room. Unable to stop her tears, she ignored his cries for her to stay.

* * * *

Arderin found Nolan in the infirmary, sitting on a stool and writing in a chart. Looking up, he smiled at her. "I started a chart for Sadie, so we can document her progress after she begins the regimen with the serum."

"Awesome," Arderin said, unable to control her grin. "I'm so excited. She's examining Miranda now and should be down shortly to finish her notes."

Nodding, he inhaled a breath. His expression turned pensive.

"What's wrong?"

Sighing, he ran a hand through his brown hair. "Are we making a mistake? We never stopped to ask if this was what *she* wanted. We always just assumed. Maybe she likes her burns. She's had them for centuries."

"Why would she like her burns? They hold her back from having a full life. I think she'll jump at the chance to heal them."

"You're smart enough to know that her burns don't hold her back from anything. *She* holds herself back. She uses them as an excuse to hide. I'm not sure she's equipped to live in a world where she's seen as normal. We should've thought of the psychological consequences of offering her this treatment. I'm kicking myself now."

"Why?" she asked, approaching him and leaning her hip on the counter. "What happened?"

He told her about their lunch and her subsequent crying jag and storm-off.

"Crap," Arderin said, biting her lip. "I didn't even think of the possibility that she wouldn't want the treatment. What should we do?"

"I don't know—"

Sadie's sneaker-padded footsteps sounded as she entered the infirmary. Smiling, she said, "Hey, Arderin. I just finished examining Miranda and Tordor. Everything's fine." Approaching Nolan, she handed him the chart. "I made notes upstairs. Everything's complete. We should be all set."

"Great," he said, taking the file and setting it on the counter.

"What's under the microscope?" she asked, lifting to her toes to glance at the eyepieces of the device.

Arderin gave Nolan a look. His shrug and wide eyes indicated that they should go ahead with their original plan.

"It's actually something we've been working on," Arderin said, smiling hopefully.

"What for?"

"Take a look," Nolan said, standing and aligning himself behind her. Grabbing her shoulders, he gently pushed her toward the microscope. "The specimen's already there."

Giving one last curious look at Arderin, Sadie placed her eyes over the microscope. "It's burnt tissue."

"Yes," Nolan said, reaching for a syringe filled with serum. "Now, look at this." Removing the slide, he placed a drop of the serum on the tissue and deposited the slide back under the scope.

Lowering her head, Sadie observed the specimen. Gasping, she brought her fingers to her lips. "It's regenerating!"

Nolan smiled, and Arderin felt that everything might just be okay. "Yes. Isn't it awesome? It can regenerate cells that have been long dead. It's a huge advance forward for any burn victim."

"Oh, my god," Sadie said, turning and lifting her hands to her cheeks. "I can think of so many soldiers who need this. Now that we have the SSW, Crimeous has turned it on about twenty of our soldiers, singeing their skin. I've healed them the best I can but this will completely cure them. You guys! This is fantastic!"

Arderin glanced at Nolan, happy that her friend was excited but worried she didn't understand the full implication of the serum. "Yes. And it could regenerate skin on anyone who was burned before the SSW too."

"Oh, yes," Sadie said, smiling broadly. "I can think of thirty or so Slayers off the bat who've been burned in house fires over the centuries. And a few welders who have been burned on the job. How exciting! I get to tell them there's a way to heal their skin! How did you guys do this? It's amazing!"

Arderin began to realize that Sadie was so selfless and so resigned to her burns that she wouldn't even consider herself as a candidate for the serum. "It's a combination of self-healing Vampyre fluids, CBD and other things. But the final ingredient was the formula I lifted from a genetics lab in Houston. It's the reason I went to the human world. I wanted to get the formula so Nolan and I could give the serum to you as a gift. We want so badly for you to live a normal life, Sadie, and we felt it would help heal your skin."

Every one of Sadie's features seemed to fall to the ground, and Arderin knew she'd made a terrible mistake. Dread filled her as she watched her friend's eyes flash with anger.

"So, you don't think I live a normal life? Is that what you're saying?"

"Of course not," Nolan chimed in, turning her to face him by touching her shoulder. "We care about you and thought that giving you the gift of regenerating your skin would be incredible. I can see now that we might have misjudged, but I assure you, we're coming from a good place. We want you to be happy, Sadie."

Arderin's eight-chambered heart shattered into a thousand pieces as twin tears rolled down her dear friend's cheeks. "I'm sorry you all think I'm so ugly that you need to travel to the human world to fix me. How awful it must be to see me like this. Well, I'll save you the trouble. I'm going home."

"Sadie," Arderin said, grabbing her unburnt arm. "Please, don't go. I'm so sorry I messed this up. I love you. I was just trying to do something nice for you. Please, don't hate me."

"How could you?" Sadie asked, fury in her tone. "You're one of the only people who tells me I'm perfect just the way I am. Have you been lying to me this whole time? Am I that hideous to you?" Shaking Arderin off her arm, she stomped out of the infirmary.

Placing her face in her hands, Arderin began to cry. "Fuck! I feel terrible."

"Let me go after her," Nolan said, squeezing her shoulder. Her body wracked with sobs, she watched Nolan jog from the room.

Chapter 27

Nolan caught up with Sadie as she was about to ascend the steps leading out of the dungeon. Grabbing her burnt arm, he turned her. "Sadie, please. Let me explain. We only wanted to help."

"Let go. You're hurting me." Angry, she shook off his grip.

Letting his arm fall to his side, he felt his own anger begin to swell in his gut. "You can't pull that off with me, Sadie. I'm a doctor, remember? I know that you don't have any nerve endings left in your arm, or anywhere else in that half of your body, so feeling pain there is impossible. How many times have you lied and told others you felt pain to keep people from touching you?"

"Screw you!" she said, wiping the tears from her face with both hands. "No one ever wants to touch me, so who cares? It's easier to lie than to remember what I look like."

"Why do you want to lie? To yourself and to me and to the world? It's time for you to stop, Sadie. This life you've created for yourself is a fabrication. You need to face the world as the person you were meant to be."

"What do you know? You don't know me. You don't know what I've been through. How many people over the years have made fun of me and thrown rocks at me and called me worse names than you can imagine? You have no idea!"

"No, I don't," he said, taking a step toward her. "All I know is that you're the kindest person I've ever met, and you put everyone before yourself. There are two people who care for you very much who are trying to put you first for once. You need to let yourself accept that there are people who love you for you."

"No one loves me," she said, her face seeming to glow in the dimness of the dungeon. "And I'm fine with that. I've been fine with that for centuries. I don't appreciate you both digging up old wounds that I tried to bury ages ago."

"Holding on to old wounds won't bring you happiness. You need to be strong enough to let them go. Someone as kind and amazing as you should be loved by a good man and a worthy family. It's time you let yourself believe that."

A harsh laugh escaped her lips. "Like any man would ever want to touch me. I'm disgusting."

Unable to stop himself, he grabbed the V of her hooded sweatshirt where the zipper separated. Pulling her to him, he wrapped his arm around her waist. She gasped, her face a mask of confusion.

"Take off your hat," he said, hearing the growl in his voice.

"Why?" Her throat bobbed as she swallowed thickly.

"Because I'm going to kiss you."

Her one perfect nostril flared. "I only have half my lips. It's impossible."

Grabbing the brim of her hat, he flung it to the floor. "Then, I'd better make it twice as good." Pulling her to him, he placed his lips on hers.

She fell limp in his arms, and his heart hurt for her, feeling the fear course through her body.

"Don't be scared," he whispered against her lips. "It's just me. Ol' human Nolan. I'm insignificant to immortals. Just remember your superiority over me and kiss me back."

He felt her relax a bit and breathe a laugh into his mouth. "I don't know how."

"Push your lips against mine and move them. And if you're feeling really bold, you can stick your tongue inside my mouth. Now, let's try it."

Cementing his lips to hers, he moved them across the silky unburnt side. The burnt side offered a natural opening, since they didn't quite fit together, and he took the opportunity to slide his tongue inside. Moaning, he found her wet tongue and lathered it with his. She placed her thin arms around his neck and pulled him in. Shyly, she touched her tongue to his, causing him to grow thick and turgid inside his dress pants.

Rotating his head, he went for another angle, loving how she panted into him. Gingerly, she extended her tongue over his bottom lip, into his mouth, battling with his. Their lips mated and consumed each other's for a small infinity. Finally, he lifted his head. Her magnificent eyes, filled with bursting colors of yellow, brown and green, smoldered back at him.

"Who says you can't kiss? That was unbelievable."

She shook her head. "I guess I just assumed. No one's ever tried to kiss me before."

"Well, you're pretty fantastic at it," he said, nipping at her bottom lip. "I'd really like to try again one day soon."

"You would?" The mystified expression on her face was so genuine that he almost laughed.

"Yes. I definitely would. You're rather remarkable, Sadie. I wish you'd let yourself believe it."

"I don't know what to say to that. This is crazy. I'm pretty sure I'm dreaming and will wake up at Uteria needing a cold shower."

Laughing, he let her go. Reaching down, he picked up her baseball cap and placed it on her head. "You're so cute with the cap, but I love seeing your hair. You should show it more."

"The burnt half of my scalp is so ug—"

"No," he said, placing his fingers over her lips. "We're not going to use words like ugly and hideous and disgusting anymore. They're beneath you. I've never met anyone as beautiful as you, inside and out. I won't let you talk that way about yourself."

"Who are you?" she asked, her expression sincerely confused.

"I'm someone who cares about you. And so does Arderin. She risked her life to get that formula for you and almost died. You can distort the reasons for her efforts, or admit that she did it because she loves you and wants to do everything in her power to see you happy."

"I just don't understand why you guys would go out of your way for me like this. I haven't done anything for you."

"You've done so much for me, Sadie. You have no idea. I'd become a robot in the way I practiced medicine, drowning in my misery at being stuck in this world. You reminded me that healing is about the patient. That doing everything we can to help them recover and be the person they were before their injuries is our main priority. It's so humbling, and I'm ecstatic you came along. I'm not sure you can truly understand the gift you've given me. I want so badly to give one back to you."

Lowering her eyes, she searched the ground, kicking it with the toe of her sneaker. "I truly appreciate it, Nolan." Lifting her gaze to his, it was filled with compassion. "And I didn't realize how unhappy you were here. I'm so sorry. I'd really like to help you change that, if I can."

"See?" he asked, smiling. "You always shift the subject to someone else. It's very nice, but why don't we agree to help each other? Can we do that?"

The corners of her lips turned up, making her look so pretty. He wished that she could see herself as he saw her. As a clinician, he'd seen so many scars and wounds that he was unfazed by them. When he looked at her, all he saw was her smooth, tanned skin, gorgeous eyes and white teeth.

"Okay, let's do that."

"Good." Extending his hand, he grabbed her burnt one. "You can hold onto me with your three primary fingers. Don't give me that nonsense about not being able to hold hands." Biting her lip, she laced her three fingers through his. "C'mon, let's go soothe Arderin. You hurt her pretty good."

"Crap," Sadie said, her eyes glassy. "I feel awful."

"Well, there's no time like the present to make it up to her." Pulling her hand, he dragged her to the infirmary.

* * * *

Arderin gave Sadie a blazing hug, repeating how beautiful and special she was. She seemed to calm down a bit and understand that their intentions were pure.

"I really appreciate you guys thinking of me," she said, her always-genuine expression making Arderin's heart constrict in her chest. "I'd like to try the serum, but I just need some time. Is that okay?"

"Take all the time you need," Nolan said, reaching down to squeeze her hand. *Bingo*, Arderin thought. Those two were going to end up together. She just knew it.

Later, Sadie joined her, Sathan, Miranda and Heden for dinner. The nice nanny also joined them, feeding Tordor from his bottle while they all laughed and enjoyed each other's company.

As she sat at the table, she thought of Darkrip. Images of him holding her, kissing her between her breasts, and telling her he cared for her flooded her. He'd only been gone a few days, and she missed him so.

Saturday, she took Sadie out bar-hopping in Astaria's main square. Surprised to hear that her friend had never done shots, she quickly ordered two Fireballs. And then two more. And two more after that.

Being quite larger than Sadie, she'd thrown the little Slayer over her shoulder and carried her home, laughing at what a lightweight she was. After helping her into bed, Arderin sat on the side, holding a glass of water.

"Come on, Sadie," she said, holding the water to her mouth. "I promise this will make you feel better. Sit up a bit and take these Advil too."

Complying, Sadie downed the water and swallowed the pills.

"No more," she said, sinking into the pillow.

"Okay." Arderin chuckled and rubbed her hand on her friend's forehead. "Do you need anything else?"

"A do-over for tonight? I'm going to be so sick tomorrow."

"I'll take care of you. Don't worry."

Sadie's gorgeous hazel eyes studied her. "You'd be such a good mom. I just realized that. You're so caring. You should have a baby."

Arderin placed her hand over her abdomen. Was it possible that she was pregnant already? She'd only had one shot tonight, surreptitiously asking the bartender to fill her shot glasses with iced tea instead of Fireball. A bit surprisingly, she found herself hoping that she was indeed pregnant. That would have to force Darkrip to face his feelings for her, wouldn't it?

"Thank you, sweetie," she said, pulling up the covers to her chin. "Do you need anything else? Besides about ten hours of sleep?"

"Nolan kissed me," she said, her eyes drooping. "Why would he do that?"

Arderin couldn't contain her smile. "Because he thinks you're beautiful, just like I do. I knew it."

"How can he think that? I'm so gross."

"Stop it. You're astonishing, Sadie. You have to tell me when you guys bone. It's gonna be so awesome. Can't wait!"

Laughing, she closed her eyes and snuggled into the bed. "I hope so. He's so handsome."

Her body relaxed, and soft, slow breaths began to exit her lips. She looked so peaceful and pretty, and Arderin's chest swelled with glee that Nolan had made a move. She deserved all the happiness in the world.

The next day, she made sure Sadie got to the train platform safely. The weekend died down, and the week began. Arderin helped Sathan as he addressed the governors and council members from each compound at the annual summit he always held at Astaria. He seemed thrilled that she was taking her royal duties more seriously. He wanted to get the councils connected on social media, so she helped them create pages and accounts for each compound.

As the days rolled by, Arderin found herself becoming bored at Astaria. Not knowing if she was pregnant, she desperately wanted to go visit Lila and Latimus at Lynia. Understanding the risk that posed, she busied herself helping Nolan see Slayer patients in his clinic. Her thoughts often strayed to Darkrip, and she found herself missing him terribly.

Where was he in the human world? Had he found Evie? Did he think of her at all? As she did yoga each morning, she would send him positive thoughts, hoping they would reach him through the ether. At night, she would hold her pillow to her chest, wishing it was the soft skin of his forehead upon her collarbone. Anticipation at seeing him again swamped her. She hoped he would return soon. Otherwise, she was sure her heart might break from missing him so.

Chapter 28

Darkrip stood atop the mountain, breathing in the fresh winter air. Frustrated, he tried to let the crispness soothe him. Sadly, it was no use. He'd been in the human world for weeks now, searching every area that Evie could possibly be, but he'd still come up empty.

He knew that she would cover her tracks well, but this was an entirely different level. If he didn't know better, he'd think she wasn't in the human world at all. Irritated at his inability to find her, he decided that he was wasting his time. He needed to get back to the immortal world and update Miranda that her trail had gone cold. Having the help of the council might point him in the direction of something he was missing.

Transporting himself to the spot where he'd entered the human world, he walked through the thick ether. Once through, he closed his eyes, locating Miranda. She was at Uteria. Lowering his lids, he materialized to the royal office chamber at the main castle.

She was sitting at her desk, furiously scribbling on the paperwork that she always complained she hated doing. Grinning, the joy of seeing her swished through him.

"Hey," she said, lifting her head and giving him her always brilliant smile. Standing, she jogged to him and threw her arms around his neck. Emotion for her, pure and true, coursed through his muscular frame. "You're back."

"Hey, yourself. Mired in paperwork, huh?" He motioned his head toward the desk.

"It's awful," she said, scrunching her nose. "Why do people need a license to own a pet? Just feed it and keep it alive. What the hell? I hate this crap."

Chuckling, he shook his head. "You're an amazing queen, but this stuff comes along with the territory. Can't Sathan do it?"

"We have a deal that he does it for the Vampyre kingdom, and I do it here. Although, I did carry his baby for over eleven months, so maybe I can guilt him into doing some for me. Good thinking. So, what did you find?" Grabbing his hand, she pulled him to sit in the chair in front of her desk. Walking behind, she sat in the leather-backed chair, facing him.

"I couldn't find her," he said, shaking his head. "I looked absolutely everywhere. Her condo in France has been sold. The new owners were nice enough to let me look around once I told them I was her brother. Nothing. I went to Japan, North Carolina, Italy, Africa. There's no trace of her. I'm not even sure she's in the human world anymore."

Miranda brought her hand to her lips, fingers tapping. "Do you think she's come back here?"

He shrugged. "I don't know. She hates it here, but it's possible."

"Where would she go? She has no ties here."

"It's feasible she's biding her time, studying us from afar. I'm praying that she doesn't approach my father. If he realizes how strong she is, he could try to sway her to fight with him. If she aligns with him, we're all doomed."

Inhaling a deep breath, Miranda looked out the window. "Okay, I need to talk to Sathan. I'll also speak to Heden to see if there's something he can build that can track her energy. Perhaps if we get an infrared energy imprint of you, we can look for that imprint in our world. She would have your same energy pattern, right?"

"More or less."

"Okay. Give me a day or two. In the meantime, do you want to stay here with me a few days? I have plenty of room and lots of expensive wine that I can finally drink now that I've had the baby. Sathan's at Astaria, and I won't get back there for a few days."

Realizing that he wanted to spend time with her, he nodded. "I'd like that."

Smiling, she gestured across the desk. "Let me finish this crap, feed Tordor and then we'll go out for a ride. I haven't ridden Majesty in a while, and it's gorgeous today. I have a fine horse that I can give you."

"Sounds good. Can I use your gym?"

"Down the stairs from the main foyer. You'll find it. I'll see you in a bit."

Heading downstairs, he used the bathroom beside the gym to change, pulling the clothes from his bag. As he rustled inside, he pulled out the folded white papers. They were the medical school applications that Arderin had procured from the human world. He hadn't been able to toss them for some reason.

The notes she'd written to her brothers were scrolled on the backs of the pages in sprawling cursive. Reading them, Darkrip remembered the helplessness he'd felt in the cave. Every time he'd contemplated giving up hope, Arderin had been there, encouraging him to forge ahead. Smiling at her strength, he stuffed the pages in his bag. She might want them as a reminder of how precious life was and how lucky they'd been to survive. Tying his sneakers, he located the treadmill and hopped on.

* * * *

Arderin screamed every single curse word she knew into the porcelain bowl of the toilet. Every last one. Then, inhaling a huge breath, she proceeded to vomit the rest of her guts out. Exhausted, she sat back, leaning against the wall. Lifting her fingers, she began to count.

She'd had one period in the cave. Then, she'd slept with Darkrip about two weeks after that, although it was hard to be precise since time had been quite indiscernible in the dim lair. Two weeks ago, she'd had some spotting and assumed that was her monthly cycle. Her body had gone through trauma with the lack of Slayer blood, so she wasn't alarmed at the light period. Despair had wracked her when she realized she wasn't pregnant with Darkrip's child, but she also accepted that it allowed them to start fresh. When he came home, she would work furiously to secure his love, not stopping until he accepted that they were meant for each other.

What if the prior spotting wasn't a period at all? Holy hell.

Cleaning herself up and brushing her teeth, she padded down to the infirmary. Thankfully, Nolan was absent. Looking at her watch, she realized it was mid-day, so he was most likely eating lunch. Grabbing multiple pregnancy tests from the cabinet above the counter, she went into the nearby bathroom and peed on one of the sticks. Several minutes later, she read the results. Positive. *Holy crap.*

Deciding to be thorough, she took another test. And then another. Finally, after six tests, she allowed it to sink in. She was pregnant. With the child of the son of the Dark Lord. Whom she was completely and totally in love with, and who wanted nothing to do with her. Fucking great.

Sighing, she threw the last test in the waste basket and washed up. Exiting the door, she saw Nolan sitting at the counter, writing in a chart.

"Hey," he said, "I didn't realize you were down here. I'm updating Sadie's chart now. She's using the serum on her forearm, and so far, the results are astounding. If this keeps up, she'll continue using it on other parts of her body. I'm so excited for her."

"Me too," Arderin said, genuinely happy that the formula was working for her friend. "I just came down here to...um..."

"Take some pregnancy tests?" he said, gesturing to the shelves above. "I realized that half a dozen are missing from the cabinet."

"Yeah. I wanted to be sure."

Standing, he came over and placed his hands on her shoulders.

"Are you okay?" Concern laced his handsome brown eyes.

Nodding, she pulled him into an embrace. "I just have to figure some stuff out. I can do it. I think the most important one is how to get him to love me back. It's not going to be easy."

His hand rubbing against her hair was so soothing. "Who couldn't love you back? You're brilliant and gorgeous. I'm sure he's already bone-deep in love with you. He just won't admit it to himself. You just need to give him time to accept it on his own terms."

She lifted her head to look into his eyes. "I hope so. I'll die if he doesn't love me back. I want so badly to build something with him."

"I know," Nolan said, wiping away the tear that ran down her cheek. "It's okay. I'm here if you need me."

Smiling, she arched her eyebrow. "You kissed Sadie."

Chuckling, he nodded. "I did."

"That's so awesome. You two would be great together."

"I hope so. She's a bit skittish. I'll have to see if I can win her over."

"You can do it. I know how lonely you've been here. I want so badly for you to find love."

"How can I be lonely when I have my bright little student around all the time? You've kept me sane."

Hugging him again, she reveled in what a good man he was. Stepping back, she winked at him. "Keep me updated. I want to hear all the juicy details. Our girl needs some good lovin'."

Laughing, he shook his head. "A gentleman never kisses and tells. Where are you headed?"

"I'm going to ask Lila if I can come visit for a few days. She's always been able to see things in a way that I can't. I need her advice."

Concern clouded his expression. "Is it safe for you to leave Astaria?"

Arderin sighed. "Probably not, but I'm bored as hell and am going to go completely insane if I don't get a change of scenery. Latimus knows about me and Darkrip. I'll get him to help me travel safely. He owes me, after all I did to help him woo Lila."

"Wow. Can't imagine he took the news that his baby sister might be pregnant with the Dark Lord's grandchild very well."

She scoffed. "Better than Sathan would've taken it—that's for damn sure. Don't tell anyone else. Only Latimus knows, which means Lila knows," she said, rolling her eyes. "They tell each other everything."

"You keep asking me not to tell your secrets. It's giving me a complex. I'd never betray your trust, Arderin."

"I know," she said, beaming as she squeezed his upper arm. "Sorry. I'm a mess. I'll blame it on *pregnancy brain*. That's a thing, right?"

Chuckling, he shook his head. "Not sure, but we'll say it is for argument's sake. Be careful, Arderin."

Giving him a peck on the cheek, she exited the infirmary.

* * * *

Arderin arrived at Lynia's train station, excited to see Lila. The two soldiers that Latimus had tasked to accompany her from Astaria ascended the stairs beside her. Breaching the top step, two more soldiers met her, took her bag and helped her into a four-wheeler. Starting the engine, they began the ten-minute trek to Lila and Latimus' home. Latimus had informed her that there would be twenty soldiers protecting the house. They were all armed with SSWs and ready to pounce if Crimeous made an appearance. Vowing not to let the bastard stop her from living, she inhaled the fresh air, eager to see her best friend.

Arriving at their home, she observed the pretty purple flowers that grew around the foundation. Latimus had them planted for Lila, one more romantic gesture that had convinced Arderin he was a romantic sap. The two-story house had a large wrap around porch. White shutters encased the windows, and the sound of a small creek could be heard gurgling behind. Tall trees surrounded the creek, giving them a nice bit of privacy and space. Arderin knew her brother hated being around lots of people and large social gatherings. Since he craved solace, it seemed a fitting place for them to build their family.

Hurtling up the stairs, she threw her arms around Lila when she opened the front door.

"Hey, sweetie," her friend said, her voice always so melodious. "Wow, that's some greeting."

"I'm so happy to see you," Arderin said, running her hand down Lila's soft blond hair. "We have so much to catch up on."

"Well, Jack won't be home from school for a few hours, so you can tell me all the juicy details." Walking into the kitchen, Arderin set her bag on the counter.

"Do you want some wine?" Lila asked, holding a bottle of pinot noir.

"My stomach's been jacked lately," Arderin said, rubbing her belly. "Can I maybe just have some Sprite?'

"Sure. I have some in the fridge. It's Jack's favorite." Opening the refrigerator, she poured her some of the soda, a glass of wine for herself, and they headed out to the porch.

"If we hear anything, it's best to head to the bunker immediately," Lila said. "For now, there are soldiers everywhere, even though we can't see them. I say, we relax and enjoy the beauty of the sun."

"Sounds perfect," Arderin said, squeezing her hand.

Lowering into two of the white rocking chairs that lined the front porch, Arderin sighed, observing the rolling mountains in the distance. "It's so gorgeous here," she said, looking at Lila. "You guys have created such a magnificent life for yourselves. I'm so happy for you."

Lila's expression turned wistful. "I can't take credit for the house. That was all Latimus. It was so romantic. I can't believe how sweet and thoughtful he is."

Arderin snorted. "My brother is not sweet. I don't know what the hell you did to him. I think you gave him a love lobotomy or something. It's amazing."

Lila's harmonious laugh surrounded them. "He's always been so thoughtful and caring. You know that because he always loved you most of all. I just helped him show it a bit more."

"Well, it's unbelievable. How did you do it? I need advice."

"Really?" Her perfect blond eyebrow arched. "Did you finally get around to saying yes to Naran?"

Huffing a breath through her lips, she waved her hand. "As if. He's nice and everything, but, good god, boning him would be like boning a plank of wood. Sorry, but no thanks."

Lila laughed, shaking her head. "Then, who?"

Arderin gave her a sardonic look. "Don't play dumb. I know you and my brother tell each other everything. It's gross and cute all at the same time. He must've told you that Darkrip banged me in the cave."

Lila chewed on her bottom lip, contemplative. "Yes, he told me. I wish you had. Losing your virginity is such a big step. I wish I could've been there for you."

Arderin clenched her hand. "I needed to process it on my own. For a while anyway. But now, I'm here, and I need your advice. Like, really bad. I've created a dilemma, and I'm scared shitless."

Inhaling a large breath, her lavender irises seemed to glow. "Is that why you're not drinking wine?"

Arderin felt her eyes well. "Yes," she said, swallowing thickly. "Damn it, Lila. What the hell am I going to do?"

Setting her glass on the wooden railing, Lila stood. Pulling Arderin into her embrace, she rubbed her hair as she cried into her shoulder. "There, there. Don't make yourself sick. It's all going to work out. Please don't cry. This is a happy time. You're going to have a baby."

Pulling back, Arderin wiped her tears with both hands. "With a man who wants nothing to do with me and is filled with the blood of the Dark Lord. What the hell was I thinking? I'm such a fucking idiot."

"Hey," Lila said, cupping her cheek. "Don't talk about my best friend that way. I'm pretty protective of her."

Arderin sniffed and rubbed her nose with her wrist. "Goddamnit. These pregnancy hormones are no joke. I'm a sopping mess."

"Hold on. Be right back." Lila jetted into the house, returning with a box of tissues. Setting them on the railing, she smiled. "I've got more where that came from. You can cry all damn night if you want."

Arderin grabbed a tissue and sat back down, Lila doing the same. Chuckling, she wiped her nose. "You curse more now than you ever did. My brother's tainting you."

Lila breathed a laugh. "I guess so. His language is so vile sometimes. We're working on cleaning it up. I told him that I won't have children who have potty mouths."

Arderin blew her nose, laughing and shaking her head. "You're so damn proper, Lila. How you two work is beyond me, but it's freaking awesome. I've never seen anything like how much you guys love each other."

"It took us a long time to get here, believe me. Darkrip is like Latimus in so many ways. He's convinced himself that he doesn't deserve love or affection. That he's evil and unworthy of building a happy life. After believing that for centuries, you're going to have to work very hard and be extremely patient to get him to change."

Sighing, Arderin contemplated the pretty blue sky. "What if I can't? I don't even know if he loves me back. He says he's not capable of feeling that deeply."

"It's a lie. Lies are indiscernible defense mechanisms that we use to protect ourselves. Look at Sadie. She does the same thing with her burns. We're all just scared little boys and girls inside, doing our best not to get hurt. Darkrip is probably terrified to believe that anyone could love him. The one person he loved was tortured and raped and murdered in front of him. He must associate loving someone with death and suffering. It's quite terrible."

"After all of that, all he went through, there's such goodness in him. I feel it from him when we're together. He resisted having sex with me in the cave, even though I could tell he wanted me badly. Of course, the inevitable eventually happened." Flipping her long hair, she smiled. "I mean, obviously. I'm irresistible."

They both snickered, enjoying each other as they talked under the late-afternoon sun. After a while, Lila's gaze settled on hers.

"So, you truly love him?"

"I do," Arderin said with a nod.

"Then, you're going to have to push him. It will be very hard for him to come to a place where he can begin to contemplate loving you back. He's going to fight and claw against it as hard as he can. I worry that someone like him will hurt you very much before he finally realizes his error."

Arderin inhaled deeply, closing her eyes and imagining Darkrip's handsome face. "I'm tough," she said, lifting her lids. "If he hurts me, I'll just have to take it and keep trying. I can't give up. I want this baby so badly."

"You do?"

"Yes," she nodded, unable to contain her smile. "I mean, I've always thought I'd bond and have kids one day. It always seemed so far away, like a picture in a book that I'd pick up and put back down when I got bored. But now, I imagine our children, and how beautiful they'd be, and how he'll smile at me while I'm holding them. I see the way Miranda and Sathan are with each other and with Tordor, and it's so incredible. I want that, and I want it with Darkrip. Am I crazy?"

"No," Lila said, shaking her head. "You're in love. I've never seen you so beautiful, Arderin. You're absolutely glowing."

"Thank you. That means a lot coming from you. You look like Gisele, Karlie and Rosie all rolled into one."

Her eyebrows drew together. "Who?"

"Whatever," Arderin said, waving her hand. "They're super-hot human models. And they have nothing on you."

"Well, thank you."

"Oh, by the way, the handcuff idea was awesome. Good stuff." She waggled her eyebrows.

"Yeah, Latimus wasn't happy I told you about that. We had to have some extra make-up sex for sure."

Laughing, Arderin sipped her Sprite. "Then, I'm pretty sure he was ecstatic that I spilled the beans."

Twin splotches of embarrassment warmed Lila's face. Arderin thought they made her look absolutely captivating.

"I'm here if you need me," Lila said, her magnificent irises glowing with genuineness. "The next few weeks and months will be hard. Please, call me when you need to talk. I want to be there for you."

"Okay. I love you, Lila."

"I love you too, sweetie."

They turned to see Jack running through the grass, his red hair flopping as he called their names.

"How in the hell is he so cute?"

"I don't know," Lila said, standing to wave to him. "He's the most adorable thing I've ever seen. I'm so lucky to have him."

Jogging down the porch stairs, Lila lifted him up under his arms and swung him around. Carrying him, she ascended the steps as he chatted endlessly about his day at school. Rubbing her abdomen, Arderin imagined her child running and embracing her, Darkrip watching them from their porch of their own home. Determined to make that happen, she stood to hug her nephew.

Chapter 29

Darkrip returned with Miranda to Astaria, riding in the Hummer as her cousin drove. He could've dematerialized, but it afforded him the ability to study Kenden a bit. Recalling Evie's attraction to him, he wondered if they could create some sort of opportunity out of it. The nanny, whom Darkrip had yet to meet, had taken Tordor to Astaria earlier that morning, so the car seat beside him sat unused. It seemed to beckon to him, taunting him to imagine a pretty blue-eyed Vampyre full with his child.

Looking out the tinted window of the back seat, he angrily shook away the vision. He'd begun imagining Arderin pregnant more times than he wished to admit. It was dangerous and futile. Furrowing his brow, he contemplated. How was she doing after all these weeks? Was she pregnant? He'd tried to read the images in her mind, but for some reason, they were incredibly fuzzy, and he'd been unable to make a clear connection. Wondering if his father had anything to do with it, his heart flooded with dread.

He needed to confront her and find out once and for all. Having his child in her womb would put an indelible mark on her, even more than she already had with his insuppressible feelings for her. Although Astaria was protected by Etherya's wall, and Crimeous had been unable to penetrate it thus far, his powers had grown immensely. They could take nothing for granted in these dark times.

Once back at the main house, he searched for her, ending up in the kitchen. Glarys informed him that Arderin had spent the last few days at Lynia with Lila and would be home around two o'clock. Fury surged within as the housekeeper gave him the news. Didn't Arderin understand that she needed to stay at Astaria? Or was that a confirmation she wasn't pregnant and felt safe to roam the kingdom?

Driving himself insane with worry, he busied himself with eating some of Glarys' chicken salad while he waited. The usually mouthwatering dish tasted like cardboard as bugs of anxiety ate away at his stomach. The maddening Vampyre princess might just be the death of him.

Finally, looking at his phone, he rose to meet Arderin, hoping she'd be home on time.

He found her in the foyer, about to ascend the stairs, bag in hand.

"Hey," Arderin said, setting the bag on the bottom stair and coming to stand a few feet in front of him. "How did it go in the human world?"

"Why are you leaving the compound?" he asked, anger evident in his tone. "We discussed this. It's imperative you stay safe."

"Latimus surrounded me with a ton of soldiers," she said, her expression unreadable. "He knows everything. He won't let that asshole touch one hair on my head."

Darkrip scowled. "You're smarter than this, Arderin. I won't have him abduct you—"

"Please," she interrupted, holding up her palm. "I don't want to argue with you. I feel like I haven't seen you in forever. I missed you." Those gorgeous eyes were wide and guileless, causing Darkrip to feel a thud in his solar plexus.

When he didn't respond, she asked, "How did it go with Evie?"

"Not well. I couldn't find her anywhere."

"Crap," she said, rubbing her palms on her thighs. "That sucks. What's your plan now?"

"I don't know," he said, shaking his head. "But right now, we need to talk. Can we go somewhere more private?"

"I'm meeting Nolan and Sadie in the infirmary at two-thirty to document her progress with the serum. Latimus is training the troops, Miranda and Sathan are upstairs with Tordor, and Heden's in the tech room. No one can hear us. This is probably the most private place in the entire house right now. Do you want to go into the sitting room?" She gestured toward the opening that led to the adjacent room.

Sighing, he rubbed his fingers over his forehead. "It's fine. This isn't really the time for tea and crumpets. I need to know if you're pregnant. I've tried to read the images in your mind, but they're garbled for some reason."

"That's strange," she said, taking a step closer. "Do you think your father—?"

Cutting her off, he grabbed her wrist and pulled her into his body. "Stop stalling. There are consequences stemming from this that you can't even begin to understand."

Her eyes narrowed, filled with hurt and confusion. "Don't act like I'm stupid. I know exactly what's at stake here."

"Then, tell me," he said, his eyes roving over her impassive face.

"And what if I was? What would that mean for us? Would you even consider doing right by me and pushing away your fear to let us raise the baby?"

"No," he said, glaring at her. "It would be an abomination. You know that. You need to stop pretending that any child of mine would be at all normal."

"Any child of *ours* would have the blood of your mother, your grandfather and my wonderful parents. How in any world could it even begin to be evil?"

"You don't know what you're dealing with, Arderin. Someone as innocent and pure as you could never understand the darkness that lies in him. That lies in *me*."

Closing the gap between them, he palmed her face, tilting it toward his. "My god, you're fucking pregnant."

Those stunning ice-blue eyes filled with tears, one of them sliding down her cheek to wet his hand.

"No," Darkrip said, placing his forehead against hers. "I can't let this happen."

"Please," she whispered, rubbing the smooth skin of her forehead against his. "Think of all we could have. It's so beautiful, what we created together when we thought we were dying. An affirmation of both our lives."

"I can't think that way," he murmured, his blood pulsing as he held her. "Even if I wanted to, I can't. We have to abort it."

"No," she said, lifting her head. "I won't kill my baby. That's not an option."

Lowering his hands, he clenched them at his sides. "Do you know what he'll do to you the second he finds out? He'll kidnap you to his cave and torture and rape you until you have the baby. Then, he'll murder you. Do you understand this, Arderin?" He struggled to keep his voice low, not wanting anyone else to hear.

"He can't break through Etherya's wall. I'll make sure to stay at Astaria once I start to show."

"And then what?" he asked, incensed. "Once you have the child? Would you lock yourself in a prison, never being able to visit Lila, or the other compounds, or the human world where you so desperately want to train? You'd last a month. You're too adventurous and curious to settle for that."

She thrust up her chin. "You'll find Evie, and she'll defeat your father soon enough. After that, I'll be able to travel again."

Giving a frustrated laugh, he rubbed his fingers over his forehead. "You've got some faith in a woman who hates us all and can't even be located. You're lying to yourself. It has to stop. You need to abort this child."

"No!" Shaking her fists at her side, those baby-blues enflamed with anger. "I'm having this baby and I'm going to raise it to be good and just and all the other things I know you to be inside. I want to bond with you and have you raise it with me, but if you're too much of a coward, then I'll do it by my own damn self."

"Bond with me?" he asked, enraged. "I'm the son of the Dark Lord and spent the first two centuries of my life torturing and murdering. You want to tie your ribbon to that horse? You're insane!"

"You did those things because you were young and your father urged you on. They weren't you. After you gave your word to your mother, you lived by your Slayer side for eight centuries. That's amazing. I can see it if you can't. And yes, I would be honored to be your bonded mate. I see you for the good person you are inside, even if you can't."

"This is ridiculous," he muttered, looking to the ceiling for patience. "Abort the child, or I'll do it for you."

"Never!" she screamed, tiny wisps of spittle escaping from between her fangs.

Unable to control his anger, Darkrip began choking her with his mind. Not enough to injure her, as that was something he could never do, but enough to make her listen. Bringing her hand to her throat, she clutched it, her stunning irises flashing with hurt.

As her pain coursed through him, wetness welled in his eyes. Unashamed, he continued denying her the full dose of oxygen she needed. Her anguish was so innocent, filled with such betrayal, that he wanted to retch.

"Arderin!" Sathan called, bounding down the large spiral staircase, Miranda behind him. When they reached the black and white tile floor of the foyer, Darkrip lifted his hand and threw them against the wall with his mind. Arderin still sputtered as he held his mental grip on her.

Standing, Miranda trained her olive-green gaze on him. "Stop it, Darkrip!" she said, looking so much like his mother as she scolded him. "You're hurting her."

"Not as much as he will!" he screamed, holding up his hand to freeze her. Unable to move, she stared at him.

"I know you're scared that he'll hurt her and the baby." Eyes widening, he regarded his sister. "I know the signs of a pregnant woman, Darkrip. You're worried it will make her a target, but I need you to calm down and let her go."

Sathan tried to rush him, and he froze him in place beside Miranda.

"I tried to tell you," Darkrip said, his chin trembling. "I tried to tell you that I was evil and awful and malicious. You didn't want to believe me."

"No, you're not," Miranda said, her eyes so full of love for him. It made him sick. How could she still look at him that way? "You're our mother's son and you're very afraid right now. I understand. I would be too. But you need to let her go so that we can discuss this calmly and rationally."

Scoffing, he shook his head. "There's nothing calm or rational about this. If she won't abort the baby, I'll have to murder it inside her body. I don't care if you all hate me. It's the only course."

"Darkrip, please," Sathan said, his voice so calm. "If you do that, you might end up hurting Arderin as well. Do you want to take that chance? Please, let us help you. There's another way. I promise."

Heden charged into the foyer, his broad chest rising and falling as he panted. "What the hell is going on in here?"

Lowering his lids, Darkrip froze him in place as well. There, he stood before them, Sathan and Miranda frozen to his left, Arderin in front of him gasping for air, Heden to his right, shooting daggers from his sky-blue irises as he stood frozen in place. The evil in Darkrip's blood reveled in the power of it all. It beckoned to him, urging him to kill them all with one snap of his hand. Unwavering in his fear and rage, he contemplated his next move.

A woman with dirty-blond hair and brown eyes appeared at the top of the staircase. Grabbing the rail, she walked down slowly, a slight grin on her lips. Looking like she was strolling into the prom instead of witnessing him hold four people hostage.

"Well, well," she said, reaching the cold floor and leisurely strolling toward them. Darkrip tried to freeze her motions with his mind but was unable to.

"Belinda, please be careful," Miranda said. "It's best not to approach him."

"Is it?" Belinda asked, giving her a faint smile. "He seems harmless to me." Strolling toward him, she patted his cheek. "Hello, brother dearest. You've really stepped in some shit here, haven't you?"

Darkrip sucked in a breath. "Evie?"

Lips turning into a slightly wicked grin, she pulled the wig from her head. Throwing it on the ground, Evie shook out her scarlet tresses. "God, that feels good. I was getting so tired of wearing that damn wig." Reaching to her hairline, she pulled off a thin mask, rubbing her hand over the skin of her slightly freckled face. Lifting her contact-covered irises to Darkrip's, she arched her brow. "Why don't we let the little princess breathe? After all, she is pregnant with your brat."

Turning to Arderin, Evie lifted her hand and waved it through the air. Arderin collapsed on the bottom step, inhaling huge gulps of air into her lungs.

"Holy shit," Miranda said.

"Holy shit is right, sis," Evie said, sighing as she turned to face Darkrip. "My, my, this is all so nasty. And I thought you said you liked these people?"

"What the hell are you doing here?" Darkrip asked through gritted teeth, still holding Sathan, Miranda and Heden frozen.

"Um, you came looking for me, you little idiot. Or do you not want my help anymore?"

"Of course, I want your help."

Her eyelids constricted. "I'm still debating. I needed to observe these immortals for a while to see if they were worthy of my time. We'll see."

"Now, now," she said, grabbing Darkrip's forearm. "Why don't you let them go and evaporate out of here? There's no way the king will let you stay now that you've tried to strangle his sister, so why don't you go find yourself a nice spot in the woods near the Purges of Methesda to contemplate the shit show you've made of your life? Hmmm? I'll come looking for you when I feel that you're ready to talk. You've made me really angry, searching for me, but you've also awoken something inside that I can't seem to squash. When I'm ready, I'll need to discuss that with you."

Darkrip eyed her, then looked at Sathan. He was indeed pissed. Knowing Evie was right, he resigned himself to the fact that he'd never be welcome on the compound again.

"Go on. And don't try to invade the princess' thoughts. I've erected a shield for her. She needs a fair shot if she's going to have your brat. I don't know why, but I feel that the child is important. Now, go. Leave these nice people to talk about how awful you are behind your back. How fun." Her eyes glowed with mischief.

"Come find me when you're ready," Darkrip growled. "I have quite a bit I want to say to you too." Closing his eyes, he disappeared.

Lifting his lids, he looked out on the lush, dense mountain forest that surrounded the Purges of Methesda. Hating himself for even attempting to hurt Arderin, he crumpled to the ground, curled up in a ball and let the wave of self-loathing overtake his soul.

* * * *

Evie watched them all regain control of their limbs, the two massive Vampyres rushing to their sister's side.

"Aw, how sweet," she mocked, as Arderin assured them she was okay.

"Wow, Evie, I had no idea," Miranda said, her expression filled with wary admiration. "I have so many questions."

Evie regarded her, about the same height as she and the perfect reflection of their mother. "Fine. I'll give you a few minutes. Can we sit down though? I think the foyer's seen enough action for today."

"Sure, let's go into the sitting room."

Miranda walked over to Arderin, extending her hand and helping her up. Together, they all walked into the adjoining sitting room. Evie and Heden lowered into the wide-backed chairs, while Sathan, Arderin and Miranda sat on the long couch.

"Thank you," Arderin said, her blue irises so genuine.

"I can see why he likes you," Evie said. "You're as innocent and pure as our mother was. It must drive him wild. You've got it too," she said to Miranda, "although you're a bit snarkier than dear old Mother was."

Miranda's lips quirked. "I'll take that. Thanks. So, when did you come back from the human world? And how did you get that family at Restia to vouch for you? Their reference was impeccable."

"Oh, them," Evie said, waving her hand. "I materialized into their house, causing them to nearly crap themselves. It was quite funny. Then, I explained who I was. Daughter of the Dark Lord with limitless powers, able to snap their necks with my mind...all the dirty details. I told them that if they didn't give me a glowing reference, their days on Earth were limited. They were happy to comply."

"Okay," Miranda said, blowing air out of her bottom lip so that it fanned the hair above her forehead. "Well, that was resilient, if nothing else. I have to say, I'm a bit fucked-up in the head that a self-proclaimed evil sorceress has been watching my child. We should've done more research," she said to Sathan.

The King's body was tense with worry. Looking at Evie, Sathan said, "If you ever hurt our child, I'll kill you myself—prophecy or not. We've already lost one child due to your malicious antics, and I won't stand for that again."

Evie shrugged. "I would say your inability to trust your wife is what killed your child, but why dredge up the past?"

Sathan's body tensed further, causing Miranda to reach her arm over Arderin's lap to hold him in place.

"Look," Miranda said, "we all have something to gain here. Nothing's going to be accomplished if we can't see the big picture. It's a complicated situation, but we need to stay cool." Sathan scowled at his wife and then trained the expression on Evie.

Evie sighed. "I know what you all think of me. Believe me, most of it is true. But I will tell you this: there has always been a line I won't cross. One very important and distinct line. I would never hurt a child. My father harmed me from a very young age, and it was...*appalling*." She rubbed her upper arm absently, shame and bitterness washing over her as it always did when she remembered the violations of her youth. "I didn't know you were pregnant, Miranda. Darkrip had erected a shield to hide your thoughts, and I wasn't able to break through. I'm truly sorry about what happened and can only assure you that Tordor has been safe with me. Even though I generally detest infants, the little dribbler is actually quite cute. Taking care of him helped to ease my guilt, if only slightly, so take that as you will."

Miranda gnawed her bottom lip. "I believe you," she said finally, her gaze firm. "And although your actions spurred the battle, it was your father who ultimately killed our child. I will always blame him and dream of the day we murder him, once and for all."

"As do I," Evie said.

"Have you come to help us defeat Crimeous then?" Miranda asked.

Evie felt her chin lift slightly. "I'm not sure. I still haven't decided if there's anything I want badly enough to put myself in danger like that. Although I'm quite powerful and much stronger than my imbecile of a brother, our father will always be stronger. He doesn't have Rina's infuriatingly sappy blood running through his veins."

"Well, I'd like to help you find something that you care about enough to make you fight. I won't stop until I do. What do you need from me to get there?"

"So willful and determined. My god, you really are everything Darkrip said you'd be. It's annoying."

Miranda grinned. "I won't let you goad me into an argument, Evie. I've wanted to meet you since I learned I had a sister. It's astonishing to me. I hope we can work our way toward becoming friends. I would like that very much."

Evie gave a good-natured scoff. "Well, okay then. I'll count the days until we have sleepovers and pillow fights. In the meantime, I need some things from you."

"Okay," Miranda said with a nod.

"First, I need a place to stay."

"You can have your choice of any of our vacant cabins by the wall," Sathan said. "Or you're welcome to have a room here at the castle."

"Thanks for the offer, but I don't really like it here. It's a tad pretentious. I've enjoyed the time I've spent at Uteria with Miranda and the baby. If there's something there, I'd rather that. Something that offers a bit of privacy."

"There are some vacant cabins on the outskirts of the compound, by the wall. You can stay in any of those," Miranda said.

"Good. Give me the one that's the most remote and secluded. I need your word that you'll leave me the hell alone while I figure this out. I know you all are desperate to rid the world of my father, but I need to process this in my own way. If I'm not one-hundred percent dedicated when I fight him, he'll surely defeat us."

"We'll give you time," Miranda said. "But, please, let me know what I can do to help you along. He's a looming threat and attacks our compounds regularly now."

Evie nodded. "Do you have a stable? I haven't ridden in a while and find that it helps me think."

"Yes, you can ride my horse, Majesty. He's magnificent and descended from the horse that Mother used to ride. I think she'd love knowing that we both enjoy riding as much as she did."

"Well, dear old Mother really never cared for me as she did for you, but that's a story for another time." Exhaling an extended breath, she regarded them. "My brother fucked up today. That's clear. But I need him if we're going to defeat my father. Although my powers are greater than his, he and I will have to work together to keep our father from dematerializing so I can strike him with the Blade."

Glancing between Heden and Sathan, she asked, "Are you two going to be able to get over him almost strangling your sister so he can help me? If we're divided, then we've already lost."

Heden and Sathan regarded each other, both of them sullen.

"Well, I can get over it," Arderin said, confident and resolute. "It's not their decision. I care for your brother very much and understand why he did what he did. My idiot brothers are just going to have to accept that I'm a big girl who's in love with a man who has a crap-ton of demons inside."

Miranda smiled at Arderin. "You love him?"

"I do," Arderin said, nodding. "I'm going to get him to love me back and raise this kid with me if it kills me."

Evie felt the corner of her lip curve. "Well, he's a lucky man. You're gorgeous. I don't understand why you want to have a child with my father's blood, but it's your life. Now, I need your word that you'll accept him back on the compound after he beats the shit out of himself for his actions today. Believe me, he'll probably try to burn himself in the Purges of Methesda. He always was such a martyr. He always tried to protect me and Mother when that bastard raped us. Although he has my father's blood, he's never been as evil as he pretends to be."

Arderin beamed. "I tell him that all the time."

Evie found herself taken with the innocent beauty.

"You have our word," Sathan said, although she could tell he was still fuming. "I can assure you that my brothers and I aren't happy about this situation, but there are bigger things at play here, and we're smart enough to see the end game."

"Good," she said with a nod. "I don't want you all to think that I'm as good as Darkrip. I'm not. I'm an evil bitch with powers that you can't begin to fathom. I've studied medieval black magic, voodoo, Satanism and every other human dark magic you can think of. It's how I was able to shield your thoughts from him," she said to Arderin. "He can only erect a shield for someone with whom he shares blood. My powers are limitless compared to his. So, let's keep that in mind, shall we?"

Standing, she rubbed her hands over her jeans. "Now, if you don't mind, I'm ready to get out of these drab nanny clothes. Sorry, sis, but you'll need to find a new caretaker. Where should I go to find the cabin at Uteria?"

Miranda came to stand in front of her. "I'll call Kenden. Meet him at the main castle, and he'll show you the stables and get you settled in your cabin. I'll also tell him to give you a phone. If you need anything at all, please call me. I'll be back at Uteria next week. Maybe we could ride together?"

Evie shook her head at her sister's genuine smile. "Maybe we could. Let's see what kind of mood I'm in then."

And then, Miranda grabbed her wrists, squeezing as she beamed. "I'm really excited to get to know you, Evie. You're my blood, and that means something."

Evie pulled her arms away. "Yikes. The sentimentality in this world is stifling. This is going to be more annoying than I thought. Call your cousin and let's get on with it."

Closing her eyes, she whisked herself upstairs to gather her meager belongings and freshen up. Then, she transported to Uteria.

Chapter 30

Arderin sat with her brothers around the conference room table. Their faces scowling, their massive bodies tense, she knew she had an uphill battle in front of her. She'd called them here after the debacle in the foyer earlier today, knowing it was best to get everything out in the open.

"Okay, guys. Let's hash this out," she said from her seat at the head of the table. "Your sister's been a very bad princess and gotten herself knocked up by the son of the Dark Lord. So, give it to me. I'm ready. Go ahead and tell me what an idiot I am."

The three of them exchanged glances, driving her insane. "Just get it out. I don't want to have any unspoken words between us. The three of you are the most important people in my life, and I would die if anything ever came between us. We have to talk about this."

Sathan sighed and grabbed her hand as it sat atop the table. "I just feel like I let you down. I'm sorry."

Her features drew together. "Let me down, how?"

"I should've encouraged another suitor for you centuries ago and ensured you bonded with someone worthy of you. Our parents trusted me to take care of you. Of all of you."

"Hey, bro," Latimus said, "you've taken care of us and everyone else in the kingdom for centuries. You can't beat yourself up."

"And I would ask you not to speak of Darkrip as unworthy," she said, enfolding Sathan's hand into her own. "I know you guys don't know him like I do, but he's a remarkable person and has such good inside."

"Even after he almost strangled you today?" Heden muttered.

"He was barely choking me," she said, rolling her eyes. "I don't think his mother's blood would actually let him cause me harm. I was just surprised."

"I don't understand how you're so flippant about this," Sathan said.

"Look," she said, releasing his hand and straightening her spine. "I'm pissed as hell at him, and he'll get a piece of my mind once he has the balls to come back here and show his face. But you all have to understand where his motivations come from. When I drank from him in the cave, I saw his memories. They're worse than anything I could've ever imagined. He watched Crimeous rape and torture his mother, the only person he ever loved, until he murdered her in front of him. I think he's so terrified that loving me or letting me have the baby will make me a target that he was protecting me in his own way."

"How can you be sure that he won't harm you if you try to build a future with him?" Latimus asked.

"I don't know. I just feel that he won't hurt me. Truly hurt me. I think he loves me very much, although he's terrified to admit it."

"What do you want us to say, Arderin?" Heden asked, lifting his hands and shrugging. "That we give our blessing for you to bond with the son of the Dark Lord?"

Inhaling, she nodded. "I think that's exactly what I want. I know that the three of you have strived to protect me my entire life. Especially you, since you're an overprotective caveman," she said, smiling at Sathan. "But I'm a fully-grown woman capable of making her own decisions. I'm competent and confident enough to choose who I love and want to build a life with. I need you all to trust me. If you can't trust him yet, I understand. But I need you to trust me."

The three of them regarded each other, and she gritted her teeth at their silence.

"Remember that if he hadn't let me drink from him in the cave, we wouldn't be having this discussion. He was against feeding me because he didn't want to expose me to his evil side, but in the end, he did it anyway. You should be extremely grateful to him. Otherwise, the three of you would be having this discussion over my gravesite."

"So dramatic," Heden said, rolling his eyes.

"Well, it's true," she snapped, scrunching her face and giving him a glare.

Latimus stretched his hand out on the table, palm up. "Give me your hand, little one."

Smiling, she placed it in his, adoring how he threaded his fingers through hers. She'd always loved him so much and felt wetness in her eyes.

"I'm not enamored with the idea of you bonding with him or having his child, but what's done is done. If you love him, then I love you enough to support your choice. But I need you to understand that his first priority must be defeating his father. If he and Evie aren't able to do that, you won't be able to build any sort of life with him. All of our lives will be doomed."

Squeezing his hand, she couldn't stop her grin. "And *I'm* dramatic?"

Chuckling, he nodded. "You are, but this is real life and death stuff, little one."

"I promise to help him focus on defeating Crimeous. I think that having me support him will make him even stronger."

"Okay, then, I'm in. Even though I hate it, I'm in. I love you, Arderin."

"Well, damn. I guess I'm in too then. Can't let Latimus one-up me," Heden said, placing his hand on top of their joined ones. "Although, I'm still going to tell myself that you guys just played tiddlywinks in the cave, and you got pregnant by immaculate conception." Winking at her, his white fangs glowed as he smiled.

"Fine," Sathan said, surly as he placed his hand on top of theirs. "I'll support you, Arderin, and try my best to accept him. It won't be easy, but I want you to be happy."

"Thank you, Sathan," she said, the tears in her eyes threatening to spill over. "He makes me happy, and I know that once Crimeous is gone, he's going to be able to give me the life I want. I'm so excited to get there. I promise, I'll support him in his efforts to kill the bastard. It's imperative that he succeeds."

Wiping a tear with her free hand, she regarded her brothers and their joined hands. By the goddess, they were all so precious to her. "I love you guys so much," she said, whispering the words since her throat seemed to be closing up.

Standing, Sathan pulled her up and embraced her. Latimus hugged her from behind, and Heden threw his arms around them.

"Look at this awesome family group hug," Heden said. "We put the Osmonds to shame."

Arderin burst out laughing. "Oh, my god, I forgot to tell you how funny that was. I was dying."

They all gave each other one last squeeze and released.

"What the hell are you two talking about?" Latimus asked.

"Don't worry about it," Arderin said, waving her hand dismissively. "You don't have the sense of humor to get it."

"Hey," he said. "I'm super funny. Ask Lila. She says I'm hilarious."

"Right," Arderin and Heden said simultaneously, causing them to break into another fit of laughter.

"Okay, leave Latimus alone," Sathan said, smiling at them. "We need him since the world's gone to shit. Our sister's bonding with an evil Deamon, and his wicked sister has moved onto my wife's compound. I think the Earth has gone insane."

"Oh, man," Arderin said. "This is going to be freaking awesome."

Laughing, they threw their arms around each other and exited the large room.

* * * *

Kenden met Evie outside the massive wooden doors that led inside the castle at Uteria. When she appeared, her lithe body illuminated by the late-afternoon sun, he felt his heartbeat quicken, if only a little.

"Well, well," she said, approaching him until there were mere inches between them. "It seems we meet again."

A sauciness glowed in her stunning green eyes, and the fire of her hair seemed to burn the air around her. Reminding himself that she was a master of seduction, usually for malicious intent, he nodded. "Hello, Evie."

She shivered, seeming to revel in it as she exaggerated the movement. "You've still got that deep voice. It's magnificent."

She was so transparent in her attempted flirtation that he almost laughed. "I'll show you the stables first and then your cabin. And here's a phone for you." He thrust the device at her.

Plushy red lips formed a pout. "Still so serious though. We'll have to work on that." Patting his face, she pivoted and began to walk. "So, show me these stables. I don't have all day."

Gritting his teeth, he followed her, eventually taking the lead to steer her toward the stables.

"This is Majesty," Kenden said. "Miranda said you can ride him, which she never allows anyone to do, by the way. If you ride together, she'll have you ride Thor. He's Majesty's son."

"Well, aren't you magnificent?" she asked, lifting her slim arms to rub her hands over Majesty's black mane. The horse seemed to purr as she caressed him, talking in a low timbre, and he wondered if there had ever been a man unable to succumb to her charm. Even the damn horse was half in love with her. Deciding that he would be the one man she could never seduce, he cleared his throat.

"Just text me when you want to ride him. I'll have the stable hands prepare him."

"Thanks," she said, still enthralled with the horse.

"So, the cabin's about a ten minute walk from here. Is that okay?"

Turning to face him fully, she gave him a brilliant smile. Although he was determined to resist her, he wasn't dead. She was absolutely gorgeous. Almond-shaped, deep green eyes sat atop a slightly freckled nose. Cheeks, flushed with the red of the outdoors, were well defined above those amazing lips.

"I could transport us, but I need the walk. And then, I can keep annoying you, as I seem to be doing. How fun."

Rolling his eyes, he pivoted and strolled out of the stable, knowing she'd follow him. They set a nice steady pace as they meandered through the open meadow toward the cabins.

"It took a lot of courage to come back here. I know you hate the immortal world. We're excited that you're our ally. I hope you'll decide to fight with us."

"I'm my own ally. Let's get that straight. And I might fight with you. I have to decide if there's anything I want enough to make that happen. We'll see."

"Well, you've met Miranda, so let me just get this out. If she's set her mind to it, you're fighting with us. You can try to resist, but she'll win you over."

"Let her try. I'm excited to see her best effort."

Eventually, they made it to the cabin.

"It's sparse," he said, walking her around the den that sat inside the front door, then the small kitchen, bedroom and bathroom. "If you need anything, just let me know, and I'll have one of the castle staff members send it over. It's been recently cleaned, and the sheets and comforter are all freshly washed."

"Thanks," she said, looking around the space. "What do I do for food?"

"Sadie and I usually eat dinner together when we're both on the compound. You're welcome to join us. The main housekeeper, Jana, is always around and about. I programmed her number in your phone. Call her anytime you're hungry."

"Well, this is some full-service shit. Maybe even better than the fancy hotel I found you at in France."

Chuckling, he nodded. "Maybe. I'm heading to do a night training with the troops. If you need me, I put my number in your phone, along with Miranda's, Sathan's and all the others. You can call me anytime."

"Anytime?" she asked, one scarlet brow arching.

"Yes," he said, unable to stop his smile, "but I might not answer. See you later, Evie." Stepping from the cabin, he closed the door behind him and headed to the training.

Chapter 31

Darkrip stood atop the hill, staring down at the boiling lava. The Purges of Methesda had always held such mysticism in the immortal world, and he could see why. Surrounded by mountains covered in thick green trees, the lake of the Purges simmered with rage and heat. Said to be over two-thousand degrees at the center, it was a lake of death. Waves of molten rock battled with each other, crashing upon the rocky shore.

Standing in solace, he let the self-hatred overwhelm him. How had he gotten here? He'd tried so hard to be the man that he promised his mother he would be, all those centuries ago. His desire to help Miranda was pure; his feelings for Arderin the strongest he'd had since Rina died.

Closing his eyes, he let his heart constrict with anguish. Although he hadn't closed Arderin's throat enough to cause her real harm, he'd hurt her. Those magnificent eyes had looked upon him with such pain. Loathing himself, he lifted his lids to look at the flaming lava below. If he had any sort of balls, he'd just throw himself in. What a waste of a creature he was. Revulsion for himself and his pathetic life threatened to choke him.

A *whoosh* of air flushed against his right side, and he turned his head, expecting to see his father. How fitting that the Deamon would come to push him to his death from the grassy hill.

Instead, the image of Etherya appeared. Waist-long red, curly hair sizzled around her body as she floated above the ground. Cursing his beating heart, he straightened, determined not to cower in the face of the goddess he detested.

"You won't bow to me, son of Rina?"

"Why would I bow to you? And, let's be clear, I'm the son of Crimeous. Rina only played a small part in my wasted life."

The goddess seemed to sigh. "I understand your hatred. I've cursed you for so many centuries, using the stalk of your seed to remind you that you were the child of rape and torture."

"Yeah, thanks. Like I needed reminding."

"When you were young, I was so sure you would turn out to be like him. I cursed you so that you would think twice before you acted. But I see now that I was wrong."

Darkrip felt his eyes narrow. "I doubt that."

"The man I truly wanted to punish was your father. We have a history that you can't even begin to understand. There was a time, many ages ago, when he was not evil. Those days have long passed. I held on to hope for so many centuries that he would change and find his goodness again. Sadly, I now know that will never happen. In the end, I must ensure his death."

"It would be really helpful if you could confirm that Evie's the descendant of our grandfather, who will kill him and get her in front of him."

"The Universe does not work that way, child. Because I am so powerful, I have control over much, but you immortals must ultimately prevail on your own. I have tried to help you as best I can."

"Well, your help is shit."

Placing her blurry hand under his chin, she turned his head. Her beady eyes bore into his.

"I will remove the curse with the condition that you truly must learn to love without fear. It is natural to worry and carry concern for those you love, but you clutch onto your fear to your detriment. It is beneath you, and it's time you change. Learn to do this, and the curse will be released."

Angry, he knocked her hand away, irritated when his arm only plowed through what seemed to be a puffy cloud. Still, she lowered her hand and regarded him.

"You could just release the curse now."

"It is not time yet. You will know. Remember, it is only when you allow yourself to experience true love and love outweighs the fear."

"Then, leave me the hell alone. I have no use for you. You've done nothing but cause me pain my whole life."

"There is a great battle before you. You and your sister will need to combine your powers in your efforts to defeat the Dark Lord. Stop wasting time contemplating your death. It is futile, and we both know you don't have the will do it."

"Maybe I do," he said, staring down at the angry molten rock. "Maybe I'll just fling myself right now. Lord knows, I don't have any sort of life to go back to."

The goddess cupped his cheeks with her airy hands. Forcing him to look at her, she seemed to smile, although he couldn't be sure. "You have so much of my beautiful Valktor in you. And Rina as well. I've done a great disservice to you. You've lived by their blood for so long, and I didn't give you proper due for that. I'm proud of you, son. Now, go claim your Vampyre and kill Crimeous. You are important. Never forget that."

With a puff of air, she vanished.

* * * *

Arderin felt so wonderful after talking to her brothers that she decided to do some moonlight yoga under Sathan's elm tree. As she contorted through the poses, she thought of Darkrip, hoping he was okay. Although she wasn't thrilled that he'd choked her with his mind, she was firm in her belief that it came from his desire to protect her.

Realizing how much he cared for her caused her to smile as she maneuvered into tree pose. Holding her hands together in front of her chest, she prayed to Etherya. Under the half-lit moon, she asked the goddess to pave a way for them to have a future. Although it wouldn't be easy, Arderin held on to hope.

That night, alone in her room, she was restless and struggled to sleep. The need to vomit woke her up in the dim light of dawn, and she battled with the toilet for almost an hour. Remembering how sick Miranda had been when she was pregnant, she cursed. Vampyre women usually didn't experience morning sickness due to their self-healing bodies. Having a baby filled with the blood of the Dark Lord threw that out the window. Realizing her pregnancy certainly wouldn't be a picnic, she resigned herself to having many more months of worshiping the porcelain gods. Just freaking great.

After drinking some Slayer blood in the kitchen, she trekked out onto the open field behind the barracks. Under the strong morning sun, she walked to Darkrip's cabin. A thin layer of dust coated the furniture, and she set about cleaning up. Once finished, she pulled back the covers and lay down. Inhaling his scent from the pillow, she smiled. Grabbing the other pillow, she lay there for hours, remembering when he'd held her there.

The feelings warred inside her: love for her complicated man, and anger that he'd used his powers against her. If they were to have a future, they would need to set some ground rules. Arderin would make it clear that using his abilities for anything other than virtuous causes, or the protection of those he loved, was unacceptable. The capabilities were important in his fight against Crimeous, but he must choose goodness over darkness. Especially if he was going to help raise their baby. The child would inherit his extraordinary gifts and needed to be taught how to use them properly.

Arderin found herself returning to his cabin almost on a daily basis. There was something calming about being near his scent and his paltry possessions. As her pregnancy progressed, the morning sickness also abated a bit. She still woke up each morning needing to puke her guts out, but her insides didn't feel like they were being pulverized. Determined not to let pregnancy kick her ass, she resolved to maintain a strong, positive outlook.

At night, she would cuddle under the comforter, silently calling for Darkrip to come to her. Missing him terribly, she would close her eyes and imagine his handsome face. Keeping her faith in him, she knew that one day he would return to her.

Chapter 32

Darkrip finished his shower and milled about the small room, throwing on the clothes he'd picked up in town. After his conversation with the goddess, he admitted to himself that she was right. He didn't possess the will to burn himself in the Purges of Methesda. Knowing this, he had transported to Restia. Although he'd rarely visited the smallest Slayer compound, he found it quite charming.

Locating a small bed and breakfast a few miles from the main town, he had checked in under an alias. Not possessing the sense of humor Heden did, he used a rather boring name instead of a human pop singer's.

After spending a few days on the quiet compound, he became quite restless. Realizing that he needed to head back to Astaria to accept the consequences of his actions, he still waited for some reason. There were so many unanswered questions. How would Sathan react to his return? Would Arderin's brothers threaten to kill him for impregnating her? Did they still want his help to defeat his father?

The questions were maddening as they swirled in his mind. The one thing that was constant? His desire to see Arderin. Thoughts of her consumed him until he thought he might go mad. How was her pregnancy progressing? Was she experiencing morning sickness? Could she possibly still care for him, even a little, after he'd treated her so terribly? Darkrip had no idea. Wanting so badly to find out, he packed his tiny bag, sucked in a deep breath and dematerialized to his cabin at Astaria. Opening his eyes, he searched the surroundings.

Turning his head, he heard retching coming from the small bathroom. Approaching, he saw her, hugging the toilet as she vomited.

"Hey," he said, throwing down his bag and running toward her. Lowering, he spooned his front against her back. "Holy shit, you're puking your damn guts out."

Arderin groaned, and he was unable to see her face as her forehead rested on the porcelain. "By the goddess, you picked a *really* fucked-up time to come back." Sucking in a breath, she proceeded to barf, the liquid brown and stringy.

"This is fucking gross," he said, hugging her to him. "I told you that you didn't want a Deamon inside you. You should've listened to me."

"Aargh, you're infuriating. Leave me the hell alone."

Unable to control his chuckle, he held her close, burying his nose in her fragrant curls. Reveling in the softness, he ran his hand over her thick hair.

"God, Arderin, I missed you so much. I'm sorry to tell you when you're hanging over the toilet, but I need you to know."

"I missed you too, asshole. I've imagined punching you in the face about a thousand times and can't wait to make that happen. Now, shut up and let me barf in peace."

Holding her, he let her get it all out. When she was done, he helped her up.

"Let me brush my teeth," she said, her expression impassive. "I'm disgusting."

"Okay," he said, walking outside and unpacking his small bag while she tidied up in the bathroom.

When she walked out, he studied her. She wore a light blue sweater over those tight-as-sin jeans he loved, her cute feet bare. "Why are you in my cabin?"

"I've decided that it's *my* cabin now," she said, the corner of her lip turning up.

"Is that so?"

"Yup."

The air between them seemed to sizzle.

"So, have you come to strangle me to death? Or perhaps knock me unconscious and send me down the river? We don't have a very good history. Should I be worried?"

His heart constricted at her words. God, he was a bastard. How in the hell could she ever forgive him? She looked so angelic, framed by her flowing hair, her eyes glowing.

Gradually, he advanced, closing the distance between them. Dropping to his knees in front of her, he placed his forehead on her abdomen. Grasping her slender hips, he inhaled her scent, rubbing his face against her. Thin fingers speared through his hair, soothing him as she rubbed his scalp. The feel of her nails scraping against his head caused him to shiver.

"I'm so sorry," he said into her stomach, his voice gravelly. "I don't blame you if you hate me. I should've never used my powers against you."

Running her hand down his cheek, she lifted his chin with her fingers. Sky-blue irises locked onto him.

"No, you shouldn't have. If you ever do it again, I'll cut off your testicles and shove them down your throat. I'm not sure who you think you're dealing with here, but I'm not putting up with that shit."

He couldn't control his broad smile. "Yikes."

"Yikes is right, buddy," she said, arching an eyebrow. Ever so slowly, she slid her palms down his upper arms, grasping his elbows and pulling him to stand. Unable to catch his breath, he panted softly as he cupped her cheeks. When she slid her arms around his neck, he placed his forehead on hers.

"Arderin," he whispered, shaking his head. "I'm so fucked. All I ever think about is you. How in the hell did this happen?"

Her laughter surrounded him, warm like the waves of the far-off beaches near the equator of the human world. "I don't know. I'm pretty irresistible."

Chuckling, he nodded. "You sure are. I think you're the most gorgeous woman I've ever seen."

White teeth almost blinded him as she smiled. "As for hating you, well, you knocked me up, so I think I'm gonna have to forgive you whether I like it or not." Those baby-blues were filled with mischief and desire. Thanking every god in the universe that she still wanted him, he lowered his arms, encircling her waist.

"I'm terrible at this. I don't know what to say. I've never felt guilt or sorrow. You make me feel so many things. It's terrifying."

"You make me feel *alive*," she said, squeezing him with her arms. "You have since I met you. It's incredible, and you bet your ass I'm never letting it go."

"How can you still want anything to do with me? I don't deserve you."

"Of course, you don't." Her grin was so cute it almost stopped his heart. What a lucky bastard he was.

Rubbing his nose against hers, he couldn't stop his lips from curving. "I've never met anyone like you, princess. When you're not irritating the hell out of me, I'm pretty sure you're my favorite person on the damn planet."

She shuddered at his words, sending a jolt of energy through him as he held her.

"We have a lot of crap that we need to hash out, but right now, I need you to carry me to that bed and have your way with me. In my mind, you haven't banged me nearly enough for me to be pregnant, and I need to even the tally. It's extremely unfair."

Breathing a laugh, he lowered his lips, unable to keep from tasting her any longer. Sliding his tongue into her mouth, he groaned as it mated with hers. She tasted of toothpaste and mint, purity and innocence. Reveling in her, blood coursed through his muscled body as it throbbed, so thrilled to be in her arms once more.

With his mind, he dematerialized her clothes, causing them to reappear in a pile on the floor near the bathroom. Standing naked in his arms, she pulled back to stare at him, her fangs glistening as she beamed.

"That was so hot. Okay, you can you use your powers to get me naked anytime. I'll give you a pass on that one."

Smiling down at her, he bent his knees and placed his arms under the backs of her legs. Lifting her, he carried her to the bed. Black, sensuous curls spread across the pillow, her beauty making his heart slam in his chest.

Sitting beside her, he stroked her cheek. "I told you that sex never meant anything to me. It didn't until I met you. Now, I wish I'd taken the time to learn how to make love properly. I want so badly to please you."

Sky-blue irises swam with compassion. "I'm a washed-up virgin. Or, I was, until I met you. So, I don't really have anything to compare you to."

Expelling a laugh, he felt himself drowning in her. "I want to make love to you, Arderin. I've never called it that before, so I guess I'm kind of a virgin too."

Her smile was so charming as her fangs sat atop her bottom lip. "So, let's do it."

Standing, he removed his shirt.

"You're wearing my ring," she said. The tears that pooled in her eyes caused him to feel a thud, right in his solar plexus.

"I never took it off," he said, grasping the beautiful trinket above his heart.

"Well, take it off now so you can fuck me. I don't want it slamming in my face."

Laughing, he pulled it over his head and placed it on the bedside table. Unbuckling his belt, he divested himself of his clothes. Sitting beside her, he gazed at her abdomen, running his hand over it. "You have a little bump."

"Just barely," she said, nodding. "You don't notice it when I'm wearing clothes."

Emotion for her swamped him, knowing that their child was growing inside her. "It's so beautiful," he said, caressing the soft skin of her belly.

"You know what else is beautiful?" she asked.

"What?"

Opening those gorgeous thighs, she arched her brow. Eyeing him seductively, she smiled.

Not needing any more of a hint, he crawled onto the bed between her legs. Lowering his mouth to her, he kissed her lower abdomen. Trailing his lips down, he nuzzled past the sexy black strip of hair, above the juncture of her thighs.

Using his hands to spread her apart, he placed his lips on the sensitive folds of her sweetest place. Reveling in her moan, he lapped at her, needing to taste her honeyed wetness. Long, sure strokes ensured that she was squirming under him, whispering his name.

Lowering her hands, she grasped onto his short hair.

"You let it grow," she said, staring down at him.

He shrugged. "You said you liked it. And it gives you something to grab onto when I suck you. Pull me into you, princess. I'm going to make you come."

Lowering his mouth to her again, he groaned when she dragged him into her core. Loving the pleasure-pain that her slim fingers triggered at his scalp, he threaded his tongue through her moisture. Licking up to her tiny nub, he flicked it several times, then sucked it between his teeth.

"Oh, god," she cried, rubbing her essence all over him.

"Do you like that?" he murmured into her.

"Yes. Bite it. That felt so fucking good."

Chuckling, he pulled her clit between his teeth again, gently biting it as he sucked it in an endless rhythm. The tip of his tongue flicked the sensitive nub as he pulled it through his teeth, over and over.

Releasing his hair, her body tensed, hips coming off the bed. Determined not to lose the momentum, he stayed latched onto her, wanting so badly to make it good for her.

"I'm coming," she wailed, her body quivering as it began to shudder. Loving how beautiful and responsive she was, he hugged her hips, needing to pull her as close to him as possible.

Silky moisture oozed from her core, and he nuzzled into it, lapping it up as her spasms began to die down.

"Holy crap," she said, panting. "That was awesome. Now, get up here and fuck me."

Laughing at how bossy she was, he slid up over her flawless body until he was stretched over her, chest-to-chest, hip-to-hip. Lifting her leg over his hip, so that her calf curved over the globe of his ass, he aligned the tip of his shaft with her wetness.

"Ready, princess?" he asked.

"Ready," she said, eyes sparkling with playful naughtiness and such genuine desire.

"You're so fucking cute," he said, lowering to kiss her. Once his tongue was warring with hers, he thrust into her.

"Yessss," she hissed, devouring his lips with hers as he loved her. "I missed you so much."

"I'm so sorry," he whispered, gazing into her as he slid back and forth, the sensation achingly pleasurable as the drenched walls of her core clutched him like a glove. "I was so afraid you wouldn't forgive me."

"*Ohmygod*," she breathed, her head falling back on the pillow. "I don't care right now. Keep pounding me like that. Holy crap. It feels amazing."

Desperately wanting to please her, he concentrated on following her directive, determined to make her scream when she came. The plushy tissues of her deepest place squeezed his swollen cock, and he struggled to understand how anything could feel so incredible. Threading his fingers through her beautiful hair at the crown of her head, he held her stationary, pummeling her as her body started to tense.

"Can I go harder?"

"Yes!"

Concentrating with all his might, he hammered into her, gritting his teeth as sweat poured down his body. The straining walls of her snug channel choked his thick shaft, and he felt his balls start to tingle.

"I'm so close," he gritted, his hips frenzied as they jutted into her. "Fuck, Arderin, you feel so good."

Calling his name, her body snapped. Throwing her head back, she lost control as he continued gyrating into her. As she convulsed around him, he felt his seed fill his cock and begin to spurt. Groaning with joy, he pulled her close, needing to feel her silky skin against him as he came. Losing control of his body, he gave in to the pleasure, letting his muscles contract and tremble as he depleted himself into her.

Finally, after what seemed like a lifetime, he regained consciousness. Wrapped up in her, he opened his eyes, realizing that he'd collapsed entirely on top of her.

"Am I crushing you? I can move."

"I swear to the goddess, if you move one muscle, I'll kill you." Her thin arms hauled him to her, almost choking him.

Chuckling, he turned his head so that his lips brushed her ear. Loving her resulting shiver, he spoke into the small crevice, "You imagined me sticking my tongue in your ear. After you stitched me up in the infirmary."

"Fuck yeah," she said, dragging her fingernails up and down his back in a soft caress. "And then, I went up to my room and rubbed one out. I thought of you the whole time. It was so hot."

Laughing, he nuzzled her ear with his nose. "I'll store that away for the future. There's a lot I can do to your ear."

"Okay, I'm down. I'm not even sure what you're talking about, but I'm game for anything."

Snuggling into her, he smiled.

They lay like that for a while, cherishing each other's nearness, stroking each other softly. Eventually, he slid off her, turning to lie on his side. Pulling her front to his, he regarded her as they shared a pillow.

"I don't even know where to start," he said.

"Um, yeah," she said, the corner of her pink lips turning up. "Should we start with the fact that I'm pregnant, that you want nothing to do with me, that your sister's back, or that my brothers are all lined up to murder you?"

"Wow, that's quite a lineup," he said, rubbing her back, his arm lying over her side. "Let's start with me not wanting anything to do with you. I think you know that ship has sailed."

"Does that mean you'll consider bonding with me?"

Terrified at the question, he studied her. "I don't want to answer that yet. There are a lot of things that need to happen before we get there. The idea of tying you to me for eternity is petrifying and very dangerous. I'm an extremely dark person, Arderin. I don't know if you really understand how evil I am."

She looked at him with such love that he felt his blackened heart flush ten shades of red. It was as if she gave the damn thing new life. "I comprehend every single part of you. Drinking from you in the cave gave me a window into your soul. I know you didn't want me to see the worst parts of you because you thought I would hate you."

Her fingers threaded through the short hair at his temple as she spoke, her voice so melodic. "But the opposite happened. I saw your struggles, your pain, your vulnerabilities. I saw your worst moments, and they didn't make me think less of you. They made me understand how unbelievable it is that you chose to honor your word to your mother. All these centuries, you've chosen the light. It was a brave and difficult choice, one that many others wouldn't have made.

"I won't push you. I know you need to figure this out on your own. But I won't let you underestimate how well I know you. I think I understand you better than anyone in your life, including your mother. I'm your soulmate, whether you want to admit it or not."

Darkrip rubbed the silky skin of her arm, humbled by her genuine compassion and acceptance of him. Unable to acknowledge her beautiful words, he teased her instead. "You know that *soulmate* is a stupid word made up by humans to sell greeting cards, right?"

She scrunched her features together. "Well, I like it, and I'll use it if I want to."

Loving her scowl, he pinched her butt. "Okay, little imp. Lord, knows there's no use in arguing with you." Growing serious, he slid his hand up to cup her cheek. "I need you to be patient with me. I'm going to try my best to sort this out. I'm scared that my feelings for you are going to get you killed. And since you're determined to have this baby, it's also a target."

"I know. I love that you want to protect me. But I'm my own woman and I deserve to build the life I want with the man I care about. Even if that man is a huge pussy."

"You can call me names all you want. I don't want to see you hurt. After what happened to my mother, I don't think I could live with myself."

"Says the man who tried to strangle me," she said, arching an eyebrow.

Sighing, he caressed her cheek with the pad of his thumb. "I felt so terrible afterward. I almost threw myself in the Purges."

Smiling, she said, "Evie said you'd try to do that. She said you'd beat the crap out of yourself."

"Well, it's warranted. I never should have done that. It was beneath me and you and whatever the hell this is between us. I'm sorry. It was extremely careless, and you deserve better."

"Okay," she said, scooching over to give him a peck on the lips. "That was a nice apology. I'll let you keep your testicles. For now."

"Man, you're one tough broad."

"Damn straight. Plus, I like your balls. I think I need to play with them more."

Throwing back his head, he laughed. "You say the weirdest shit. I've never met anyone who makes me laugh like you do. You're funny as hell."

"Well, if the world's crashing down, we might as well have a sense of humor about it." Grinning, she wiggled into him.

"So, how pissed are your brothers?"

She told him about the discussion they'd had around the conference room table. When she finished, her ice-blue eyes gazed into his. "They're prepared to accept you as my mate and the father of my child. If you get up the courage to ask me."

Nodding, he reached for her hand, bringing it to his lips to give it a sweet kiss. Lifting it to his face, he maneuvered it so that she palmed his cheek. "Give me some time, princess. I've spent my whole life telling myself I couldn't have children and that I was a wretch who didn't deserve a mate or any sort of happiness. And now, I have this gorgeous, brilliant woman who wants those things with me. It's unbelievable and so fucking frightening. I'm so scared I'll mess everything up. Part of me feels it would be best for you to raise the baby on your own and find a man who doesn't have my fucked-up blood and fucked-up past. He could protect you both, since my father will surely come looking for you."

Anger flashed in her eyes. "No way in hell. You got me into this mess, and you're sure as hell stuck with me now. Got it?"

Laughing, he rolled onto his back and pulled her to splay over him. "I'm the luckiest bastard in the world. I feel like I'm dreaming. I don't deserve you. I don't deserve any of this."

"You don't give yourself enough credit," she said, kissing him with her soft lips. "You played a significant role in reuniting the species. You kept your word to your mother for all those centuries. You fight valiantly by my brother's side against your father. I love you, Darkrip. So much. I need you to know that."

His nostrils flared, and her face blurred, as wetness gathered in his eyes. Pushing the emotion away, he said, "I don't want you to love me. I don't understand that word."

"Yes, you do" she said, kissing him again. "You just don't want to admit it. When you're ready, I'll be here. Don't wait too long. I'd like to hear it from you."

Wrapping his arms around her, he pulled her into his chest. "You're too much. I don't know what to do with you."

"Well, since we're here, I'm thinking you could bang me again. We know you don't really need any recovery time."

Rolling over, he reveled in her squeal as he took her advice and loved her with his body, since he couldn't with his words.

Chapter 33

That afternoon, Darkrip texted Miranda, letting her know he was at Astaria.

Miranda: That's great. Welcome home. Can't wait to hug you. I'm at Uteria for a few days. I just texted Sathan that you want to talk to him. He, Latimus and Heden will be waiting for you in Sathan's office at 4:30. You're welcome. ☺

Darkrip: I always knew you hated me. But thanks for ensuring I won't be a coward.

Miranda: I love you. You know that. Now, go convince my caveman husband that you want to marry Arderin. And maybe convince yourself while you're at it.

Darkrip: I don't deserve her, but that doesn't seem matter to her. I'm determined to do right by her. I promise. How's Evie?

Miranda: Fine. I think she wants to bone Kenden. Did you know about this?

Darkrip: Yes. She has some interesting images of him in her mind. Probably too dirty to text.

Miranda: Yikes! Can't wait to hear. TTYL.

Smiling, Darkrip placed his phone in his back pocket. Unable to deny it any longer, he admitted that he loved his amazing half-sister. So unfamiliar with that word, he acknowledged that the emotion that sat warm and deep for her in his heart must be love. It was so genuine and true, and it coursed through him with such bright energy.

At four-thirty, he materialized into the royal office chamber, Arderin's three hulking brothers standing in front of Sathan's desk, arms crossed over their massive chests.

"Wow. This is gonna be fun," he said, rubbing his hand over the back of his neck as he regarded them.

"You've got a lot of fucking explaining to do, Darkrip," Sathan said. "I'm going to do my best not to annihilate your face with my fist while you get to it."

"Look, I get it, guys. I'm not going to stand here and give you excuses. My actions are unforgivable. Although I can snap your necks with a thought and disappear before you lay a hand on me, I'll stand here and let you beat the shit out of me if it will help make my case."

Muscles corded in their strong jaws as they clenched their teeth. "And what case is that?" Heden asked.

"Can we at least sit down?"

"No," the three of them responded in unison.

"Okay," he said, puffing out a breath, his cheeks expanding. "After living in the Deamon caves for centuries, I thought I'd lost the ability to be intimidated. Wow." Running a hand over his hair, he contemplated.

"I don't know where to start," Darkrip said, shrugging. "She's a beautiful and exceptional woman. I wanted to rape her the night I knocked her unconscious and sent her down the river."

Sathan stepped forward, most likely to punch him, and Latimus extended an arm to hold him back. "Not a good start, man," Latimus said.

Nodding, he said, "I'm telling you this not to piss you off, but for you to understand how hard I fought not to touch her. Once I came to live at Astaria, the need to be with her almost drove me crazy. But I never laid a hand on her, even though I think I could've seduced her if I wanted to. She was always too important to me, and I knew that I would never be good enough for her.

"My mother came to me many centuries ago and asked me to live by my Slayer side. I've done my best to honor that request. I regret how evil I was when I was young, but my father urged me on, and I didn't have exposure outside the caves. I haven't been that man for so long, but I know that I will never even come close to being worthy of Arderin. I swear, I was determined not to touch her in the cave. But even the best intentions aren't always honored. I'm sorry for creating a mess, but I'll never be sorry I made love to her. It was one of the best experiences of my wretched life. I don't know what else to say."

Sathan's eyes narrowed. "And what are your intentions now? She's prepared to bond with you and raise the child. Do you want the same?"

"I'm working through that. It's something that I need to give a lot of thought to, and I know that's not the answer you're looking for. But I don't want to lie to you. She deserves a full life with someone who can make her happy, and I need to make sure I can do that. I'm hoping that you all can understand what I'm struggling with. It's imperative that I get this right."

"I understand," Latimus said. "And as much as I want to rip your arms out of your sockets, I know that Arderin pursued you as well." Addressing his brothers, he said, "I've spoken to Arderin, and Lila's also told me some things they discussed. She put some moves on him. I know that's hard for us to think about, but we need to give Darkrip some credit."

They scowled, remaining silent.

"Her happiness is of utmost importance to us," Latimus said. "We need to know that you'll do right by her."

"I'm determined to do just that. It's all I think about. I'm not sure what that looks like yet, but I'm dead set on figuring it out. I promise."

"Do you love her?" Heden asked.

The cold rush of fear that he always felt when examining his feelings for Arderin flashed through him. "I'm working on that too. Love is a word I only associated with my mother my entire life. Every time I showed her any affection or love, he raped her in front of me. It was awful, and after a while, I convinced myself that I would never feel that deeply again. It doesn't have the same meaning for me that it does for all of you. But I need you to know that I care for her more than anyone since my mother died. The feelings I have for her run very deep, and, honestly, that terrifies me. If he kidnaps and tortures her, I don't think I'll survive. It's why I really need to think about the best course for our future."

The three colossal Vampyres just stood, studying him in silence.

"I can lie to you if you want, but I think that's beneath all of us."

"I appreciate your honesty," Sathan said. "The fact that you've lived by your Slayer half for many centuries is admirable. I'm not sure how many would've been able to for so long. What you went through in your early life is heartbreaking, and I'm truly sorry that you had to endure that."

"Thank you," Darkrip said, giving a nod. "It was certainly no picnic, that's for sure."

Sathan uncrossed his arms, letting them fall to his sides. "When our willful sister makes up her mind, it's impossible to change it. She's decided that she loves you and wants to build a life with you. We accept that, even though it's extremely difficult for us." Walking toward him, Sathan extended his hand. "If you promise to honor her and put her first, I will accept your relationship with her."

"I promise," Darkrip said, shaking his hand. "Nothing's ever been more important to me. I'm determined to get this right."

"And we need you to focus on working with Evie to defeat your father," Latimus said, approaching him as he let go of Sathan's hand. "She's still unsure on whether to fight with us, and I need you to help sway her."

"Absolutely," Darkrip said, shaking his hand. "I hope to all the gods that she's the descendant to kill my father. If not, the burden will pass on to our children, and I don't want them to live in a world where he even exists."

Heden came forward, offering him his hand. "Arderin's a little brat half the time, man. Good fucking luck."

Laughing, Darkrip shook his hand. "Don't I know it. She drives me insane about ninety-five percent of the time."

Heden held up a finger. "But I love her to pieces and will mutilate you if you ever hurt her. Capisce?"

"Got it," Darkrip said, smiling. "Thank you all for being so understanding. I know it's hard to discuss this stuff about your sister. She loves all of you so much, and I'm honored that you can accept me. She's...*everything*. I'm so damn lucky."

"I hate to tell you, man, but you love her," Latimus said, patting his shoulder. "Stop being a coward and admit it. From one coward to another, it's just fucking easier that way."

Darkrip chuckled. "Good advice, man. Thanks."

"Do you want to continue to live in the cabin?" Sathan asked. "It's yours if you want it."

Darkrip shot him a sardonic glare. "Your sister informed me that it's actually hers now. Stubborn woman. But yes, she and I discussed it, and we'd like to live there together. Only if you all are okay with it though. I don't want to make you uncomfortable."

"Dude, you knocked up our sister. I think that train has left the station."

The corner of his lips curved. "Fair enough."

"It only seems right," Sathan said. "And having you with her will make her happy. That's our ultimate goal here. Just do us a favor and let us pretend that you sleep on the couch."

"Sorry, man, but we said no lies," Darkrip said, chuckling. "She's the most stunning woman I've ever seen. I'm so honored to be with her that way."

"Thanks for meeting us here, Darkrip," Sathan said. "I'm heading to Uteria to see Miranda and Tordor tonight and will be back in the morning. If you need anything, let me know."

They all shook hands once more, and Darkrip headed to the kitchen to find some food. Glarys gave him a warm embrace, glowing with excitement about the baby. As he sat at the counter, eating her scrumptious buttermilk pie, he thanked the heavens that the three massive Vampyres hadn't taken him up on his offer to kick his ass.

* * * *

Darkrip materialized back into the cabin, finding Arderin sitting at the desk by the window in front of her laptop. Slender fingers maneuvered around the keyboard as she stared intently at the glowing screen. Walking over to her, he placed his hands on her shoulders.

"Hey," she said, beaming up at him. She wore tiny black reading glasses that made her look absolutely adorable. Pulling them off, she threw them on the desk. "How did it go with my brothers?"

"Fine. They decided to let me live. For now," he said, massaging her.

"*Ohmygod*," she sighed, leaning her head back on his abdomen and closing her eyes. "That feels so good. I've been writing for hours."

"What are you working on?"

"Now that we've finished the serum, I'm writing a thesis on the psychological implications of healing patients who have been burned for many decades. I have to use that timeframe since I hope to publish it in the human world someday."

Pride in her intellect speared though him. He'd never met anyone with her voracious mind and lightning-quick aptitude. "You're amazing," he said, not even beginning to understand how she could possibly love a black-hearted devil like him.

"Thanks," she said, opening her eyes. Gazing up at him, as the back of her head still rested on his abdomen, she asked, "So, did they crap themselves when you told them we're going to be living together?"

Breathing a laugh, he grinned. "They weren't thrilled, but since I've knocked you up, I think they realize that we're already having sex."

Closing the laptop, she stood and slid her arms around his neck. "Living together is a big step. Are you freaking?"

"No," he said, placing a peck on her soft lips. "I'm so honored that you want to live with me. It's such a gift."

Lifting her leg to wrap around his hip, he palmed her sweet ass and held her as she wrapped both legs around his waist. "Don't think for one second that I'm letting you live with me and not cuddle with me every night. If you're too much of a wuss to bond with me, I'm at least putting my foot down on that."

Chuckling, he kissed her, lapping at her tongue with his. "I think I can live with having your gorgeous body wrapped around me every night. It'll be tough, but I'll survive."

"Jerk," she said, thrusting her tongue in his mouth. "You know, my friend Naran is head over heels for me and would cuddle with me every night. I can go live with him if it's too much for you. He'd be happy to snuggle anytime—"

Yelping, she laughed as he rotated and threw her on the bed. Sliding on top of her, he cupped her flushed cheeks with his palms.

"If he touches you, he's dead. You're mine, Arderin. All mine. Do you understand?"

Black curls framed her face as she bit her lip. "Prove it."

Groaning, he muttered something about how exasperating she was and proceeded to love her until she was screaming his name. Damn straight. That would be the only name she'd ever scream again.

That night, he held her, pulling her so close he thought he might choke her. But his resilient little Vampyre just snuggled into him, sighing into his neck that he was a born cuddler, laughing when he pinched the tight globe of her perfect butt.

The next day, they went to the infirmary for her first ultrasound. She was almost three months along, and Darkrip thought she'd never looked more beautiful. Pregnancy seemed to give her a glow, those stunning eyes pulsing, her cheeks always splotched with the most magnificent blush of color.

Holding her hand, he watched Nolan squirt the clear gel on her abdomen and then place the wand on top.

"There you go," Nolan said, pointing to the screen. "There's the head and the feet and the hands," he said, moving his hand around. "It's too early to tell the sex, but if you want to know, we can try and look at the sixteen-week ultrasound."

Never believing that he would ever have children, Darkrip felt his throat close up, and he brought Arderin's hand to his mouth, kissing it as he watched the screen.

"It's okay," she said, love for him shining in her eyes. "We're not going to let anything happen to this kid. I promise. It's gonna have an awesome life. I can't wait."

"What if it's evil?" he asked, knowing his eyes were glassy, not caring that the human doctor was there.

"It won't be," she said, squeezing his hand.

How fitting that his strong woman would be giving him hope as she lay on the bed. Realizing that he had to pluck up the courage to be the man she needed, he nodded. "Okay. I'll choose to believe that. We have to raise it right. Thank god you're its mom. I'm a wretch."

"Hey," she said, compassion flashing across her flawless face. "You're not that bad. Most of the time," she teased, scrunching her nose at him.

Laughing, he kissed her hand again and thanked Nolan as they finished.

Two days later, Darkrip transported to Uteria, wanting to speak to Evie. They saddled the horses, her riding Majesty, and he riding Thor, and headed out beyond the wall of the compound. Once outside, they tied the horses to a nearby tree and sat on the plushy green grass.

"So, the spunky princess forgave you for strangling her?" Evie asked, her scarlet eyebrow arched.

"Yeah." Darkrip nodded, pulling at the grass. "She's mad for me. I've got her eating out of the palm of my hand."

His sister shot him a look, knowing he was full of shit.

Laughing, he shook his head. "I'm so fucking in love with her. I need to tell her. I'm just such a damn coward. I know that once I do, she'll insist we bond. Then, she'll have the baby, and, bam, I've got two people who will always be marks for him. I'm scared shitless."

Evie shrugged her slender shoulders. "Then, we'll just have to kill him."

"So, you're ready to fight with us?" he asked, gazing into her eyes, so much like his; like Miranda's.

"I've figured out something that I want. Before you ask me, let me tell you that I'm not quite ready yet. But I will be soon. Once I am, we'll need to train together on uniting our powers. There are a lot of dark magic techniques from the human world that I need to teach you."

"I hope they don't call too much to my Deamon half. I've done so well for so long and want to make sure I continue living by Mother's blood."

"I don't think you have anything to worry about," she said, giving him a knowing glare. "You might as well be made up entirely of her. You're so good now. It's quite a transformation. It gives me hope."

"You can do it too," he said, smiling at her.

"Don't hold your breath," she muttered. Kicking the grass with her riding boot, she sighed. "But we'll see. For now, go marry your Vampyre, and let's have a party. I miss dancing, and maybe I can shimmy up to someone at your reception and get laid."

"No luck with Kenden?"

She rolled her eyes. "He's infuriatingly stubborn and fights his attraction to me like I've never seen. It's quite absurd really. I can see how much he wants me from the images in his mind. It's only a matter of time. I haven't had to chase anyone this fervently in...well, maybe forever. It's annoying but also just a tad bit fun." Her smile was brilliant under the afternoon sun.

"How strange would it be if I married Miranda's husband's sister, and you married her cousin? That's some next-level 'keep it in the family' shit."

Laughing, she threw back her head. "You're not kidding. Although, Kenden doesn't have our mother's blood, so, technically, we're family in name only. That said, I was raped by our father for decades. I'm so fucked-up, there's probably nothing that would be off-limits to me."

Grabbing her hand, Darkrip threaded his fingers through hers. "I'm so sorry I wasn't able to stop him from violating you. I tried so many times, but he was always so strong. He would freeze me in place and make me watch while he tortured you and Mother. I should've done better by you."

Evie squeezed his hand and then disengaged, bringing her knees to her chest and wrapping her arms around her legs. Setting her chin on her knees, she stared off into the distance. "He's a fucking son of a bitch. He tortured all of us. I hate him so much. I can't wait to look into his eyes as I murder him. Fucking asshole."

Darkrip nodded, remaining silent as they released the horrible memories to the bright, sunny air of the meadow.

"But let's not bring up marriage again," she said, wrinkling her nose. "How absolutely boring. Why people want to tie themselves to one penis or one vagina for eternity is beyond me. Arderin is gorgeous, but you'll eventually get tired of her."

"No way. She's everything I've ever wanted in a lover and a mate. I'm extremely lucky that she even speaks to me, much less loves me."

"Gross. You sound ridiculous."

Chuckling, he arched a brow. "Well, maybe Kenden will make it so good for you that you'll change your mind."

"Screw that. I'm going to give him the best lay of his life—or maybe the best ten lays, depending on how much I like it—then, I'll let him get on with whatever he does in this poor excuse for a world. After we kill Father, I'm heading back to the human world. It's so boring here."

"We'll see. I never thought I'd ever have a mate or a child, but shit happens."

"No kids for me, thanks. I have enough to deal with, controlling my evil half. Not really interested in creating another little monster to manage. Although, Tordor was pretty damn cute. I only despised him half the time." She winked, acknowledging her teasing.

"Famous last words. Wear Kenden down, and then, we'll talk."

"Come on," she said, standing and extending her hand down to him. "Let's ride some more. It's a gorgeous day, and I want to take advantage of it."

Taking her hand, they straddled their horses and rode the open fields outside the wall of Uteria, much as their mother had done centuries before.

Chapter 34

Arderin walked into their cabin, heart bursting after leaving Sadie at Uteria. She'd gone to visit her today, excited to check up on her progress with the serum. She'd been using it on her arm, abdomen and thigh, and the results were astounding. Smooth skin now replaced the burnt tissue and blood flow could be seen through her pale skin.

She agreed to try it on her cheek, starting next week. Arderin realized that this much change was quite overwhelming for her dear friend and wanted to make sure she didn't push too hard.

Speaking of not pushing too hard, she closed the door behind her, anxious to see Darkrip. He'd been at Uteria for two days, sequestered with Evie as she taught him some human magic, and she missed him terribly. In the month they'd been living together, he seemed to slowly be accepting his feelings for her. Arderin hoped he grew a pair one day soon. She was ready to bond with him and didn't want to walk down the aisle looking like a pregnant whale.

A dim light shone on the bedside table, and she looked for him as her eyes adjusted. Inhaling, she smelled something yummy coming from the small kitchen that adjoined their bedroom.

"Hey," she said, stopping in the doorway of the kitchen to observe him straining pasta from a large silver pot.

"Hey," Darkrip said, setting the pasta down so that it could cool. Lifting a wooden spoon, he swirled some red sauce in a pot that sat atop the stove.

"Didn't know you could cook," she said, smiling. "I actually love pasta. Jack and I eat it all the time."

"Good," he said, giving her a sexy smile. "I asked Glarys to teach me how to cook a few things, so I didn't have to keep raiding the kitchen in the main house. Pasta is actually really easy." He wore those expensive tailored clothes that she loved, the black pants hugging his muscular thighs. A thin black belt sat below his buttoned shirt. His feet were bare, and her mouth started to water. He was way yummier than the pasta, for sure.

"I set out a bottle of red," he said, jerking his head toward the table. "Nolan said you could have a small glass each week. Want to pour us one?"

"Sure. Let me just change." Throwing her bag on the dresser, she exchanged her sweater for a soft tank and kicked off her ankle boots and socks. Leaving on her comfy but tight jeans, she headed into the kitchen. Pouring them both a glass, she sat at the two-seater table that aligned the wall in the tiny kitchen. He'd set it for two, with plates and silverware.

Coming over, he sat a full goblet of Slayer blood in front of her, winking as he bent and gave her a kiss. Walking back to the stove, he resumed stirring. Narrowing her eyes, Arderin sipped it gingerly. Something was up. What the hell was he after?

"Someone's in a good mood," she said.

He shrugged, spooning out the red sauce into a bowl. Licking it from his fingers, she caught a glimpse of his tongue and felt wetness rush between her thighs. Good god, she wanted to bone him against the stove. It would be so freaking hot. Literally.

"Evie and I had a good session today. Her powers are insane. I never even realized. If she's the descendant to kill him, then he'll be dead. I can't wait for that day."

He set the pasta, sauce and butter-slathered garlic bread on the table. Sitting across from her, he smiled with mischief. "Bon appétit."

Throwing her head back, she laughed. "This spread is way better than the dead rats you had in the cave. They were disgusting." Dramatically, she shivered.

Giving her a good-natured glare, he said, "Well, you weren't the one who had to eat them."

"Thank the goddess. You food-eaters are all so strange to us. Although, the taste is amazing. Gimme." Reaching for the pasta, she scooped a healthy portion onto her plate and spooned sauce over it.

"You've been ravenous lately," he said, chuckling when she arched an eyebrow, giving him a come-hither look. "For *food*, princess. I think the baby likes it."

"I think so too."

They chatted as they ate, catching up on the past two days. "Do you like the wine?" Darkrip asked.

"Mmm hmm," she said, chewing. "It's really good."

"I found a bottle of this red on a picnic blanket outside Latimus' cabin the first night he seduced Lila. Then, I transported to the river where you were trying to heal the bird."

"I remember," she said, gazing at him as she sipped her wine. "You pissed the hell out of me."

"I was trying so hard not to shove my cock in your mouth. You were so passionate and captivating under the moonlight."

She rolled her eyes. "I would've cut it off. Good thing you restrained."

Laughing, he nodded. "I guess so. Man, you're tough."

"Don't forget it."

They finished, and he cleared the table. Asking her to pour him another glass, he departed through the kitchen door, returning with a pile of papers and folders stacked high. Sitting down, he regarded her, the documents in front of him on the table.

"What are those?"

His green eyes darted over her face, and she struggled to read his mood. "They're our future. Or, what I hope will be our future, if you let me give it to you."

Her eight-chambered heart began to pound in her chest. "I'm listening."

"I've struggled with how to do this with you, Arderin. You're so incredible, and I don't even know how to go about making you happy."

Love for him coursed through her pulsing body. "You already make me happy."

"Not nearly enough. You deserve to have everything you've ever wanted. It's the only way that I'll let you tie yourself to me. I have to make sure I give you the life you're entitled to."

"Okay," she said, nibbling her lip in anticipation.

"I kept these," he said, holding a few of the papers in the air and shaking them. She realized they were the medical school applications she'd absconded from the human world. The notes to her brothers were scrawled on the backs of the white sheets.

"California, huh?" Those gorgeous olive eyes glowed as he smiled at her.

"Yep," she said, shrugging. "It just seemed more my style. And it's where the Kardashians live, so, obviously, it's awesome."

Laughing, he sat straighter in the chair. "If you say so." Lifting what looked to be a course book, he said, "This is an MCAT prep manual." He continued down the stack, pointing as he spoke. "These are medical school applications to every prominent school and residency program in California."

The curious wheels of her mind were firing. "While I appreciate all that, I'm about to have a baby with a crap-ton of immortal blood. I can't really go to the human world right now."

"I know," Darkrip said, standing and closing the small distance between them. Taking the glass from her hand, he set it on the table. Bending at the knees, he slid her across the chair until her legs encircled his waist. As she clutched her arms around his neck, he carried her to the bed. Sitting on the edge, he held her as she straddled him, her ankles locked behind his back.

"In a few years, once my father is dead and the baby is old enough, we're going to go to California. You're going to take the MCAT and get into whatever medical school you want. After that, you'll apply for residency. I've talked to Nolan about the track you need to take and the time it will take to complete it. Heden has assured me that he can forge your undergraduate credentials, and Nolan says you've already learned more than any human undergrad would ever know. Medical school and residency will take seven years, and then, we can decide if you want to stay there and practice or come back to the immortal world."

Tears burned her eyes as she regarded him. His face was filled with such love, and she knew he'd finally embraced the emotions he felt for her.

"But you hate the human world," she said, squeezing her arms around his neck.

Breathing a laugh, he nodded. "I do. But if I'm there with you, I'll be able to muddle through. I'll take care of our son or daughter while you complete everything."

"Are you sure?" she asked, rubbing her fingers over the soft skin on the back of his neck. "I don't want you to live somewhere you won't be happy."

"Arderin," he whispered, kissing her so sweetly. "Haven't you realized that I can't even be remotely happy unless I'm near you?"

Unable to contain it, a tear slipped down her cheek. "This is so amazing. I never expected you'd be willing to do anything like this for me. Now, tell me why you're doing it."

"Because I want you to be happy," he said, wiping the wetness from her cheek.

"That's a good start," she said, knowing that he was playing with her. "Why else?"

"Because you're a brilliant woman and you've earned this."

Smiling, she rubbed her nose against his. "Getting warmer. Why else?"

Cradling the back of her head with his hands, he stared into her. "Because I love you so damn much," he said, the timbre of his rich baritone so sincere. "I never even realized that I could feel this deeply. You've given me so much, princess, and I want to try and give a little piece of that back to you."

She began to cry in earnest then, tears streaming down her cheeks. "It's about time. I was getting worried."

"You don't ever have to be worried about my feelings for you," he said, rubbing the moisture away with his thumbs. "They've latched onto my dead heart and made it beat again. Thank you, Arderin. You'll never know how much I love you."

"I love you too," she said, pulling him to her for a firm embrace. Head buried in his neck, she cried tears of happiness, wetting his fancy dress shirt.

"It's okay," he soothed, running his fingers down her hair. "You still drive me batshit crazy about ninety percent of the time, so don't get too excited."

Laughing, she nodded against him. "It wouldn't be fun if I didn't keep you on your toes."

Fisting his hand in her hair, he gently pulled her head back so that their gazes locked. "Now, if you're done crying, I'd very much like to fuck you."

"Well," she said, waggling her eyebrows, "I'd very much like to fuck you back. And maybe I stopped at the barracks on the way home to grab a little something for us, since I haven't seen you in two days."

Lifting from him, she walked to her bag and pulled out two shiny pairs of handcuffs.

"Fuck yes," he said, his eyes flashing with desire. Standing, he began to unbutton his shirt.

"Use your powers," she whispered, thinking it was so hot. Closing his eyes, he dematerialized his clothes, causing them to appear in a pile at the foot of the bed. Grabbing onto his cock, he began to jerk it back and forth.

"Do mine too," she said, her voice gravelly.

With a whoosh, he divested her clothes with his mind, depositing them beside his on the floor.

"Now, lie on the bed," she commanded, sauntering toward him. "This time, I'm binding *you* up, little boy."

"Is that so?" he asked when she was just inches from him.

"Oh, hell yes." Pushing his chest, he fell to the bed. Laughter filled the room as she shackled one of his wrists to the bedpost, and then, the other. Straddling him, she panted, "You're so sexy." Running a nail down his abs, she reveled in how the muscles quivered.

"Crawl up here and sit on my face," Darkrip commanded.

Complying, Arderin climbed his body and straddled him, placing her ankles under the juncture of his arms and chest. Lowering, she palmed the wall as she placed her center over his mouth. Groaning, he lapped her, murmuring how sweet she was. As her breath became more labored, she gyrated on top of him, jutting her hips, loving how his tongue followed her. Gasping, she felt him spear it inside her. Arching her spine, she leaned back, palms on the comforter, arms outstretched. Mouth open, she stroked her core over his face and tongue, every inch of her body on fire.

Her long hair shimmied over his shaft as he sucked her clit through his teeth. Undulating, she teased him, leaning her head back so that the silky strands stroked his cock. Finally, when his pace became frenzied and every nerve ending felt that it might explode, she came. Wailing with joy, she climaxed around him, squeezing his face with the soft skin of her thighs. Sucking in air, she lifted her head.

His gorgeous eyes gazed into hers, so full of love and longing. Inching down his body, she flung her hair over her shoulder. Grasping the base of his thick shaft, she slid her lips over the thick head.

"Goddamnit," he groaned, pulling at the cuffs. She could see why he liked this binding thing—it was so freaking erotic. Determined to make it good for him, she worked her mouth over his straining cock, dousing it with saliva, the strokes of her tongue firm and thorough.

"Don't stop," he said, throwing his head back on the pillow. "Fuck, you're amazing at this. How in the hell are you so good at giving head?"

"I'm a natural," she said, loving his chuckle.

"Hell yes, you are. Wrap both hands around the base and keep sucking. I'm so close."

Following his directive, she tugged him with both hands, pulling the head into her wet mouth over and over. His muscular body tensed, and he screamed her name. Pulses of his release began to jet over her tongue, and she collected them all, loving how salty and spicy he tasted. Taking it all in, she waited until his body had relaxed against the bed and swallowed. His eyes were locked onto her as her throat bobbed.

"You're so fucking beautiful."

Smiling, she climbed over him. Aligning his shaft with her core, she slid over him. Closing her eyes, her head tilted back as she rode him.

"God, you're so tight, princess. Good girl. Milk my cock." His hips rose to meet hers, undulating, as she clenched around him with her snug channel. Hearing the cuffs clink open, she opened her eyes. Sitting up, he grabbed her and spun her around. Stretching out his legs, he impaled her, his front to her back. The perfect globes of her ass pounded his upper thighs as she sat atop him.

"Ride me this way," he commanded into her ear.

"No fair," she said, her head lolling back on his shoulder as she moved up and down. "You unlocked the cuffs. Cheater."

"Take it like a good little princess," he said, clutching her hair and devouring her lips. Swirling her tongue over his, she slid her back up and down his front, loving how the crisp black hairs on his chest tickled the skin between her shoulder blades.

Breaking the kiss, she trailed her lips down his neck. Baring her fangs, she pierced him, his body arching up into hers as he groaned.

"You little bitch. You know that feels so good."

Purring, she sucked him while he increased the maddening pace. Bringing his hand to her clit, he rubbed her. Flushed and throbbing, she began to come.

"Oh, god," she said, ending the ministrations on his neck to throw her head back on his shoulder.

"I love coming in your tight little pussy," he said, clutching her to him. "God, Arderin, I love you so much." Holding onto her, he spurted into her. Their bodies crashed and shuddered, achieving release as they clung to each other. Finally, they collapsed in a heap, him falling onto his back and pulling her to sprawl over him. Finding the energy to turn over, she snuggled into his chest.

"Did we kill each other?" she asked, her hair covering her eyes, obstructing her view. Too sated to push it out of the way, she lay over him.

"Not sure. Ask me in a few minutes."

They lay panting as their sweaty bodies attempted to return to normal.

Running her hand over his abdomen, she loved how his muscles shook under her palm. Sliding her hand down, she softly brushed his shaft.

"Hey," Darkrip said, lifting his head. "He's tired."

Realization swept over her. Grabbing him ever so gently, she tested. "It's soft. Holy crap."

His shuttered eyes looked down and he placed his hand over hers, squeezing lightly. "That's impossible." Assessing, he pulled her hand from him and felt his cock. As his eyes grew wide, she knew he was accepting the truth. "Holy shit. She removed the curse." His features were contorted with shock and awe as awareness set in. "She told me she'd remove it, but I didn't believe her."

Arderin smiled, filled with such joy that the goddess had finally rid him of the curse that caused him to feel so much pain and humiliation. He'd told her of their conversation at the Purges, and she knew the terms of the curse's removal.

"She said she would when you learned to experience true love without fear. So, I guess you really do love me." Placing her elbow on his chest, she rested her head in her hand. Gazing at him, she caressed his cheek with her free hand.

His grass-green eyes welled, and she knew he was fighting tears. "I'm sorry. I'm just overwhelmed. I've had that curse for ten centuries. I'm trying not to look like a fucking pansy right now, but I'm experiencing some pretty intense emotion."

A lone tear trailed down his cheek, and she wiped it away. Sliding over him, she kissed the wetness, lapping it with her tongue. Remembering to close his wound, she lowered to his neck and licked that closed as well.

Placing his hands over his face, his thick frame began to wrack with sobs. "I'm so sorry. I don't want to show weakness in front of you. It's just been so long since my body hasn't been straining for release. It's unbelievable."

Sliding her arms around him, she let him shudder and weep against her as he set free a thousand years of self-loathing and shame.

"It's okay to be emotional. You've been good for so long. She should've removed the curse ages ago. I'm so proud of you. And I can't wait to claim you as my bonded, for all the world to see."

Shaking his head on the pillow, he wiped his cheeks with his hands, sighing. "Good grief, she could've given me some warning or something. I look like a fucking idiot."

"You look so handsome," she said, running the backs of her fingers over his wet cheek. "I'm so happy for you. Although, now, I need to figure out your recovery time. I'm used to you just boning me until I can't breathe."

Laughing, he ran a finger down her face. "Don't worry. There will *never* be a time when I won't be ready to fuck you. Let's get that straight."

She smiled, and they stayed that way for a while, staring into each other as their bodies recovered.

"My beautiful Arderin," he said, tracing the pad of his finger over her bottom lip. "I don't deserve you, but I'm ready to bond with you. I'm sorry I'm not more romantic. I should've bought you a ring and gotten down on one knee. That's how it's done, right?"

"For me, a stack of MCAT practice exams and medical school applications far outweighs all that crap. You did a good job." Smiling, she gave him a soft peck on the lips. "And I gave you a ring. That's pretty kick-ass. Gloria Steinem would be proud." When his eyebrows drew together, she waved her hand. "She's a human feminist. You'll hear a lot about her in California."

"Great," he muttered, causing her to playfully scrunch her face at him.

"Let's do it soon, so we can focus on the baby," he said. "I don't need the ceremony of it all. I just need you. But whatever you want. I know you like parties and dancing. I want to make you happy."

"Let's do a small ceremony by our spot at the river. We must've had at least ten epic arguments there, so it seems fitting. Just family and close friends. And then, yes, I'd really like to have a reception afterward, so we can dance."

"We can do something grander if you want," he said, threading his fingers through her hair. "I don't want to deny you anything."

"What I want most is you. I know you hate social gatherings. Latimus does too. How you two introverts bagged me and Lila is beyond me."

Laughing, he nodded. "Okay, I'll ask your brothers for your hand tomorrow. I won't feel right unless I do."

Her eyebrows drew together as she grinned. "You already knocked me up and moved in with me, but whatever floats your boat."

"Well, at least I can do one thing right. Now, shut up and let me. Stubborn woman." Kissing the top of her head, he gently pushed it to his chest. As he stroked her hair, he seemed so relaxed under her.

"I love you so much," she said, running her palm over the scratchy hairs of his chest. "I'm so happy she rescinded the curse."

"Me too," he said, hugging her. "I feel like it's one more step on the path to being worthy of you. One day, down the road, I might actually get there."

"Can't wait," she said, snickering when he pinched her butt.

Soaking up his warmth, her eyelids grew heavy. Snuggling into each other, they fell into slumber.

Chapter 35

Two weeks later, they bonded at Arderin's favorite spot by the river. Darkrip had asked her brothers for their blessing, and they each had consented, threatening his life if he ever caused her one ounce of unhappiness. Assuring them it would never happen, he affirmed his commitment to love and cherish her for eternity.

Staring at Arderin under the blazing sun, he took a moment to think of Rina. So long ago, she'd come to him, promising he would have a happy life. Never even imagining it was possible, gratitude swelled in his chest.

Arderin's ice-blue eyes glowed as she spoke words of love and forever to him. They had decided to write their own vows to recite first, before the traditional vows. Lila had styled her long curls into some fancy half-up style, driving him mad. He longed to pull her from the ceremony and bury himself in her. Not understanding how someone as beautiful as she could ever choose him, his throat closed as she finished her vows.

Miranda and Lila stood behind her, both gorgeous in their deep blue dresses. Latimus and Heden stood behind him, Sathan officiating the ceremony between them. Evie, Kenden, Jack, Glarys, Sadie and Nolan stood on the soft grass, forming a half-circle around them.

Sathan nodded to Darkrip, acknowledging it was his turn to speak. Squeezing Arderin's hands, his gaze bored into hers.

"I'm not really great at this stuff, so I thought I'd have a tough time coming up with what to say. But then, I realized that it came down to one thing. You." Darkrip's heart constricted at the love that shined from her magnificent face.

"All those years ago, I loved someone and learned that love meant pain. But then, you came along and changed that for me. For centuries, I assumed I was evil and unworthy, but you burrowed into my soul, believing in me in a way no one ever had. You saw something in me that I thought was long dead. I convinced myself that I couldn't feel, but you challenged me and resuscitated my blackened heart, bringing it to life again. Everything is because of you, Arderin. I love you so much."

Her eyes swam with tears as she blinked to keep them from falling.

Lifting a ring from the pocket of his suit, he slid it onto her left middle finger. "This was my mother's. She took it off to go riding and never returned to Uteria. Miranda kept it and gave it to me when we connected. I hope it will give Mother some peace, knowing that it transferred from her finger, when she was still alive and happy, to the finger of the woman I love with my entire heart."

"Well, there goes my makeup," Arderin garbled, wiping a tear from her cheek. After the surrounding chuckles died down, he ran the pad of his thumb over the diamond. Repeating after Sathan, he spoke the traditional words of the bonding ceremony. Promising to love her for eternity, through darkness and despair, light and peace. While their family cheered and clapped around them, he pulled her into his embrace, kissing her so sweetly and passionately.

Afterward, they headed to the ballroom at Astaria. They'd invited sixty people to the reception, wanting to limit the earlier ceremony to family. As Darkrip flitted around the room with her, thanking people for coming, he reveled in her happiness. It was nice to see Aron, who'd brought a lovely woman named Moira as his date, Larkin, Jack's Uncle Sam and others.

Standing with his back against the wall, he watched Arderin dance with Lila.

"Aren't you going to join your wife, man?" Latimus asked, patting his shoulder and sipping the drink in his hand.

"No fucking way. I don't dance."

"Yeah, I didn't either. Get ready for bonding. You'll do shit you never even dreamed of." Laughing, they chatted as Sathan and Heden walked over.

"All right, I've got a bottle of Macallan here and four glasses," Sathan said. "Let's get to it."

Pouring two fingers into each of the tumblers, Sathan dispersed them, and they lifted to toast.

"To the man who bonded with our sister," Heden said. "May he be able to withstand her dramatics and infuriating tantrums."

Chuckling, Sathan said, "And if he ever hurts her, we'll dismember him and throw him in the Purges of Methesda."

"Hear, hear," they all said, clinking their glasses.

"Tough room," Darkrip muttered, enjoying the smoothness of the Scotch.

Later, he allowed his stunning bonded mate to pull him onto the dance floor.

"We have to share one dance together."

"I suck at this," he said, pulling her close and swaying with her to the awful human slow song.

"Hey, this is Madonna. It's so good. It's called 'Crazy for You.' Seems pretty appropriate for us."

Laughing, he nodded. "I guess so, since you drive me nuts eighty percent of the time."

"These percentages are quite inconsistent. We're going to have to work on quantifying them."

Smiling, he kissed her temple. "You look so beautiful."

"Lila's a whiz at these formal hairstyles. I feel so fancy. Like a Real Housewife of Beverly Hills. Once we move to California, I need to get on that show."

"Kill me," he muttered, admiring the pale skin of her throat as she threw her head back and gave a hearty laugh.

"Wait until I make you watch Vanderpump Rules. I guarantee, you're gonna love it. You're totally a Tom Sandoval, with a hefty dose of Jax thrown in."

"Good god, woman, what have I signed up for?"

"I'd say that you could still let Naran have me, but he seems very cozy with a pretty little thing in the corner over there. So, it looks like you're stuck with me."

"I'll shatter his eyeballs if he ever looks at you in any way but platonic again," Darkrip murmured, the words counteracted by the curve of his lips.

"God, I love it when you get all jealous," she said, twining her arms tighter around his neck. "It's so hot."

Resting his forehead on hers, he sank into her as they rocked to the rhythm of the music.

Later that evening, as she lay entwined with him, Arderin twirled the diamond on her finger. "I thought you said you weren't romantic."

"I'm not. I wish I could be for you. You deserve that."

Cupping his face, her fangs seemed to shimmer in the light of the bedside lamp. "Your vows today, and the ring, they were so romantic. Thank you. I'm so honored to wear your mother's ring."

"And I'm honored to wear yours," he said, grasping it as it hung from his neck. "It's the most amazing gift."

"You're my gift," she said, pulling his hand to cover her slightly distended abdomen. "You gave me our child, and soon, once you defeat that bastard, you're going to give me the gift of training in the human world. Thank you, Darkrip. I love you."

"You're so optimistic about our future. I hope it happens."

"It will," she whispered, snuggling into him.

There, in the tiny cabin, they spent their first night as bonded mates, knowing it was only the beginning of the life they would build together.

Epilogue
Seven years later...

Darkrip sat in one of the folding chairs that lined the soft grass of the park beside UCLA Medical Center's main hospital. As with most days in California, it was sunny, with a soft breeze that brushed across his face. His hair whipped in the wind since he kept it a few inches long, knowing his wife liked it that way.

His infant son slept against his chest, soft snores emanating from his tiny, wet lips. The little kid was a slobberer, that was for sure. Although humans were a pain in the ass, they'd created the BabyBjörn, which he thought was just a tad shy of ultimate brilliance. The thing allowed you to strap your child to your chest, leaving your arms free. Fucking genius.

"Daddy," his daughter said, tugging on the sleeve of his shirt. "I'm so bored. When is Mommy coming?"

Looking down to his right, he smiled at the little imp wiggling in the seat beside him. She was a carbon copy of Arderin, with waist-long curls, a smattering of freckles across her nose and tiny pink lips. Except for her irises. They were a beautiful combination of her parents, olive-green in the middle surrounded by a circle of vibrant ice-blue. She was the epitome of everything virtuous and sweet, and his heart constricted as he gazed at her.

"She'll be walking across the podium soon," he said, pointing toward it. "I need you to help me look for her."

"Okay," she said, nodding and attempting to stand in her chair.

"Whoa, let's stay seated," he said, gently pulling her down by her thin arm. "You can see her just fine from your chair."

Her lips formed a pout. "No, I can't. I need to stand."

God, she reminded him so much of Arderin, the exasperating little cherub. "No, you don't. Now, help me look. You can do it."

The members of Arderin's residency class walked out to sit in the front row of chairs, closest to the podium. Locating them in their seats, Arderin waved, excitement glowing in her gorgeous blue eyes. Blowing them a kiss, Calinda grabbed it with her hand, giggling.

"You caught it, Callie. Good job."

Nodding up at him, he thought he might drown in her eyes. He'd never seen anything as adorable as her innocent face.

The ceremony dragged on for a bit, Callie squirming but remaining quiet. Thanking all the gods for her good behavior, he promised her they would get ice cream on the way home. Arderin accepted her certificate of residency on the platformed stage, her eyes locking with his as she held it high.

I love you, she mouthed to him from the stage.

Love you too, he mouthed back.

After the ceremony, they went to greet her, Callie's black curls bobbing behind her as she ran.

"Hey, baby," Arderin said, picking her up and balancing her on her waist. "Were you good for Daddy?"

She nodded furiously. "He said we could get ice cream on the way home."

"Really?" she asked, giving Darkrip a stern yet playful glare as she arched her eyebrows. "That will extend your bedtime by several hours. How wonderful."

"I couldn't help it," he said, smiling and giving his bonded a peck on her soft lips. "She's too damn cute. It's all your fault."

Chuckling, she hugged Callie close and sat her down. As she went to pluck at the flowers growing in the grass beside them, Arderin kissed their son on the top of his head, swathed with black hair. "I can't believe he's still sleeping," she said, peeking into the BabyBjörn.

"Me either. Let's try to keep it that way," he muttered.

The waves of her laughter surrounded him as their gazes fell to Callie. She was talking to a bluebird that had landed on the ground a few feet away. Thrusting out her hand, she focused on the bird, slowly dragging it toward her on the soft grass with her mind. The bird's wings fluttered, and Arderin rushed to her, crouching down beside her.

"Let the bird fly away, baby," she said, pulling her to her side. Callie released her invisible hold on the bird, watching in awe as it flew away.

"What did we say about your powers?" she asked quietly.

Callie frowned. "That I can only use them in the house when you and Daddy are there."

"Yes, ma'am," Arderin said, smoothing a hand over her curls. "That's a very important rule, and I need you to promise me you'll remember it."

"I'm sorry, Mommy," she said, her eyes filling with tears. "He was just so pretty. I wanted to hug him."

"I know, baby," she said, embracing her. "But you have to be careful. Remember what we told you? That you're very special and it's so beautiful that we need to keep it a secret between you, me and Daddy. It would break my heart if you broke your promise and showed your powers to someone else."

"I'm sorry," she said, rubbing her wet cheek with her stubby fingers. "I promise, I won't. I like being special."

"I like it too," Arderin said, rubbing her nose against Callie's. "Now, did I hear something about ice cream?"

"Yes!" Callie yelled, jumping up and down. "I want vanilla and chocolate and strawberry and rocky road."

"Wow, that's a lot," Darkrip said, shooting a look at Arderin. "Sorry. I've created a monster. Literally."

Laughing, Arderin threw her arm around his waist and extended her hand to her daughter. After loading everyone in the car, Creigen fastened tight in the car seat, they headed for ice cream.

Once home, Callie scampered into their three-bedroom rented house that sat in the suburbs of Los Angeles. Arderin pulled a frozen lasagna from the freezer and heated it up, Creigen sucking on a bottle in his carrier, while Darkrip played with Callie in the living room. He was teaching her how to use her powers, slowly but surely, intent on ensuring she only ever used them for good.

As the day wore on and the sun hugged the horizon, the kids fell to sleep. Once Callie was in her bed, draped with pink like a proper princess, and Creigen was asleep in his crib, Darkrip walked downstairs holding the baby monitor.

"He's out for several hours at least," Darkrip said, setting the monitor on the counter.

"Thank the goddess," she said, sliding her arms around his neck as he leaned back on the island in the middle of their large kitchen. "They're exhausting."

"Tell me about it. And their mother's no picnic either, dramatic woman. I don't know how I have the energy to put up with all three of you."

"You'll pay for that," she said, scrunching her features at him. "I was going to bang you right here on the counter. Now, you're never getting laid again."

"Wanna bet?" he asked, palming the sweet globes of her ass and lifting her as she squealed. Reveling in her laughter, he proceeded to show her exactly how he liked to be banged on the counter.

* * * *

Later, as they lay entwined, facing each other on the couch in the darkened living room, Arderin regarded her husband.

"I'm a doctor," she said, biting her lip as she ran her fingers through his hair. "I did it."

"You did it," he said, placing a sweet kiss on her lips. "You're so fucking amazing. I can't believe you finished medical school in three years. I'm pretty sure you're a genius."

"Obviously," she said, rolling her eyes.

Chucking, he pulled her closer. "So, what do you want to do now? Do you want to stay here and practice, or go home? I'm fine with whatever you decide."

Arderin felt her eyes burn as they filled with moisture. Cupping his check, she asked, "How did I get so lucky? You've given me everything I ever wanted."

"Thank god," he said, so gorgeous as he smiled at her. "It's important to me that you're happy, Arderin. It's all I care about. Along with the little beasts we created."

She breathed a laugh. "I know you don't love it here, but you've put up with humans for six years. I think it's about time I focused on making you happy for once."

"You make me so happy," he said. The sincerity swimming in his olive-green irises made her heart slam in her chest. "You'll never know how much."

"I'm glad," she said, stroking the clean-shaven skin of his jaw. "But I'm ready to go home. I miss our family. Now that I've completed residency, I want to open some clinics. I think I'll start at Astaria and eventually work with Sadie and Nolan to open one on each compound. Now that Slayers occupy all the compounds, we need clinics to service them."

"Are you sure?" he asked.

"I'm sure," she said, kissing his thick lips. "And thank you for being so awesome. I don't know what the hell I did to deserve someone who always puts me first like you do, but it's freaking incredible. I love you so much."

"I love you too, princess," he said, threading his hands through her hair and pulling her to him. Against her lips, he murmured, "So much. You saved me from a life of self-loathing and misery. Your belief in me helped me become someone I never even imagined. Thank you for being my wife. I'm so honored to be your mate."

Smiling at each other, they relaxed until the baby monitor began to beep. Groaning, they went upstairs to throw on their PJs and feed Creigen. As she sat in her son's room, feeding him from her breast in the russet rocking chair, Darkrip walked in to stand behind her and massage her shoulders.

"Are you worried to go home?" Arderin asked softly.

"No," he said, his ministrations soothing her. "We're stronger when we're not divided. That's been proven. I want to help Miranda secure peace. Mother would want it that way."

The slight twinge of worry that always seemed to fill her gut when she thought of the threats in the immortal world, old and new, took hold. Feeling her body tense, Darkrip increased the pressure.

"Don't worry, princess. I've got you. Nothing will happen to us as long as we're together. I promise."

"I know," she whispered, staring up at him as she squeezed his wrist. "I'm just concerned for our babies."

"We're going to ingrain them with every ounce of goodness we can, sweetheart. I'm certain the darkness won't tempt them. We need to have faith."

She nodded. "I know. I believe in them. And in you. I want to help heal our people and rid the kingdoms of every speck of evil."

"We will," he said, placing a sweet kiss on her head. "Count on it, princess."

Resolved, Arderin sat in between her two men, her daughter sleeping a few feet away. Thankful for her beloved husband, she knew that together, they were unstoppable. Although the future was unclear, Arderin was ready to go home. To her brothers and Lila and her incredible family. The immortal world of Etherya's Earth called to her. The stories of the centuries ahead were still unwritten, but how could they be anything but magnificent with her cherished bonded mate and children by her side? Closing her eyes, tentative excitement for their future pulsed through her eight-chambered heart.

Before you go...

I hope you loved Darkrip and Arderin's story as much as I did. I adore a dark, reformed hero, and our princess is so sassy yet sweet. Get ready for Evie and Kenden's book, available on Amazon now! Our complex Slayer-Deamon heroine is desperately in need of some TLC from a strong, sexy man, and I think Kenden might just be the one to draw out her goodness. We'll see! Happy reading. RH

Please consider leaving a review on Amazon, Goodreads and/or BookBub. Indie authors survive on reviews and they are so appreciated. Your friendly neighborhood author thanks you from the bottom of her heart!

Acknowledgments

Well, folks, I never dreamed I'd say this: thanks for reading my THIRD book! The dream of publishing these novels, filled with the awesome characters that have lived in my head for so long, always seemed so far away. Now, it's a reality, and I am tremendously thankful that you all are with me on this journey!

Thanks so much to Melanie and Jaime, whom I consider my Goodreads gurus. I've had my issues with that platform but you two always talk me off the ledge and help me out. The site is essential to my success, and I truly appreciate your support!

Thanks to my awesome friends who read these books and review them, even though this genre might not be everyone's cup of tea. I'm always so thrilled to get a text about sexy Latimus from Aleks or Margaret (um, hello!! Obvi, Houston was for YOU! #twinning!) or laugh at the "tingly" parts with Lori and Stacey. So many of you came to my first book signing, held at the fabulous Ambience boutique in Edgewater, NJ, and I can't even begin to find words to express my gratitude. You ALL are amazing!

Thanks to Dorothy and Grace for your unwavering support. I've never met two more compassionate and supportive women. You are truly incredible.

Thanks to John and James for offering to dress up as Sathan and Latimus for the upcoming RomantiConn conference. I WILL be taking you up on that!

Thanks a TON to Laura and Keira at The Book Corner (on IG @thebookcorner19). Your love of paranormal romance equals mine, and I'm thrilled you like these books. Also, you're both just pretty darn cool and I'm glad to have made two new friends!

Thanks to Debbie T. for leaving such thoughtful and thorough reviews on GR for TEoH & TES. I woke up to them the day I was uploading TDW to Kindle and it was amazing to say the least. Those of you who review our books are incredible, and I think I can speak for most authors when I say we truly appreciate it!

Thanks to Megan McKeever for the superb editing, as always. You help me make these stories better, and I appreciate your thoughtful observations. It's such a pleasure to work with you on this series!

Thanks to Susan Olinsky for the fantastic cover, yet again, and the map of Etherya's Earth.

What are your dreams? Believe me, if I can follow mine, YOU CAN TOO! Go seize the day, peeps, and don't let anyone deter you. Stay awesome!

About the Author

Rebecca Hefner grew up in Western NC and now calls the Hudson River of NYC home. In her youth, she would sneak into her mother's bedroom and raid the bookshelf, falling in love with the stories of Judith McNaught, Sandra Brown and Nora Roberts. Years later, that love of a good romance, with lots of great characters and conflicts, has extended to her other favorite authors such as JR Ward and Lisa Kleypas. Also a huge Game of Thrones and Star Wars fan, she loves an epic fantasy and a surprise twist (Luke, he IS your father).

Rebecca published her first book in November of 2018. Before that, she had an extensive twelve-year medical device sales career, where she fought to shatter the glass ceiling in a Corporate America world dominated by men. After saving up for years, she left her established career to follow the long, winding and scary path of becoming a full-time author. Due to her experience, you'll find her books filled with strong, smart heroines on a personal journey to find inner fortitude and peace while combating sexism and misogyny. She would be thrilled to hear from you anytime at rebecca@rebeccahefner.com.

Books by Rebecca Hefner

Etherya's Earth Series (Fantasy/Paranormal Romance)
Book 1: The End of Hatred
Book 2: The Elusive Sun
Book 3: The Darkness Within
Book 4: The Reluctant Savior
Book 5: The Impassioned Choice

Prevent the Past Series (Sci-Fi Dystopian Time Travel Romance)
Book 1: A Paradox of Fates
Book 2: Claire and Cyrus' story (coming soon!)
Book 3: The conclusion of the trilogy (coming late 2020!)

Books also available in Audiobook and eBook format!

Please Follow Rebecca on Social Media! Find her here:
BookBub

Goodreads

Instagram

Facebook

Twitter

www.rebeccahefner.com

Made in the USA
Middletown, DE
31 May 2020